MATTHEW REILLY

THE TWO LOST MOUNTAINS

MATTHEW REILLY

THE TWO LOST MOUNTAINS

MACMILLAN
Pan Macmillan Australia

This is a work of fiction. Characters, institutions and organisations mentioned in this novel are either the product of the author's imagination or, if real, used fictitiously without any intent to describe actual conduct.

First published 2020 in Macmillan by Pan Macmillan Australia Pty Ltd
1 Market Street, Sydney, New South Wales, Australia, 2000

Reprinted 2020

A catalogue record for this book is available from the National Library of Australia

Typeset in 11/14 pt Sabon by Post Pre-press Group
Printed by IVE

The top image on page 34 is by Alexei Kouzaev, modified by the author and IRONGAV, and used under CC BY 2.0 licence
The top image on page 126 is by vwalakte/iStock
The image on page 344 is by Nephiliskos, modified by IRONGAV and used (and shared alike) under CC BY-SA 4.0 licence
The images on pages 192, 221, 345, 346 and 347 are sourced from the public domain
All other internal illustrations and endpapers by IRONGAV

The author and the publisher have made every effort to contact copyright holders for material used in this book. Any person or organisation that may have been overlooked should contact the publisher.

The paper in this book is FSC® certified. FSC® promotes environmentally responsible, socially beneficial and economically viable management of the world's forests.

This book is dedicated to
first responders everywhere,
those who run toward the danger.
Thank you.

Hear the sound of the Sirens' song,
Ride its rolling waves.
But beware that song
And the bliss it brings,
For you may wake as slaves.

INSCRIPTION ON A LARGE ANCIENT BELL
KNOWN AS 'THE SIREN BELL'
PRIVATE COLLECTION, MOSCOW

The woods are lovely, dark and deep,
But I have promises to keep,
And miles to go before I sleep,
And miles to go before I sleep.

'STOPPING BY WOODS ON A SNOWY EVENING'
ROBERT FROST

I don't believe in the no-win scenario.

CAPTAIN JAMES T. KIRK

A QUICK RECAP . . .

After unexpectedly winning the Great Games—recounted in *The Four Legendary Kingdoms*—JACK WEST JR discovered that in order to prevent THE OMEGA EVENT, the cataclysmic collapse of the universe, he had to complete two ancient 'trials': the Trial of the Cities and the Trial of the Mountains.

In *The Three Secret Cities*, racing against the superior forces of the four kingdoms, he successfully completed the Trial of the Cities, but at great cost. As part of that trial, unbeknownst to Jack, an Oracle of Siwa had to be ritually sacrificed in a chamber inside the Rock of Gibraltar.

Jack's adopted daughter LILY, twenty years old and the current Oracle, was captured by a new player in the game, SPHINX. Ruthless, calculating and knowledgeable in ancient matters, Sphinx was the watchman of the city of Atlas who had long planned to overthrow the kingdoms and seize their power.

In the final moments of *The Three Secret Cities*, Sphinx took Lily to the altar inside the Rock of Gibraltar and there he performed the sickening ritual sacrifice.

Jack arrived at that chamber soon after, to find Sphinx and his men gone and what appeared to be Lily's body encased in a slab of hardened liquid stone. But he had to flee and so didn't linger there.

Three days later, Lily's friend, ALBY CALVIN—accompanied by STRETCH and POOH BEAR—ventured to the Rock to retrieve Lily's body.

Upon breaking open the stone slab, however, Pooh Bear's face lit up.

'Good God,' he gasped. 'It's not—' Then, smiling, he told the others to call Jack immediately.

Maybe it *hadn't* been Lily who had been sacrificed.

Having completed the Trial of the Cities, Sphinx and his forces— including the cunning **CARDINAL MENDOZA** of the Catholic Church and the ambitious **CHLOE CARNARVON,** the former assistant to Jack's ally **IOLANTHE COMPTON-JONES**—raced off to commence the second trial, the Trial of the Mountains.

Other forces, such as the mysterious **ORDER OF THE OMEGA,** a fanatical group of monks from Venice, were also on the move.

Now, with the Omega Event fast approaching, Jack and his intrepid team—including his formidable wife **ZOE;** his feisty mother, the historian **MAE MERRIWEATHER;** and **HADES,** the ultra-wealthy former King of the Underworld—find themselves wounded and scattered, a long way behind their rivals in this race, and desperate to know what happened to Lily . . .

PROLOGUE

THE EMPTY CITY: MOSCOW

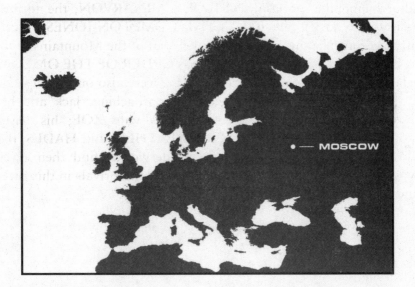

But this mighty music, produced by the revolution of the whole universe, at the highest speed, cannot be perceived by human ears, any more than you can look straight at the sun, your sense of sight being overpowered by its radiance.

CICERO, REFERRING TO PYTHAGORAS'S THEORY OF THE MUSIC OF THE SPHERES

MOSCOW, RUSSIA
23 DECEMBER, 0900 HOURS

Lily West woke with a jerk, startled and terrified, and freezing, *freezing* cold.

She was bound and gagged, tied to a thick wooden chair and sitting out of doors, atop some steps overlooking a very wide square.

She was not alone.

Seated on either side of her, also bound to wooden chairs, were two headless corpses.

Lily recoiled, aghast.

Jesus . . .

Looking more closely at them, she saw that the corpses were female and that they wore the black habits of nuns.

The wounds to their necks were horrific: jagged and torn. Their heads had not been cut off. They had been wrenched off.

Pinned to the chest of one of the grisly corpses was a sheet of paper. It fluttered in the icy wind. On it were five handwritten words:

YOU
WILL
WAKE
AS
SLAVES

Snow fell.

Wind whistled.

It was a bleak overcast day.

Looking around the wide plaza before her, Lily saw some buildings that she recognised—albeit only from books—and suddenly she knew exactly where she was.

She was in Red Square.

In Moscow.

Off to her right was the Kremlin. Its 200-foot-high blood-red walls and imposing towers stood like gigantic sentinels in the morning light, every flat surface on them caked in a layer of snow.

Lily blinked, trying to restart her brain. Her head ached terribly. She vaguely recalled coming here, but then someone had hit her, knocked her out.

She tried to think, to remember.

Red Square itself—the vast parade ground used by the Russian government to host military spectacles and national events—was almost completely deserted, even though the clocktower atop the Kremlin's main gate, Spasskaya Tower, announced that it was nine in the morning.

Almost deserted, because of one striking thing.

The many bodies that lay scattered around the square.

There were maybe thirty of them, all lying face-down on the snow-dusted ground, seemingly dead. There were men in uniform— Russian Army guards and police officers in parkas—and civilians of both sexes. They all looked like they had fallen abruptly, collapsing in mid-stride. Small piles of snow had formed on their backs.

Aside from the drifting snow, there was no movement.

Lily stared at them in horror.

Suddenly, an animal whipped across the square. A street dog. It stopped to sniff one of the immobile bodies and then scurried away.

Swivelling in her chair, Lily saw that she was sitting at the base of some stairs in front of the south face of a building known throughout the world.

St Basil's Cathedral.

With its nine enormous onion-shaped towers, it was the most famous building in Russia, the symbol of Moscow.

The historic cathedral's onion domes were the pride of Russian architecture although no-one actually knew their origin. In modern times, the ornate domes were painted in twisting rainbows of colour—gorgeous reds and greens, pastel blues and pure whites—but that had not always been the case.

Moscow . . . Lily thought. It was starting to come back to her.

Sphinx had brought her here.

After the ceremony at the Rock of Gibraltar. That terrible ceremony.

He had wanted to go to Moscow, to some . . .

. . . convent.

Lily shivered.

The cold was beginning to physically hurt her. Dressed only in jeans, sneakers, a t-shirt and a military jacket that she had acquired somewhere along the way, she was not equipped to be outside in the Russian winter.

Her teeth began to chatter.

With her hands bound behind her back, she couldn't even hug herself for warmth.

What had Sphinx said?

An old convent in Moscow. Something kept there.

He'd talked about it after the ceremony at Gibraltar.

Oh, God, Lily thought. *The ceremony.*

For as long as she lived, she'd never forget what had happened there . . .

A GIRL NAMED LILY

PART VII
THE SACRIFICE AT GIBRALTAR

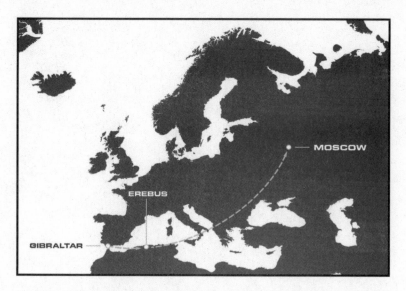

If you want to test a man's character, give him power.

ABRAHAM LINCOLN

THE ALTAR OF THE COSMOS
GIBRALTAR, U.K. TERRITORY
3 DECEMBER, 20 DAYS EARLIER

Lily lay face-up in a small sacrificial pool, trapped beneath its golden grille, resigned to die. She was inside a ceremonial chamber cut into the heart of the mighty Rock of Gibraltar.

As the Oracle of Siwa, she had to be sacrificed in order to save the world.

Directly above her was a wide slanting shaft—it looked like a colossal ancient chimney that bored upward through the Rock—and through it she could see the night-time sky and a thousand glittering stars.

Sphinx stood over her, gripping the fabled sword, Excalibur, holding its gleaming blade poised directly above her heart, ready to run her through and thus carry out the necessary ritual.

Lily closed her eyes and waited for the end—

Gunfire.

Loud and sudden.

Her eyes sprang open.

They were pistol shots.

She saw Sphinx turn, confused and enraged, as a bullet nicked his shoulder, spinning him, making him drop the sword and cry out in pain.

Lily heard four more pistol shots—single shots echoing loudly in the ancient chamber—before they were drowned out by the louder and faster clatter of automatic-rifle fire.

Then there was silence.

Gunsmoke filled the air.

And the acrid smell of cordite.

Hurried footsteps—the sound of Sphinx's men coming to his aid.

From her position in the shallow pool, Lily saw Cardinal Ricardo Mendoza step into view, kneel beside his master and say, 'Sire, sire! Are you all right?'

Sphinx rose, shoving the cardinal away. 'I'm fine. It's a flesh wound. How the fuck did he get out?'

'We don't know. It looks like he surprised his guards on the boat—'

'Is he alive?' Sphinx growled.

'Yes, sire.'

Gripping his bloody shoulder, Sphinx stalked out of Lily's view.

'You little shit,' Sphinx said to someone.

A weak voice answered him: the quivering, agonised voice of a young man or boy.

'You killed . . . the only people . . . who ever loved me.'

The voice sounded vaguely familiar and at first Lily couldn't place it.

Then she could.

It was—

'Get her out of the pool and put him in,' Sphinx said. 'He's going to bleed out and die soon anyway.'

Suddenly, there was movement all around Lily. The golden gate confining her to the shallow pool was swung open, its hinges squealing, and Lily was lifted out of the pool by a pair of soldiers.

And she saw him.

Saw the young man who had stormed the ceremonial chamber and opened fire on Sphinx and his crew with a single pistol. But now his body was punctured all over with bullet wounds as two of Sphinx's men dragged him to the pool. He was alive, but only barely.

Lily hadn't seen him in years, but his features hadn't changed.

Like her, he was twenty. He had longer hair now—dark and

straight, it dangled down carelessly into his eyes, making him look like a disaffected college kid or a member of a grunge band.

But his face was the same. His small elfin nose and dark eyes were just like Lily's.

Exactly like Lily's, to be precise.

For he was her brother, her twin brother.

Alexander.

And in that fleeting moment as they were carried past each other, their identical eyes met and Lily saw that Alexander was glaring right at her.

In his eyes was a fire, an apology, a plea to action. All in one look.

'Don't let them wi—' he whispered before he was swept by her.

Things moved fast from there.

To Lily, what happened next inside the chamber, and outside it, went by in a blur.

First, Sphinx carried out the sacrificial ceremony with ruthless efficiency.

He lay the wounded Alexander in the shallow ceremonial pool, slammed the gate closed on top of him and then without pause, reflection or remorse, stabbed the lad through the heart.

The sword went right through his body before it was halted by the stone bottom of the pool beneath him.

Alexander screamed as blood blasted out of his chest and his dead body sank into the shallow little pool, its clear waters turning red.

Silence followed.

Lily stared in mute shock at her brother's corpse, lying motionless in the pool. But for his actions a few moments earlier, that would've been her. She didn't know what to think or what would happen next.

And then the whole chamber glowed an eerie shade of crimson, illuminated by a strange light that emanated from the bloodstained water around Alexander's body.

In the sickly red glow, a series of symbols came to life on one wall: glyphs written in the Word of Thoth, the ancient language that Lily could read by sight.

She translated the symbols silently in her head:

> *The Supreme Labyrinth awaits*
> *With the ultimate throne at its core.*
> *Perform the Fall at an iron mountain*
> *And acquire the Mark.*
> *For only one with the Mark may open the Labyrinth and sit*
> *on the throne.*
>
> *Take armies if you choose.*
> *Use the Siren bells if you wish.*
> *But know that only success at the Labyrinth*
> *Will prevent Omega.*

Lily saw that Cardinal Mendoza had a computer program on a laptop translating the symbols at the same time she was.

Next to Mendoza, she saw the pretty young Englishwoman who accompanied Sphinx. She was Chloe Carnarvon, the former assistant to Iolanthe Compton-Jones, the Keeper of the Royal Records.

Lily remembered Iolanthe saying once that when Chloe Carnarvon had worked for her, Chloe had essentially been Iolanthe's second brain. When it came to historical matters, she knew everything Iolanthe did. But when Iolanthe sided with Jack after the Great Games, Carnarvon had sided with—and slept with—Iolanthe's brother, Orlando, the King of Land, only to betray Orlando here at the Rock in favour of Sphinx. Chloe was now filming the entire event on a digital camera.

With a great rumbling, a stone panel in the wall slid open, revealing five sparkling gold signet rings positioned in a row on a shelf.

Each ring bore a huge gem on it. One was a little larger than the others. Its gem was red. The gems on the other four rings were amber in colour.

And then the ethereal crimson lightshow stopped and the cavern was plunged into relative darkness again, lit only by the electric lights Sphinx's people had erected.

Sphinx picked up the five rings and carried them over to the pulsing Mace of Poseidon.

As he held them close to the Mace, the Mace's glowing gem diminished in intensity . . .

. . . while the gems on the five signet rings began to glow with increased power.

'The power of the Mace is transferring to the rings,' Mendoza said.

When it was done, Sphinx held up the largest ring.

Its giant red gem, now gleaming with light from within, had a raised image cut into it: the image of a crown.

It pulsed with fierce power.

Sphinx put it on.

Chloe gasped.

Mendoza bowed.

'My emperor . . .' he whispered.

Sphinx gazed at the ring.

It was a singularly beautiful thing, formidable and commanding. It was neither flashy nor gaudy. Just a clear symbol of power.

Chloe nodded at it. 'The ring of the emperor. Now all the bronzeman armies are yours to command.'

Sphinx handed one of the other rings to Dion, his protégé, and another to Jaeger Eins, the leader of the Knights of the Golden Eight and thus essentially his military commander. The other two he kept for himself. 'There are four battalions of bronzemen around the world: one at each of the three secret cities and one at the Underworld. My ring gives me command of *all* of them. But whoever wears these other rings can command certain battalions, too. Dion, I give you the ring that controls the bronzemen from the city of Atlas. Eins, you shall command those from the Underworld. Gather these bronzemen from the around the world. We will need them.'

'Planes have been requisitioned for the purpose, sire,' Jaeger Eins said. 'Ten U.S. Air Force C-5M Super Galaxy cargo planes equipped with ADS containers. They're the only ones large enough and powerful enough to carry the weight of the bronzemen. It will be done within the next week.'

Cardinal Mendoza read aloud from his computer's screen. His translation, Lily noted, was identical to hers. His program was good.

Sphinx said, 'Cardinal. The first iron mountain . . . ?'

'. . . awaits your arrival,' Mendoza said. 'The High Astronomer, Father Rasmussen, is there right now, preparing everything for you. He is the Church's foremost expert on the iron mountains, the lunar alignments and the Fall.'

Sphinx nodded. 'I also want the bells.'

A hush fell over the group when he said this.

'Sire,' Mendoza said. 'You do understand that they are not necessary to complete the trial.'

Chloe added, 'And are notoriously dangerous—'

'I want them,' Sphinx said firmly, 'because they are key to my ruling plans. This means paying a visit to the lovely ladies of Novodevichy Convent in Moscow.'

'Whores,' Mendoza spat. 'Women who are too clever for their own good.'

'I like them,' Sphinx said. 'They're committed. To their code and their cause. They have been for five thousand years. They outwitted your Church for all that time, Cardinal. When is the next series of alignments?'

'Sometime around the solstice, according to Father Rasmussen. Christmas Eve or thereabouts. I will get the exact times and dates from him promptly. We have about three weeks.'

'You have all the data on the Apennine Mountains and the Sea of Rains?'

'Yes, sire,' Mendoza said.

'And the observatory is ready?'

'All prepared, sire.'

'Then let us go to Moscow,' Sphinx said. 'Except we shall make one stop on the way.'

'Where might that be, sire?'

'The Royal Prison at Erebus,' Sphinx said.

Then he turned on his heel and casually tossed a pill of greystone into the sacrificial pool containing Alexander's dead body.

The moment the pill hit the water, the surface clouded over, going dark and opaque. There followed a series of foul cracks as the black-grey water solidified into a concrete-like substance that wholly encased Alexander's corpse, hiding it from view.

And then they were moving.

Lily was shoved toward the exit stairs.

She managed to grab a final, sad glance back at the sacrificial pool containing the brother she'd hardly known, now entombed in solid stone.

His last act, he had said, had been on behalf of 'the only people who had ever loved him'.

Lily knew who that referred to.

Sky Monster's sweet and loving parents, who had taken Alexander into their home as a boy and raised him as their own.

Sphinx's men—the Knights of the Golden Eight—had killed both of them horrifically.

Then Lily was pushed out of the chamber as Sphinx and his people whisked her away from the Rock and onto a plane headed for Erebus.

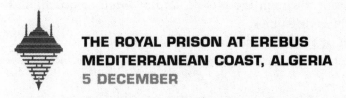

THE ROYAL PRISON AT EREBUS
MEDITERRANEAN COAST, ALGERIA
5 DECEMBER

Roland Rubles was singing happily in the pitch darkness of the abandoned royal prison.

'When Irish eyes are smiling, sure, 'tis like a morn in spring . . . !'

Rubles was, of course, clinically insane.

Once upon a time, he had been the refined butler of a minor royal household in Luxembourg. But then, when his master had gone away one weekend, Rubles had killed and then eaten his master's wife, two children and dog.

Sentenced to spend the rest of his life half encased in a stone slab on Erebus's infamous Wall of Misery, Rubles had been terribly disappointed when Jack West Jr—his next-door neighbour on the Wall—had escaped from the prison and not taken Rubles with him.

That Jack had been the first person ever to escape from the notorious prison had not impressed Rubles, even though he was aware that it was a prison whose location was known to perhaps three individuals in the whole world.

'In the lilt of Irish laughter, you can hear the angels sing . . . !'

A small consolation for Rubles, however, had been a new neighbour: no less a figure than the Governor of the Royal Prison himself, Count Yago DeSaxe, the younger brother of Hades, the King of the Underworld.

After being rescued by the bounty hunter, Aloysius Knight, Jack had unceremoniously imprisoned Yago in a liquid-stone slab of his

own and mounted him on the Wall of Misery: imprisoning the jailer in his own jail.

'When Irish hearts are happy, all the world seems bright and gay . . .'

But now, a few days later as the prisoners around him sagged with hunger and thirst and Rubles sang, flashlights suddenly appeared, sabring through the gloom, and a dozen armed figures appeared in front of Rubles.

At the sight of them, Rubles increased his gusto.

'And when Irish eyes are smiling, sure, they—'

Bang!

Rubles's head exploded, shot, his forehead blasting apart in a spray of blood and brains. His head, still embedded in its vertical stone slab, could not even loll to one side. Rubles just hung there, still, his eyes wide, his mouth hanging open, blood oozing out of a hole in his skull and down his face.

Sphinx stepped out of the darkness and lowered his gun.

He stood in front of the slab containing his friend, Yago.

'Get him out,' Sphinx commanded.

It took thirty minutes to free Yago from his slab.

While everyone was gathered around Yago, one of Cardinal Mendoza's assistants, a young Serbian priest named Father Miroslav Cilic slipped away from the larger group.

Moving quickly by the light of a small flashlight, he wended his way down several dark passageways, moving ever deeper into the ancient prison until at last he came to the innermost dungeon of the whole ghastly place: a square-sided stone-walled chamber with a broad pit in its middle.

It was hard to tell how deep the pit was.

It could have been bottomless for all anyone knew.

A thick iron cage hung out in the centre of the pit, twenty feet from the cavern's walls, suspended above the drop by a single sturdy chain.

An inescapable cell.

A huge hulking figure stood inside the cage, cloaked in shadow. He did not move.

The young priest gazed at him with eyes that were wide with fear and . . .

. . . adoration.

Although the prisoner's face was bathed in shadow, it was clear that he was looking directly at the young priest.

Father Cilic said softly, 'General Rastor. My name is Cilic. I am a loyal disciple. You commanded my brother during the troubles in my homeland. Here.'

He threw a key across the chasm to the figure in the hanging cell.

Whip-quick, the figure's hand reached out through the bars and caught the key.

When he spoke, his voice was a low rasp that sent a chill up the spine of the young Serbian priest.

'You will be rewarded in the next life, my son,' the prisoner said.

'Thank you, General,' Father Cilic said. 'Forgive me, but I must get back before I am missed.'

'You have done well,' the prisoner said. 'Go. I will follow later.'

The young priest hastened away from the innermost dungeon of the royal prison, leaving the prisoner in it hanging in darkness, in his cage, but now with the key to unlock it.

Thirty minutes later, Sphinx and his people left Erebus, with Yago in their midst.

Sphinx had also ordered the release of eight other rather unusual prisoners. They were taken, too, although they were transported in cuffs and chains, and with leather gags covering their mouths.

Father Cilic walked quietly behind Cardinal Mendoza, glancing furtively about.

'Let us regather our people and bring all our forces together,' Sphinx said. 'Then we will go to Moscow. To the convent.'

NOVODEVICHY CONVENT
MOSCOW, RUSSIA
23 DECEMBER, 0000 HOURS

Novodevichy Convent lay silent in the cold Moscow night.

It had begun life as a fortress—or to use the Russian term, a *kremlin*—and it still retained the colossal walls and defensive towers of the citadel it had once been.

But in the 1500s, under the reign of Vasili III and his psychotic son, Ivan the Terrible, it had been converted into a convent to imprison royal women forced to take the veil.

Today, it is famous for three of its features: first, its stupendous belltower; second, its cemetery containing the graves of many famous Russians; and third, the glorious white Smolensky Cathedral that stands in its centre with its five gold-and-grey onion domes, domes that resemble those of its cousin, the larger and more famous St Basil's Cathedral, a few miles away.

For five hundred years, the convent has been a symbol of stoic endurance, surviving wars with Napoleon and Hitler, and even making a cameo appearance in Tolstoy's *War and Peace*.

It is also a symbol of decidedly feminine endurance.

For since its conversion from fortress to cloister, Novodevichy Convent has been the exclusive domain of women, an order of nuns known to most as the Order of Serene Maidens, or the Sereneans for short, and by a much older name to a select few.

That would change on the night of 23 December, for at the stroke of midnight, Sphinx's forces attacked it.

★ ★ ★

It was not a silent attack. It wasn't even a stealthy attack. And it was not small.

It was big, bold and loud.

Four long dark boxes that looked like armoured black shipping containers came roaring out of the sky and *slammed* into the snow-covered grounds of the convent.

BAM!

BAM!

BAM!

BAM!

As they hit the ground, the earth shook and snow was thrown into the air.

In military circles, these dark containers were known as ADS-IRM—Aerial Delivery System for Impact Resistant Material.

In regular English, this meant they were precision-guided containers that, because of their non-human or non-mechanically sensitive contents, *didn't* need to land softly. And with the advent of GPS and high-tech guidance features on the containers themselves, ADS containers had become very adept at landing on small targets very quickly.

They were mainly used to drop food, weapons or ammunition into remote war zones or cities suffering humanitarian crises.

These four ADS containers came down hard inside the fortified walls of Novodevichy Convent, landing at the four points of the compass, so that they blocked each of the four exits from the complex.

A moment later, the walls of the containers dropped open with loud slams and out of each container ran thirty bronzemen, racing for the central living quarters.

Sphinx and his human companions arrived minutes later in two low-flying Chinook helicopters loaned to them by the Russian Army.

Sphinx emerged from the first chopper, guiding Lily behind him, her hands bound with flex cuffs.

They were followed by Cardinal Mendoza and Chloe Carnarvon; Jaeger Eins and four of his Knights; twelve bronzemen and the eight unknown men they had sprung from Erebus prison.

As a prominent figure in the shadow world of the four kingdoms, Sphinx had forewarned the appropriate people at the top of the Russian military of his arrival, so there was no local intervention, not from the police or the army.

Sphinx did not want to be disturbed as he stormed the convent.

Because he had important things to do.

Minutes later, inside a dark crypt deep beneath the five-domed cathedral, backed by his two advisers, the five Knights, the twelve bronzemen and the eight other men, Sphinx stood in front of the twenty female residents of Novodevichy Convent.

All the nuns knelt on the floor except for their leader, the abbess of the convent, Sister Beatrice, who stood defiantly in front of Sphinx.

Some of the nuns sobbed quietly.

Most of them cast wary glances not at Sphinx or even at the exotic bronzemen, but at the eight other men Sphinx had brought along.

For those eight men were the stuff of nightmares.

They were short and skinny, with wiry muscles and hunched shoulders. But it was their faces that were truly terrifying: these men had teeth filed to sharp points and the skin on their foreheads, tattooed red, was stretched over surgically inserted subdermal horns.

Upon seeing them enter, one of the younger nuns had gasped involuntarily, 'Vandals . . .'

The cathedral's crypt was bitingly cold.

It was essentially one long underground corridor with vaults and caged side-chapels lining its walls; monuments to great Russian women over the centuries. Some of these little chapels had altars, others had waist-high stone sarcophagi.

The abbess eyed Lily, standing behind Sphinx with her hands bound.

'You are the Oracle . . .' the old nun breathed with realisation, before she snapped to look in horror at Sphinx.

'High Priestess,' Sphinx said formally.

'Watchman,' the abbess replied evenly.

Sphinx smiled brightly. 'It's good to see you, Beatrice. You've aged well.'

'And you, Hardin, are still clearly a prick of the highest order.' The old nun glared at him. 'You were a shit when you were a child and I was your babysitter, and you're obviously still a shit now. So, you've finally made your move?'

'I've waited a very long time for this,' Sphinx said.

'You always were patient, I'll give you that,' Sister Beatrice said. 'Patient, watchful . . .'

'Why, thank—'

'. . . and cruel,' the nun finished. 'I never forgot what you did to the Ludovico boy.'

'He stole my new sunglasses.'

'You blinded him.'

'Thou shalt not steal.'

'You were thirteen years old, Hardin,' the old nun said. 'Normal psychopaths, when they are children, torture small animals and pets. You tortured a boy.'

Sphinx gave her a wan, indulgent smile.

'I want the bells,' he said flatly.

'They are not here,' Sister Beatrice replied. 'They haven't been here for a hundred years—'

'They are in the crypt of Tsarevna Sophia Alekseyevna right behind you,' Sphinx said curtly, nodding at the enormous stone vault behind her, the largest one in the entire subterranean complex.

The vault was a great square thing, made entirely of grey stone, and it was the size of a double garage. On its door was carved the severe frowning face of a heavy-browed, matronly woman wearing a crown.

Sphinx stroked the grey stone face of the statue.

'Tsarevna Sophia,' he said. 'Daughter of Tsar Alexis and once all-powerful regent of Russia. But it ended badly for her, didn't it, Beatrice?'

The abbess said nothing.

Sphinx said, 'During the height of her power, the tsarevna rebuilt this convent and supported its nuns, but when her grasp on power collapsed, she was herself imprisoned here for the final years of her life. Do you recall what the new tsar, Peter, did with her supporters, Beatrice?'

The abbess said softly, 'He hanged them by the neck right outside the windows of her room, so if she looked outside her prison, she saw them.'

'Got to hand it to Peter,' Sphinx said, 'he was an inventive sadist.'

His eyes narrowed.

'Tell you what, Beatrice, let's have a wager. Let's open this crypt right now. If, as you say, the Siren bells are not inside it, I will kill you and your sisters here quickly and painlessly, with bullets to your heads.'

He held up a finger.

'But, if the bells *are* in there—and you're lying to me—I will leave you to my ghastly friends.'

He waved at the eight Vandals, with their horrific teeth and 'horned' heads.

Sister Beatrice swallowed.

Lily froze.

'Open it,' Sphinx said to Jaeger Eins.

Minutes later, the door to the great crypt was blasted open with controlled explosives and Sphinx beheld its interior.

Sphinx was not a man who was easily impressed, but his breath caught in his throat.

A giant, nine-foot-tall, gold-and-silver sphere stood before him.

It was a glorious piece of metalwork, polished to a brilliant sheen, its gleaming sides perfectly curved. It was astonishing in its flawlessness: far too precise for people of previous centuries to have built; perhaps too precise even for people of today.

It stood there, heavy, ancient and ominous, reflecting the light dully. It was mounted on a slab, which allowed one to see the wide round hole at its bottom. This great sphere was hollow, a huge bell of some kind.

Behind it stood thirteen more spherical bells, lined up in two long rows, all of similar gigantic size, all made of silver and gold.

'The Siren bells . . .' Chloe said.

Sister Beatrice's face fell.

Sphinx just shook his head sadly.

'Oh, Beatrice. You lied to me.'

'Don't toy with me, Hardin. I'm too old for games,' the abbess snapped. 'You've got what you came for. You have your emperor's ring on your finger and now you have the Siren bells. You did it. You won. As a boy you were a petty tyrant, and now, as a man, you can be a full-blown one. Leave us. Go to one of the five mountains and perform your Fall. Then go and claim your throne at the Labyrinth and make us and everyone else in the world your servants, just like you've always wanted. Only spare me the fucking speeches.'

Sphinx was silent.

He stared at the defiant old nun.

'You lost our wager,' he said softly.

The way he said it made Lily's stomach tighten.

'I am no tyrant,' he added. 'Far from it. I am a merciful man. To demonstrate, I will spare your nuns the price of the wager and give them quick deaths. *But not you.* You made the bet so you shall pay the full price.'

Without warning, Sphinx shoved Sister Beatrice into another adjoining side-chapel, then he had the eight fearsome-looking Vandals released into it after her, with their mouth-gags removed.

'She is all yours, my hungry friends.'

The eight Vandals scurried into the chapel like slavering dogs. Sphinx slammed the gate shut behind them.

A second later, Sister Beatrice's screams—inhuman, and agonised—pierced the air as the Vandals tore into her flesh with their hideous teeth, eating her alive.

Lily squeezed her eyes shut, trying not to hear it, but she couldn't.

★ ★ ★

After a minute, the abbess's screams stopped and the only noises that came from the chapel were the sounds of crunching bones and sloppy chewing.

Sphinx was true to his word regarding the other nuns. Within a few minutes, they were all dead, each ruthlessly shot in the head.

The giant bells were removed from the crypt with forklifts.

Lily scowled at Sphinx. 'You're a monster.'

'Young lady,' Sphinx said, 'I haven't even started. Come, let us test one of the bells.'

A few hours later, Lily was flying inside one of Sphinx's Chinook helicopters high above the outskirts of Moscow, sitting beside Sphinx in the cockpit.

The vast Russian capital lay spread out before her, stretching toward the horizon, a colossal metropolitan basin that was home to twelve million people.

Moscow was an incongruous mix of the old and the new, the beautiful and the ugly: sleek glass skyscrapers towered over brutish Soviet-era apartment blocks; charcoal-black factories flanked the limestone aristocratic neighbourhoods of the 19th century; high-walled kremlins and beautiful churches nestled beside huge public parks, many of them containing frozen ponds for ice-skating.

All of it was covered in ice and snow, blanketing the city in grim greyness.

Clouds of steam rose from chimneys both residential and industrial: evidence of the heating systems required to withstand the Russian winter.

Carving a broad swathe through the entire cityscape was the Moskva River, snaking along in wide bending curves, its surface white and hard-frozen.

It was just before dawn and the Russian capital was stirring.

A thin stream of cars cruised around the ring roads. Buses rumbled down the boulevards. The icebreakers that would cut canals in the frozen Moskva River were not yet out, but they would be soon.

A few ice-skaters were on the river doing graceful spins and crossovers. A couple of early-morning dog walkers strolled down the paths by the shore.

Garbage trucks roamed the streets of the residential districts and alleyways of the city.

And then suddenly something rose up from within the walls of Novodevichy Convent, flying quickly and vertically into the sky, as if pulled upward by a string.

It was a huge double-rotored Chinook heavy-lift helicopter, only this Chinook had blacked-out windows.

Lily felt her chest constrict.

She had seen a helicopter like this one before. In London, a few weeks ago, when the Knights of the Golden Eight had drawn Jack out into the open by suspending a red London bus from a similar chopper above the Thames.

It was a drone, operated by the Knights of the Golden Eight.

Suspended beneath the drone Chinook in some rope netting was one of the mighty spherical bells that Lily had seen at the convent.

Looking out at the sleeping city with the drone chopper now high above it, Sphinx handed Lily a pair of military-grade protective earphones, the kind worn by special forces operators.

'Here, you will want to wear these.'

Lily knew this type of headset: it was a 3M Peltor ComTac ear-protection headset with air-sealed gel cushions that covered the ears.

While they looked like regular commercial over-the-ear head-phones, these units were much more than that.

They had external noise-cancelling microphones, but ones that operated several levels above those available commercially. These Peltor headsets were worn by special forces units around the world and for good reason: they digitised all noise around their wearers, giving the wearer almost superhuman hearing, while at the same time protecting them from deafening sounds like gunshots and explosions, preventing their eardrums from rupturing.

Lily noticed that all of Sphinx's people now wore similar protective earphones. She hurriedly put hers on.

'Ring it,' Sphinx said.

Suddenly the drone chopper rocked, causing the great bell hanging from it to swing . . .

. . . making something inside it clang.

A long, high-pitched note rang out from the ancient metal bell, reverberating mightily, blaring out over the city like an unearthly chime.

Lily heard it as a digitised sound through her earphones.

What the people of Moscow heard *without* any aural protection was difficult to describe.

It was at the same time both beautiful and terrible, joyous and painful. A moment of pure yet fleeting ecstasy.

But more than anything, the ringing sound was authoritative, penetrating, irresistible.

It rippled out from the mysterious ancient sphere, expanding in invisible waves over the entire city.

Lily saw the reactions immediately.

A garbage truck beneath her veered off the road and slammed into a building.

Cars collided on the ring road. The buses on the boulevards crashed into light poles, traffic lights and shopfronts.

Lily watched in helpless horror.

Her searching eyes found the skaters on the Moskva River below her.

Lily watched as they all—all of them, at the *exact* same time— collapsed like marionettes whose strings had been cut.

Lily zeroed in on one woman in particular.

After she fell to the ice, the woman seemed to pause, confused, looking around herself in an effort to understand what had just happened.

She struggled to her hands and knees, trying to get back onto her skates, but for some reason she couldn't, so instead she crawled desperately on her belly, straining to reach the shore.

After about fifteen seconds of this, the woman slumped to the ground and lay motionless.

A few of the other skaters had done the same and they, too, now lay on their bellies, still.

Whether they had lost consciousness or died, Lily couldn't tell.

She also noticed the dog walkers beside the river.

They'd also dropped in mid-stride while their dogs howled, yelping in pain as the stinging sound of the sphere hit their differently configured hearing. The dogs, Lily saw, hadn't collapsed.

'Are they dead?' she said flatly to Sphinx.

'No,' Sphinx said. 'Not yet. It is a kind of sleep or coma. Nor are they in pain. According to the ancient texts, as they enter the Siren sleep, they experience a moment of incredible rapture.'

'Everyone in the city?' Lily asked.

Sphinx nodded. 'To a radius of about thirty miles, we estimate.'

The city below Lily was now still.

The whole city.

Every car, every bus, every garbage truck, every person: all still.

Horns blared from drivers who had collapsed against their steering wheels. Car alarms wailed from the many collisions.

The only movement was the constantly rising steam from the chimneys.

'Some of them will die soon,' Sphinx added. 'That cannot be helped. The skaters on the ice and the drivers of those cars will almost certainly die. Not from the sleep but from exposure or thirst.

'Those in their beds should be okay for a few days, perhaps a week, but they too will die of thirst or starvation if the sleep lasts too long. That is why I wanted to do this now—at this time of day, early—while most of the population are in their beds. They will just continue sleeping, only now they will be sleeping in the coma created by the bell. When they wake, they will find themselves in a new world.'

Lily shivered.

She didn't quite know what to make of that statement. This day had already held too many horrors.

'What kind of world?'

Sphinx gazed out over the subdued city of Moscow. 'One ruled by me.'

He turned to face Lily and smiled brightly.

'Come now, my dear. Do not dwell on such grim topics. It's time for you to play your part and do what I brought you here for.'

'And what's that?'

'Somehow, your adoptive father, Captain West, escaped from the City of Atlas. It was caught on my security cameras. He is a determined one, I must admit. He will, I have no doubt, come looking for you, so we must give him what he seeks.'

And with those curious words, Sphinx struck Lily in the face with the butt of his pistol and her world went black.

She would wake later that morning on the steps on St Basil's Cathedral in the middle of Red Square, bound to a chair with a sore head and flanked by two headless nuns.

FIRST OFFENSIVE

THE MOSCOW RESCUE

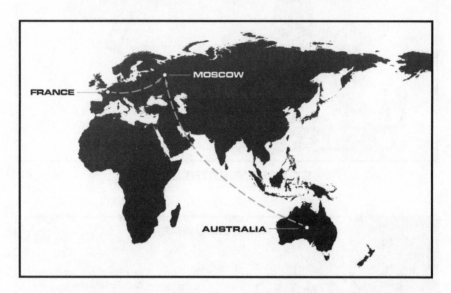

In Greek mythology, the Sirens were three beautiful maidens
who lived on a rocky island.
They sang a song that was so sweet and entrancing that any
sailor who heard it fell into an enraptured sleep. His ship would
then be dashed on the rocks of the island.
The only person to hear the Sirens' song and live to tell the tale
was Odysseus, who, ever curious, was determined to hear it.
He survived the encounter in a characteristically clever way: he
had himself tied to the mast of his ship while his men rowed
past the island with balls of wax stuffed in their ears . . .

GREEK MYTHOLOGY
MURRAY BODINE (MACMILLAN, SYDNEY, 2010)

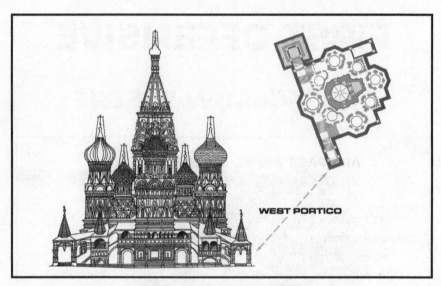

ST BASIL'S CATHEDRAL

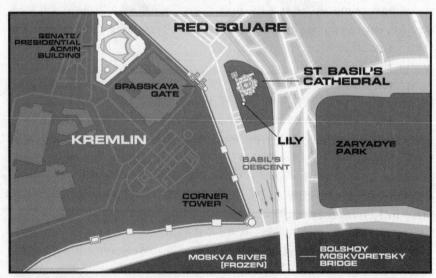

RED SQUARE, THE KREMLIN AND ST BASIL'S CATHEDRAL

AIRSPACE ABOVE RUSSIA
23 DECEMBER, 0845 HOURS

Jack West's plane sped toward Moscow.

Unusually, however, Jack West was not in it.

Rather, inside the plane were his friends, Pooh Bear and Stretch, plus their pilot, Sky Monster, all racing toward the Russian capital as fast as the sleek Tupolev Tu-144 could carry them.

Jack was also on his way, but he had been further out when the news had come in: that Lily had been found in Moscow, in Red Square, on the steps of St Basil's Cathedral. He had been returning from Australia with Aloysius Knight and Alby in Knight's Sukhoi Su-37 fighter-bomber.

Stretch and Pooh Bear had been much closer, in eastern France, so they had come straight here in the Tupolev.

The two soldiers—one a tall and lean Israeli sniper whose actual name was Benjamin Cohen, the other a short and chubby Arabian prince named Zahir al Anzar al Abbas—could not have been more different in appearance or temperament. Indeed, when they had first encountered each other in the early years of Lily's life at a remote farm in Kenya, they had barely been able to tolerate each other.

But one moment had changed all that.

During a firefight at the farm—when their enemies had ambushed them—Stretch and Pooh Bear had done an extraordinary thing: seeing Lily in danger, they had both, at the exact same time, leapt from cover, guns blazing, to rescue her.

In that moment, all of their differences had vanished and in the ensuing years, they had become the closest of friends, sharing homes and holidays, missions and milestones.

And when Lily was spotted—captured by facial-recognition software on a CCTV security camera in Red Square—there was no way on Earth that they were not going to dash to her rescue.

Sky Monster felt the same. The gentle big-bearded pilot from New Zealand had doted on Lily since she'd been a baby—although it had to be said that no-one in their little extended family, except maybe Jack, had any clue what his actual name was.

The three of them had weaponed up, boarded the *Sky Warrior* and taken off for Moscow immediately.

In the weeks after Stretch, Pooh and Alby had made the shocking—and thrilling—discovery at the Rock of Gibraltar that Lily had *not* been sacrificed during the ceremony there, Jack's team had regrouped.

At first, they had been scattered around the world, variously at the Rock and at the three secret cities of Thule, Atlas and Ra.

They had two main goals in the following weeks.

One: *find Lily.*

And two: figure out what Sphinx—having completed the Trial of the Cities—would do next in his quest to rule the world during the coming Omega Event.

But before they could do either of those things, they all had to get to safety.

Hades's apartment in Rome was deemed both too small and too vulnerable. If they were discovered there, escape would be difficult. It also couldn't accommodate the whole team.

They needed a place that could hold them all and allow them to do their ancient research, yet which also offered quick access to a runway or other means of rapid getaway.

Of course, as a former king in the shadow royal world, Hades owned just such a property, albeit one that he kept off the books.

It was a horse farm in Alsace-Lorraine, nestled in a classically Germanic forest just outside the medieval town of Lembach. Vast and rambling, he had once kept his many polo ponies here. When they'd been younger, he had brought his two sons to the estate for family vacations.

Then, a few years ago, Hades had sold it. But the sale had been a front; he had basically sold it to himself: it was now a hideaway in plain sight.

The estate met all their key requirements.

It had plenty of space; in fact, inside the main house, some of them got their own *wings*.

More interestingly, the enormous property contained within its boundaries a massive old concrete entry blockhouse—or *ouvrage*—to the Maginot Line, France's enormous complex of concrete forts, gun emplacements and connecting tunnels, built in the 1930s, which had spectacularly failed to stop the Nazi invasion of May 1940. The Germans had just swept *around* the Maginot Line, bypassing it by going through Belgium and the Netherlands.

In addition to the huge grey ouvrage, Hades's estate included a lake and lake house, a concealed runway and an old World War II military hangar which Hades used to garage his private jet.

One final group of team members also arrived: Jack's beloved animals—his falcon Horus and his dogs Roxy and Ash—brought by their earnest minder, the sweet Neanderthal known as E-147. They had taken a private plane from Australia, paid for by Hades, that had landed at nearby Strasbourg. Jack's mother, Mae, who had taken a shine to the short Neanderthal, had driven there to pick them up.

When they arrived at Hades's estate, the former minotaur from the Underworld emerged from the car carrying Horus and flanked by the two delighted bounding dogs.

'Hello, Captain Jack,' he said. 'All animals be well. I good dog minder. I feed dogs and walk dogs. I not eat dogs.'

Despite everything that was going on, Jack couldn't help but smile at that.

'I'm glad to hear you didn't eat my dogs, buddy. Nice work.'

The Neanderthal nodded enthusiastically.

Jack, of course, was consumed with their first objective.

'We find Lily,' he said. 'There's no point saving the world if she's out there, alone, with that bastard, Sphinx.'

To find her, they tapped into the U.S. government's top-secret facial recognition system known as TITAN, a system that used a worldwide network of closed-circuit security cameras, airport face scanners, social media apps, and even cell-phone facial locks, to geolocate individuals and pinpoint their locations.

If Lily stepped in front of a camera somewhere, they would know.

Police and military frequencies were tapped, as well as satellite feeds of aeroplane movements, but it would take time to get a hit.

On the ancient side of things, they began researching the next trial, the Trial of the Mountains.

Hades, Mae and Iolanthe took the lead on that, pulling up its description from the Zeus Papyrus. This was the papyrus that had been written at the command of Zeus himself after his champion had won the Great Games and he had received the Mysteries that showed one how to overcome the two trials that preceded the Omega Event. It was this that had introduced them to the Trial of the Cities. Now they focused on the second trial it mentioned:

THE TRIAL OF THE MOUNTAINS

Five iron mountains. Five bladed keys. Five doors forever locked.
But mark you, only those who survive the Fall,
May enter the Supreme Labyrinth
And look upon the face of the Omega.

While all this was happening, Jack went to two places.

First, he went with Zoe and Hades to a nearby but potentially very dangerous place: the Gallerie dell'Accademia in Venice, the home of the Fraternal Order of St Paul, or as they were known in the secret royal world, the monks of the Order of the Omega.

It was only *after* all the chaotic events surrounding the finding of the Three Secret Cities that Jack had learned what had become of the Omega monks.

They had vanished.

It had even been reported on the TV news: the secretive order had abandoned their lodgings adjoining the Gallerie dell'Accademia, taking with them all of their possessions, including many priceless works of art and sketches.

To the TV news anchors, they were just a group of quirky monks.

But to Jack they were something far more deadly.

They were experts in all the astronomical events connected to the Omega Event.

'They also showed themselves to be singular haters of women,' Jack said to Zoe and Hades as they broke into the Gallerie dell'Accademia in Venice a couple of days later. 'They think of women as baby-makers who were put on Earth to serve men.'

'So we're talking about very modern thinkers,' Zoe said drolly.

'The worst thing is these guys really believe it.'

Jack recalled when the leader of the monks, High Brother Ezekiel, had winced in almost physical pain when Lily had spoken to him.

'*Do not speak!*' he'd squealed. '"*Do not permit a woman to speak or to have authority over a man; she must be silent.*"'

Jack said to Zoe, 'Their leader, Brother Ezekiel, said that the female voice is a foul and disgusting thing.'

'*O-kay . . .*'

Hades said, 'The man you call Ezekiel was born Nicolai Niculescu. That was his name before he took on his holy name, Ezekiel. For the Omega monks, that holy name always starts with an *e*.

'Like many of his Omega brothers, Ezekiel is Romanian by birth. Some while ago, the Order became a haven for ultra-conservative

Romanian priests and monks, men who found the regular Church too *permissive*. To this day, the Order of the Omega maintains links to hardline Catholic soldiers within the Romanian armed forces.'

Zoe went to check the living quarters while Jack explored the innermost sanctum of the monks' realm: the main underground vault of the museum.

Police tape was stretched across its door, but he just tore it away and stepped inside.

The Omega monks had indeed taken pretty much everything they could carry.

That hadn't included the striking life-sized stone statue that stood in the centre of the vault.

It still stood here, the pained image of a man with his hands bound behind his back, his face pointed skyward, mouth open in an agonised scream.

Jack said to Hades, 'Ezekiel told me this statue is actually a *man* encased in liquid stone: an intruder who had been discovered inside the museum. Can that be true?'

'Entombment alive in greystone has long been a punishment in religious circles,' Hades said. 'That pained scream looks real enough to me.'

'I do *not* like these guys,' Jack said.

He crossed to several steel cabinets he had seen last time; they contained wide pull-out drawers that had been filled with parchments and sketches.

This was where he and Lily had found the tracing of the entire triangular stone tablet that had been the key to fulfilling the Trial of the Cities.

Jack recalled seeing among the other parchments here a star map on a papyrus sheet labelled in Latin, MAGNUM VIAM PORTAE QVINQVE: *The Five Gates to the Great Labyrinth*.

Now, however, most of the shallow drawers were empty, cleared of their contents. But some still contained random documents and scraps of paper.

On one such scrap, Jack saw some scribbled words: INCA INCERCAND SA DETERMINE LOCATIA CELUI DE-AL DOILEA.

'What language is that?' he asked.

'It's Romanian,' Hades said. 'It translates as: "Still trying to determine the location of the second mountain."'

'They're already in this race,' Jack said. 'That's what I was worried about.'

He found another note near the first one that read: INCA INCERCAND SA GASEASCA STATUIA SARELUI.

'What's this one say?'

'"Still trying to find the statue of the serpent,"' Hades said.

'Any idea what the statue of the serpent is?'

'No . . .' Hades said thoughtfully.

On another loose sheet of paper, Jack found a list of numbers: coordinates of some kind expressed in degrees of latitude and longitude:

Original Davies et al, 1987

	Latitude Deg N	Longitude Deg E	Latitude Deg N	Longitude Deg E
11 LRRR	0.6875	23.4333	0.67337 0.67409	23.47293 23.47298
12 ALSEP	-3.1975	23.3856	-3.01084 -3.01381	-23.42456 -23.41930
14 LRRR ALSEP	-3.6733	-17.4653	-3.64422 -3.64450 -3.64544	-17.47880 -17.47753 -17.47139
15 LRRR ALSEP	26.1008	3.6527	26.13333 26.13407 26.13224	3.62837 3.62981 3.63400
16 ALSEP	-8.9913	15.5144	-8.97577 -8.97341	15.49649 15.49859
17 ALSEP	20.1653	30.7658	20.18935 20.18809	30.76796 30.77475

He took it. He'd crosscheck the coordinates on a map later.

'Hey, Jack,' Zoe said, returning from the living quarters. 'Apart from a few Bibles left on bedside tables, this is all I found. Spotted it in a closet, in the pocket of an old jacket.'

She held in her hand a curious little hourglass hanging from a slim chain. Inside the hourglass was a fine-grained black-grey powder that Jack knew well.

Greystone.

Gorgon Stone.

The deadly powder that turned water to stone.

Jack took the little hourglass from Zoe and gazed at it. 'The Omega monks wear these around their necks.'

He looked about himself and shook his head. 'Come on. Let's get out of here. These assholes are long gone.'

After dropping Zoe and Hades back at Hades's estate, Jack had then dashed to his second destination, his secret farm back in Australia.

He took Alby and Aloysius Knight with him and they flew in Knight's plane.

Jack wanted to retrieve some ancient texts and files he kept in a bio-secure vault there. In particular, he was after a collection of documents related to his very first mission with Lily, the one involving the Great Pyramid at Giza and the Seven Wonders of the Ancient World.

He recalled that a couple of those documents—in the course of describing some of the booby-trapped places Jack had encountered during that mission—had mentioned ancient Egyptian labyrinths. Since the vault was biometrically sealed, only Jack could open it, so he had to go himself.

In addition to this, he had hoped to find an old Warbler of Wizard's that he had kept for many years. With its ability to deviate a bullet's flight, he figured the Warbler might come in handy in the coming days but he couldn't find it anywhere at the farm.

He also wanted to pick up one other thing . . . for Alby.

One of his old artificial hands.

During the mission to find the three cities, Alby had been cap-tured by Dion DeSaxe and the Knights of the Golden Eight. Using a supersharp ancient filament weapon, Dion had cruelly severed Alby's left hand. Over the years, Jack had upgraded his own pros-thetic titanium left forearm a few times, so he figured he could retrofit one of the old ones for Alby.

Having collected everything they needed at the farm, Jack, Alby and Aloysius had started their return flight to France and were in the air over the Persian Gulf when word came in.

Lily had been found . . .

. . . spotted by a security camera . . .

. . . in Red Square, Moscow.

AIRSPACE OVER MOSCOW
23 DECEMBER, 0910 HOURS

Stretch shot down through the sky at astronomical speed, buffeted by the freezing wind, his head pointed downward, his body shaped like a spear, his face covered in a high-altitude facemask.

The mask was actually Jack's. So was the high-altitude dropsuit Stretch wore and the carbon-fibre wings on his back known as gull-wings.

Stretch didn't care whose gear he wore. He wanted to rescue Lily.

Three miles below him was Moscow.

The city looked like a freezing mix of mottled white and grey, the combination of snow, slush, and grim Russian architecture.

With one shining exception.

In the heart of this monochromatic metropolis lay a precinct that was painted in the most vivid and striking colours.

The Kremlin district.

The famous fortress is painted in a deep shade of red: rich blood-red. It is this colour that inspired the name of the square beside it. Some think Red Square was a Soviet name, but this isn't true. The name preceded the Soviets.

And in that square, next to the Kremlin, also exploding with colour, is St Basil's, with its colourful onion domes and red and green walls.

The city's three concentric ring roads gave Moscow a roughly circular shape, with Red Square nestled in the innermost ring.

Cutting across the three concentric rings was the thick white line that was the frozen Moskva River.

While Stretch zoomed downward, soaring high in the sky above him in a holding pattern were Pooh Bear and Sky Monster in the *Sky Warrior*, ready to dive in fast and low with a retrieval hook-and-cable when Stretch found Lily.

As Stretch fell further, the details of Moscow became clearer: in the innermost circle, he could make out the blood-red Kremlin and the domes of St Basil's Cathedral.

As he came in low, Stretch hit a switch and his gull-wings sprang out from their swept-back position into gliding mode and suddenly he banked in a controlled swoop, shooting in fast over the Moskva River, following its twisting curves, heading toward St Basil's.

Then he saw the bodies.

And the side-turned cars and buses.

And the crashed garbage trucks.

The people lay on riverside walks, face-down, arms wide, as if they had crawled in their final moments. One man's dog was still tethered by its leash to his wrist. It barked forlornly.

'Pooh, Sky Monster, are you seeing this?' Stretch said into his throat mike. A camera on his facemask was recording everything.

'*Good Lord*,' Pooh Bear's gruff voice said in his ear. '*We're seeing it.*'

'*Are they dead?*' Sky Monster's voice said.

'Don't know,' Stretch said. 'But the whole city looks like a ghost town.'

'*Be careful, old friend,*' Pooh Bear said.

Stretch flew over the white-frozen river until he came to the Kremlin and Red Square.

Still no movement.

And then he saw St Basil's Cathedral . . .

. . . and three tiny figures seated on its front steps.

Stretch's heart leapt.

The middle one was Lily.

Lily watched from her bound and gagged position on the west portico of St Basil's as the winged figure swooped in to a perfect landing on the cobblestones of Red Square twenty metres in front of her.

At first she thought it was Jack: the outfit, the gull-wings and the opaque black visor of the high-altitude facemask.

She strained against her bonds, her eyes bulging, yelling uselessly through the gag in her mouth.

Then the man flipped up his visor and she saw that it was not Jack but Stretch.

'Lily! Oh, thank God,' he said, clambering up the steps. He spoke into his mike as he ran: 'Guys, confirmed. It's her, and she's alive.'

Stretch raced to Lily's side and yanked the gag off her mouth.

'It's okay, Lily. I'm here now. I'm here to get you out.'

Her body quivering from the cold, Lily sobbed, 'Oh, Stretch! No! You shouldn't have come . . .'

'A lot of people care about you, kid,' Stretch said kindly. 'Everyone you know has been trying to find you. I got Pooh circling above us with Sky Monster, and Jack is en route—'

Lily shook her head. 'No, Stretch, I didn't mean it that way. I meant you shouldn't have come because this is a trap!'

At the exact moment that Lily said those words to Stretch, they were being watched.

By four individuals.

Two of these watchers stood about half a kilometre away, over by the river, atop the high corner watchtower of the Kremlin.

They were both Knights of the Golden Eight and they observed Lily and Stretch through high-powered digital binoculars.

They were Jaeger Zwei—translation: *Hunter Two*; the second most senior member of the Knights—and Jaeger Acht, *Hunter Eight*, the most junior of the ruthless knights-for-hire.

The other pair of people watching Stretch and Lily did so from a different vantage point, the opposite side of Red Square.

They hid behind the snow-flecked trees of Zaryadye Park. They wore bulky white parkas, white reflective goggles and state-of-the-art headphones. White woollen scarves masked their faces and they made sure not to be seen.

Standing on their watchtower, Jaeger Zwei and Jaeger Acht gazed down at Stretch. They had tracked him on their scanners all the way into Moscow.

Jaeger Zwei keyed his radio-mike: 'Sir, this is Zwei. West just arrived here. He came in on those gull-wings that he used against us at Aragon Castle.'

'*Put him to sleep,*' Jaeger Eins's voice said through Zwei's

headphones. '*I would very much like to remove some of Captain West's body parts when he wakes.*'

'Copy that, sir,' Jaeger Zwei said. 'It will be our pleasure.'

Then he picked up a remote-control unit beside him and hit a switch on it.

It rose quickly from behind a building near St Basil's Cathedral, shooting vertically into the sky.

Catching the movement out of the corner of his eye, Stretch spun.

Lily gazed up at it in horror. 'Oh, shit.'

It was the drone Chinook helicopter that she had seen used earlier. Still suspended from its underbelly was the ancient spherical bell.

The Chinook rose in the way of robotic drones: up, up, up, fast, fast, fast.

Stretch frowned. 'What's going on?'

'We're in trouble,' Lily said as he cut her hands free. 'Big trouble.'

She snatched the sheet of paper pinned to the chest of one of the headless nuns beside her, the sheet with the grim handwritten warning:

YOU
WILL
WAKE
AS
SLAVES

'Sphinx left this for whoever came to rescue me. I think he figured Jack would be the one who found me first.'

'What does it mean? *You will wake as slaves . . .*' Stretch said.

In answer, Lily just craned her neck to look up at the drone chopper now hovering high above the coloured domes of St Basil's.

'We're about to go to sleep. You got a pen?'

Stretch was now really confused, but he did have a Sharpie in his suit's breast pocket. He handed it to Lily.

She started writing hurriedly on the sheet. 'You say Pooh Bear and Sky Monster are circling above us in the *Sky Warrior*?'

'Yes. Why?'

'Shit, they'll be within thirty miles. The soundwave will knock them out. Call Sky Monster right now and tell him to put the plane on autopilot and, if he has them, to put on full noise-cancelling headphones. Pooh as well.'

Stretch knew better than to argue so while Lily kept writing, he did just that.

Then, high above them, the drone helicopter rocked . . .

. . . causing the spherical bell hanging from it to ring out.

The eerie sound rippled across Moscow again, fanning out in an invisible wave.

Stretch looked up at the noise: it was so beautiful, so true, so perfectly—

'We don't have long,' Lily said, scribbling fast.

A second later, she and Stretch collapsed together to the ground.

They were still awake, for now.

Stretch's eyes boggled in confusion. 'What the—?'

Lily had never felt anything like it.

It was as if her legs had been kicked out from under her.

'I just have to . . .' she gasped as she crawled on her belly, her legs useless, dragging herself on her elbows to the pen and paper she had dropped as she'd collapsed.

She wrote on it some more, but her pen strokes were getting slower as her mind and body faded.

'. . . have to . . .'

Sleep overtook her.

And as Lily slumped to the ground on the front steps of the famed Russian cathedral, she realised that Sphinx had been well informed about the effect of the spheres.

An almost electric charge of something that could only be

described as pure bliss—joy, ecstasy—ran through her, tapping the pleasure centres of her brain in an almost chemical way, and suddenly falling asleep seemed like the most wonderful and desirable thing in the world.

Lily and Stretch's heads dropped to the ground as they fell into matching comas.

From their position atop the corner watchtower of the Kremlin, Jaegers Zwei and Acht saw them go down.

Jaeger Zwei smiled thinly.

'Jaeger Acht,' he said, 'if you would be so kind, please go down there and secure the bodies of the girl and Captain West. It will be our honour to present them to our lord emperor, Sphinx, later.'

'Yes, sir.' Jaeger Acht hurried for the stairs behind them.

A short while later, Jaeger Acht stepped out of Spasskaya Gate and crossed the deserted expanse of Red Square, gripping his gun as he approached St Basil's.

He came to the southern end of the west portico and beheld the slumped bodies of Lily and—

It wasn't West.

It was one of his companions.

The Israeli, wearing West's gull-wings and drop gear.

Jaeger Acht keyed his radio. 'Zwei, come in! It's not—'

Acht never saw the blow coming.

Someone hit him in the back of the head with a pistol butt and he fell, knocked out cold.

A figure stepped out from behind Jaeger Acht, emerging from the shadows of the portico, dressed in a thick brown parka, tan cargo pants, sturdy boots and a fireman's helmet.

'It's not *me*,' he said, standing over the fallen man.

It was Jack West Jr.

BENEATH MOSCOW
15 MINUTES EARLIER

The ultra-modern train boomed through the tunnel underneath southern Moscow, rushing toward the Kremlin and Red Square.

The train belonged to the Russian president, Vladimir Putin, but he wasn't travelling in it today.

No, today it held Jack West Jr, Aloysius Knight and Alby Calvin.

They were the only occupants of the train and they all stood in the driver's compartment.

Jack gazed out through the forward windshield, watching the tracks sweep by beneath him at speed.

His eyes were fixed.

His jaw was set.

His entire body was energised like it had never been before.

Lily was here.

And he was coming to get her.

The train in which Jack was travelling—and the tunnel around it—was exceedingly modern.

For it was not a regular Moscow subway train. Nor was this a regular subway tunnel.

It had been Knight's suggestion to enter Moscow this way.

His reasoning: only a select few people knew about the secret railway; it led directly into the heart of Moscow; and it could get them there both unseen and fast.

In his dark past as an international bounty hunter, Aloysius Knight—or as some knew him, the Black Knight—had done a job for Vladimir Putin.

The details of the mission were murky, but it had involved an incident early in Putin's presidency: the kidnapping of his niece and the delivery of some of her fingers to Putin.

When Russian intelligence and its military had failed to locate the child, Aloysius Knight had been called in.

He'd rescued the girl—minus the fingers—killed her captors and returned her to her uncle.

His reward had been his plane, a hover-capable Sukhoi Su-37 fighter-bomber and refuelling privileges at any Russian base in the world. (For a bounty hunter this was a worthy prize, especially the refuelling part.)

What the mission had also revealed to Aloysius Knight was this secret train line that ran *underneath* the southern sector of Moscow's subway system.

'It's known as "Subway 2" or, in intelligence circles, "D-6",' Aloysius said as their high-speed train blasted through the tunnel. 'A secure subway line that can get you from the Kremlin to Vnukovo Airport south of the city in ten minutes flat. It was designed to allow senior leadership figures a rapid escape from the city, should such an evacuation be required.'

'A secret presidential train line,' Jack said.

'That's some nice insider knowledge you got there, Captain Knight,' Alby added.

'You think this is nice,' Aloysius said, 'let me know when you want to take over an aeroplane remotely. A few years ago, a government that shall not be named gave me a nice little hack of the GPS satellite system used for navigation by most military and commercial aircraft. The hack of the nav-system lets you take over a plane's controls. Doesn't work every time, but it got me out of a couple of pretty tight situations.'

Alby nodded. 'Love your style, man.'

'Hey,' Aloysius said. 'You guys got your secret ancient world, I got my secret government one.'

As Stretch and Lily had been collapsing on the steps of St Basil's, Jack, Aloysius and Alby had been landing in Knight's Sukhoi Su-37 at Vnukovo Airport.

They found the entire airport still.

All the staff lay motionless on the ground, a light snow falling on their bodies.

Jack had checked the pulses of two of them.

'They're alive,' he said. 'It's like they're *sleeping*.'

Aloysius slapped one comatose man hard across the face. He didn't wake.

'This isn't sleeping,' he said sourly. 'I think this is more of your weird ancient shit, Jack.'

Cynical and dry at the best of times, Aloysius Knight had been consistently struck by the stranger elements of Jack's world after he had been brought in by Shane Schofield to rescue Jack from the Royal Prison at Erebus.

They dragged the comatose ground crew members into shelter and hurried—unchallenged, since all the guards had also collapsed—into the bowels of the airport and to its secret presidential train line.

As they rushed into central Moscow on Vladimir Putin's private bullet train, Jack turned to Alby.

'You getting anything from Stretch?'

'Not a word,' Alby said from his portable radio console. 'Stretch, Pooh and Sky Monster are not responding. Jack, *all of Moscow* is silent. No radio, no TV. Nothing.'

Jack frowned. 'What happened here?'

Stretch had made it to Red Square and confirmed that it was

indeed Lily seated out in front of St Basil's Cathedral and that she was alive.

But then, moments later, Stretch had suddenly and inexplicably gone off the air.

There was no word from Lily.

Or from Pooh and Sky Monster in the *Sky Warrior*.

Jack swore.

He was racing into an empty city whose citizens lay unconscious and where three of his friends and his daughter had just gone unexpectedly and ominously silent.

The secret train squealed to a halt inside a concrete-and-steel station buried beneath the presidential palace in the Kremlin.

Jack emerged from the engine car, gun up and hyper-alert, flanked by Knight and watched by Alby.

It was a very modern station, clean and well lit.

Every single uniformed guard lay slumped on the floor or inside glass booths.

'This way,' Knight said. 'There's a tunnel that leads under the square to St Basil's. I think it's best we get to your girl as unobserved as possible.'

'I concur,' Jack said. 'Alby, you stay here. Go to the engine car at the other end of the train, start it up and keep the engine running, in case we need to make a quick getaway.'

'Jack—'

'I know you want to come, son,' Jack said. He glanced at the high-tech metal hand now affixed to Alby's left wrist. They'd successfully attached it on the flight back and Alby had spent most of the journey practising with it, grasping and holding large objects then smaller ones. It would still take time to get fully used to it. 'You're more help to her here and you know it.'

Alby nodded. 'Okay.'

Jack and Aloysius swept out of the deserted underground train station, dashing into a long foot tunnel that cut eastward.

Aloysius led the way and after a few minutes, they emerged in a crypt underneath St Basil's Cathedral.

'This way,' Aloysius said, hurrying up some stairs.

Up they went, before they arrived inside the nave of the cathedral. It soared above them for hundreds of feet, decorated with paintings of Jesus Christ and the Virgin Mary.

Jack and Aloysius didn't stop to gawk.

They ran across the wide empty nave, guns up.

As he ran, Jack heard the distant thump of a helicopter somewhere outside.

He kept going, knowing that his desperation to get to Lily was blinding him.

He didn't care.

He had to find her.

With his gun raised, he hurried with Aloysius down the covered steps of the cathedral's west portico, until suddenly, at the base of the stairs, he saw a man dressed in the black uniform of the Knights of the Golden Eight standing over the slumped bodies of Lily and Stretch.

Jack pistol-whipped the Knight and the man fell to the ground.

Then Jack hurried over to the prone bodies of Lily and Stretch.

Behind him, Aloysius stopped dead in his tracks, gazing out at the empty square and the scattered bodies all over it.

'Jesus, it's *all* of Moscow,' he breathed.

As he came closer to them, Jack saw that Lily and Stretch lay slumped beside two headless bodies perched on a pair of chairs.

He raced past them, going directly to Lily, sliding to his knees beside her, snatching her up in his arms.

She lolled lifelessly, her eyes closed.

Was she dead?

He checked for a pulse.

Found one, a weak one.

Thank goodness . . .

'Lily! Wake up!'

She didn't respond.

'Lily! Come on, *please* . . .' Jack had tears in his eyes.

She was cold, very cold, but alive and by the look of it, in the same somnolent state as the other people they'd encountered on the way here.

He held her tight against his body, trying to warm her.

As he gripped her, Jack closed his eyes for a moment.

He recalled his anguish three weeks previously when, at the Rock of Gibraltar, he'd thought she was dead, the victim of Sphinx's cruel sacrificial rite there. It had been the lowest point of his life. He had felt that everything he'd ever lived for was gone.

Now it was the opposite. Now he was energised beyond measure. That she was in this mysterious unconscious state was unexpected, but he didn't care.

She was alive and he'd found her.

★ ★ ★

At that moment, as he held Lily in his arms, Jack was being watched.

Jaeger Zwei scowled. 'Fuck.'

The first guy hadn't been West.

But here he was now.

Zwei reached for the remote that controlled the drone Chinook helicopter with the bell while at the same time lifting his radio to his mouth and yelling: 'West is here! Squires! Bring in the trucks!'

Jack turned to Aloysius.

'We're lucky we got here when we did. If she was out in this weather much longer, she'd be dead of hypothermia.'

Aloysius's eyes were searching the area. 'We need to leave. Right now . . .'

His voice trailed off as four huge trucks emerged from the four corners of Red Square, tyres squealing, and skidded to matching halts around St Basil's Cathedral, surrounding it.

They were not regular trucks.

They were big semi-trailer rigs, but with unusual trailers. They were full-sized Scandia car-carriers, equipped with superlong skeletal trailers designed to carry upward of ten cars each.

Except these four car-carriers did not carry cars.

On their platforms stood dozens of bronzemen.

As Jack held Lily, he and Aloysius snapped round to look at the four rigs loaded with bronze automatons now surrounding their position.

Both men had encountered the bronzemen before. Silent, faceless, robotic and remorseless, they had resided for thousands of years in coffins at the Three Secret Cities and the Underworld. At the completion of the Great Games at the Underworld in India, the deadly bronzemen had been awakened. They were impervious to bullets and could not be reasoned with.

'Not these things again,' Aloysius said.

Jack bit his lip. 'If they're here, I'm guessing that Sphinx must somehow now control them.'

It was at that moment that Aloysius looked down and saw a sheet of paper on the mushy ground beside Lily.

He picked it up and read it.

'Oh, *fuck* . . .' he said, spinning around suddenly. 'Fuck, fuck, fuck!'

Jack turned. 'What?'

And then Aloysius did the strangest thing.

He looked Jack in the eye and said, 'The world needs you right now more than it needs me.'

And with those peculiar words, Aloysius snatched his own helmet off his head—complete with its attached ear-protection headphones—*and threw it to Jack.*

'Put the headphones on, Jack! Put them on now! Or we're all done for. Don't let me do this for nothing.'

Confused, Jack looked from Aloysius's eyes to his helmet with its dangling earphones.

Aloysius Knight was a soldier's soldier and a seriously tough motherfucker. Jack had never heard him speak like this before.

So he whipped off his own fireman's helmet and put on Aloysius's helmet, sealing his ears inside its headphones.

A bare second later, a massive double-rotored Chinook helicopter rose into view above them, appearing from behind the spires of St Basil's, and Jack saw the enormous, ancient, gold-and-silver bell suspended from its underbelly and then the chopper rocked and the bell rang out.

At the sound of the spherical bell, Aloysius Knight's eyes rolled up into his head and he collapsed instantly.

He hit the ground and groaned, clawing with his fingers for a few seconds, before all his muscles relaxed and he went still, unconscious.

Jack had seen many things in his adventures, but nothing like this.

Aloysius's words echoed in his mind.

The world needs you right now more than it needs me.

Then he'd thrown him his protective headphones.

That had been after he'd read the note.

Jack snatched up the note.

He saw the original message on it, written in bold black letters:

YOU
WILL
WAKE
AS
SLAVES

But after that were scrawled additions in Lily's distinctive handwriting:

Sphinx has a sonic weapon
Protect ears!
He also knows about Omega:

Newton's planet, Friedmann + Einstein k>0.
I love you, Daddy.
I knew you'd come for m

The final word was unfinished.

Me.

Lily's pen had trailed off as she'd evidently lost consciousness.

But her warning had done its job.

It had galvanised Aloysius Knight to sacrifice himself and give his helmet with its protective earphones to Jack. If the world was to be saved from Sphinx and the coming Omega Event—Aloysius had deduced in that split second—it was Jack West Jr, with all his historical knowledge and experience, and not Aloysius, who had the best chance of saving it.

Jack looked desperately around himself.

He was alone, on his knees, out in front of St Basil's Cathedral in Red Square, wearing another guy's helmet and earphones, with the limp body of Lily in his arms and the slumped bodies of Stretch and Aloysius on the ground beside him . . . while at least one hundred bronzemen had arrived around the cathedral, flanking it on every side.

'You have got to be kidding . . .' he said to no-one.

And then the small army of bronzemen stepped off the car-carriers in unison and started striding toward him.

The four groups of bronzemen closed in on the cathedral from all four of its corners.

In the face of their approach, Jack did the only thing he could think to do.

He threw Lily over his left shoulder. He detached the carbon-fibre gull-wings from Stretch's body and grabbed hold of him by a strap on his dropsuit. As for Aloysius, Jack clipped his own fireman's helmet onto Aloysius's head, snatched him by the hard collar of his body armour and hauled him along the ground into the west portico of the cathedral.

He moved awkwardly backwards, dragging two men and holding one young woman on his shoulder.

Lily wasn't a huge burden. Twenty years old, slim and fit, she didn't weigh much. In any case, Jack would have dragged her out of Hell itself with his last dying breath.

But Stretch was a full-grown man and Aloysius was heavier still.

It was a huge amount of weight for one man to pull, but Jack did it, grunting with the exertion, heaving with all his strength.

The four ranks of bronzemen kept advancing.

Jack dragged his companions under the portico's awning, panting desperately, glancing back at the approaching bronzemen as he did.

There must have been thirty bronzemen in the group nearest to him. Four groups meant over a hundred in total.

Their footfalls boomed in the chilly air.

The body of a Russian Army trooper lay face-down on the ground between Jack and the bronzemen nearest to him.

The first bronzeman stomped on the man's head, smashing it under its metal foot, making his skull burst like a tomato.

The following ranks of bronzemen, marching forward, ground the rest of the man to nothing, crushing his remains into the slush, discolouring the snow with his blood.

None of them even noticed what they were stepping on.

Jack did. 'Shit.'

He kept staggering backwards under the weight of his daughter and his friends further into the portico.

If he could get back to the tunnel under the main nave, he might be able to—

And then Jack fell.

His foot slipped on some ice and he toppled onto the steps of the portico, losing his grip on Stretch and Aloysius and almost dropping Lily.

It was simply too much to carry all three of them on his own.

He couldn't do it alone.

But he couldn't leave them.

Wouldn't leave them.

Jack bowed his head, exhausted, beaten.

'Need a hand?' a voice said from behind him.

Jack spun.

Alby stood at the top of the steps: a young black man of twenty-one, with one natural hand and one prosthetic one, and nothing protecting his ears.

Yet somehow he was okay . . .

He must have entered the cathedral via the underground tunnel from the Kremlin.

Alby said apologetically to Jack, 'I know you told me to wait at the train, but I just couldn't. I had to come for Lily—'

Jack clambered to his feet. 'Alby! Shut up! I'm so glad you came! Get down here and help me!'

★ ★ ★

Jack had entirely forgotten about Alby, waiting back at the secret presidential train station.

But then, he supposed, if he had remembered, he'd have assumed Alby had succumbed to the bell when it had taken out Aloysius.

But he hadn't.

Because there was something special about Alby.

Alby was deaf.

He was only able to hear because of the brilliant device implanted in his skull: a Cochlear implant that turned natural sounds into digital ones.

The bell hadn't affected him.

Jack leapt into action.

He handed Aloysius to Alby while he kept Lily on his shoulder and dragged Stretch himself. Alby hoisted Aloysius up into a fireman's carry.

Relieved of the extra weight, Jack moved much faster now and he and Alby fled into the beautiful nave of St Basil's.

They ignored the splendid high-ceilinged nave, instead just scampering down some side stairs, heading one level down, until they spotted the secret tunnel to the Kremlin—

—when suddenly ten bronzemen emerged from that tunnel, blocking that escape route.

'Damn it, no!' Jack breathed. 'We can't get out that way!'

'What do we do?' Alby said.

Jack spun, thinking fast.

Then he had a thought and he keyed the radio-mike on his headset, Aloysius's headset.

'Rufus? You there?' he asked.

'*Cap'n West?*' came the confused reply. It was the voice of Aloysius's gentle-giant pilot, Rufus. He was still at Vnukovo Airport on the southwestern outskirts of the city.

Jack breathed with relief. As he'd hoped, Rufus wore the same ear-protecting headphones that Aloysius did.

'Rufus! We're in trouble! Aloysius is out cold! We're stuck inside St Basil's Cathedral and we need an immediate evac! Can you come and get us?'

'*You bet. Where do you want me to pick you up?*'

Jack looked upward and swallowed.

'From on top of the cathedral.'

Jack and Alby hauled ass up the tight stairwells of St Basil's Cathedral, carrying their friends.

While the nine onion-shaped domes atop the spires of St Basil's Cathedral seem irregularly placed, they are actually arrayed in a symmetrical pattern: the four bigger domes form a + while the smaller domes form an x around them.

The ninth dome occupies the highest and most central point of the cathedral, the top of the colossal spire above the nave. It is the only onion dome that is unpainted since it is made of gold.

The cathedral ascends gradually in essentially three levels: its wide base, made of red bricks; a middle level comprising small sections of green-painted roofs that connect the trunks of the spires; and finally, the spectacular spires themselves.

Jack kicked open a window and emerged on the western side of the middle roof level, standing between two of the spires and above the awning of the west portico.

The slanting green awning of the portico sloped away from him in a step-like manner, heading both north and south.

From this vantage point, he could see two of the car-carriers down on the square: they had almost finished disgorging their loads of bronzemen.

At the northern end of the portico's roof, he saw a crashed garbage truck. When its driver had been incapacitated by the first ringing of the spherical bell, he must have smashed up against the portico.

Right now, the bronzemen from the car-carrier nearest to the garbage truck hurried past it, entering the cathedral.

They moved fast, racing into the building via the portico's ground-level doors.

Alby stepped up beside Jack. 'What do we do?'

'Rufus isn't going to get here in time,' Jack said.

He jerked his chin at the crashed garbage truck.

'We get on that and drive outta here,' he said. 'Come on.'

Down onto the roof of the portico they ran, carrying Lily, Aloysius and Stretch, while below them, the bronzemen invaded the cathedral via every available door.

Jack and Alby came to the edge of the roof just above the garbage truck.

'You go first,' Jack said. 'I'll lower them down to you.'

Alby lay Stretch down on the roof and leapt down to the garbage truck's flat steel top.

Jack passed Lily down to him first. Alby caught hold of her and slid her gently into the garbage truck's cab.

Jack lowered Stretch next. Working with his new artificial hand, Alby struggled a little as he guided Stretch's body safely down into the garbage truck's cabin—

A sudden thudding noise made Jack spin.

He looked behind him and his eyes boggled.

He and Alby had been spotted by some bronzemen on the ground . . .

. . . *and so they'd started climbing the outer wall of the nearest spire!*

The bronzemen climbed with brutal efficiency.

With their metal claws and shocking strength they just *punched* holes in the brickwork and scaled the vertical walls, climbing quickly.

'Goddamn . . .' Jack breathed.

'Jesus . . .' Alby agreed.

Jack did the calculations in a split second.

There wasn't enough time for him to lower Aloysius and himself onto the garbage truck before the bronzemen swarmed it.

He had to get Lily away.

'Alby! Go! Get Lily outta here! We'll catch up!'

'How?'

'I don't know yet! Just go!'

Alby knew not to argue, so he just hopped down into the cab, shoved the comatose driver out the door, gunned the engine and zoomed away from the cathedral.

On the roof of the portico, Jack hoisted Aloysius Knight onto his shoulders, grunting under the weight.

'Shit, shit, shit.'

There was only one way he could go and survive.

Up.

With the limp body of Aloysius Knight on his shoulders, Jack pounded up the tight spiral staircase inside the tallest spire of St Basil's.

He could hear the bronzemen ascending the stairs below him: a chorus of heavy footsteps.

If anyone had been awake in Moscow to see St Basil's from the outside at that moment, they would have seen quite a sight.

It was literally crawling with bronzemen.

They were scaling it on every side, dozens of them, punching handholds into its red brick walls and swarming like ants up its snow-covered flanks.

They slithered around its onion domes, clambered up the vertical walls of its towers, converging on the central spire.

At that instant, a small window up near the summit of the tallest spire was kicked open from within, sending a deposit of snow on the ledge outside it flying into thin air, and Jack emerged on the tiny ledge with Aloysius on his shoulders.

Breathless and gasping, he looked down.

A dizzying drop fell away from him. Greater Moscow spread out to the horizon.

He also saw, directly below him, two dozen bronzemen coming for him, scaling the walls of the main tower like relentless metal demons: they were brilliant climbers, oblivious to the deadly height. They punched their hand- and footholds easily, and, worst of all, they never tired.

'Damn,' Jack said. He'd been climbing for two people and he was sweating and exhausted.

He drew his Desert Eagle pistol and fired it at the nearest bronzeman.

Ping!

The bullet bounced off the metal face of the automaton with a spark. The bronzeman hardly noticed. It just kept climbing.

'Oh, come *on*,' Jack said. 'All right, then . . .'

Jack fired again, this time at the brickwork near the bronzeman's clawed hands, causing two brittle old bricks around the bronzeman's fingers to shatter and give way . . .

. . . and this time the creature fell!

It dropped away from Jack and Aloysius, collecting two of its fellow automatons on the way down.

But the others just kept on coming.

They climbed relentlessly, closing in around Jack.

Jack fired at them anyway.

His rounds pinged off their skulls harmlessly.

The nearest bronzeman rose to its feet on the same parapet on which Jack now stood with Aloysius, only fifteen feet away.

Jack levelled his pistol at it and fired—

—and the bronzeman was blown off the parapet with violent force, as if hit by a cannonball, not a pistol round!

'What the—?' Jack looked incredulously at his gun.

Vrooooom!

With a deafening roar, Aloysius Knight's black hover-capable Sukhoi Su-37 fighter-bomber—the *Black Raven*—came swooping into a hover behind Jack, right beside his high tower.

It fired it cannons again, blowing the nearest bronzemen off the tower, sending them sailing off it and falling hundreds of feet.

If the sight of the bronzemen swarming all over the famous cathedral was something to behold then the appearance of the Sukhoi beside its highest spire was simply spectacular.

The Sukhoi edged in close to the spire, the thunderous downblast of its thrusters sending snow billowing everywhere in wild flurries.

A steel cage on chains descended from the underbelly of the Sukhoi, swinging wildly, arriving next to Jack . . .

. . . just as the first bronzeman—entirely oblivious to the swirling snowstorm around it—slammed one of its metal hands down on the ledge right next to Jack's feet, its claws digging into the stone.

Gripping Aloysius's limp body on his shoulders, Jack leapt for the steel cage.

Because he was holding Aloysius, he couldn't reach with his hands. He had to dive *into* the open basket.

Jack flew through the air, high above St Basil's Cathedral and the hoard of climbing bronzemen—

—and landed inside the basket, rolling to a halt within it, holding Aloysius tight.

'Rufus! Go!'

In response, the plane banked wildly, lunging away from the historic cathedral, engines roaring, thrusters flaring.

Two bronzemen tried to leap into the basket after Jack and they almost made it, their outstretched claws missing it by millimetres.

But the Sukhoi was away, clear of the building.

'*Where to?*' Rufus's voice said in Jack's headphones.

Jack didn't hesitate.

'Catch up with Alby! He got away with Lily and Stretch in a garbage truck! Follow that truck!'

As Jack was climbing up the inside of St Basil's highest spire, Alby Calvin had been in the middle of his own private car chase.

He was driving like a maniac across Red Square with two unconscious passengers in the cab with him and six bronzemen clinging to the sides of his speeding garbage truck.

If that wasn't bad enough, close behind him were two of the gigantic car-carriers that had brought the bronzemen into the square around St Basil's.

When the drivers of the car-carriers had seen Alby back out from the west portico in the garbage truck, they had powered up and come after him, their engines roaring and still with maybe ten bronzemen on each of their long multi-levelled trailers.

As Alby had gunned his truck away from St Basil's into the wider square, one of the two car-carriers had swept in close beside him and some bronzemen had leapt off it onto his moving garbage truck!

Alby swerved wildly, but the bronzemen hung on.

He swept right, grinding the right flank of his truck against the towering red wall of the Kremlin, and suddenly the three bronzemen clinging to that side were no longer there.

'Take that, you metal assholes,' Alby said.

Right then, with a loud *boom*, Aloysius's black Sukhoi Su-37 swept in low over him, rushing in from the southwest, heading for St Basil's.

Rufus had arrived.

Alby hoped he could keep driving—and stay alive—long enough to meet up with the Sukhoi.

He glanced in his left side mirror and saw two bronzemen on that flank of his truck, edging their way toward the cab.

The garbage truck was now careening wildly down the steep brick-paved slope that connected Red Square to the Moskva River.

The slope had a name: Basil's Descent. The descent ran all the way down to the river beside the on-ramp to the Bolshoy Moskvoretsky Bridge.

Alby swung left and ground that flank of the garbage truck against the on-ramp's foundations and the bronzemen were swept off—

—only for one final enterprising bronzeman to attack suddenly from above him, from the roof of the garbage truck's cabin.

With the howling squeal of rending metal, this creature peeled back the roof of the truck, and the winter air rushed into the cab and Alby looked up in horror to see the faceless automaton glaring down at him, crouching, preparing to jump into the cab.

In a panic, Alby slammed on the brakes.

The inertia sent the bronzeman on the roof flying off the truck and tumbling, bouncing, cartwheeling down the descent before disappearing over the low fence guarding the river.

The sudden braking movement, however, also locked the garbage truck's wheels, sending it into a wild skid on the icy cobbled pavement of Basil's Descent.

Alby looked ahead, aghast, as his garbage truck aquaplaned down the hill, totally out of control, toward the river's edge.

There was no way to regain traction or to steer the heavy truck out of the skid. Indeed, the truck itself was *rotating* laterally as it shot toward the river, so that as it came to the guardrail, it was travelling ass-end first.

Alby saw the future a second before it happened.

The garbage truck, now sliding backwards, shot at speed off the bottom of the descent, blasting through the low fence, and dropped into the broad Moskva River below.

Alby's garbage truck fell, rear-end first, for a full twenty feet before it landed with an almighty crash not in water but on solid ground.

Well, almost solid ground.

It slammed into the frozen surface of the river.

On most winter mornings in Moscow, icebreakers carved through the frozen-over river, opening paths in the ice for ferries.

But with the city in a collective coma, the morning icebreakers had not done their usual job and now the wide Moskva River looked like a vast snow-covered field, frozen and white, with a crust of ice maybe twelve inches thick, more than enough to hold a car or even a large truck . . .

. . . but not nearly thick enough to withstand the impact of a falling ten-ton garbage truck.

Alby was thrown into his backrest as the garbage truck's rear bumper smashed into the ice-covered surface of the river only a few metres from the Moskvoretsky Bridge.

Like a hammer striking glass, the steel bumper of the truck cracked the ice instantly into a dozen spiderwebs.

In any other circumstance, it would have looked comical: the garbage truck lying there nose-up and vertical, its wheels pressed against the embankment wall, its rear hopper embedded in the iced-over river.

But not now, for with the ice broken, the garbage truck immediately and inexorably began to sink.

★ ★ ★

Alby was moving in an instant.

With the whole truck around him sliding downward, he threw off his seatbelt, kicked open the driver's door and hurled Stretch out onto the ice.

He grabbed Lily next and just as the sinking truck's cab came level with the ice-crust and was about to go under, Alby leapt clear of it with Lily in his arms.

They landed on the ice in a clumsy heap, with the unconscious Lily flopping like a ragdoll, just as the garbage truck disappeared completely into the hole it had created and was swallowed by the freezing waters of the Moskva.

Alby gasped for air, his face pressed against the snow-dusted ice.

'Man, this is hardcore—'

They were the only words he got out before he saw a figure appear at the guardrail of the embankment high above him: another bronzeman.

Alby didn't know what to do.

He still had Lily and Stretch to protect but he no longer had a vehicle to carry them in.

He could hear the Sukhoi over at the cathedral: too far away.

Six more bronzemen joined the one at the guardrail.

'No,' Alby said softly.

His escape was over.

It appeared suddenly from behind Alby, speeding out from under the nearby bridge, sliding to a controlled halt on the ice a few feet away from him, Lily and Stretch.

It was a compact thing that looked like a motorcycle-snowmobile hybrid.

The forward half was the motorbike part, with handlebars, a saddle and a ski instead of a front tyre. The rear half was like a little truck bed with two tracks underneath it. The logo of the Moscow Department of Parks was on its side.

Two figures in bulky white parkas rode it—one astride the saddle, the other crouched in the rear tray—their faces obscured by

reflective white goggles, white helmets with headphones and white scarves over their faces.

The second pair of watchers.

The rider tore the scarf and goggles off, to reveal herself to be a pretty young woman in her late twenties.

'Quick!' she yelled to Alby. 'Get them on the tray! We gotta get outta here before—'

With an almighty crash, one of the car-carriers came bouncing down the steps of a ferry platform further down the river. It rampaged down the stone steps, careless of the damage to its shock absorbers, before blasting out onto the ice-covered surface of the river.

It was followed by a second transporter and a third, all of them speeding out onto the river, coming after Alby and the others.

The second white-clad figure on the snowbike threw off her scarf to reveal herself to be significantly older than the rider. She was a woman of maybe seventy, with a wrinkled but kind face.

'Move your ass, kid! We're not here to hurt you!' the older woman barked as she leapt nimbly down from the tray. 'We're nuns, we're fans of the Oracle and we're pissed as hell because these mother-fuckers killed all our sisters at the convent! Now, haul ass!'

Alby hauled ass.

'You're *nuns*?' he said as with the older one's help he loaded Lily and Stretch into the tray of the snowbike.

'Kick-ass nuns,' she said. 'She's Sister Agnes and I'm Sister Lynda.'

With Lily and Stretch safely in the tray, Alby and Sister Lynda leapt into it and the old nun yelled, 'Agnes! Punch it!' and the younger nun in the saddle gunned the engine.

The snowbike peeled out, its rear tracks kicking up snow as it sped away down the wide frozen river, now chased by the three enormous car-carriers.

It zoomed southwestward, following the curves of the Moskva, heading toward a bunch of road-bridges that spanned the river.

Sunken twenty feet below the level of Moscow's riverside

boulevards, the frozen-over river was essentially a broad trench with high walls on both of its sides.

As the nimble snowbike sped down this trench, the big-engined car-carriers thundered over the ice behind it, gaining.

Alby looked back anxiously: the three car-carriers were huge and still bearing on their skeletal trailers at least a dozen bronzemen each.

And then, as Alby watched, a man in black combat gear— a Knight or squire of the Golden Eight, he guessed—leaned out from the cabin of the first car-carrier with a rocket launcher mounted on his shoulder.

He fired.

A rocket-propelled grenade lanced out from the launcher, issuing an extended trail of smoke behind it, and slammed down into the ice right in front of the fleeing snowbike.

A geyser of snow and ice blasted up into the snowbike's path.

Sister Agnes cut right, avoiding by bare centimetres the gaping hole that the RPG had created in the ice.

'They're trying to break holes in the ice layer!' she called.

'Sons-a-bitches . . .' Sister Lynda yelled.

Then another RPG came in.

Another explosion of snow and ice.

The snowbike banked hard around it before it whipped underneath the next bridge spanning the river—the Bolshoy Kamenny Bridge—shooting under its low steel arch *just as* the bridge's north-side pylon was hit, devastatingly, by a missile.

This was not the work of a shoulder-launched RPG.

It was the work of a *full-size* air-to-ground missile . . .

. . . fired from the wing of Rufus's Sukhoi Su-37, which now swooped in low over the frozen river behind their pursuers!

The Sukhoi's engines boomed as it half flew, half hovered over the river.

Alby blanched at the sight of it.

This chase now involved one snowbike, three car-carriers and a Russian fighter-bomber flying over the frozen Moskva River in the middle of a comatose Moscow.

The Sukhoi's air-to-ground missile had blown the north pylon of the Bolshoy Kamenny Bridge to smithereens—

—causing the entire steel bridge to collapse!

With its northern end blown away, the bridge toppled that way and fell.

The lead car-carrier managed to speed under it before the bridge came down, but not the second.

The immense steel bridge slammed down *right on top of* the second car-carrier, *flattening* the long vehicle and its occupants, before driving it down through the ice and under the surface!

The third and last car-carrier had nowhere to go.

The collapsed bridge was entirely blocking its path and it was travelling way too fast to stop.

Its driver hit the brakes, but it was no use, not on a surface this slippery: the speeding car-carrier smashed into the collapsed bridge, nose first, crumpling like an accordion.

'Thanks, Rufus!' Alby yelled.

Inside the Sukhoi, Jack looked down on the speeding snowbike now pursued down the wide river by only one car-carrier.

Jack was sitting in the rear seat of the cockpit, at the missile controls.

'Keep us low, Rufus,' he said to the big-bearded pilot. 'I gotta make one more shot.'

He fired another missile.

A second air-to-ground missile lanced out from the Sukhoi's right wing and thundered directly into the surviving car-carrier.

For a brief moment, the car-carrier lit up with white light before it blew apart in a colossal explosion.

The wild chase over, the snowbike pulled into a ferry dock at the same time as the Sukhoi landed on the roadway above the dock.

Alby rushed to Jack with Lily in his arms.

'Thanks, Jack,' he said.

'Hey, thank *you*,' Jack said. 'I'd be dead if you hadn't shown up at the cathedral before.'

He turned to the two women dressed in their bulky white snow gear.

'We also owe you a debt of gratitude, ladies,' he said. 'I'm Jack West Jr. This is Lily and Alby. Who're you?'

The older nun said, 'Sisters Lynda and Agnes from the Order of Serene Maidens at Novodevichy Convent. Although to be honest we never really went in for all the nun shit, did we Agnes?'

'Celibacy sucks,' the younger nun agreed.

Jack blinked ever-so-briefly. 'I appreciate you helping us out just now, but you'll understand if—here, now, in an empty city—I'm a little wary of anyone I don't know.'

'Captain West,' Sister Lynda said. 'We know who you are. Everyone in our world knows who you are: the fifth greatest warrior and the surprise winner of the Great Games who threw the ruling royal elites into turmoil. A thoroughly deserved turmoil, in my opinion. And you and I have actually met before, although you were too young to recall it. I held you in my arms when you were a month old.'

Jack cocked his head, confused. 'Wait. You knew my—'

'Yes, I knew your mother,' Lynda said. 'A long time ago. Before she married that gigantic douchebag, Jonathan West Sr. I'd say marrying him was the biggest mistake of her life, but then she gave birth to you and you became the fifth warrior and all that.'

Lynda nodded at the unconscious Lily. 'And we also know who she is: the Oracle of Siwa, the one you raised as your own daughter.'

'And we know the nature of the sleep that grips her,' the younger nun, Agnes, said meaningfully.

Jack eyed the two nuns closely.

Sister Lynda took a deep breath, collecting herself.

'Captain, we've had a shitty fucking morning, so let me say this: you need not fear our motives or doubt our loyalty. Our order cheered your actions at the Great Games from afar and we have

no love for Sphinx. He just murdered all of our sisters, a singular group of intelligent, kind and wonderful women.

'Agnes and I were lucky. It was our turn to be designated survivors: every night two nuns have to stay offsite, in case something like this happens. Tonight was our night.

'We were listening to it all on a live radio link,' she added. 'It was horrible. Sphinx toyed with our abbess Sister Beatrice before he threw her to some cannibal Vandals he brought with him and had all of our fellow sisters shot.

'We are now alone in this world, but we are not powerless. We have knowledge that can help you stop Sphinx and we *want* you to stop him. We know all about the ancient bells he took from our convent and the sleep they cause, and maybe even someone who can undo it.'

'Undo it?' Jack said.

'Yes. This will be vitally important given what Sphinx intends to do with the bells in the coming days. We also know about the trial he must perform to claim his throne.'

'The second trial,' Jack said. 'The Trial of the Cities was the first one. The Trial of the Mountains is the second. "*Five iron mountains, five bladed keys . . .*"'

'"*. . . and five doors forever locked,*"' Sister Lynda finished. 'I can also tell you something else.'

'What?'

'When the Omega Event will occur.'

Jack looked long and hard at the old nun before he jerked his chin at the plane.

'Get aboard, then, and let's get out of here.'

They boarded the Sukhoi, took to the sky and shot away from Moscow.

The fighter-bomber was not designed to carry so many people and was kind of crowded.

In addition to Jack, Rufus, Alby and the two nuns, it now also carried the comatose bodies of Lily, Stretch and Aloysius.

Sitting in the gunner's seat in the cockpit, Jack keyed the secure radio. 'Sky Monster? Pooh Bear? You guys out there?'

No reply.

Jack repeated his question.

Still nothing.

'Rufus,' he said, 'Can you track the *Sky Warrior*? See where it's got to?'

It took Rufus a minute.

'Found 'em, but it don't look good, Cap'n West.'

'What do you mean?'

Rufus nodded at his radar screen. A lone dot on it was flying northward in a dead-straight line.

'I mean, they're flying due north, totally straight, but they ain't responding,' Rufus said. 'That usually means a ghost plane. It happens when a plane loses cabin pressure and everyone on it passes out and the plane keeps flyin' on autopilot. But here, well . . .'

Jack nodded, understanding.

'Sky Monster and Pooh Bear got knocked unconscious by the ringing of that bell in Moscow and now the plane is flying itself on autopilot.'

'Yup.'

'What's going to happen to it?' Alby asked, standing behind them in the doorway to the bomb bay.

Rufus said, 'Usually, a ghost plane just keeps on flyin' till it runs outta fuel and crashes.'

'We're not going to let that happen to our friends,' Jack said determinedly. 'Chase it.'

Twenty minutes later the Sukhoi Su-37 caught up with the sleek black Concorde-like Tupolev Tu-144.

It was a tiny black dot several miles in front of them, flying in a steady straight line toward the northern horizon.

Sky Monster and Pooh Bear returned no hails.

The *Sky Warrior* just flew silently northward.

Jack, Alby and Rufus watched the distant plane from the cockpit of the Sukhoi.

'Cap'n West,' Rufus said, seeing something on his scopes.

'Yes?'

'Three aircraft just took off from Moscow behind us and are coming our way. They're all C-5 Super Galaxy heavy-lift cargo planes. Those are big-ass planes, sir.'

'You'd need some big-ass planes to carry all those bronzemen,' Jack said. 'And those Super Galaxies are some of the biggest you can get. They following us?'

'Either us or your plane.' Rufus nodded at the silent *Sky Warrior*. 'To finish us off.'

Jack looked out at the tiny Tupolev, flying high in the grey sky far ahead of them, zooming dead straight, with its occupants Sky Monster and Pooh Bear not responding—

It came from above them, slamming into the *Sky Warrior* so suddenly it made Jack jump.

An orbit-to-air missile.

The *Sky Warrior* exploded, cracking in the middle before blowing apart in a billowing ball of fire. The broken pieces of the

Tupolev Tu-144 peeled downward, trailing ribbons of black smoke as they fell out of the sky.

Jack's mouth fell open.

Sky Monster and Pooh Bear . . .

Shot down. Killed in their sleep . . .

'Oh, Jesus.' Jack stared in shock at the smoking wreckage dropping out of the sky.

Rufus was also stunned, but he wasn't looking *down*.

He was looking up.

'I got a second one!' he shouted as he yanked on his control stick and the Sukhoi banked hard left.

Jack and Alby were thrown sideways. So were the nuns in the back.

'Initiating electromagnetic countermeasures!' Rufus yelled, flicking switches.

An instant later, a second missile roared out of the cloud-strewn sky, coming at them vertically from directly above.

But it shot past, thanks to both the electromagnetic jamming signals Rufus had initiated and his quick banking manoeuvre. The missile screamed by so close Jack saw its white-hot tail flame.

'Get us out of here!' he called.

'On it!' Rufus replied.

The Sukhoi swept left as three more missiles rained out of the sky, launched from low-orbit Russian military satellites. The missiles, of course, were illegal, built in breach of every major treaty about weaponising space, but both Russia and America had them.

And clearly now Sphinx had the use of them.

Rufus's countermeasures, however, sent these new missiles streaking harmlessly by and as the Sukhoi sped westward, away from Moscow and Russia, back toward Europe, Jack gazed sadly back at the spot where the Tupolev had been blown apart—with Sky Monster and Pooh Bear on it, unconscious and defenceless.

The remnants of the fiery explosion receded into the distance, wisps of smoking debris that floated down to the snow-covered landscape below.

'Damn,' Jack sighed. '*Damn.*'

He swallowed deeply, trying to process everything he'd seen that morning.

Moscow: struck down.

Lily, Stretch and Aloysius: unconscious.

Sky Monster and Pooh Bear: dead.

The *Sky Warrior* lost.

Missiles coming at them from orbit.

And three cargo planes filled with bronzemen chasing them.

Sphinx was rampaging toward his destiny with superior knowledge of the Trial of the Mountains and almost unlimited firepower. Christ, he had space-launched missiles at his disposal.

Plus, of course, the coming Omega Event.

Jack turned to the others.

'Alby, call our team at Hades's estate: Zoe, Hades, my mother and Iolanthe. Tell them we're on our way and tell them I need to know everything they've got about the Trial of the Mountains, specifically the five iron mountains. We are now *way* behind Sphinx in this race. We need to put our heads together and figure out how we're gonna catch up before it's too late.'

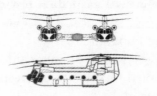

The giant four-rotored military helicopter landed in the middle of St Peter's Square, right beside the gigantic Egyptian obelisk that stands out in front of the largest and most important church in Catholicism.

The Pope himself stood waiting for it, his vestments billowing in the big chopper's downdraft. He was a portly man, fat and jowly, unlike his predecessor, Francis. Also unlike Francis, this pope enjoyed the finer things in life.

Thousands of tourists, Christians from all over the world, gawked and took photos with their camera-phones, wondering who could possibly land a helicopter on the Vatican's doorstep with the clear permission of the Pope.

The helicopter was one of the largest rotored aircraft in the world: a giant Mi-4000 quadcopter. It was a Russian-built heavy-lift troop carrier/gunship that was essentially two Chinooks bolted together side by side with steel crossbeams, creating a superchopper with four rotors.

The massive chopper dominated St Peter's Square and from it emerged . . .

. . . Sphinx and Cardinal Mendoza.

They had flown here from Moscow.

Sphinx extended his hand to the Pope. Rather than the other way around, the Pope dropped to his knees and kissed the ring on Sphinx's hand.

Some people in the crowd gasped. A few crossed themselves in shock.

'Greetings, sire,' the Pope said.

'Do you have what we need?' Sphinx said.

'I do.' The Pope waved forward two priests.

One carried a bronze globe.

It was obviously ancient, its surface covered in scratches and dents, yet it was still stunning: it was a glistening orb depicting the planet Earth. Protruding from it like tiny spikes were three little mountains.

The second priest carried a file filled with old documents and rumpled pieces of parchment.

The Pope said, 'The ancient globe and every document we have on the location of the Orphean Bell.'

The priests handed them to Sphinx's men.

Sphinx smiled his big leonine grin at the Pope. 'Thank you, Your Holiness. A new world order is approaching.'

'We cannot wait, sire,' the Pope said. 'The world has become a den of wickedness and sin. It is time to cleanse it. Restart it anew. Recommence things with our noble Church as the world's moral leader at the top of the social hierarchy.'

He turned to Mendoza. 'You have done well, Cardinal Mendoza, as I would expect of one so devoted to the precepts of Amon-Ra. I appreciate your work.'

Mendoza bowed his head.

Sphinx snorted.

Then he turned his back on the Pope and twirled his fingers in the air, indicating to his people that it was time to leave.

And then he did one more thing.

He quickly put on his ear-protecting headphones.

So did Mendoza.

The Pope frowned. 'What are you—?'

He didn't get out another word, for right then a second chopper rose up into view above Rome and a spherical bell hanging from it rang out loudly and the Pope collapsed.

★ ★ ★

It was quite a sight.

The thousands of tourists staring at the superchopper in the middle of St Peter's Square all toppled as one, falling like dominoes.

It was the same across the whole of Rome.

Inside St Peter's, inside coffee shops, inside cars, buses, planes and trains—people collapsed, succumbing to the mysterious sound of the Siren bell . . .

. . . until only Sphinx and his people, protected by their military-grade headphones, remained standing.

Sphinx drew his gun, walked over to the immobile Pope lying on the ground and calmly shot the defenceless pontiff in the head.

The Pope's head blew apart, splattering the cobblestones of St Peter's Square with blood.

Sphinx holstered his pistol and shook his head. 'Honestly, "a den of wickedness". "The world's moral leader". This from a man whose organisation protects child molesters. I could never stand him.'

He took the papal ring off the Pope's dead finger and threw it to Mendoza.

Mendoza caught it and put it on. 'Thank you, sire. Thank you so much. I appreciate this more than you know.'

Sphinx nodded. 'This is what I promised you: to be Pope in my new world. Later, you can wake whichever cardinals and priests you choose and rebuild the Church in whatever image you desire. Congratulations, Your Holiness.'

A MINOTAUR NAMED . . .

AUSTRALIA/FRANCE
3–23 DECEMBER

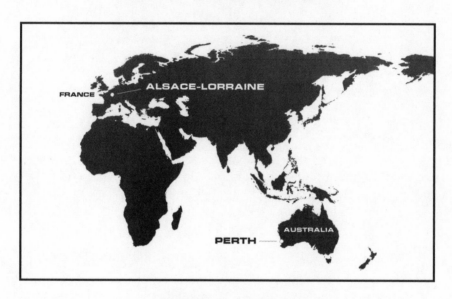

What's in a name?

WILLIAM SHAKESPEARE
ROMEO AND JULIET

JACK'S FARM/HADES'S ESTATE
3–23 DECEMBER

In the three-week period between the chaotic ending of the global race to find the Three Secret Cities and Jack's dash to Moscow to save Lily, one individual came to observe and experience the unique world of Jack West Jr.

That was E-147, the Neanderthal minotaur whom—to the shock of the assembled royal spectators—Jack had saved during the Great Games at the Underworld.

In the days immediately after the Great Games, E-147 had lived and recuperated with Jack and his team at their remote farm in the Australian desert.

It was a culture shock for him in many ways.

First of all, E-147 got a new name.

'Young man,' Mae declared, 'we are *not* going to call you by a number.'

Suggestions were made, most of them starting with the letter E— Eric, Eldrick, Edward—but in the end, it was the origin of E-147's alpha-numeric name that became the source of his new one.

The E in 'E-147' indicated that he hailed from the eastern sector of the minotaur city in the Underworld. The other clans were similarly designated N, S or W, for the north, south and western sectors.

'How about Easton, then,' Alby had suggested. 'It's a nice name and it's kinda close to *eastern*.'

That was the one he chose.

Easton loved his new name.

In addition to his new name came a new look.

As a Neanderthal in the Underworld, Easton hadn't had to subscribe to any kind of grooming regimen, so his black hair was unkempt, his whiskers were wild and his monobrow pronounced.

So Mae gave him a haircut, and Pooh Bear and Stretch taught him how to shave. (Of course, they disagreed on whether or not he should have a beard; Pooh was naturally pro-beard, while Stretch voted for a clean-shaven look.)

When he emerged from the bathroom, Easton looked like a new man.

He had two neatly trimmed eyebrows, a shorter hairstyle parted on the side, longish sideburns and a clean-shaven chin.

Some new clothes completed the makeover.

Now, he looked like a regular short stocky guy with dark hair, olive skin and a large rock-hard jaw that by three in the afternoon had a five o'clock shadow.

He was no longer E-147.

He was Easton.

Another thing that E-147 noticed—*no, Easton,* he corrected himself— was the unusual concept of family that was prevalent in Jack's group.

Of course, minotaurs knew the idea of family: they had clans; they had marriages; they even had a ruling bloodline that produced the minotaur king.

But Jack's concept of family included people who were *not* related to him by blood or marriage.

Alby, Easton saw, was not Jack's relative, but Jack treated him as if he were his son.

Pooh Bear and Stretch were like his brothers, as was the big hairy guy with the funny accent who flew Jack's plane.

One day during that three-week hiatus, Easton asked Jack about it.

'Because I care about them, Easton,' Jack answered. 'I've never understood why people limit the idea of *family* to blood relatives. It seems unnecessary to me, unnecessarily self-limiting. Look at these people.' Jack waved his hand at the team around them, working away at their various tasks. 'I'd do anything for them. That's how much I love them.'

'Even though they are not of your blood?'

Jack smiled. 'There's an old saying, "You can choose your friends, but you can't choose your family." I don't subscribe to that notion at all. You *can* choose your family. Because "family" are those people who lift you up, who help you reach the heights you can't reach by yourself. Why should that group be arbitrarily limited to blood relatives? Life is short, Easton, so it's best spent with those you love.'

The final illumination in Easton's life had been his experiences with Jack's animals.

For when Jack and the others had gone off in search of the secret cities, Easton—himself nursing a partially broken foot from an incident during the Great Games—had remained at the farm to watch over Jack's beloved falcon, Horus, and his two dogs, Ash and Roxy.

Or as Easton called them: 'the smart bird and the doggies'.

After being shot in the wing at Pine Gap, Horus had spent most of the time recovering. She cooed weakly but appreciatively when Easton fed her and rebandaged her wound.

As for the dogs, well, Easton had never known *pet* dogs before.

In the Underworld, the only times minotaurs encountered dogs were when they ate them. To care for dogs and enjoy their company was nothing short of a revelation to him.

He loved it.

He adored Roxy's irrepressible nature, especially given that she had one gammy leg—kind of like he did. He delighted in the way

her tail wagged with unbridled joy at the sight of him and how the little black poodle bounced up and down with anticipation when he prepared to throw the tennis ball for her to fetch.

Ash, the labrador, was older than Roxy and more docile. She only ever wanted Easton to rub her stomach. She ignored the ball when he threw it for her.

Jack had commented about that: 'Yeah, Ash used to fetch the ball, and then one day, she just decided she didn't want to anymore. Don't take it personally, she won't fetch it for me either, no matter how much I try to coax her.'

And so Easton maintained Jack's farm for that time, sweeping the floors, tending to Horus and playing with the doggies.

For anyone else, it might have seemed like a lonely life, but Easton didn't mind it at all. He was a simple soul and having lived his whole life in the crowded confines of the minotaur city in the Underworld, he quite liked the combination of open space and solitude.

And then, on the third morning of his time there, he woke to find that, during the night, both doggies had climbed into his bed, nestled beside his legs and fallen asleep there.

They had been inseparable after that.

When Easton had rejoined Jack and the others after all the secret cities stuff, even though Jack was bloodied and bruised, Jack had said, 'Thank you for looking after my furry friends. They look very happy.' Easton had beamed with pride.

And when Easton had proudly reported that he hadn't eaten the dogs, he had actually meant: *I adore these dogs.*

Jack understood.

He loved them, too.

Even if Ash wouldn't fetch the ball for him anymore.

When Easton relocated from the farm in Australia to Hades's estate in France, he watched the goings-on there with curious interest.

He had arrived just as Pooh Bear, Stretch and Alby had returned from the Rock of Gibraltar with the news that it was *not* Lily who had been sacrificed on the Altar of the Cosmos.

He had also seen them return with the three fabled weapons—the sword Excalibur, the Mace of Poseidon and the Helmet of Hades—all three of which had been left at the Rock.

One day Easton had watched, intrigued, as Jack, Aloysius and Stretch worked on the sword with a grinder while Alby analysed the helmet with a spectrometer.

'What Alby doing?' he asked.

'We want to know how this helmet makes its wearer invisible to the bronzemen,' Alby said.

'Magic?' Easton asked.

'No.' Alby smiled. 'It's not magic. Usually, there's a reason. We just have to find it. In this case, I'm detecting that this helmet emits faint pulses of low-level gamma particle resonance.'

'Why is this helpful to know?' Easton asked.

'By our count, Sphinx could have as many as five thousand bronzemen at his command,' Alby replied. 'This helmet's resonance confuses them, blinds them. If we can replicate it, then maybe we can make ourselves invisible to the bronzemen and beat them in a fight.'

'Alby very clever,' Easton said.

He looked over at Jack and the others working on the sword with the grinder.

Sparks flew from the fabled sword's blade as Stretch worked away at it with the fast-spinning grinder.

'And the sword?' he asked.

'The sword kills the bronzemen,' Alby said. 'Stretch has an idea how to use that ability to our advantage. For that he needs some slivers of its blade, but it turns out, Excalibur's blade is pretty tough. Eventually, he'll get some slivers, but there'll only be one way to test his theory and that'll be hairy.'

Easton didn't know what that meant.

'What about the Mace?' he asked.

Alby pursed his lips. 'It looks like the Mace is now inert, dead. According to our scanners, it gives off no detectable particle emissions or resonance at all. Its power seems to have, well, gone out of it.'

Stretch worked on his project with Excalibur right up until the day they had got word that Lily had been spotted in Moscow and he had dashed off with Pooh Bear and Sky Monster to save her.

Before Stretch left, however, he gave Easton a task on that project. It wasn't a very exciting task—in fact, to anyone else, it would have been exceedingly tedious—but Easton, once again happy to contribute to his new family and with the dogs curled up beside him, took to it with gusto.

THE SECRET ROYAL WORLD

THE FIVE IRON MOUNTAINS

Then is doomsday near.

WILLIAM SHAKESPEARE
HAMLET

HADES'S ESTATE
ALSACE-LORRAINE, FRANCE
23 DECEMBER, 1600 HOURS

In was mid-afternoon on the 23rd of December when the Sukhoi arrived at the private airstrip of Hades's horse farm in eastern France.

It landed in front of a small group of people: Jack's wife, Zoe; Hades, the former King of the Underworld; Iolanthe Compton-Jones, former Keeper of the Royal Records for the Kingdom of Land; the famed oceanographer Professor David 'Nobody' Black; Jack's mother, the noted historian Mabel Merriweather; and last of all, Easton.

Jack, Alby and Rufus emerged from the plane carrying the sleeping bodies of Lily, Stretch and Aloysius. The two nuns came out cautiously after them, lingering near the plane.

At the sight of the three limp bodies, Nobody said, 'Are they—?'

'They're alive,' Jack said, not stopping. 'But unconscious. Some kind of ancient sleep.'

'The Siren bells . . .' Iolanthe said.

'Yeah, them,' Jack said. 'Folks, we can't linger. We've got an army of bronzemen in cargo planes on the move from Russia. Sphinx's people knocked out Sky Monster and Pooh Bear in the *Sky Warrior* and then shot them down while they were defenceless.'

Mae said, 'Oh, God, no.'

'They didn't deserve to go out that way,' Jack said. 'Killed in their sleep. They at least deserved a stand-up fight. We only got out of there alive because of some fancy flying by Rufus.'

There was a short silence as the group digested this loss.

They all knew that death was a possibility, but that didn't lessen the blow when it occurred, and this blow hit them all hard.

'Jack,' Zoe said seriously. 'Moscow has been all over the news and social media, but it just happened again, literally a few minutes ago.'

'Where?'

'Rome. The whole city just went silent: people collapsing in the streets; hundreds of car accidents; planes falling out of the sky. Just like Moscow. Twitter's gone crazy with hashtags about "SleepingCities" and people are scared out of their minds, looking for a pattern, wondering which city will be next. Sphinx must have gone to Rome and rung another of his bells.'

Sisters Lynda and Agnes were still standing beside the Sukhoi.

They took in their surroundings: the chateau, the lake, the grim concrete fort of the Maginot Line and the forest-covered hills ringing it all.

Sister Lynda's gaze landed on Jack's mother.

'Mae Merriweather . . .' the old nun said.

'Lynda Fadel . . .' Mae said.

A tense pause followed . . .

. . . and then the two women embraced each other warmly.

'It's good to see you, Lynny,' Mae said. 'Gosh, it must have been thirty years.'

They followed Jack and the others into the main house.

'Closer to forty,' Sister Lynda said. 'You look good, Mae. I must say I was so pleased when I heard you divorced that shithead of a husband.'

'How do you know each other?' Jack asked as he lay Lily down on a couch and threw a blanket over her.

Sister Lynda said, 'When your mother was a young woman making a name for herself in archaeological circles, I tried very hard to get her to join our order. But she was *in love*. In love with some big tough smart military guy named Jonathan West—*Wolf* was his nickname—and she went off and married him instead. I never liked him. He just *looked* like a wife-beater and it turned out, he was. Mind you, I suppose it was a good thing, since their union brought you into existence.'

She turned to Mae. 'What ever happened to Wolf? He just disappeared off the face of the Earth.'

'Jack killed him,' Mae said simply. 'It was kind of a showdown.'

'Oh,' Lynda said. 'A father versus son thing?'

'Something like that,' Jack said. 'But that's in the past. Folks, I hope you've been doing some research because what I need right now is information. If he's put Rome to sleep, then Sphinx is on the move and getting further ahead of us. I need information and I need it fast.'

'What should we look at first?' Zoe asked.

Jack turned to Sister Lynda.

'The Omega Event. When is it going to happen?'

'In six days,' Lynda said simply. 'On December 29.'

'You're sure about this?'

'Captain, the Church has known about this date for a very long time. Its astronomical observatory in Arizona is solely devoted to tracking the expansion of the visible universe down to the micrometre. So, yes, I'm sure.

'In six days time, at precisely 3:06 a.m. GMT on the 29th of December, the expansion of the universe will cease and then, in a single crushing instant, it will collapse inward in an all-consuming rush, withdrawing into a singularity, destroying every planet, every star, every single thing in existence. The end of all things is less than a week away.'

Everyone assembled in the lounge of the main house. Computers and projector screens were set up.

When they were settled, Jack said, 'All right, then. Six days till doomsday. Tell me about the Trial of the Mountains, the five iron mountains, these sphere-bells and how they are connected to the Omega Event?'

Hades said, 'This is *all* connected to the Omega Event, Jack. The best place to start is here, with the Zeus Papyrus. We've been looking into it.'

Hades projected the image of the Zeus Papyrus and its translation of the second trial onto the screen:

THE TRIAL OF THE MOUNTAINS

Five iron mountains. Five bladed keys. Five doors forever locked.
But mark you, only those who survive the Fall,
May enter the Supreme Labyrinth
And look upon the face of the Omega.

Hades said, 'After Zeus's champion, Hercules, won the Great Games of their time, Zeus won the title "King of Kings". It was thus his honour and responsibility to complete the two trials and prevent the Omega Event of that age.

'When he stood inside the obelisk atop the Underworld, Zeus received the solutions to the two trials—the Mysteries—and performed the trials without any complications. He also, thankfully, wrote down what he did, which has proven to be enormously helpful to us.

'For after Jack won the Games, Jack *prevented* his sponsor, Orlando, the King of Land, from standing inside the obelisk and receiving those secrets to the trials. This wasn't necessarily a bad thing: Orlando was an evil and foolish man. But it did complicate matters. It meant we had to figure out how to complete the trials.'

Jack said, 'I didn't mean to complicate things, I just—'

'Jack,' Iolanthe said firmly. 'Don't beat yourself up. Trust me, this is much better than having Orlando enjoying unlimited power.'

She indicated her face: the result of the unspeakable torture inflicted on her on the orders of Orlando, her own brother. The bruises to her eyes had healed and her hair had grown back slightly. But her nose was still damaged by the bull-ring that had been thrust through it.

'At least the world now has a *chance* to live free,' she said.

Hades went on: 'As it happened, we successfully completed the first trial at the Three Secret Cities of Thule, Ra and Atlas.'

Mae said, 'But it was Sphinx who reaped the reward for our efforts, since it was he who performed the hideous sacrifice at the end of it all.'

'Correct,' Hades said. 'One reward for performing that ritual sacrifice, clearly, is being able to command the bronzeman armies, although I'm not sure how Sphinx does this.'

'Rings,' Sister Lynda said. 'Some call them the Rings of Dominion or the Rings of Command. There are five. One all-powerful ring and four lesser rings that allow their wearers to command the automatons that reside at the three cities and the Underworld. Whoever wears them directs the actions of the bronzemen, the silvermen and the goldmen from each city.'

'Goldmen?' Zoe asked. 'There are *gold*men?'

Sister Lynda said, 'The bronzemen are the worker ants, the foot soldiers. The silvermen are guards. The goldmen are the elite, the most ruthless silent sentries of them all.'

Nobody muttered, 'I thought the bronze and silver ones were bad enough.'

Jack was gazing at the text of the Zeus Papyrus. 'Okay. Five mountains. Five keys. Five locked doors. Something called the Fall. And a Supreme Labyrinth. This is what Sphinx is up to now and apparently it includes putting whole cities to sleep with those bells. He left this for me in Moscow. A final taunt.'

Jack held up the rumpled sheet of paper that Aloysius had found on the ground in front of St Basil's Cathedral, the one Lily had re-used to warn them about what was coming.

Its cruel words blazed:

YOU
WILL
WAKE
AS
SLAVES

'Explanations?' Jack asked.

It was Sister Agnes who answered.

'It wasn't just a taunt, Captain West. It was a very specific reference to an ancient poem, one that is connected to the Trial of the Mountains. It goes like this:

> '*"Hear the sound of the Sirens' song,*
> *Ride its rolling waves.*
> *But beware that song*
> *And the bliss it brings,*
> *For you may wake as slaves."*'

Sister Lynda took over. 'It's an old verse, long known to our order and the secret royal world. Sphinx does not wish to just rule the world. He wishes to rule it as the ultimate tyrant: to plunge everyone into a coma and have them literally awaken as his slaves.'

'Say that again,' Jack said.

'Let me explain it another way, Jack,' Hades said. 'We are coming to a climactic time. The Tartarus Rotation, the Six Sacred Stones, the Great Games, the two trials—they all lead to one place at one time: the Supreme Labyrinth during the Omega Event on December the 29th.'

He pulled up an image from his laptop. It showed an inscription in ancient Greek. Hades read it aloud, translating it:

> '"*When the Three Cities are opened*
> *Make haste*
> *To the Mountains*
> *And the Fall!*
>
> *The survivors may then enter*
> *The impossible maze*
> *And decide the fate of all.*"'

'This is from Plato,' he said. 'Just as he knew fragments about the Trial of the Cities, he was aware of the Trial of the Mountains or, as it is sometimes called, the Fall.'

'An impossible maze?' Alby said. 'That's the Supreme Labyrinth?'

'Yes,' Hades said. 'It is a maze of extraordinary magnitude and complexity, a maze of mazes, some believe.'

'Do we know where it is?' Nobody asked.

'No,' Iolanthe said. 'Its location is one of the ancient world's

most closely guarded secrets. It must be remote, since no-one has ever found it, but given that Zeus went there in classical times, it can't be too far from the Mediterranean Basin.'

Hades added, 'I believe that Imhotep the Great, the renowned Egyptian architect and Chief Priest of the Cult of Amon-Ra, made a pilgrimage to the Labyrinth around 2600 B.C.E. so it can't be far from Egypt, either.'

'What happens at this maze?' Alby asked.

Hades said, 'At the centre of the Supreme Labyrinth sits a great throne. When the Omega Event occurs, so long as someone who has completed the Trial of the Mountains is sitting on that throne, Omega will be averted. That person will also be crowned ruler of the planet. This is what Sphinx desires.'

'So why use the bells?' Jack asked.

'The bells are a powerful weapon,' Sister Lynda said. 'By putting large segments of the world's population to sleep, Sphinx can prepare the world for his reign. Since they are comatose, he can place troublesome people or even entire populations wherever he wants—deserts, islands, prisons—or simply kill them where they lie. He can even choose who he wakes, if he wakes any of them at all. And those who do wake will do so to find him as their undisputed overlord.'

There was silence as this sank in.

Nobody whistled. 'Whoa.'

'So how do you wake someone from the sleep?' Alby asked, looking over at the room containing Lily, Stretch and Aloysius.

'The blue bell,' Sister Agnes said.

Sister Lynda said, 'There are fifteen bells in total. Fourteen are of immense size and made of gold and silver. Those are the ones we kept in our convent. One bell, however, is very small. This smallest bell is silver-blue in colour, so it has become known as the blue bell, although to some it is known by its older name, the Orphean Bell, after the legendary musician in Greek mythology, Orpheus.'

Jack nodded. 'Because during the voyage of the Argonauts, Orpheus's music overcame the deadly song of the Sirens.'

'Very good, Captain,' Lynda said. 'You've read the *Argonautica*. According to legend, the blue or Orphean Bell is exceedingly small—it can be held in one hand—but it is very powerful, for it possesses the singular ability to *awaken* those who succumb to the Siren sleep of the other bells.'

'Did Sphinx acquire it when he stormed your convent?' Jack asked.

'No, the location of the blue bell is unknown. It's been lost for over two thousand years,' Sister Agnes said.

'You don't know where it is?' Jack asked.

'No-one knows where it is,' Lynda said. 'It's said that the Church has documents related to the blue bell in its Secret Archives at the Vatican. And one of our nuns, Dr Tracy Smith, did some extensive research into its properties, but she left our order some time ago and has since, sadly, disappeared.'

Sister Lynda's voice trailed off.

'All right,' Jack said. 'So, the Trial of the Mountains flows on directly to the final test at the Supreme Labyrinth: only someone who completes the Trial of the Mountains—this "Fall" thing—can enter the Labyrinth?'

'Correct.'

'Then the Fall is everything,' Jack said. 'Let's hear about it.'

'Well, first, look at the Zeus Papyrus,' Mae said. 'Five iron mountains, five bladed keys, five doors, forever locked: at the mountains you get the keys, which you then take to the Labyrinth—with its five entrances—open it and enter it, although what is meant by "bladed keys", I don't know.'

'That translation is disputed,' Lynda said. 'A Siwan Oracle in the 14th century said it was wrong. It should have been translated as five "burned" or "blazing" keys.'

'Either way, you do the Fall, you acquire a key to the Labyrinth and a ticket to the final main event,' Mae said.

'So what's the Fall?' Zoe asked.

Hades paused.

'"*He cannot be emperor who does not risk his own blood,*"' he recited softly. 'It's an old royal maxim related to the Fall. For it is

a test like no other, the ultimate test for anyone who would aspire to rule the world, a deadly challenge of strength, will and, most of all, nerve.'

'And that is?'

'Standing on a massive ancient stone temple while it freefalls down a four-kilometre-deep shaft underneath one of the iron mountains at a specific astronomical moment.'

Jack swallowed. 'Is that all?'

'Let me explain,' Hades said. 'It all relates to this image.'
He brought up a picture on his computer:

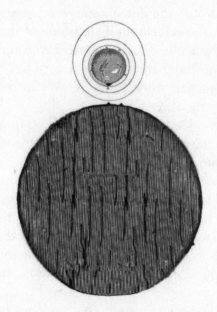

'As you know, this image is called Newton's Mountain, but
it should be named Newton's Planets. It's from his most famous
book, the *Principia*, and it is the only drawing in the book that
Isaac Newton drew himself. Even then, he disguised it a little by
flipping the top planet upside down.

'Note the two planets. The smaller one is the moon. The larger one is Earth. Look closely now. Can you see the mountains on them?'

Jack leaned in closer and peered at the image . . . and he saw them.

'Well, I'll be . . .'

He hadn't noticed them before but there they were.

They looked like tiny black pimples on the two orbs, protruding slightly from their otherwise smooth outer surfaces.

There was one little mountain on the moon, pointing downward, and three on the Earth, pointing up and out.

One of the upward-pointing mountains on the Earth was in perfect alignment with the downward-pointing one on the moon.

Hades said, 'You perform the Fall at one of the iron mountains when that mountain is in direct alignment with the lone one on the moon. For on that lunar mountain is a very strange object that is not natural: an ancient stone pedestal, grey in colour, rectangular in shape, roughly the size of an altar.

'Of course,' he added, 'due to the differing rotations and orbits of the Earth and the moon, the moments of alignment only happen at very specific times.'

Mae looked hard at Hades. 'Back when we were at Jack's farm, before we found the cities, I asked you a bunch of questions about the royal world, like whether it was involved in the JFK assassination and fixing elections. When I asked about the moon landing, you said not only was it necessary but that the fourth landing was the important one. I looked it up. That was *Apollo 15*. Is that relevant here?'

Hades nodded. 'Very relevant. That pedestal is the reason why *Apollo 15* landed where it did. You have to understand, humanity didn't fly to moon out of some noble spirit of adventure. The entire space program was initiated by the royal world for precisely this time, to locate that pedestal.

'*Apollo 15* was also the first moon mission to use a lunar rover. This was important. Because by using that rover, the astronauts were able to explore much farther from their landing site and locate the lunar mountain and its pedestal. They were also able to cover it up from prying eyes here on Earth with a sheet of silver thermal Kapton foil.'

Mae's eyes widened.

Alby gasped.

Hades went on. 'While America is the only nation to have successfully sent astronauts to the moon and back, other nations have sent probes and robot vehicles to the moon. Russia sent a remote-controlled rover to the same site as *Apollo 15* back in the 1980s. China tried to send an unmanned probe there, but for some reason they never recovered it on its return.'

'Back up a second,' Jack said. 'Let's focus on Earth for now. For unless we find an iron mountain, we've got nothing. The papyrus says there are *five* iron mountains, but there are only *three* pictured on Newton's drawing of the Earth.'

Iolanthe said, 'Since ancient times, scholars and students of the ancient world—including Newton, Pythagoras and even Albert Einstein—have debated the identities of the five mountains. We only know one of them for sure.'

'Just one?' Jack said.

'Like many things in the ancient world, due to wars, royal rivalries and simple human carelessness, the identities of the five mountains have been lost through the ages. There are many contenders: Mount Kilimanjaro in Africa. A string of volcanoes in Uganda, including the one in which Lily was born. The hanging monasteries of Bhutan. Some even say Potala Palace in Tibet sits atop a giant *underground* mountain. So, yes, only one of the iron mountains is known for certain.'

'And that is?' Nobody asked.

'Mont Saint-Michel in France,' Sister Lynda said. 'There have long been claims that it contains a mysterious structure within it, but none of the Land Kings have ever let anyone but a few trusted priests inside to see it.'

Jack knew about Mont Saint-Michel.

It was a spectacular island-monastery located on a tidal island on the French shore of the English Channel. It was known for the magnificent church built high on its summit and the surging tides that cut the island off from land when they came in.

It was the sister-island to St Michael's Mount over on the English side of the Channel, the home of the Land Kingdom's Hall of Royal Records, where Iolanthe had worked—and been tortured.

'So how do you know this?' Jack asked.

Lynda said, 'I heard it from a nun who saw the Vatican Globe.'

'What's the Vatican Globe?'

Iolanthe said, 'Jack, I actually told you about it when we were in London, after Zoe rescued me from St Michael's Mount and just before the Knights of the Golden Eight launched their attack there.'

Jack remembered that attack all too well: it had involved a drone tank, two drone choppers, the death of Lachlan Adamson and his young family, and the dropping of a London bus filled with innocent passengers into the Thames. Jack tried to recall what Iolanthe had told him about some globe connected to the Vatican.

'Wait, I remember. It's the metal globe that once sat at the peak of the obelisk in St Peter's Square,' he said.

'That's the one,' Iolanthe said.

'Uh, excuse me. Explanation for those present who are not experts in superancient global history, please,' Nobody said.

Iolanthe smiled. 'The most sacred shrine in all of the Catholic Church stands proudly out in front of its headquarters, St Peter's Basilica in Rome: a massive stone obelisk.'

'I thought obelisks were Egyptian monuments dedicated to the worship of the sun,' Nobody said.

'They are. This is because the Church is actually a sun-cult that came out of ancient Egypt. Its true name is the Cult of Amon-Ra.'

'Wait, the Catholic Church worships the sun—?' Nobody began.

'Long story. I'll tell you later,' Alby whispered to him.

Iolanthe said, 'For thousands of years, atop that obelisk sat a very mysterious bronze orb . . .'

She paused. 'Hmmm. You know, maybe—'

Iolanthe stood suddenly. 'Excuse me a moment. I just had an idea; an idea about someone who might be able to help us. A quirky old mentor of mine who may well have got swept up in all this. Hades, can you take over?'

Iolanthe stepped out of the room, clutching her phone.

Hades stood. 'The obelisk outside St Peter's is actually unique for several reasons, one of which is the simple fact that *no-one knows where it came from.* The mad Roman emperor Caligula had it brought to Rome from Egypt in 37 A.D. It is said to have come from Heliopolis but this has never been confirmed. The main reason for its uniqueness is that it is also the *only* obelisk in the world that is surmounted by a small bronze orb or sphere.

'In 1585, Pope Sixtus V replaced the original metal orb with a brass forgery. The original was taken to a vault deep within the Vatican—the Church's most secure vault, the famous Vault XXII—and has remained there ever since.

'Few have seen it but those who have say it is amazing. For this orb—which stood undisturbed for two thousand years in ancient Egypt—is a *globe*, a map of the world, crafted millennia before man flew into space. According to those lucky enough to have laid eyes on it, it depicts the world's oceans and landmasses *plus the locations of the three secret cities and the five iron mountains.*'

There was a short silence as everyone digested this.

'You think this is why Sphinx just silenced Rome?' Jack asked. 'To get this globe?'

'And maybe to silence anyone else who has seen it,' Hades said. 'If he has the globe, he could complete the Fall at one mountain and destroy all the other mountains and thus stop anyone else from following him into the Labyrinth and competing with him.'

'I thought Sphinx was working *with* the Catholic Church,' Alby said. 'With Cardinal Mendoza. There's no need for him to put the Vatican to sleep.'

Zoe said, 'Maybe Sphinx isn't the most loyal ally—'

'Wait!' Iolanthe burst back into the room, holding her phone up. 'We may still have a chance!'

Iolanthe showed her phone to Jack, indicating a text conversation on the encrypted app, Telegram.

'This is a chat I just had with my one-time mentor and tutor, Brother Dagobert de Montreuil. He's an old Jesuit and an adjunct scholar at the *Specola Vaticana*, the Vatican Observatory. He has doctorates in history, astronomy and astrophysics. He was my tutor when I was a teenager. I wondered if the Church might bring him into this.'

The chat read:

MOON4
Bertie,
Desperate times. I'm
with some folks trying to
stop Sphinx succeeding
during Omega. Need the
Vatican Globe to find the
five mountains. Thoughts?
Animadversions?

BERTIE
Which folks?

MOON4
Fifth warrior and his people.

BERTIE
Ooh, I like him.
Vatican Globe is not the

only way to find the Iron
Mtns. Only shows three,
and even those not very
accurately. Javier Journal is
another option. It's in Vault
IX. (If they'd listened to me,
it'd be in Vault XXII.) Things
moving fast. I'm at MSM and
Sphinx's people are en route.
Can't talk. Snarky young
boss is hovering. Meet me at
MSM ASAP while there is still
time. Use the English tunnel.

'Moon4?' Jack gave Iolanthe a look.

'Io,' she said. 'The fourth moon of Jupiter. It's what Bertie called me as a child.'

'What's MSM?' Alby asked.

'It's an old shorthand Bertie and I once used for Mont Saint-Michel,' Iolanthe said.

Jack looked at Iolanthe, at her shaved head and facial wounds. He jerked his chin at the messages on her phone.

'Your buddy says the Vatican Globe only shows three of the mountains, not five? Is that true?'

'Bertie would know better than me. When I glimpsed it, I only saw one side of it, the hemisphere showing the Atlantic Ocean and a sliver of Europe. So I only saw the city of Thule and the mountain of Mont Saint-Michel. I was young and kind of overwhelmed. It's pretty mind-blowing.'

'If the globe only shows three, then that would mean there are two mountains out there that Sphinx doesn't know about and which can still be found,' Jack said.

'It does.'

'Two lost mountains . . .' Jack said. 'This Bertie. Can we trust him?'

'I'd trust him with my life,' Iolanthe said firmly. 'Brother Dagobert was practically my surrogate father. He is a classic Jesuit: gentle, sweet, entirely sexless and *very* intelligent. He must be pushing eighty by now. He simply loves knowledge for knowledge's sake.'

'So why join a religious order as strict as the Jesuits?'

'Because the Jesuits, like him, prize knowledge and wisdom above all else. They're constantly getting into trouble with the Vatican elites. Bertie only ever wanted to be left alone to study history, the planets and the stars. For the last ten years he's been working for the Vatican Observatory at the VATT, but old Bertie is a dinosaur and not very good at office politics. He was replaced by a much younger—and *very* ambitious—German priest named Father Felix Rasmussen. This annoyed Bertie very much.'

'What's the VATT?' Rufus asked.

'The Vatican Advanced Technology Telescope in Arizona. One of the finest telescopes in the world.'

Jack said, 'He says Sphinx is heading to Mont Saint-Michel and may even already have people there. What's the English tunnel?'

Iolanthe said, 'It is a secret entrance to Mont Saint-Michel, a tunnel dug by the English when they laid siege to the Mont in 1434. It starts on a nearby island called Tombelaine. The tunnel is dangerous but it's the only way to get to Mont Saint-Michel undetected.'

'Okay,' Jack said. 'Here's what we're gonna do. If Sphinx is going to Mont Saint-Michel, that's where I'm going. To either stop him or to get one of those keys and use it to enter the maze. Iolanthe, you're coming with me to introduce me to this Bertie. Hades, you, too. Nobody, I'll need you to fly us.

'Zoe and Mum, I need you two to go to Rome. Go to the Vatican. If the city is asleep, see if you can get in there and find any clues to the location of the blue bell, the globe or that journal in Vault IX of the Archives.'

Mae turned to Sisters Lynda and Agnes. 'Wanna bust into the Vatican Secret Archives with us?'

Sister Lynda said, 'Love to. Be nice to see the Church's inner sanctums and go where no girl has gone before.'

Jack turned to Rufus. 'Can you fly them in on the Sukhoi?'

'Be my pleasure, sir.'

Jack added, 'What's the status on those cargo planes filled with bronzemen that followed us out of Moscow?'

Rufus checked a portable satellite radar. 'They're coming over Europe now, sir. Heading toward northern France on a direct course for Mont Saint-Michel.'

Jack said, 'Alby, Easton. You get the most important job of all. I need you guys to watch over our unconscious friends here—Lily, Stretch and Aloysius. They can't fight for themselves, so you need to guard them and keep them out of the reach of our enemies.

'Stay here for now, but be ready to run in case the bad guys turn up. While you're waiting, see what you can find out about that Supreme Labyrinth. Check out my stuff from the farm, too: I recall that some of it mentions labyrinths and Imhotep the Great. Also, look into the fourth moon landing and that pedestal. And Alby?'

'Yeah?'

'Find out everything you possibly can about the five iron mountains, especially the two lost ones.'

There was movement all over Hades's palatial estate as everyone prepared for their missions.

Alby and Easton were prepping three rolling hospital beds on which they could lay the sleeping bodies of Lily, Stretch and Aloysius.

Alby hooked up some IVs that would keep the comatose bodies nourished in their sleep. He also set up some computers nearby so he could do his research while watching over them.

Rufus refuelled the Sukhoi as Zoe, Mae and the two nuns loaded everything they needed.

A short distance away, near Hades's lake house, Nobody flight-checked a compact little seaplane.

It was one of two identical seaplanes that Hades kept on his private lake, although technically the planes did not belong to him.

They had been bought by his sons—his two nasty sons, Princes Dion and Zaitan—for quick hops to mountain lakes at exclusive ski resorts in Switzerland and Austria.

The two seaplanes were custom-built ICON A10s. Regular people couldn't buy these. They were made to order.

Small and state-of-the-art, the two A10s were slightly larger than the famous ICON A5, which can only carry two people. These could carry five: two up front, three in the back. Like the A5, their big selling point was their ability to take off and land on short bodies of water, like remote alpine lakes.

Painted on the sides of the two seaplanes were their names:

Sexy Prince One and *Sexy Prince Two*.

Nobody shook his head.

'Jackasses,' he muttered.

When the sleeping room was ready, Jack carried Lily into it, wrapped in a blanket.

He handed her to Alby who laid her down gently on one of the hospital beds. They handled her like precious cargo, like the most important thing in their lives, which she was.

Once Lily was safely in her bed, Jack went to get Stretch.

He passed Rufus on the way. The big pilot was carrying his unconscious friend, Aloysius, to the sleeping room in a similar manner: gently, tenderly.

After he had laid Aloysius on one of the beds, Rufus approached Jack, holding something in his hands.

It was a black gunbelt, with two sawn-off silver Remington shotguns in its holsters: Aloysius Knight's signature weapons.

'Jack,' Rufus said. 'I want you to take these. They're the best in the business. They make an impression. Aloysius would want you to use 'em, you know, to do some damage.'

Jack gave Rufus a long look. Then he nodded, took the gunbelt and strapped it around his waist, affixing the holsters' Velcro straps around his thighs.

'Appreciate this, Rufus,' he said.

'Do him proud, Cap'n,' Rufus said, before ambling off with his huge shoulders hunched.

When Lily, Aloysius and Stretch were in their beds, Easton put down some blankets for the dogs nearby. Horus watched it all from her perch.

Easton showed the set-up to Jack. 'We will keep a good watch, Captain Jack.'

'You're a fine man, Easton,' Jack said. 'Thanks.'

Easton beamed and went off to grab some more medical supplies with Alby.

Jack sat for a moment in the room with the three sleeping figures and his pets.

It was a rare quiet moment and he used it to bring up two emails kept in special folders on his phone: two Messages from the Other Side pre-written by Sky Monster and Pooh Bear.

In the silence of that room, Jack read them.

First, Sky Monster's:

Well, hey there Jack, my buddy, my bro,

I imagine this is a time to say something profound, but I never really was any good at all that kind of stuff. I was always just a dumb ol' pilot.

So all I'll say is this: thank you.

Thank you for taking me along on your adventures, for giving my life meaning, a purpose, something to fight for.

Running and flying and fighting alongside a guy like you makes a guy like me a little taller, a little braver, a little less fat.

Speaking of which, I will never forget our battles together during those crazy Great Games. All those other brilliant warriors brought with them fit and strong companions while you only had me by your side: a dumb, fat Kiwi who should shave more.

But fuck me, we did it, and I'll always have that. Always.

And now, I guess I'm gone.

Damn, I hope I went out fighting.

Your friend,

Ernest Q. Shepherd II

a.k.a. Sky Monster

P.S. Go the All Blacks!

Jack sniffed back a sob. 'Damn New Zealanders. It's always about the rugby. And you used your name, Ernie.'

He turned to Pooh Bear's email. It was easily the shortest of the messages he'd seen so far. It read:

Jack,
My hero.

Lily,
My light.

Stretch,
My friend forever.

I'm sorry I had to go.
Pooh

Jack sat there for a moment, his head bowed, a tear trickling down his cheek.

Jack was clicking off his phone when Alby returned to the bedroom.

'Jack, I just did some calculations. The moon is going to be directly over Mont Saint-Michel at 8:37 p.m. tonight. It'll be over it for approximately thirteen minutes. I don't have an exact location of the pedestal on the lunar surface, but I'm guessing it'll be aligned.'

'Good work, Alby. Now keep my girl safe while I'm away.'

'I will.'

Jack left the room and called to the others. 'Time to go, people!'

Goodbyes were said before everyone made for their respective planes.

An air of sombreness hung over the moment.

It was as if many of them sensed they might not see each other again.

Jack and Zoe embraced and kissed.

'You look after yourself, okay,' Zoe said. 'Don't make me have to come rescue you from somewhere.'

Jack smiled. 'I only take those risks because I always know you'll be there to save me. See you soon, honey.'

Hades made to shake hands with Mae, only to be unexpectedly hugged by her.

'Good luck, Anthony,' she said. 'You may have been the King of the Underworld once, but you've grown on me.' She jerked her chin at Jack. 'Look after my boy.'

'I will, Mae,' Hades said. And then he added, 'Mae. Can I ask you a question?'

'Shoot.'

Hades looked over at Jack, now striding toward one of the sea-planes with Iolanthe and Nobody. 'How did you raise him? How did you create a man like that?'

'I'll show you,' Mae said. 'Hey, Cubby!' she shouted suddenly.

Jack spun instantly at the name.

'Sorry, *fifth greatest warrior*,' Mae called, smiling. 'I'm so proud of you, Cub. Be careful out there. Love you.'

Jack gave her wry smile in return. 'Love you, too, Mum.'

Hades said, 'Cubby?'

'My pet name for him as a kid,' Mae said. 'His father went by Wolf, so right from when he was a baby, Jack always went by Cub or Cubby. How did I make him the way he is? I don't know. I do know that every time I see him I tell him how proud I am of him. I hear he does the same with Lily. It's parenting, right?'

Hades sighed sadly. 'Mae, during the Great Games my two sons plotted to kill me and seize my throne. The younger one, Zaitan, died, and Dion now works with Sphinx. My brother, Yago, hates me. I failed both as a parent and as a brother.'

They watched in silence as Jack climbed into the seaplane.

'He's going to die doing this,' Hades said softly.

'Say again?' Mae said.

'He's entirely overmatched. Sphinx has more knowledge, more experts, more resources, more weapons plus an entire army of automatons at his command. Jack cannot win this.'

'Maybe,' Mae said. 'When he was a kid, I only ever gave Jack one piece of advice: *choose good friends*. Look at all these people helping him now. He chose well. And they help him because he'd step in front of a bus for them.

'Did Alby tell you what Jack did in Moscow? He dragged *three people* away from those bronzemen, when he could have run and saved himself. Look at how he just carried Lily and Stretch to their beds. Everything he's doing now is for his friends. He fights for them, for their world, for their right to live free.

'Jack may be overmatched on paper, but never count him out,'

Mae said. 'The odds don't mean anything to Jack. And that makes me very proud.'

The team split up.

Jack's seaplane—*Sexy Prince One*—took off from the lake for the short flight to Mont Saint-Michel in northern France.

Rufus's Sukhoi flew south toward the Vatican.

Alby stayed behind and watched them go.

SECOND OFFENSIVE

THE FALLING TEMPLE AT MONT SAINT-MICHEL

The moon, Earth's closest neighbour, is among the strangest
planetary bodies in the solar system.

SCIENCE DAILY, 2016

MONT SAINT-MICHEL

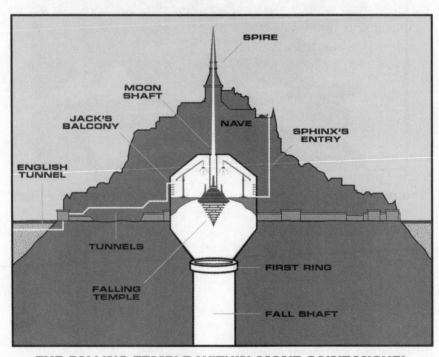

THE FALLING TEMPLE WITHIN MONT SAINT-MICHEL (X-RAY VIEW)

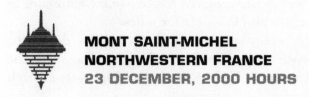

**MONT SAINT-MICHEL
NORTHWESTERN FRANCE
23 DECEMBER, 2000 HOURS**

Mont Saint-Michel is stupendous.

There is no other word for it.

Like its companion island in England over on the other side of the English Channel, St Michael's Mount, it is a tidal island with a medieval structure on its back.

But that is where the similarities end.

While the castle that sits on St Michael's Mount in England is squat, square and utilitarian, the structure atop France's Mont Saint-Michel is striking, soaring and breathtakingly beautiful.

Over time, some historians have used the name 'Mont Saint-Michel' to describe both the abbey and the island, but this is not strictly correct. The island's full name is actually 'Mont Saint-Michel au péril de la Mer': *The Mount of St Michael at the peril of the sea.*

It is well earned.

For the island stands a kilometre out from the shore, in the middle of a wide bay. The tides of this bay are both strong and enormous, rising and falling a full fifteen metres twice a day.

It is one of the largest and fastest tidal movements in the world and it is lethal: even modern-day tourists have been caught unawares by its speed and been overwhelmed by the incoming waves. Victor Hugo himself described it as '*à la vitesse d'un cheval au galop*': 'as swift as a galloping horse'.

When the tide is out, the bay around the magnificent island is no less dangerous. The exposed seabed becomes a deadly wasteland of sucking mud and quicksand-filled potholes.

The peril of the sea.

The abbey itself is an architectural marvel. If it was built at ground level, it would be an iconic wonder of the world to rival Notre Dame, but it stands *five hundred feet* above the landscape at the summit of the mount and is visible for miles.

The multi-levelled, many-spired cathedral cascades down the mountain in a sequence of enormous step-like walls that shade the sprawling medieval town nestled at the base of the island, itself protected at the waterline by battlements.

At the very top of the abbey, at the tip of its steeple above the heart of the cathedral, at the very highest point of the whole forti-fied island, is a golden statue of the archangel Michael.

The dangerous tides and battlements have proved to be an excellent defence for Mont Saint-Michel: it withstood not one but three sieges by English forces during the Hundred Years War. The English even made camp on the second island in the bay, the nearby uninhabited island of Tombelaine, but they never took Mont Saint-Michel.

In the 1800s, those same tides and battlements worked in the opposite way when Napoleon used the mount as a prison: a 19th-century Alcatraz.

One final feature is worth noting: long before the Catholic Church gained a foothold on it, Mont Saint-Michel contained many stone circles and ancient pagan religious sites both on and inside it. For over a thousand years, the Church has banned access to these sites.

On the evening of 23 December, Mont Saint-Michel was ablaze with light.

A full moon lit up the entire bay and newly erected floodlights mounted on the island's lower walls illuminated the abbey's upper reaches. They had been set up by Sphinx's advance team, the members of which could be seen moving all over the upper reaches of the Mont, especially around the cathedral.

The tide was coming in. Swiftly.

The inrushing waves sloshed against the battlements at the base of the mighty island.

The only road connecting the tidal island to the mainland was a long sweeping causeway bridge. It was also lit up by floodlights and on it, blocking it, were four jeeps, two troop trucks and . . .

. . . twenty bronzemen, all facing impassively outward, barring the way.

In the other direction, out in the wider bay to the north, the island of Tombelaine lay low and dark in the night.

But underneath it, there was movement.

Jack and Iolanthe raced through a tight tunnel that had been dug under the seabed between Tombelaine and Mont Saint-Michel.

They had left Nobody and Hades back at Tombelaine, with the seaplane that had brought them there. The plane was hidden inside a rickety old fishing shack, part of a cluster of abandoned hovels that hung off the northern tip of the uninhabited island.

Down in the tunnel, Jack and Iolanthe were well aware that in the world above them, the tide was coming in.

For a rising tide *above* meant a rising tide *inside* the tunnel.

This was because the tunnel—built by English forces six hundred years earlier—was not entirely watertight. Over half a millennium, its ancient walls had become porous, allowing silty water to slowly seep into it as the tide came in overhead.

'We have to hurry!' Iolanthe said as she ran, the rising water slapping against her knees, her flashlight's beam bouncing up and down.

'When the tide outside comes in, water gradually fills the tunnel, making it a deathtrap. The English only used it once to try to storm Mont Saint-Michel, but the tide came in too fast and two hundred

soldiers drowned. The sheer number of corpses left inside the tunnel blocked the way so badly that it couldn't be used again without clearing them out. Then the war ended and the English left and it was forgotten.'

The grim evidence of that mass drowning was all around them, even now, six hundred years later.

The flesh and bones of the dead invaders had long ago crumbled to nothing—largely clearing the way—but their 15th-century armour and weapons remained.

Jack found himself hurdling rusted chestplates, fallen swords and blackened shields as he hurried down the tight, rough-walled tunnel.

The water rising around his shins was a foul milky sludge, a mix of mud and silt. The idea of drowning in it was sickening.

The tunnel was about two kilometres long and by the time they reached its end, the sludge—fed by the incoming tide above them seeping through the walls—had risen to their thighs.

At last they came to a medieval wall with a ragged hole punched in it, where an old man with a wild shock of white hair, a Roman collar and a kind face stood waiting for them.

It was Brother Dagobert de Montreuil.

And he was waving anxiously at them to stop.

'Stop, stop, stop! Hold it right there!' Brother Dagobert said in a hushed whisper. 'There's a laser trip-wire just in front of you!'

Jack stopped instantly, looked down and saw it through the murky water.

A faint red beam spanned the tunnel at knee height.

He and Iolanthe stepped carefully over it, joining the old priest.

At first, Brother Dagobert smiled when he saw Iolanthe, but then his grin vanished.

'Goodness me . . .' he said as he scanned her partially-shaved head and bruised face.

When he had last seen her, Jack guessed, she had probably had her lush auburn hair and flawless complexion. She looked very different now.

Bertie leapt forward and hugged her warmly. 'Oh, Io! It's so good to see you.'

'You, too, Bertie.' She indicated Jack. 'Brother Dagobert de Montreuil, meet Captain Jack West Jr.'

Bertie nodded at Jack, impressed. 'You, young man, have disturbed the universe. Big fan. Love your work. Those entitled royal families have been ruling this world for far too long. Welcome to the first iron mountain.'

'Nice to meet you, too,' Jack said.

'Quickly now, we cannot linger,' Bertie said, turning suddenly and striding into the dark bowels of Mont Saint-Michel. 'Sphinx's advance team arrived here not long ago. I don't know where Sphinx is, but I overheard someone say he is on his way. The advance team

is led by Cardinal Mendoza, who now sports the papal ring and a Ring of Command, and Dionysius DeSaxe. And my snivelling snake of a boss, young Father Rasmussen—ever alert to the possibility of impressing a senior member of the Church—has his lips permanently attached to Mendoza's ass.'

Iolanthe and Jack hurried after the old Jesuit.

He moved quickly, like a power-walker.

They wound left and right, through a maze of old passageways, before they came to some narrow stairs going steeply upward.

Bertie didn't stop as he started up them. 'This is the priests' entrance to the ancient temple within the mountain. Lots of these old shrines and temples have back doors for caretaker-priests to enter them without using the main entrances.'

He turned to Iolanthe as he walked.

'Oh, Io, whatever happened to your lovely hair?'

'My brother had me tortured, Bertie,' Iolanthe said.

'Orlando, hmm. He was a nasty boy and no doubt a nastier man. Resentful lad. Spoilt. And not very bright. That's never a good combination in a king.'

Jack said, 'You knew Orlando and Iolanthe when they were children. Did you know Sphinx, too?'

'Ooh, yes,' Bertie said, never stopping. 'Yes, I did. Back then, Sphinx was just Hardin. Hardin Lancaster. Even when he was young, he was old. Shrewd beyond his years. Cunning. Patient, too. And he could hold a grudge against a teacher or another child like you wouldn't believe. As I recall, there was an incident with a boy from the Ludovico family. I'm not surprised Hardin has made his move now.'

For the first time, Bertie paused on the stairs, nodding at Iolanthe.

'But Io, here'—Bertie gave her a genuinely affectionate smile— 'she was my best student. Wilful, yes. Headstrong, yes. Naughty, oh my, yes. But gifted and brilliant like no other student I ever taught.'

He spun and started climbing the steep stairs again.

'Thanks,' Iolanthe said wryly.

Bertie was disappearing into the darkness. 'Hurry now. I can't be away for too long before I am missed by Father Rasmussen. They are preparing to perform the Fall.'

Back on Tombelaine Island, Nobody sat huddled in his seaplane—
parked inside the old fishing shack—watching and listening to the
video feed from Jack's helmet-mounted camera.

Hades stood on a hill a short distance from the dock, gazing out
at Mont Saint-Michel a couple of miles to the south.

The great island monastery was gloriously lit by the full moon
and the artificial lights.

Through an earpiece, he listened to the audio from Jack's helmet-
camera, noticing the second reference to his son: '*Sphinx's advance
team arrived here not long ago . . . led by Cardinal Mendoza, who
now sports the papal ring and a Ring of Command, and Dionysius
DeSaxe*—'

Hades gazed in silence at the island, thinking.

Dion . . .

He glanced at a small stone shack built into the hillside near him.
Ostensibly, it was a shepherd's hut, designed to shield the herders
of old during the sudden storms that were common here, but in
reality it housed the hidden entrance to the English tunnel to Mont
Saint-Michel.

A few minutes later, Nobody came out from the plane.

'Yo, Hades,' he called. 'Can you tell me about—'

He cut himself off.

Hades was gone.

Huffing and puffing as he struggled to keep up with Bertie, Jack hustled up flight after flight of ultra-narrow stone stairs.

It was so tight, his shoulders brushed against the walls.

He got the impression that the many steep flights they were climbing were built *inside* the medieval walls of Mont Saint-Michel's colossal abbey.

Brother Bertie climbed the stairs with the energy of a younger man. He spoke with equal sprightliness.

'I'm sorry I couldn't write it all out in that message, Iolanthe. My superiors could have happened upon me at any moment. So I'll tell you now: the Vatican Globe that originally sat atop the obelisk outside St Peter's is incomplete.'

'What do you mean, incomplete?' Iolanthe said.

'What I mean,' Bertie said, 'is that the globe that Caligula had transported to Rome from Egypt in 37 A.D. was *defaced* and thus rendered incomplete.'

'How so?' Jack asked.

'It's always been believed that that obelisk came from Heliopolis,' Bertie said. 'But it doesn't. It comes from Siwa, the famed oasis way out in the Egyptian desert, the birthplace of the Oracles. When the priests of the Cult of Amon-Ra at Siwa were informed that the mad Roman emperor, Caligula, was planning to move their sacred obelisk to Rome, they were horrified.

'They knew that the globe on that obelisk showed the locations of the three secret cities and the five iron mountains. They were aghast at the idea that a man as insane as Caligula might possess

such knowledge. Don't forget, Caligula was so mad, he declared his horse to be a god. His *horse*!'

Jack watched the old monk as he marched up the stairs, speaking quickly. He clearly loved all this history. Jack liked him.

Bertie continued: 'So the priests of Amon-Ra at Siwa immediately began defacing the globe, *filing down* the mountains on it, so that Caligula wouldn't obtain its sacred knowledge. It was difficult work—that globe is made of a metal not found on Earth—but they managed to scrape off two of the mountains before Caligula's men arrived and took the globe and killed all the priests. Thus the globe is incomplete.'

Jack said, 'Leaving two unknown mountains . . .'

'Yes. The two lost mountains. Even then, because the Vatican Globe is so small and lacking in detail, deducing the locations of the three mountains actually depicted on it is not that easy. Mont Saint-Michel's location is clear enough: it's right there on the coast of modern France. But the other two mountains, which we call the second and third mountains, well . . .'

He shrugged.

'The second mountain is definitely in the French Alps—we know that—but it could be any one of several mountains: Mont Blanc, the Matterhorn, or even the Jungfrau. The third mountain is somewhere in central Asia in the Himalayas: it could be Everest or Annapurna, it could be in Bhutan, it could even be underneath Potala Palace, as some believe.

'And then there are the last two mountains that were erased from the globe completely. Over the centuries, the Church and the royal families have sent many men to find them: Columbus, Magellan, Drake, Cook and, of course, Javier, whose journal is reputed to mention them, as I said in my text to Iolanthe. Ah, here we are.'

They came to an old wooden door cut into the wall of their rough-hewn stairwell. They pushed through it—

—and suddenly Jack found himself in a curving stone-walled corridor that swept out of view in both directions. Unlike the stairwell, its walls were beautifully carved, clean and smooth.

Bertie hurried down the curving hallway.

Jack said, 'We've sent some people to find Javier's journal in the Vatican Archives.'

'Nice to know someone takes my advice,' Bertie said. 'Unlike the stupid Church. I might have told them the same thing if they hadn't made my former student, Rasmussen, my boss.'

And there it was, Jack thought. The older man passed over by his protégé. He felt for poor Bertie.

'As you would be aware, Captain, over the course of sixty years of study, one acquires a considerable amount of arcana. I'm an old man. I *own* nothing. I *am* nothing. I *have* nothing but the knowledge in my head. When Rasmussen was my student, I didn't tell him *everything* I know. But that is not our immediate concern. This is.'

They came to a small stone balcony branching off the inner side of the curving passageway.

'Careful, now. Stay back a little, so they don't see you,' Bertie said.

Staying in the shadows, Jack peered out from the balcony.

'Oh, wow,' he gasped.

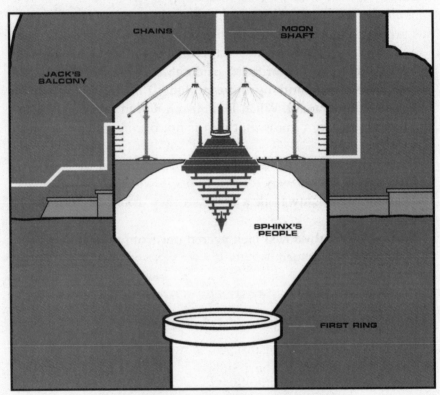

THE HALL OF THE FALLING TEMPLE

A vast cavern lay below Jack, lit by two huge floodlights that Sphinx's advance team must have erected.

It was an immense space, at least two hundred metres wide, and it had no floor.

Its sheer stone walls—cut from the heart of the island mountain—just fell away into darkness.

Five levels of balconies ran in a wide circle around the space, the highest of which was Jack's. They looked like VIP boxes at an opera house.

In the middle of the chamber's soaring ceiling was a round hole through which a thin shaft of moonlight lanced downward, almost perfectly vertical.

But it was the enormous structure in the exact centre of the cavern that seized Jack's attention.

A superancient temple.

It was the shape of a gigantic spinning top: it had a wide round waist while it tapered to sharp points at the top and bottom.

And it was absolutely immense, perhaps sixteen storeys from tip to tip, with eight storeys above the waist and eight below.

The temple was suspended from the ceiling by four mighty chains, hanging in such a way that its wide middle was perfectly level with four leaping half-bridges that reached out to it from ceremonial doorways in the walls of the cavern.

Looking down on the gigantic temple from his balcony, Jack saw immediately that it comprised two distinct parts: an upper half and a lower half.

The upper half appeared to be made of solid stone and was visibly heavy. Five gorgeous obelisks surmounted it: four smaller ones ringing a larger central obelisk that stood proudly at the very peak of the hanging temple. That obelisk alone must have been sixty feet tall.

Markings in the distinctive symbols of the Word of Thoth covered the obelisk. Jack wished he had Lily with him to read them.

The lower half of the hanging structure was very different from the upper half.

Whereas the upper half was all weight and mass, this half was skeletal.

It had eight open-air levels, each one smaller than the one above it, so that its bottommost level—the lowest tip of the immense temple—was basically a small open-sided cupola.

And in the centre of that bottommost level, Jack spied a waist-high altar.

All of the lower levels were made of brilliant white stone. They were connected by glistening golden pillars, each of which was inset with ladder-like rungs.

Jack peered down into the vast shaft below the hanging temple.

In the shadowy darkness down there, he saw that it narrowed to a circular shaft barely wider than the temple itself.

'What is this place?' Jack whispered.

'This,' Bertie said reverently, 'is the Hall of the Falling Temple at the First Iron Mountain.'

There were some figures down on one of the bridges, looking positively tiny against the scale of the gigantic temple.

Jack recognised one of them as Cardinal Ricardo Mendoza, head of the Vatican's Congregation for the Doctrine of the Faith, or as it was once known, the Holy Inquisition.

The man beside him was younger and he wore a plastic half-facemask to cover his hideously disfigured jaw.

Dion DeSaxe, Jack thought. Hades's psycho son.

Wearing his cardinal's skullcap, Mendoza was gazing up studiously at the temple while a blond-haired priest beside him pointed out various things on it.

'That's Father Rasmussen,' Bertie growled. 'Little German snake. The other Church man is Cardinal Mendoza, Sphinx's expert and the leader of his advance party. He's a clever one, well versed in ancient matters. He is the one who perfected their Thoth translator.'

'We know Mendoza,' Jack said. 'And that guy in the mask with him is Hades's son, Dion. Unfortunately, we know him, too.'

'What happened to his face?'

'My friend shot him through it,' Jack said simply.

He scanned the ceiling of the cavern.

'Are we below the church at the summit of the Mont?'

'Yes, directly beneath the nave. Mendoza's men moved the tip of the spire that sits atop the church. They also pushed aside the altar, revealing a moon hole in the floor. The moonlight comes directly down through the spire and then through the hole and into this cavern.'

Jack looked down at the shaft beneath the suspended temple.

'Bertie,' he said. 'How deep is that shaft?'

'It is exactly 3.8 kilometres deep,' Bertie said, 'with sheer stone walls.'

'And at the bottom?'

'Solid rock.'

'And the temple falls into the shaft?'

'Yes. With the claimant on it,' Bertie said.

'The claimant?' Jack asked.

'The person who lays claim to the ultimate throne.'

Jack was silent as that sank in.

The ultimate throne . . .

Bertie added, 'The temple is a remarkable piece of engineering. It is perfectly balanced. *Perfectly.* It will fall straight and true, directly into the lower shaft. For this is the test of the claimant.'

'How so?'

Bertie nodded again at the dark round shaft beneath them, plummeting into the Earth.

'There are two giant ancient metal rings embedded in the round wall of the shaft: one annulus at the top, another a further three kilometres down.

'The claimant stands atop the temple and releases it from its chains, causing the whole structure to fall . . . with the claimant on it. As the temple drops into the shaft and passes through the *first* metal ring, the claimant must have his palm pressed against one of four hand-shaped marks on the base of the upper obelisk.

'Then the claimant must move quickly. For by the time the temple passes through the *second* giant annulus—exactly 52 seconds later—the claimant must have dashed down *to the lowest level* of the Falling Temple and placed his hand on a second altar down there. His hand *must* be pressed against a hand-mark on the surface of the lower altar at the moment the Falling Temple passes through the second ring. Only that will stop the temple's fall.'

'And what if the claimant doesn't make it to the lower altar in time?' Jack asked.

Bertie said, 'Then the entire structure—falling at incredible speed—will crash into the solid stone base at the bottom of the shaft and the heavy upper half will crush the spindly lower half in an instant, killing anyone on it.'

Bertie gave Jack a look. 'Do you see those Thoth markings on the main obelisk?'

'Yes.'

'According to our records, it translates as: "*He cannot be emperor who does not risk his own blood.*" Not just anyone can rule the world. This is a test of courage. And it is demanded as part of the Trial of the Mountains. "*Only those who survive the Fall may enter the Supreme Labyrinth and look upon the face of the Omega.*" This, my good Captain West, is the Fall.'

Bertie stood.

'I must leave you now. I told Father Rasmussen I had to fetch something from the library and I must get back before I am missed.'

He handed Iolanthe an envelope. 'For you, my dear Io. As a nineteen-year-old, you were a horrible little strumpet: wilful, insolent and entitled. All of your other teachers thought you would become a truly nasty princess, but—well—I always thought you had some good in you.'

Iolanthe smiled.

Bertie nodded at Jack. 'He's a fine man, this one. If you're traipsing around with him, then maybe you've turned out all right. I'm glad to see it. You might have proved this silly old man correct.'

He gave her an affectionate peck on the forehead and a final hug and dashed off.

Jack gave Iolanthe another sideways look. 'Should I tell him that you *did* try to kill me once? And seduce me.'

'Shush. Let me have my moment—'

The roar of a helicopter cut her off, loud and close.

The wobbling yet powerful beam of a chopper's searchlight came spearing down through the moon shaft, lighting up the space.

Jack leaned back further into the shadows.

'I'm guessing that's Sphinx,' he said.

★ ★ ★

It was Sphinx.

At that moment, high in the sky above Mont Saint-Michel, an aerial motorcade was arriving at the island monastery.

Five choppers, flying in an arrowhead formation—their searchlights playing over the fortified mountain—arrived at its summit.

The lead chopper, Sphinx's, was an Mi-4000, identical to the one he'd used in Rome.

It was followed by four big double-rotored Chinooks. Normally a Chinook would have been the biggest bird in any aerial motorcade, but not this one. With its steel crossbeam and four mighty rotors, the Mi-4000 was the alpha dog in this pack.

The lead chopper touched down on a broad balcony at the summit of Mont Saint-Michel and, followed by silvermen and bronzemen, the tiny figure of Sphinx strode out from it and headed inside.

On his balcony, Jack saw Bertie reappear beside Mendoza, Dion and Rasmussen down by the Falling Temple.

Even from this distance, he could hear Rasmussen shout, 'Brother Dagobert! How dare you keep the cardinal waiting!'

Humiliated, Bertie bowed apologetically.

Jack empathised with the old monk and saw him glance furtively up at their balcony.

A minute later, there came a commotion—

—and suddenly four silver automatons marched into the temple chamber, followed by fifty bronzemen who were followed by—

—Sphinx.

It was a procession, the procession of the most powerful man in the world, the King of Kings, the Emperor, escorted by his loyal guards.

He was also accompanied by Yago DeSaxe, Chloe Carnarvon and Jaeger Eins.

Jack gazed hard at Sphinx.

He hadn't seen Hardin Lancaster XII since their meeting

at Sphinx's mansion in Morocco on the southern shore of the Mediterranean Sea; a mansion that sat atop the lost City of Atlas and across the strait from the Rock of Gibraltar.

Jack would remember that meeting for a long time.

It was where Sphinx, holding Lily hostage, had forced Jack and Aloysius Knight to do his dirty work for him at the City of Atlas.

Back then, Sphinx had been wearing the clothing of a landed aristocrat: collared shirt, pressed trousers, smart shoes. Tall and powerfully built, he was fit for a man in his late fifties. With his broad leonine face, he cut a striking figure.

Now he wore a military shirt, cargo pants and sturdy boots. He was dressed for action.

For her part, Iolanthe glared at her old assistant, Chloe Carnarvon.

Mendoza rushed to meet his lord and master. 'Sire! All is in readiness. Jaeger Vier is at the observatory in the Alps. His rover team has exposed the pedestal on the lunar surface. Jaeger Vier says it will be in position in exactly seven minutes.'

'Excellent.'

'Sire, would you like Dion to do the Fall with you? It is permitted.'

'No,' Sphinx said firmly. 'This is historic, Cardinal, and when the history of it is written, it must record that I did it alone, with only courage as my companion. Come. It is time for me to do the Fall.'

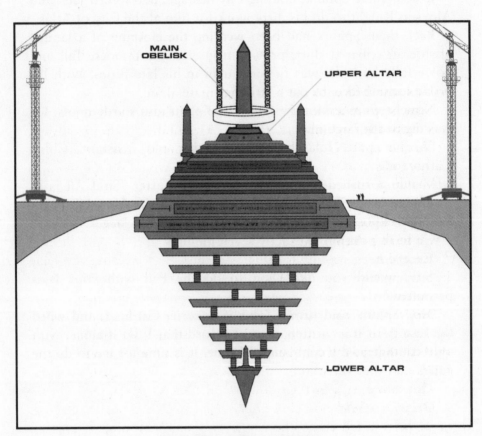

MAIN
OBELISK

UPPER ALTAR

LOWER ALTAR

THE FALLING TEMPLE

Sphinx marched onto the hanging temple, alone.

Some steps ascended the slanted sides of the temple's upper half, leading to the large obelisk at its tip. He climbed them steadily.

'*Sire, it is 8:35,*' Mendoza's voice said in his ear. '*Jaeger Vier and the observatory team report that the pedestal on the moon is almost in position. 90 seconds to start time.*'

Sphinx eyed the shaft of moonlight lancing down through the ceiling of the cavern, illuminating the towering obelisk.

He took a deep breath.

He had been waiting for this moment for a long time. Studying it, training for it.

He cannot be emperor who does not risk his own blood.

Monarchies and royal families only went so far, he thought, because hereditary rule had a fatal flaw: gifted rulers could give birth to dullards. It had been shown time and again over the centuries that they often did.

This, however, was the test of a real ruler.

Orlando could not have done this, Sphinx thought. He had never been tested and so he would not have been prepared for an examination like this.

But Sphinx had been tested.

And he was ready.

He had analysed an old drawing of this Falling Temple many times over the years, planning his route down its slopes and ladders.

'*Sire,*' Mendoza's voice said. '*60 seconds.*'

Sphinx stepped up onto the highest level of the Falling Temple.

The main obelisk loomed above him. The colossal ancient chains holding up the temple gripped it with a circular metal 'collar'.

From this position directly beneath the narrow moon shaft in the ceiling, Sphinx could actually see all the way up that shaft.

He saw the full moon up there, blotting out the stars.

And on the moon, directly facing him—impossible to see with the naked eye, but possible from an astronomical observatory—was a matching mountain with a pedestal on it that was at that very moment coming into perfect alignment with this ancient place.

'*40 seconds . . .*'

Arriving at the summit of the temple, Sphinx now beheld the magnificent altar on which the obelisk stood.

It was a very unique kind of altar.

Trapezoidal in shape, solid and sturdy, it was cut from a cloudy type of translucent stone that looked like unpolished diamond.

On each of the four slanting faces of this diamond altar, one on each side, Sphinx saw a sunken impression of a human hand or palm.

Inside each image of the hand—running up the thumb and first two fingers—was a raised marking that roughly formed the shape of a W.

'*20 seconds . . .*' Mendoza's voice said. '*Please place your hand in position, sire.*'

He held his hand above one of the four palm-shaped indentations, aligning his thumb and first two fingers with the raised W in it.

From his balcony overlooking the hanging temple, Jack watched in silent awe.

He didn't quite know what to expect.

He was still playing catch-up to Sphinx, a rival who already possessed too many advantages: men, time, resources and, most of all, knowledge of this vitally important ceremony.

★ ★ ★

Sphinx held his palm poised above the ancient image of a human hand.

'He cannot be emperor who does not risk his own blood,' he said softly to no-one.

Mendoza's voice said, '. . . *Observatory team reports that the moon pedestal will be in position in . . . three, two, one—*'

—WHAM!—

At that precise moment, a dead-straight beam of vertical green light sprang forth from the pedestal on the moon, leaping across 240,000 miles of space in an instant, and shot down through the narrow shaft in the chamber's ceiling, piercing the darkness of the cavern, and *slammed* into the top of the main obelisk!

In response, Sphinx immediately pressed his palm flat against the image of the human hand on the diamond altar.

It appeared as if the brilliant green light from the moon had shot right through the obelisk, because the translucent altar at the obelisk's base—the one Sphinx was now touching—blazed with the same green glow.

The combined action of the arrival of the green beam and Sphinx pressing his hand against the image had another effect:

It caused the chains and the metal collar holding up the temple to release their grip on the obelisk . . .

. . . and the whole supersized temple, with Sphinx on it, dropped suddenly and sickeningly into the dark shaft below.

Jack jerked up at the sight of the temple dropping from its mounts.

He'd been so thoroughly entranced by the otherworldly green light lancing down into the chamber and hitting the obelisk that the sudden falling of the temple caught him by surprise.

The building-sized structure—it must have weighed a thousand tons—dropped like an anvil, its enormous mass creating a *whooshing* sound as it scythed down through the air . . .

. . . and whipped into the narrower shaft at the base of the chamber, disappearing from view.

Wind battered Sphinx's body as he stood atop the Falling Temple, his hair whipping wildly.

With a heavy rushing sound, the temple shot into the narrow section of the shaft. The walls of this lower section rushed upward in a blur, bare feet from the edges of the huge falling thing.

But such was the precision of the temple's construction—such was its perfect balance—that it never touched those walls. It just fell through the shaft as it would have fallen through empty sky.

As the Falling Temple rushed into the lower shaft, it passed through a colossal silver ring embedded in the shaft's round wall.

Sphinx made sure to keep his hand pressed against the diamond altar as the temple plummeted through the ring . . .

. . . and as it did, he roared in pain as the raised W beneath his palm suddenly became scalding hot and something was *seared* into his hand and he knew that the first part of the ceremony had been completed.

And then he was off . . .

. . . moving fast . . .

. . . bolting down the stairs on the upper half of the Falling Temple . . .

'*You're through the first ring. 52 seconds to the second ring,*' Mendoza's voice informed him.

Sphinx bounded downward on the fast-falling structure.

Wind blew all around him.

The green light from the moon bathed him in its eerie glow.

The sixteen-storey structure fell down the shaft like a giant out-of-control elevator.

He arrived at the midpoint of the falling structure, at a ladder-hole cut into the temple's waist level giving access to the lower half.

'*40 seconds, sire . . .*'

Sphinx clambered down the ladder, gripping its hand- and footholds.

He'd practised this on a mock-up at his mansion many times.

The massive temple *whooshed* down the shaft, accelerating . . .

Down Sphinx went, climbing to the lower levels of the Falling Temple.

It was a curious sensation to be descending so frantically while the temple itself fell. Sphinx didn't have long: when the temple stopped accelerating, both he and it would be in perfect freefall and he would experience weightlessness and it would be impossible to move . . . if he didn't hit the bottom first.

'*26 seconds . . .*'

Sphinx pushed downward, hurrying to the next level, ignoring the walls of the shaft zooming upward in a blur of speed.

'*15 seconds . . .*'

And then he was there.

At the bottommost level . . .

. . . where he found a waist-high diamond altar, with four more

indented hand images on it, and inside those images were different raised markings, this time resembling a V.

'*10 seconds to the second ring . . .*'

Sphinx slammed his right palm down on one of the hand images, feeling the raised image press into the skin of his two unscalded fingers . . .

. . . as with a *whoosh*, the Falling Temple shot down through a second enormous annulus embedded in the circular wall of the shaft . . .

. . . and the altar under Sphinx's hand came alive with heat and a second image was seared into his hand . . .

. . . as, with a deafeningly loud screech, a circular section of thick shiny metal *extended out* from the waist of the Falling Temple—in an instant making that waist a few feet wider all the way around—and thus it acted like a brake, grinding against the sheer walls of the shaft, kicking up thousands of sparks . . .

. . . and slowing the fall of the temple.

A few moments later, the temple came to a grinding, shuddering halt, with Sphinx still standing on its lowest level.

He looked down.

A few hundred feet beneath him was the base of the shaft: a floor of solid rock.

Adrenalin surged through him.

He looked at his right hand.

Five red-hot lines now ran up his five fingers, seared deeply into them: the three prongs of the W and the two prongs of the V had become one five-pronged symbol branded into the five fingers of his hand.

He had done it.

He had survived the Fall.

And acquired the key to enter the Labyrinth, *burned* into his palm.

'*Sire, are you there?*' Mendoza's voice invaded his consciousness. '*Are you all right?*'

'I'm fine,' Sphinx said. 'It is done. Lower the chains and haul me up.'

As the mighty chains were lowered into the shaft, clanking and clattering from some unseen mechanism in the ceiling, Dion DeSaxe felt his cell phone buzz.

He glanced at it. It read:

MY SON,
I AM HERE. UP IN THE NAVE.
PLEASE, LET US SPEAK AGAIN.
YOUR FATHER

Dion looked around himself to see if anyone near him had seen the text, but no-one had.

As the others all watched the great chains descend into the gargantuan pit, he slipped out the nearest door.

Minutes later, Dion DeSaxe entered the nave of the church at the summit of Mont Saint-Michel.

It was a beautiful old cathedral, with a soaring ceiling, stained-glass windows and dozens of high medieval pillars.

Right now, the whole space was lit by the eerie green glow of the moon.

By that light, Dion could see that the tip of the church's spire had been removed to allow the brilliant green light from the pedestal on the moon to shoot into the cathedral and down through a hole in the floor, a hole that had until today been hidden beneath the altar, which itself now lay askew.

There was no-one here.

Everyone was downstairs inside the Hall of the Falling Temple.

Then the green light moved on and pale silver moonlight illuminated the nave once again.

Hades emerged from behind a pillar, his eyes locked on Dion's. 'Son.'

'Father,' Dion said evenly.

Hades stepped out fully into the moonlit nave.

'I failed you, Dionysius. I made you into the man you have become.'

Dion said nothing. His disfigured jaw twitched beneath the half-mask.

Hades said, 'I was too stern, too unyielding. I put my duty ahead of my family and I made you hate me.'

He paused, swallowing back tears. 'By God, I never even had a nickname for you. Dion, I just wanted to say I'm sorry.'

Dion stared at his father, uncomprehending.

Then, slowly, he removed his facemask.

Hades couldn't help doing it. He winced at what he saw.

The lower left half of Dion's face was a mess of twisted skin and bone: the result of a gunshot fired by Alby Calvin in the Underworld during the chaos after the Great Games. It looked like foul melted plasticine.

'*This* is the man I have become, Father,' he said, lisping slightly as he spoke, a consequence of the wound.

'Disgusting and grotesque, both on the outside and within. Do not overstate your role in my making. You did not make me hate you. For years, I have been in contact with Sphinx. It was he who convinced me—with Zaitan—to plot your death at the conclusion of the Games. It was he who became our surrogate father and made us both hate you.'

'I forgive you, son,' Hades said, suddenly and passionately. 'I forgive you for that. I suppose, as the world rushes toward the end of all things, I just . . . I just seek your forgiveness.'

Dion glared at him, blank-faced and cold.

'Forgiveness, Father? I'll give you forgiveness.'

Dion clicked his fingers and out of the shadows sprang Jaeger Eins and three of his Knights, with their guns raised.

Down in the Hall of the Falling Temple, Jack watched in awe as the temple rose into view, hauled up by the mighty chains of the chamber, with Sphinx standing triumphantly on it beside the main obelisk.

He smiled broadly, waved a fist.

He leapt off the temple to be embraced by Mendoza. Yago slapped him on the back. Chloe clapped vigorously as she smiled broadly.

As Jack watched, Sphinx showed his hand to his companions, displaying an image of some kind that was now seared onto his fingers.

'My *hand* is the key . . .' he heard Sphinx say. 'The translation really was *burned* not *bladed*.'

Mendoza said, 'Sire, would you like to have Dion also do the Fall as a back-up? If any of our rivals find another iron mountain and the maze becomes a competitive situation, it could be helpful. We can have Dion do the Fall here or at the second iron mountain near the observatory.'

Sphinx thought for a moment. 'I must go. Have him do it here after I leave.'

'As you command,' Cardinal Mendoza said, bowing.

Sphinx started striding for the exit. 'To the Labyrinth, then. Ms Carnarvon, Cardinal, you come with me. Cardinal, do you have Imhotep the Great's notes for overcoming the maze? Just in case the Emperor's Way is closed to us.'

Jack perked up at that.

Imhotep.

The ancient Egyptian architect and adept of Amon-Ra had made a guide to the Labyrinth?

'I carry the Church's copy of his notes with me everywhere I go, sire,' Mendoza said.

Sphinx kept walking. 'We mustn't linger. The Omega Event is coming in a matter of days. It is time to claim my throne.'

'Sire, one more thing,' Mendoza said, rushing to catch up with him. 'What should we do with Father Rasmussen, Brother Dagobert and the other monks here?'

Sphinx stopped.

He looked at Rasmussen and Bertie and the other three monks of the monastery as if they were a minor detail that he had forgotten.

'Well, they cannot be allowed to live and tell anyone about what they have seen here,' he said lightly. 'Have a bronzeman tear off their heads and throw their bodies into the shaft.'

Bertie blanched.

Rasmussen's face went red with shock. 'My Lord, I implore you, I only wish to serve—'

'Sire!' a voice called, silencing Rasmussen and making both Jack and Sphinx spin; Jack on his balcony, Sphinx down on the eastern bridge.

Dion entered the chamber.

He was followed by Hades who was covered by Jaeger Eins and the armed Knights.

'Oh, Jesus . . .' Jack breathed.

'How did he get here—?' Iolanthe gasped.

'If it isn't Lord Hades.' Sphinx smiled broadly, his cool grey eyes flush with success. 'Well, the *former* Lord Hades.'

Hades stood there defiantly, surrounded by his enemies: by Sphinx; by his bitter son, Dion; and by his furious brother, Yago, the Royal Jailer.

'You stole my son, Hardin,' Hades said flatly. 'Turned him against me.'

'It wasn't hard, Anthony,' Sphinx said. 'You ruled like an old-school king. You *expected* loyalty solely because of your crown. But people need more than that.'

He gestured toward Dion: 'Royal sons need to know their future.' And to Yago: 'Royals brothers need more than faraway postings. And I don't think you should lecture us on loyalty, Anthony. Since the end of the Great Games, you have forsaken the royal world and sided with Jack West.'

Sphinx shrugged. 'As for Dion here, I offered him more than you ever could: power of a kind never seen in the modern age of the world. He is *my* son now and, as such, he will be *my* heir, making him heir to the throne of the whole world, not a backwater kingdom like the Underworld.'

Jack watched as Hades bowed his head.

Throughout his time with the former Lord of the Underworld, Jack hadn't truly considered the effect on Hades of his sons' betrayal or of the hatred of his brother, Yago.

Now Hades stood here, beaten.

Sphinx stepped forward so he stood right in front of Hades.

'Once you were a king, Anthony. Now, you are nothing. Kneel before your emperor.'

Hades dropped to the ground, kneeling before Sphinx.

Sphinx turned to Dion and Yago.

'Gentlemen? You are the ones who were wronged by this man during his rule. What sentence would you ask of me?'

'Death,' Dion said immediately.

'Death,' Yago said.

Sphinx raised his eyebrows at Hades. 'The decapitation of Hades.'

He turned to one of the four silver automatons standing nearby like a chrome statue.

'Silverman!' He pointed at Hades. 'Tear off that man's head.'

Up on the balcony, Jack's eyes popped as he heard the command.

'Oh, Jesus . . .' he whispered.

★ ★ ★

Down in the chamber, the silverman took four striding steps over to Hades and without so much as a pause, clamped its glistening silver claws around his skull.

Sphinx watched impassively.

Dion watched, grinning.

Yago watched silently.

Jack watched in absolute horror.

As the silverman's claws gripped his head tightly, Hades said proudly, 'You will never win, Hardin. West will beat you—'

With shocking strength, the silverman twisted Hades's neck . . .

. . . snapping it . . .

. . . and then it wrenched his head from his body with a sickening tearing sound.

With a blast of arterial blood, Hades's head came free of his shoulders. So violent was the action that a whole section of his spinal column was torn out of his back. His headless body collapsed to the ground.

From his position on the balcony, Jack swallowed back the nausea that rose in his throat. Beside him, Iolanthe was aghast.

Sphinx said to the silverman, 'Throw his body into the shaft.'

The silverman obeyed, tossing Hades's head and corpse off the thin eastern bridge on which Sphinx and his people stood.

Sphinx watched Hades's body disappear from view.

Then he did something that Jack did not expect.

He called out, 'Well? Did you enjoy the show, Captain West?'

Jack's first instinct was to duck back further into the shadows of his balcony.

Sphinx's voice called: 'We know you are here, Captain! You came in via the English tunnel, which was really rather brave considering how unstable it is. Hades triggered a laser trip-wire at this end when he arrived. We checked the entrance and found more footprints: the prints of one man in hiking boots, a woman and a monk. I can only assume it's you. Show yourself!'

Iolanthe said, 'Jack, don't—'

Jack stood up on his balcony . . .

. . . in full view of Sphinx and his people over on the other side of the vast hall.

Sphinx smiled. 'Why, hello.'

Behind Jack, Iolanthe scowled. 'Oh, hell. Guess I'm all-in with you now.'

She stood up, too, rising into view beside him.

Sphinx looked quizzically at her—taking in her shaved head and scarred face—before he recognised her. Beside him, Chloe Carnarvon just gazed up coldly at her.

'Iolanthe? Is that you? Oh, dear,' Sphinx said.

'The handiwork of my brother's torturer,' Iolanthe said, her voice carrying easily across the chamber.

'You look truly ghastly,' Sphinx called. 'But I mean, really? You're siding with Captain West?'

Iolanthe held his gaze. 'Life is choices. I questioned mine. What about you, Chloe? Is that what you did when you allied

yourself with my brother and then betrayed him for Sphinx?'

Chloe snorted. 'You might say I questioned my choices, too. Honestly, working for you was holding me back, and by the look of things now, I think I chose better than you did.'

Sphinx smiled slyly at that. 'Well, Captain? Did you enjoy the show? My Fall and the sad demise of Lord Hades?'

Jack stared at Sphinx. 'Hades made his peace with the world before he died. That's not going to happen with you, asshole.'

'Captain, when it comes to what is going to happen, *you do not have the first clue*. Honestly, do you have any *idea* what I intend to do with the world when I rule it?'

Jack said nothing.

He wondered how much time he had. He guessed there were bronzemen, silvermen and some Knights of the Golden Eight converging on his balcony right now.

Sphinx said, 'The current system has collapsed. Order has been lost. Failed states, poverty, famines, refugees. Civilisation is broken. On top of that, it is *infected*. Infected with weak people. The dregs of humanity. Humans with the brains of sheep.

'Entire populations live like animals: fighting, rutting and killing each other. African nations are little more than the tribes of three centuries ago. Many of them still believe in witchcraft. India lives in squalor. China is overpopulated. Africans flee across the Mediterranean to escape poverty, while Latin Americans try to sneak into America to do the same. All this while America itself is beset by opioid addicts and fools who believe that Noah's Ark actually existed.

'I want a better world. A world for intelligent men and women. For *advanced* Homo sapiens. The rest—the dregs—need to be culled. And, as a wise but firm ruler, I will do the culling. I will use the Siren bells to put most of humanity to sleep . . . and I will only wake those who make the world better. The weak will not be woken. They will just be allowed to starve in their slumber and die.'

Jack's eyes widened at the breadth of Sphinx's plan.

It was insane.

Sphinx looked up defiantly at Jack. 'And I will rule this world with an iron fist. People need a ruler who demarcates the boundaries of life clearly. A ruled world is a better world. I fight for that better world, Captain. Tell me, what do you fight for? Do you even know?'

Jack frowned. This was all too much. He heard rushing footsteps in the levels below his balcony. They were closing in on him and here was Sphinx asking him to justify why he fought.

Sphinx said, 'Do you fight for the oppressed? Are they oppressed or are they just ignorant? Too stupid to know that there is a wider universe out there?'

'I fight for those who can't fight for themselves,' Jack said.

'Oh, please! This is your fatal weakness, Captain. You *care*. This compassion of yours will be your downfall.'

'If I'm the only one who stands up to you, then that's fine by me,' Jack said.

'That is your other great weakness, Captain. *You do not know your place.* Mark my words when I say that when this is over and your loved ones are lying bloodied and dead around you and I am standing over your battered body with my boot on your throat, you will know your place.

'The poet Robert Browning famously wrote that a man's reach should exceed his grasp. Browning was wrong. Every man should know his place. He should *not* reach beyond his station, and you have already attempted to reach well beyond yours.'

Jack said, 'I'm in this till the end.'

'And I will fight far longer than you will,' Sphinx roared. 'I believe in what I want, Captain. I am *committed* to creating my new world on a level you cannot even imagine. What about you? What do you really believe in?'

Jack didn't reply.

Sphinx scowled, waved dismissively and turned to leave.

'Goodbye, Captain West. Sadly, you will not live to see my world, for you will not leave this island alive. There are two

hundred bronzemen on it whom I will now task with finding and killing you.'

Sphinx raised his voice. 'My loyal bronzemen! Kill these monks and'—he pointed up at Jack—'kill that man and that woman! Dion! Manage this. When it is done, perform the Fall and join me.'

'Yes, sire,' Dion said.

Then Sphinx swept out of the Hall of the Falling Temple, followed quickly by Mendoza, Chloe and Yago, leaving Dion behind.

Near Dion, beside the Falling Temple, stood Bertie and Father Rasmussen, while Jack and Iolanthe were up in their balcony . . .

. . . with two hundred deadly automatons coming to kill them.

'Jack, we need Bertie and all the information in his head!' Iolanthe cried.

'Okay!' Jack said, whipping out his trusty mini-Maghook.

Down on the eastern bridge, Bertie didn't know what to do. He'd seen many things in his life, but nothing like this.

He whirled as suddenly, right beside him, a bronzeman lunged quickly forward and seized Father Rasmussen by the head and, with a gruesome twist, tore it clean off.

Blood sprayed and the young priest's body fell to the ground, headless.

The faceless bronze automaton dropped his head as if it meant nothing and turned to face Bertie.

Behind the automatons, Dion snorted cruelly.

Jack took advantage of the distraction. 'Bertie! Get to the temple now!' he shouted.

Shocked at Rasmussen's fate, Bertie bounded onto the temple as fast his legs could carry him, pursued by twenty bronzemen and three silvermen.

At the same time, over on his balcony on the other side of the hall, Jack fired his Maghook at the floodlight crane closest to him.

The Maghook's magnetic grappling hook thudded against the crane's metal frame and held . . .

. . . and without a moment's hesitation Jack leapt off his balcony and swung in a long swooping arc across the western side of the chamber and landed on the temple itself, right beside its main obelisk.

He saw Bertie clambering up the sloping sides and stairways of the temple's upper half, pursued by bronzemen and silvermen.

'Bertie! Come on!' he yelled.

Bertie reached the main obelisk just as a bronzeman lashed out at his ankles, tripping him—

—and he fell to the ground at Jack's feet.

The bronzemen and silvermen kept swarming up the flanks of the temple, faceless monsters climbing and climbing, hellbent on catching and killing Jack and Bertie.

Jack had wanted to swing back to his balcony with Bertie but the automatons had come up too fast and now, surrounding him, they were blocking that escape.

Laughing, Dion called, 'There is no getting away this time, Captain! Time for you to die!'

'Aw, screw it,' Jack said under his breath.

He leaned forward and pulled Bertie up.

'Hang on to me!' he yelled as he aimed one of Aloysius Knight's Remington shotguns at the chains affixed to the Falling Temple's metal collar.

And he fired . . . at the collar.

Boom!

The collar sprang open . . .

. . . releasing its grip on the Falling Temple . . .

. . . and the temple dropped . . .

. . . with Jack, Bertie and the thirty-plus bronzemen and silvermen on it.

Dion's mouth fell open as the temple on which he had planned to do the Fall disengaged from the ceiling.

With a colossal *whoosh*, the temple fell through the air, just like it had done before, plummeting into the darkness of the shaft below while Jack, gripping the Maghook, swung up and clear of it, with Bertie hanging from him!

Jack and Bertie swooped away to the west, arriving at a balcony a few levels below Iolanthe's.

Iolanthe leaned over the rail of her balcony and called to them.

'We have to get back to the English tunnel! Meet me at the priest's entrance! Move it, boys!'

Jack and Bertie hurried for the rear door of their balcony.

A little over fifty seconds later, a resounding *boom* rang out from the bottom of the shaft as the great temple slammed into its base with shocking force.

Jack and Bertie joined Iolanthe inside the tight, dark, switch-backing stairwells of the priest's entrance.

Down the stairs they ran.

Fleeing, panting, running for their lives.

Jack led the way, taking the steps three at a time, pivoting at each landing then bounding down the next flight, closely followed by Iolanthe and Bertie.

The heavy footfalls of dozens of bronzemen echoed above them, coming after them.

At length, they came to the English tunnel.

It was now chest-deep with muddy water, still filling with the incoming tide.

'Can we make it to the other end before it fills completely?' Iolanthe said.

There was only about three feet of space between the surface of the rising water and the ceiling of the crumbling tunnel.

'No choice,' Jack said.

They forged ahead into the tunnel, plunging into the milky chest-deep water.

They were barely fifty metres down it—wading through the muck—when Jack turned back and saw the first bronzeman enter the tunnel, splashing into the water behind them.

It was followed by a second, then a third, then a fourth.

'Shit,' he breathed.

He keyed his radio. 'Nobody! We're coming out via the tunnel and we're coming out hot! Got a lotta bad guys on our tail!'

Nobody's voice came in. 'I got some bad news for you, Jack. They're out here, too. A Chinook chopper just landed on Tombelaine and unloaded about forty of those bronzemen. They ran straight into the English tunnel from this end and then the chopper took off.'

Jack froze in mid-stride, stopping so abruptly that Iolanthe bumped into him from behind.

'We're cut off. Caught in the middle of this tunnel with two sets of bronzemen at each end. There's no way out.'

Jack's mind raced.

The bronzemen behind them continued to push through the rising water, their faceless heads and necks visible above the waterline, their burnished metal skin glinting in the beams of Jack and Iolanthe's flashlights.

And more were coming from the other end.

The tight and not very stable tunnel loomed around him: its rough earthen walls pressing close against his sides; the crumbling wooden beams holding up its ceiling low over his head.

And the foul water all around him was rising relentlessly, creeping up to his shoulders now, nearly five feet deep.

'Talk about being between a rock and a hard place . . .' he said before cutting himself off.

'A rock . . .'

Iolanthe said, 'What are you talking about?'

But Jack was now rummaging through the pockets of his cargo pants.

He found it.

The tiny hourglass of greystone that Zoe had found in Venice at the headquarters of the Omega monks; one that had once been worn around the neck of a monk.

Iolanthe saw the grey powder inside the hourglass. She knew full well what it was and what it could do.

'What are you thinking?' she asked.

Jack was now scanning the ceiling, assessing the wooden beams holding it up. A few of them, he saw, had creases and seams in them that they could use as handholds and to wedge their feet against.

'Quick, up and out of the water, now!' Jack ordered. 'Go! Before the water rises too far! Grab hold of a beam and be sure to keep your whole body above the waterline.'

Bertie threw a puzzled look at Iolanthe.

She just shrugged. 'You get used to it.'

And then they were all moving, reaching up for the ceiling beams, grabbing handholds on them and pressing their feet against other beams.

Within moments, the three of them were hanging from the ceiling of the tight tunnel—facing up; their hands gripping the beams, their feet wedged against other beams; their backs only inches above the steadily rising water.

Jack risked a glance behind them.

The bronzemen were twenty metres away now.

Almost on them.

He aimed his flashlight forward . . .

. . . to illuminate the first of the bronzemen coming from that direction. Dozens of others glimmered in the gloom behind the first one, pushing through the now neck-deep water, approaching.

'Fuck it,' Jack said.

And with those words, he smashed the hourglass filled with greystone powder against the beam he was gripping and poured its contents into the foul water filling the 600-year-old tunnel.

At first, nothing happened.

The bronzemen kept advancing from both directions.

Then the milky brown water below Jack began to change colour . . . going dark.

The bronzemen kept advancing.

Ten metres away . . .

The water became a deep grey.

Bertie clung to the ceiling like a kid on a jungle gym, his eyes wide. Iolanthe did the same.

Five metres . . .

The bronzemen coming from the Mont were now so close, Jack could see the intricately carved beaks on their faceless metal heads.

'Jack . . .' Iolanthe urged.

'Just a couple more seconds . . .'

Then the water went darker still and—

—*Craaaack!*

It began to harden.

What happened next was really quite stunning.

As Jack and the others clung to the ceiling, mere inches above the surface of the water filling the tunnel, the neck-deep liquid around the advancing bronzemen turned to stone . . .

. . . and stopped all the bronzemen dead in their tracks.

And suddenly Jack found himself hanging inches above a slab of solid grey stone, a five-foot-deep slab that extended for the full length of the centuries-old tunnel.

And embedded in that slab, their faceless heads sticking up from it, their bodies encased in it, were the bronzemen.

'Jack West Jr,' Iolanthe said. 'If you weren't already spoken for, I'd kiss you on the lips.'

Bertie was equally impressed. 'Ooh, my.'

Jack released his grip on his ceiling beams, lowering himself onto the solid greystone slab a few inches below him.

The slab was now basically a new floor for the tunnel; a floor five feet higher than the original one; which essentially turned the tunnel into a superlong crawlspace only a couple of feet in height.

Jack didn't waste a second.

He rolled onto his stomach and started belly-crawling north-ward along the slab.

He noted immediately that milky running water was already beginning to pool on top of it.

'Come on,' he said. 'We're not out of this yet. The tide's still coming in and we have to crawl the rest of the way before this tunnel floods all the way to the ceiling!'

And so they crawled hurriedly down the length of the English tunnel, skirting the heads of the bronzemen trapped in the stone.

It was scary stuff, crawling so close to the deadly automatons.

As Jack and the others went by them, the bronzemen struggled against the stone, wriggling, but it was in vain: the stone was too strong.

Jack had never been so close to a bronzeman before and now he could see the details of their faces and their heads. Their beak-like noses were truly alien. And covering their shiny metal heads were all manner of etched markings and Thoth symbols.

For the last hundred metres of the tunnel, Jack belly-crawled through one-foot-deep water, with his head held awkwardly above the surface, bumping occasionally against the tunnel's ceiling.

And then, long after he passed the last bronzeman in the tunnel, he came to the shepherd's hut and emerged into open air.

Iolanthe and Bertie came out close behind him, filthy and dripping wet, but alive.

In the distance behind them, Jack saw the towering bulk of Mont Saint-Michel, glorious in the moonlight and the glare of the floodlights.

Looking the other way, Jack spotted Nobody over by the fishing shacks, waving to him.

'Jack!' Nobody said. 'Thank God you got out! There was nothing I could do to stop them.'

'It's okay,' Jack said. 'We found a way.'

'While you were in there, the scanner intercepted some digital radio signals coming out of the Mont,' Nobody said. 'The signals were going from Mont Saint-Michel to a location in the French Alps. I pinpointed that location: the Aiguille du Midi Observatory near Mont Blanc. It's a mountaintop astronomical observatory.'

Jack nodded. 'When Mendoza and Sphinx did the Fall, I heard them corresponding with one of the Knights of the Golden Eight—Jaeger Vier, Hunter Four—at some kind of observatory in the Alps. They were talking about the pedestal on the moon.'

Jack shook his head. 'This has been a disaster. Let's hope Zoe and my mother are having better luck in Rome.'

THE SECRET ROYAL WORLD II

THE INNERMOST SANCTUM OF THE VATICAN

ROME

[T]he Catholic Church is merely the current name for a cult of priests that has survived for over five thousand years since Egyptian times. It is a cult devoted to the worship of the sun and the stars and the wisdom of an ancient civilisation that once flourished on this Earth. It is the civilisation that built the Sphinx and the pyramids, the stone circles of England and the three secret cities of Thule, Atlas and Ra. The civilisation that gave us the two sacred trees and the Life Stone itself.

CARDINAL MENDOZA TO JACK
THE FOUR LEGENDARY KINGDOMS P. 235
(MACMILLAN, SYDNEY, 2016)

THE VATICAN
ROME, ITALY
23 DECEMBER, 2000 HOURS

At the exact moment that Jack had been venturing into Mont Saint-Michel in France, Zoe and Mae had been arriving in Rome with Rufus and Sisters Lynda and Agnes.

It was evening and crowding behind Rufus in the cockpit of the Sukhoi, the four women saw the glow of Rome's lights on the horizon long before they laid eyes on the city itself.

As their plane came closer, however, they saw the columns of smoke rising into the night-time sky.

Then the Eternal City came into view and Mae gasped.

'A Siren bell was definitely rung here, just like in Moscow,' she said.

Zoe said, 'Only *unlike* Moscow, it looks like this one went off sometime during the day, while the population was awake.'

The results had been devastating.

Fires burned everywhere.

Commercial airliners had crashed at Leonardo Da Vinci International Airport and in the suburbs around it.

Zoe could see at least twelve planes variously smashed against apartment blocks, office towers, freeways and homes. Ten of the planes were still ablaze.

All over the city, cars and buses had crashed.

A couple of open-topped tour buses lay crumpled against the Colosseum, their comatose passengers strewn every which way.

More tourist buses had toppled into the Tiber River.

At the city's enormous railway station, a giant column of black smoke rose into the sky: the result of two bullet trains that had slammed at full speed into the terminal when their drivers had been struck unconscious.

Judging from the remains—smashed and burning engine cars and crumpled carriages that lay on their sides, twisted like giant dead snakes—the impacts had been colossal.

And then there were the people.

They lay everywhere, having collapsed where they stood when the bell had rung.

Tourists, locals, workers, the homeless. They all lay sprawled on the ground, unconscious.

'Jesus H. Christ . . .' Rufus breathed as he surveyed the sleeping city. 'Oh, sorry. Blasphemy,' he added when he saw Sisters Lynda and Agnes in the rear of the cockpit.

'Never mind,' Sister Lynda said. 'By the way, his actual name was Jesus of Nazareth and he was just a man. A very charismatic and influential man, to be sure, and part of the royal world, but still just a man.'

Zoe was scanning the empty city.

Her eyes landed on the gigantic dome of St Peter's Basilica, towering over the rest of Rome. The verdant gardens of the Vatican flanked it, a rare splash of green amid the otherwise grey-white metropolis.

'Take us in, Rufus. All the way to St Peter's.'

As they zoomed in over the silent city, Zoe turned to Sister Lynda. 'All right, tell me more about this Javier Journal. What is it and who's Javier? I don't know of any famous Javiers.'

Lynda smiled. 'Oh, you know him. He was one of the Church's greatest explorers and missionaries. You just know him by his anglicised name. In the Church, he goes by the name Francisco Javier, but to the wider world he is known as Francis Xavier.'

'The Jesuit priest who went to India and Asia to spread the faith?' Zoe said.

'The very same,' Lynda said. 'Francis Xavier was sent to Asia in 1541 by Pope Paul III ostensibly to convert the heathens there, but what few people know is that Pope Paul also gave Xavier a secret mission to accomplish.

'Xavier's efforts to achieve that secret task were chronicled in a journal he sent back to the Vatican just before his death in 1552. To those who know about it, it is called Javier's Journal, and according to one of our nuns who saw it centuries ago, it mentions the locations of at least one of the iron mountains. For nearly five hundred years, it has resided in the Vatican Secret Archives.'

A few minutes later, its engines booming, the Sukhoi hovered over St Peter's Square.

The usually bustling square was unnaturally still.

Thousands of tourists lay on the ground, struck down by the bell. Tour buses and cars had crashed into bollards and buildings. One bus lay up against the towering obelisk that rose up out of the centre of the square.

Rufus landed the Sukhoi right in front of the steps of St Peter's Basilica, since that was the only place to land it without accidentally crushing some poor sleeping soul.

Zoe and the others emerged from the plane's bomb bay and gazed out over the ancient city of Rome, the Eternal City, now the silent city.

Mae gazed at all the bodies. 'Look at them all.'

'*You will wake as slaves* . . .' Zoe said softly.

Sister Lynda grimaced. 'Let's try to avoid that.'

It was then that they saw the Pope's dead body.

The Pope lay flat on the ground with a star-shaped splatter of blood around his blasted-open head.

'Looks like things didn't end well for him,' Lynda observed.

'Sphinx was here,' Zoe said. 'And he wasn't friendly.'

Lynda said, 'I imagine he got what he needed from the Pope and then killed him. That's Hardin. He uses people until they are no longer of value to him and then discards them.'

'Where should we start?' Mae asked.

'Well,' Zoe said, 'with everybody knocked out, getting into the inner sanctums of the Vatican isn't going to be too much of a problem.'

Lynda said, 'I suggest we check two places: the Secret Archives and the Pope's private study in the Apostolic Palace.'

'The Pope's *private* study?' Sister Agnes said.

'Every day the Pope receives a briefing on all pressing matters, security and otherwise. He will have got one today and I imagine it'll contain information relevant to our mission. That briefing will be in his private study.'

'And the Secret Archives?' Rufus asked.

Zoe answered him. 'That's where the journal is, in Vault IX. The Archives are one of the most heavily guarded repositories of ancient knowledge in the world. If the building were ever opened to the public, it would be a museum to rival the Louvre.'

Lynda nodded in agreement. 'Few outside of the most senior members of the Church have been allowed to see its collection of artefacts. Largely, that's because many of those artefacts do *not* support Catholic teaching. But I can't say that from personal experience, since I've never been down there, because it's strictly no women allowed.'

'Not today,' Mae said.

'No, not today,' Zoe said. 'Lynda and Mae, you go to Vault IX in the Archives and find the journal. Agnes and I will go to the Papal Apartments to check out the Pope's daily briefing.'

'Got it,' Mae said.

'What about me?' Rufus asked.

'Find somewhere close by yet out of sight to park your bird,' Zoe said, 'but, Rufus, keep the engines running.'

For a thousand years the Pope's private offices and study were off limits to women but Zoe and Sister Agnes just pushed open the door and strode into them unchallenged.

Bodies lay strewn around the entry vestibule: Swiss Guardsmen dressed in their vividly coloured uniforms; cardinals with red sashes and skullcaps; priests in black shirts and white collars.

All the furnishings were gilt-edged and plush, lavish in the extreme. The Church's wealth was eagerly on display.

Zoe stepped right over the bodies and hurried into the corner suite that was the Pope's private quarters.

'Check his secretary's desk,' she said to Agnes as they passed through an anteroom.

'Got it.'

Zoe opened the ornate oak doors to the Pope's private study.

She saw the artwork first: originals by Raphael, Botticelli and Michelangelo.

'Very nice,' she breathed.

In the anteroom, Sister Agnes sat at the Pope's secretary's desk. A young priest lay sleeping on the floor under the desk, having slipped out of his chair as he had succumbed to the bell's song.

Agnes clicked on his mouse to awaken his computer while she rifled through his desk drawers.

'Really?' she said, spotting an Italian gay porn magazine hidden deep within one drawer.

Inside the papal study, Zoe sat down at the Pope's broad mahogany desk, flanked by his priceless paintings.

She saw it instantly, among some other documents on the desk, a red folder marked in Italian: SEGRETISSIMO.

TOP SECRET.

She flung it open and started reading.

The gargantuan nave of St Peter's Basilica is usually a place of sombre reflection, reverent movement and the odd echoing prayer or hymn.

Today, Mae and Sister Lynda ran down its length at full speed.

The nave is truly an architectural marvel: 211 metres long and 136 metres high, it can hold 20,000 worshippers.

Most of those worshippers would usually be intensely focused on Bernini's *baldacchino*, the 90-foot-tall bronze canopy in the heart of the cathedral that covers the Altar of St Peter and, buried beneath that altar, the reputed tomb of St Peter the Apostle himself.

Mae and Lynda ran right past it.

They were heading for the Vatican Secret Archives and this was the quickest way there.

From the basilica, they turned right, charging through the Sistine Chapel—ignoring the ceiling famously painted by Michelangelo with its notoriously heretical depiction of God emerging from the human brain—and into the private dressing areas of the cardinals.

Sister Lynda paused in mid-stride as they hurried through the Sistine Chapel's dressing chamber.

'Mae,' she said, 'you do realise that no women have *ever* been through here.'

Mae grimaced. 'Isn't it sad that none of the three Abrahamic religions—Christianity, Judaism and Islam—treat women well?'

Sister Lynda said, 'More than anything, it's just a waste of talent.'

They hurried toward the Secret Archives.

In the Pope's private study, Zoe read the pontiff's daily briefings for the last week.

Various incidents leapt out at her.

Sphinx had visited the Vatican earlier that day and he had wanted two things: the Vatican Globe and the blue Siren bell, which he called the Orphean Bell.

The Pope had written to his senior advisers:

. . . we will give the globe to Sphinx but not all of our historical notes about the Orphean Bell. We should keep the bell from him for now, to ensure that he keeps his promises. Our key notes about its location have been safely taken to Albano's emissary . . .

'Albano's emissary?' Zoe said aloud. She called to Sister Agnes in the anteroom. 'Do you know anyone named Albano? Or who his emissary might be?'

'I think there's a Duke of Albano,' Agnes called back. 'His emissary would be an underling, I suppose.'

'We'll have to figure out who he is—oh, God,' Zoe said.

'What? What is it?' Agnes poked her head inside the study.

Zoe was looking at another pair of documents in the file.

The first was a message to the Pope.

Zoe read it aloud:

'Your Eminence, our agents went in search of the rogue nun, Dr Tracy Lynn Smith. We located her working in a refugee camp in Sicily. But by the time we arrived there, she had fled.

'We have intelligence that she is now working with Médecins Sans Frontières somewhere in Syria. We are following up those leads.'

The Pope's response was on a second document, clipped to the first one:

'Find her and kill her.'

Zoe turned to Agnes. 'Dr Tracy Smith. Lynda mentioned her back at Hades's estate. Something about her doing research into the Siren bells. She was one of your nuns.'

'She *was*, yes,' Agnes said. 'Tracy *left* our order a year ago, then went off the grid.'

Zoe said, 'Must be some woman for the Church to put out a hit on her.'

'She was,' Agnes said. 'Sister Tracy was a brilliant doctor. An ear-nose-and-throat specialist. Before she left, she was one of our

order's foremost experts on the Siren bells. She did detailed studies on them in soundproof chambers: measured their acoustic wavelengths, how they affected the inner ear, all sorts of things.

'But she was also passionate about the plight of migrants and the poor. In the end, she left our order in disgust, saying that it was foolish to be consumed with high celestial matters while ordinary people starved. It doesn't surprise me to hear she ended up tending to refugees in Sicily or that she might have gone to work with Doctors Without Borders in some war zone in Syria. That was Tracy.'

'And now the Catholic Church wants her dead,' Zoe said. 'Whatever war zone she's in, we need to find Dr Tracy Smith before their assassins do.'

The entrance to the underground vaults of the Vatican Secret Archives can be found in the Belvedere Courtyard, a wide rectangular space with a gorgeous lawn.

Mae Merriweather and Sister Lynda Fadel strode straight across that lawn and into the Archives, passing several security officers and Swiss Guards lying slumped at their posts.

They took an elevator down to Sub-Level 4, the lowest level of the Archives.

A single long corridor opened onto many vaults on both sides. The farthest vault was the most secure one, Vault XXII. It was equipped with airtight doors and high-tech locks to safeguard its treasures.

Mae and Lynda didn't have to go that far.

They pushed through the doors of Vault IX, a lesser vault, the one that Bertie had mentioned in his text to Iolanthe.

Mae said, 'My memory of Francis Xavier is hazy. If this journal is so important, why isn't it in Vault XXII?'

Lynda said, 'Pope Paul III was the one who sent Xavier on his secret mission. But by the time Xavier sent his journal back to Rome, Pope Paul had died. I'm guessing that the mission was *so* secret, Pope Paul hadn't told anybody else about it. So when Xavier's journal arrived back in Rome from the Indies, the two men who knew about its importance—Pope Paul and Xavier himself—were both dead. The journal, I suppose, was then just kept as a historical memento of a famous saint. This is how great knowledge dies, on bookshelves in plain sight.'

It took them a few minutes, but soon they found the shelves devoted to St Francis Xavier and in an air-sealed container, they uncovered the journal.

It was a battered 16th-century leather-bound book.

It looked like it had seen all kinds of adventures: it was water-damaged, sun-damaged and salt-damaged. Its pages were dry and crisp. They looked like they had not been touched or read in five hundred years.

'A forgotten book,' Mae said. 'Filled with priceless information.'

Lynda flipped through the pages, turning them delicately, reading St Francis Xavier's handwritten Latin text.

'*Here,*' she said suddenly.

Mae leaned in close.

Lynda translated the Latin:

> '*Holy Father and First Son of Ra,*
>
> *I have confirmed the location of the third mount.*
>
> *It is indeed where we suspected: in the ancient city of Lhasa and not in Bhutan as others have thought from their studies of the Globe.*
>
> *In Lhasa there is a small hill that the heathen locals call Avalokitesvara—Lord of the World. It is a grand name for a rather simple hill. But then, this hill is the peak of a gigantic landform, the bulk of which lies under the earth.*
>
> *It is the summit of the Third Iron Mountain. I went inside this hill and saw the Falling Temple within it with my own eyes.*
>
> *The hill can be identified by the small wooden fort that sits atop it.*
>
> *You may add these to the two mountains we know already: the first on the tidal island of St Michael and the second at Poeninus Mons.*'

Sister Lynda gasped.

'Avalokitesvara, in Lhasa, Tibet,' she said. 'I know that place. Only it's not topped by a simple fort anymore. On top of that hill sits one of the greatest palaces in the world: Potala Palace.'

'And I know what Poeninus Mons is,' Mae said. 'It's the Roman name for the mountain pass that runs beside Mont Blanc in France. That makes Mont Blanc the second iron mountain while Potala Palace sits on the third.'

Lynda was reading another page in the notebook.

'Wait, there's something here about the fourth mountain.'

She read aloud:

> *'In his secret report to the Pope, the great wandering monk, the Venerable Laurent of the Levant, wrote that "He who wields the blade of the archangel will find the fourth mountain."*
>
> *Ignatius and I both believe this means that the fourth mount is either Sacra di San Michele in Turin or the Sanctuary to the Archangel at Mount Gargano near Foggia.'*

'The blade of the archangel,' Lynda said thoughtfully. 'Do you think that means—?'

'Yes. The Sword of St Michael,' Mae said. 'We gotta call this in.'

She yanked out her phone and called Jack.

He answered immediately. '*Mum. Talk to me.*'

Mae didn't know it, but he had just emerged from the English tunnel at Tombelaine after encasing the bronzemen in stone.

'Jack, we just hit paydirt here at the Vatican regarding two of the iron mountains. The second is Mont Blanc and the third is under Potala Palace in Tibet. We've got a lead on the fourth, but nothing on the fifth. I'm going to send you a couple of photos of pages from Javier's Journal, one regarding Potala Palace and another about the fourth mountain.'

She quickly took two photos of the journal's pages with her phone and texted them to Jack. 'How did you go at Mont Saint-Michel?'

'*We got out alive but otherwise, not well at all. Great work, Mum. Get out of there and follow up those leads.*'

'You got it,' Mae said.

She hung up and smiled at Sister Lynda. 'Our work here is done. Now let's—'

'*Hey!*'

A man's voice, loud and sharp, came from behind them.

Mae and Lynda whirled, their hearts stopping—

—only to see a man rush past Vault IX's open door and continue at a sprint down the long corridor outside.

'It's down here!' he added as he sped off.

He hadn't seen them.

He was calling to someone else.

Mae exhaled with relief.

She and Lynda quickly hid behind a bookshelf as three more men raced down the corridor after the first fellow. All four were heading in the direction of Vault XXII.

'We're not the only ones who want information from this place,' Lynda whispered.

Mae peered out after the four men, her eyes narrowing.

'I wonder who they are and what they're after. Let's find out.'

While most of the Vatican Secret Archives have remained largely unchanged for five hundred years—with its many miles of shelves in its many vaults, it resembles the underground stack of a large city library—Vault XXII is different.

It is exceptionally modern.

It is part laboratory, part airtight chamber. Its temperature is always maintained at a cool sixteen degrees Celsius and its humidity at zero.

One wall of the vault contains large metal drawers fitted with glass doors that show their contents.

The other side of the vault looks like a surgery in a teaching

hospital: it has a glassed-in viewing balcony so that observers—like the Pope—can watch as experts inside the vault handle delicate treasures with extreme care. This balcony is accessed by a separate door from the long corridor.

Mae and Lynda crept silently into the viewing balcony and peered out from it to see the four men who had rushed past their vault now standing inside Vault XXII, gathered around a large object in its centre.

'Whoa, baby . . .' Mae gasped.

She wasn't sure what she had expected to see inside Vault XXII, the innermost sanctum of the Catholic Church.

Christ's cross, maybe, or perhaps the chalice from the Last Supper, or maybe some ancient text written by Jesus of Nazareth himself.

But nothing had prepared her for this.

On one wall, encased in glass cabinets, were two large stone slabs marked with similar images. Both were a mix of interconnected circles:

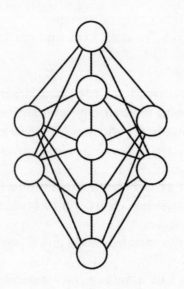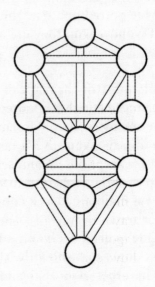

Mae said, 'That one on the right is the Sephirot from the Kabbalah. The Tree of Life.'

'And the one on the left is Norse,' Lynda said. 'It's *Yggdrasil*, the tree from which Odin was hanged, also known as the Tree of Death.'

In any other room, the two slabs would have dominated. But not in this one.

Taking pride of place in the centre of the sterile vault was something even more striking: an enormous sandstone statue of a rearing cobra.

It was huge, easily eight feet tall.

It took up most of the space.

And it was scary, too: the big stone snake appeared frozen in mid-pounce, up on its tail, jaws bared in a furious snarl.

'What . . . the actual . . . hell?' Sister Lynda said. 'A big snake statue?'

'The statue of the serpent,' Mae whispered, remembering the notes written in Romanian that Jack and Zoe had found at the home of the Order of the Omega in Venice. 'This is what the Omega monks were searching for. And it's not just any old statue. It's a *uraeus*.'

Lynda frowned. 'But here? In the Vatican?'

As a historian, Sister Lynda knew what a uraeus was: it was the upright cobra that was affixed to the brow of an Egyptian pharaoh's crown or *nemes*. It was the ultimate symbol of royalty and authority in ancient Egypt. Statues or busts of pharaohs would always include the uraeus on the pharaoh's crown.

As they examined the giant stone uraeus, the men in the vault consulted some old leather-bound folios in the drawers around it. Inside those folios, Mae caught sight of two images she had seen before.

Both showed the Great Sphinx at Giza.

The first was a very famous sketch of the Sphinx's head. It had been drawn by Vivant Denon in 1798, when Denon had accompanied Napoleon on his well-known expedition to Egypt.

It showed the Sphinx almost fully buried by the desert sands with French scientists standing on its head, taking measurements:

View of the Sphinx, near Cairo.

The second image also depicted the Sphinx and it, too, was well known in historical circles. It was a blurry black-and-white aerial photo taken in the 1920s from a hot-air balloon that showed the Great Sphinx half buried in sand:

Mae's breath caught in her throat as she suddenly realised the source of the giant uraeus in the vault below her.

Of course, she thought. *The Catholic Church is the Cult of Amon-Ra, a sun cult born at the Siwa Oasis in Egypt. It would keep its most important treasure in its most secure vault.*

'Lynda,' she said softly. 'That isn't any old uraeus from some random Egyptian statue. That's the most famous missing uraeus of them all. It's the one from the Great Sphinx at Giza.'

The four men who had hurried past Mae and Lynda's vault to Vault XXII gathered around the huge stone cobra statue. They peered at it closely, examining it with cameras and studying its hieroglyphs.

Mae and Lynda could hear their voices, muffled through the glass:

'—*Brother Ezekiel said the multiple is to be found carved somewhere on the uraeus*—'

Mae glanced at Lynda. 'Ezekiel. These guys are from the Order of the Omega.'

'The women-hating monks,' Lynda said. 'This could get awkward.'

As the other three expertly examined the cobra, a fourth monk watched a radar-scanner closely.

Suddenly he said to one of his companions, '*Brother Enoch! I've got an incoming aerial signal, coming in fast from the direction of Malta.*'

'*Malta? Helicopter or plane?*' the leader of the group of monks said. Mae guessed he was Brother Enoch.

'*A large aeroplane.*'

'*We have time. Whoever it is will have to land at the airport before they can come to the Vatican,*' Enoch said. '*Here! Got it!*'

He leaned in close to the cobra's bared fangs, reading some hieroglyphs carved into them.

As he did, Mae took some quick photos of the lab, including the giant uraeus, the four monks and the folio images they were consulting. Then she fired off those photos to Jack and the rest of the team.

As she did, she thought about the source of this uraeus.

The Great Sphinx at Giza has long been one of the most mysterious statues in the world.

It is the world's largest monolithic statue, carved from the rock of the Giza plateau in front of the second pyramid there, that of the pharaoh Khafre.

And it is huge: 240 feet long, 70 feet high.

To this day, no-one really knows when it was carved. Estimates range from 4500 years ago to 10,000 B.C.E., but no-one is certain.

Adding to this genuine sense of mystery is the Sphinx's infamously vandalised face.

Most people are aware of the great statue's missing nose and beard—which were *not* shot off by Napoleon during artillery training; ancient writers had remarked on the missing facial features centuries before then—but fewer people are aware of its missing uraeus.

But the evidence is there for all to see: a large shattered segment of rough stone just above the Sphinx's unblinking eyes shows the spot where a uraeus was once mounted.

Given the size of the Sphinx, the rearing cobra would have been huge, easily eight feet tall.

Like this one, Mae thought.

The lead monk, Brother Enoch, was translating the glyphs: '*Sixteen schoinos from my eyes*.' He smiled broadly. 'Sixteen! The multiple is sixteen! We got it. Call Brother Ezekiel at Potala and let him know.'

Mae frowned and turned to Lynda. 'Do you know what this multiple is?'

Lynda said, 'No. It must be connected to—'

'You shouldn't be here,' a low voice said from behind them. 'Vile whores.'

This time the comment was definitely directed at them.

Mae and Lynda turned.

Two additional Omega monks stood in the doorway behind them, blocking the exit and gripping Glock pistols in their hands.

Zoe was still in the Pope's study, now reading from his personal computer with Sister Agnes by her side.

They were scanning an email the Pope had sent to Cardinal Mendoza earlier that day.

It read: *The surface-point of the Labyrinth lies directly below the fourth red horizon star. See you in a few hours in Rome. You have done fine work, Cardinal.*

'The surface-point of the Labyrinth,' Zoe said.

'And what's the fourth red horizon star?' Agnes said.

'We'll have to find out. The Pope also arranged to meet Cardinal Mendoza in Rome today. I think we can safely say that meeting didn't go well for the Pope—'

BOOM!

The walls around them shuddered.

The two women rushed to the nearest window and looked out.

'Oh my God . . .' Agnes gasped.

Zoe just stared at the shocking sight before her.

The dome of St Peter's Basilica was cracked and smoking, struck by a missile of some kind.

Then, as they watched, another missile came *shooming* out of the sky and hit the damaged dome.

The whole dome blew apart, blasting outward in a spectacular explosion before . . .

. . . it crumpled in on itself and dropped *into* the body of the basilica, leaving a giant gaping hole in the roof of the church.

'What the hell just happened?' Agnes asked.

'Someone is making a big entrance,' Zoe said.

Down in the Archives, Mae and Lynda were being shoved out into the long main corridor when the leader of the team of monks, Brother Enoch, emerged from Vault XXII to look at them.

He turned up his nose in outright disgust.

'Women are not permitted here. You have desecrated this place with your presence.'

Sister Lynda snorted. 'The presence of our vaginas, you mean. Do they offend you?'

Enoch glared at her. He was a bulky man with small dark pits for eyes. 'The last woman I met, I strangled to death.'

'Fuck you, you misogynist asshole,' Lynda spat. 'Do your worst—'

BOOM!

The walls shook. Dust fluttered from the ceiling.

The first explosion was muffled down here in the Archives.

Brother Enoch looked up at the noise, as if he could see through the four levels between him and the world outside.

Then came the second missile impact—the one that destroyed the dome of the basilica—and one of his monks came rushing up.

'Brother Enoch! Someone just fired on the basilica!'

Enoch paused for a second as he took in the situation.

'It can't be . . .' he said softly. 'If it is who I think it is, we have to flee now if we want to escape this place with our lives. Bring the women, but if they slow us down for a moment, shoot them both in the head and leave them.'

They hurried for the elevator—the six monks, Mae and Lynda.

They bustled inside it and rose skyward.

The elevator doors opened at ground level . . .

. . . to be met by a barrage of machine-gun fire.

Two of the monks immediately exploded all over with bloody bullet holes and were slammed into the back wall of the elevator.

Mae ducked, covering her head, shielding her face from the gunfire.

When she turned to look again, all four of her remaining captors had their hands raised, as did Sister Lynda.

Standing before them, with Steyr AUG assault rifles trained on them, were six armed grey-clad soldiers, their faces masked by opaque visors, their ears covered with high-tech protective headphones.

Brother Enoch held up his hands. 'Please! We are not your enemies. Please don't—'

'Be silent, monk!' the lead soldier barked through his mask. 'You live for now. General Rastor would like a word with you.'

Mae and Lynda were marched at gunpoint with the four surviving Omega monks from the Secret Archives into the nave of St Peter's Basilica, or at least what was left of it.

The remains of its enormous dome lay in ruins on the floor of the cathedral: giant chunks of concrete and glass lay in huge piles around the wreckage of the *baldacchino*, which itself had been crushed by the cataclysmic collapse of the dome.

The night sky could be seen through the massive new hole in the basilica's roof.

When they first encounter St Peter's, dazzled by its awesome scale, visitors often miss the most important object in the cathedral. For it is *not* the main altar or the *baldacchino* covering that altar. Rather it is a gigantic golden throne at the very back of the space.

It is called the Throne of St Peter and it is a massive raised chair that occupies the rearmost wall of the basilica. Although it seats only one, it is four storeys tall and covered in golden images of eagles, angels, cherubs and, oddly, many blazing sunbeams.

A man now sat on the Throne of St Peter.

A very large man.

Mae eyed him closely.

He was an enormous specimen of a human being: broad-shouldered, muscular and well over six feet tall. He wore grey military fatigues.

His head was completely bald and his eyes blazed with an intensity that bordered on madness.

'So. The monks of Omega . . .' he said slowly. 'Making your play for the Labyrinth, are you?'

Brother Enoch said, 'We have no quarrel with you, General Rastor.'

'Oh, but you do,' the big bald man said mildly. 'We are at cross-purposes in our quests. You want what I do not.'

'We only want a world that operates in accordance with the natural order,' Enoch said, raising his chin righteously.

'I know what you monks want: a world where women bow before you,' Rastor said. 'How is Ezekiel, by the way? Has he recruited his equally zealous Catholic brothers in the Romanian military to help him in this matter?'

'We could work together, you know—' the monk Enoch rallied.

'No, we could not,' Rastor said. 'As I said, we are at cross-purposes. You want a warped world, whereas I do not want a world *at all*. I do not want it to continue to exist. You have discovered the multiple, I gather? Give it to me now.'

Enoch hesitated.

Rastor nodded to one of his soldiers and—*bang!*—the soldier blew out the brains of the Omega monk to Enoch's left.

The dead monk fell.

'Give me the multiple,' Rastor said again.

'We didn't get it—' Brother Enoch lied.

Bang.

A second Omega monk was shot and fell.

Sister Lynda started hyperventilating.

Mae stood stock-still.

Rastor said again, 'The multiple.'

Enoch visibly slumped. 'Sixteen. It is sixteen.'

Rastor smiled. 'Thank you.'

Then he nodded to his captain again and the soldier calmly shot Enoch and the last Omega monk.

It was only then that Rastor turned his gaze to Mae and Sister Lynda.

'Goodness me, where are my manners,' he said. 'I haven't introduced myself. Ladies, my name is General Garthon Rastor, Commander of the Elite Royal Guard, a force that for two thousand years has threaded itself into the world's leading military forces. From the Roman legions to the armies of Napoleon to various national militaries of today, the Royal Guard has always been present in some way to represent the interests of the four kingdoms.

'That said, I have been absent from royal society for a couple of years due to a *misunderstanding* I had with some members of the royal world. Their ruling philosophy and mine no longer agreed. This resulted in a short stay at Erebus. But now I am free once again and in my absence the world seems to have changed for the better.'

He eyed them keenly.

To Sister Lynda: 'You have the look of a Vestal.'

Lynda nodded. 'I am a member of that order. I am Sister Lynda Fadel.'

General Rastor turned to Mae. 'And you?'

Mae began, 'I'm—'

'You are Mabel Merriweather, or Mae to those close to you.' Rastor grinned. 'You are the mother of the man named West and were once the wife of the one known as Wolf. Before my unfortunate fall from grace, I studied your son, in case I needed to kill him. The first thing I did was determine the people he loved.'

'Cut the bullshit, then, what do you want?' Mae said.

Rastor smiled.

He stroked the armrest of his glorious throne. 'Do you know the history of this throne? It is a true work of art, sculpted by Gian Lorenzo Bernini himself. But because of his glorious *baldacchino* and the impressive interior of this basilica, few visitors ever actually heed it.

'This is a shame because this throne is actually the most significant artefact in this place, for it was made in honour of a far more important throne that resides in the Supreme Labyrinth. What do I want?'

'To rule the world like a tyrant?' Mae prompted.

Rastor shook his head. 'Some who seek the World Throne desire it so that they may rule unchallenged. Others like the monks of Omega want it so that they may subjugate women. I want neither of those things. I delight in rage, chaos, nihilism. Madam, what do I want? I want to stop *anyone* from sitting on that throne and thus gain a front-row seat to the greatest event in all of history: *the end of the universe.*'

He looked hard at the two women.

'You, Vestal, I have no need for you. But, you, Ms Merriweather, have value to me.'

With those words, he nodded to his captain, who pressed his pistol to the back of Sister Lynda's head and pulled the trigger.

A gunshot rang out—

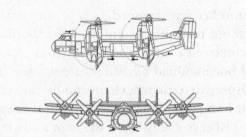

—and the captain's head blew apart, shot from the side, and to Lynda and Mae's surprise, he collapsed in a heap.

Zoe emerged from behind one of the pillars of the basilica, her smoking pistol trained on Rastor and his men. Agnes was close behind her.

'The famous Ms Kissane,' Rastor said. 'The wife of Captain West. A pleasure to meet you.'

'Mae. Lynda. Over here. We're leaving,' Zoe called. She kept the gun aimed at Rastor. 'Don't make me kill you, buddy.'

He shrugged mildly. 'I do not fear death. Indeed, I welcome it.'

'Rufus, come on in,' Zoe said into her mike.

With a deafening roar, the black Sukhoi Su-37 fighter-bomber swept vertically down through the hole in the roof of St Peter's Basilica, the blast of its engines booming loudly throughout the space.

Mae could see Rufus in the pilot's seat, expertly flying the jet *inside the gigantic basilica*!

The Sukhoi landed on the wreckage of the dome and Zoe guided Lynda, Agnes and last of all, Mae, up the pile of rubble to the open bomb bay doors in its belly.

Rastor watched, unperturbed.

'You're not the only one who has a hover-capable aircraft, you know,' he called.

At that moment, a *vast* shadow moved across the big hole in the roof of the basilica, a shadow the size of a cargo plane but with four rotors that blurred with motion.

Zoe saw it and her jaw dropped.

She'd read about these planes but never actually seen one. They had only just come out of the prototype phase.

It was a Bell Boeing Quad TiltRotor aircraft, the next generation of the V-22 Osprey. It didn't have an official name yet but those who knew of it had taken to calling it the V-88 Condor.

Where the Osprey was a two-rotored mid-sized plane, the Condor was several times larger. It was a massive four-winged and four-rotored aircraft with the fuselage of a C-130 Hercules. It was also widely regarded as the airpower of the future: a plane with enormous range and the ability to land in places that did not have airstrips. There were plans for various versions of the Condor, including cargo versions, troops versions and even hovering flying fortresses armed with all manner of cannons, mini-guns and missiles.

This Condor, it seemed, was one of those.

Mae gazed in awe at the massive aircraft hovering above them.

It explained how Brother Enoch had been so wrong.

He had thought, being a plane, the aircraft would need a runway to land on. But since this mighty plane didn't need a runway, it had simply swept into a hover above the Vatican and unloaded its cargo of killers with shocking speed.

And right now it was blocking the way out. The noise its engines made was deafening. The downblast was like a mini-hurricane.

It was amid all this noise and movement that, quick as a whip, Rastor drew a rare and devastating pistol—a Glock 18C, a handgun capable of firing on full auto—and unleashed a fusillade of gunfire at Zoe's group beneath the Sukhoi.

Lynda and Zoe were already half inside the bomb bay when he pulled the trigger and they dived inside the plane, out of the way of the line of fire.

Sister Agnes wasn't so fortunate. Rastor's withering spray of bullets cut viciously across her body and her stomach blew open with bloody holes and she was thrown down the large mound of rubble.

Mae was also hit. Pure luck had placed her behind Agnes when Rastor had opened fire, so poor Agnes had taken the brunt of the burst. Mae was still hit twice in the thigh and she also fell down the rubble mound, away from the plane.

'Agnes!' Sister Lynda cried.

'Mae!' Zoe shouted.

Zoe took in the situation. Rastor's men were moving toward them, running fast, guns up. Agnes lay face-down, not moving. Zoe couldn't tell if she was dead. Beside Agnes lay Mae, teeth clenched in pain, wounded but alive, yet too far away to save.

'Zoe!' Mae yelled above the din. 'Go! You and Lynda have to get away! You both have to go help Jack!'

Zoe locked eyes with Mae and she knew she was right. Beside her, Lynda looked from Mae to Agnes, torn.

'Rufus!' Zoe called. 'Get us out of here!'

Then she shut the bomb bay door and lost sight of Mae and Agnes.

In the Sukhoi's cockpit, Rufus was looking all around himself for a way out: left, right, up, down, in front and behind.

'Oh, well, I guess I'm going to Hell anyway for flying in here in the first place,' he said.

He gunned the engines and swung the Sukhoi around, swivelling his jet *inside* the giant walls of St Peter's before hitting the afterburners and racing down the length of the nave, toward the massive front doors of the enormous church.

Then he opened fire on those doors.

The doors blew apart under his hail of gunfire, but they were too narrow for the Sukhoi to fly through, so as he picked up speed, Rufus banked the *Black Raven* onto its side and shot through the main doorway of St Peter's Basilica with only a couple of feet to spare at either wingtip, and the Sukhoi zoomed away over the city of Rome, unseen and unnoticed by its inhabitants, comatose on the ground.

★ ★ ★

Back in the nave of St Peter's, Mae lay on the debris-covered floor, grimacing with pain, pressing hard on the two bullet wounds to her thigh.

A groan from beside her made her turn.

It was Agnes. She was still alive, if only barely—

—then Agnes's head blew apart in a short burst of gunfire.

A shadow fell over Mae.

Rastor. He lowered his smoking pistol.

'I have no need for clever nuns,' he said. 'But the mother of Captain West. You are very valuable.'

One of his masked troops came running up.

'Shall we pursue their plane, sir?'

Rastor stared off in the direction the Sukhoi had taken, entirely unconcerned.

He looked back down at Mae and a cruel smile crept across his face.

'No,' General Rastor said. 'We have a more important mission. With the multiple, we can calculate the location of the Supreme Labyrinth. Which means we now must find ourselves an iron mountain.'

A GIRL NAMED LILY

PART VIII
2007–PRESENT

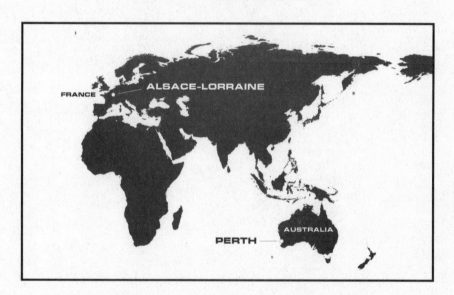

If you seek his monument, look around you.

INSCRIPTION ON THE TOMB OF CHRISTOPHER WREN,
ARCHITECT OF ST PAUL'S CATHEDRAL, LONDON

PERTH, AUSTRALIA
JULY 2007

When Lily and Alby were in sixth grade, their school for gifted children in Perth put on a careers day.

Naturally, Lily begged Jack and Zoe to attend and give presentations on their careers. And so Jack and Zoe left their isolated farm and went to the city for a few days.

This was in the gloriously quiet days after their mission to re-erect the capstone of the Great Pyramid at Giza but before the overwhelming attack on the farm that had precipitated their mission to find the Six Ramesean Stones.

Throughout that morning at the school, Jack had sat in a little chair at the back of Lily's classroom, watching all the other parents give their talks.

As a guy who had spent much of his life going to incredible places to do dangerous things—and who, more than anything, enjoyed hiding away from the world when he wasn't doing that—Jack liked seeing real people in the real world. Their interests and their passions fascinated him.

One girl's mother was a paramedic: she was awesome.

There was also a lawyer, an accountant and a hedge-fund manager.

The accountant was Tilly McCarroll's dad, Phil. Jack had met him a couple of times because Tilly and Lily were friends.

Phil McCarroll was a short, balding, bespectacled man who was not the most gifted public speaker.

In fact, poor Phil was awful.

He sweated and stammered as he told the kids what he did. 'I went to Girraween High School right here in W.A. I . . . er . . . got my CPA while I was working nights delivering pizzas, then got my CFA while I was working at a firm in the city . . .'

The kids shifted and coughed, the surest signs that Phil had lost their attention.

He finished with a mumbled 'Thank you' and shuffled away from the whiteboard to tepid applause.

Jack's heart went out to him and he patted Phil on the shoulder as the sweet accountant sat down beside Jack at the back of the room, wiping his brow in relief.

The next speaker, the hedge-fund guy, bounded to the front of the class.

Don Dalton was the exact opposite of Phil McCarroll: fun, charismatic and he kept the kids enthralled, chiefly by telling them how much money he made at Dalton Funds Management.

Jack went next—occupation: historian—and gave a short but sharp presentation that began with the statement: 'Do you know the Great Pyramid?'

'Yes,' the kids answered.

'Did you know that it's nine feet shorter than it should be?'

He then put up an image of the Giza pyramids and sure enough, there was the Great Pyramid with its flat top, its capstone missing. He didn't go on to say how he'd found the pieces of that capstone and put it back in place just in time to avoid global annihilation, but he gave an interesting talk nonetheless.

Then Jack sat down and gave the stage to Zoe.

She came into the classroom in full battle gear—helmet, body armour, laser-sighting device, camos, boots and guns, lots of guns—and the kids gasped in absolute awe.

Zoe stole the show.

To have a special forces soldier in full battle dress was one thing, but to have a female one was even better.

At the back of the room, as the kids peppered her with questions,

Jack smiled quietly to himself.

Only then, however, did he hear the snort from the guy next to him, the hedge-fund guy, Dalton.

'Hmph, wait'll they discover how much the army pays,' he whispered.

After school that day, Jack and Zoe had dinner with Lily and Alby.

'So, Lily,' Jack said. 'What did you learn from those talks today?'

Lily pursed her lips thoughtfully. 'I learned that Zoe kicked ass. And if I want to make lots of money, I should own a hedge fund like Liam Dalton's dad, although I'm still not quite sure what a hedge fund is.'

'I'm not either,' Zoe said.

Jack said, 'Let me rephrase the question. Apart from Zoe and me—we don't count because you know us—who did you find the most impressive today?'

Alby said, 'I liked the paramedic lady.'

'I liked her, too,' Lily said, 'but Mr Dalton was the best speaker.'

'Okay,' Jack said, nodding. 'Do you know who I found the most impressive?'

'Who?'

'Tilly's dad. Mr McCarroll.'

'Mr McCarroll? Why? He was kinda boring and he didn't speak well at all.'

'First, young lady,' Jack said sternly, 'no-one is boring. We never call anyone boring. *Everyone* has an interesting story. You just have to listen to them and find out what it is. When I listened to Mr McCarroll—and to Mr Dalton for that matter—I learned a lot about both of them.'

'Like what?'

'Well, I learned that Mr McCarroll went to a public high school and then he studied to be a CPA, a Certified Practising Accountant, and that's not easy. And he did it *while he was working as a pizza delivery guy*. But then, *then*, he said he got his CFA qualification.

Now that's a big deal. CFA stands for Chartered Financial Analyst and it's a *really* hard qualification to get, one of the hardest in the world. It takes years of study and you have to pass a series of brutal exams.

'Mr Dalton, sure, he put on a good show and, yes, he makes lots of money, but did you know that Dalton Funds Management was started by his father? Mr Dalton didn't have to get *any* qualifications to get into his position and make all his money.

'Mr McCarroll may not have been the most engaging presenter, but if you listened to what he had to say, you would've seen someone who worked his way up from humble beginnings at a public school in outer Perth to the very admirable position he's in today. That's the kind of guy I respect.

'And I imagine if, the next time you see him, you give him a compliment on his speech, he'd really appreciate it.'

As it happened, Lily saw Mr McCarroll the next morning when he dropped off Tilly at school, so she said, 'Mr McCarroll, I really enjoyed your presentation yesterday.'

Mr McCarroll swelled with pride. 'Really? Why, thank you, Lily. Thank you for saying that.'

Lily never forgot it.

About a month after that day, she asked Jack another question.

'Dad, at my careers day, why did you say you were just a historian? I mean, you're a bad-ass soldier who saved the world. You fought evil people and beat them. You're a great man and yet you didn't say so. Why didn't you reveal that?'

Jack looked away.

'Lily, studying history has taught me a lot of interesting things, but it's taught me one lesson above all else: not all great people are *good* people.

'Julius Caesar. Genghis Khan. Napoleon. All great men. All assholes, too. As for me, I guess I have a certain set of talents that make me the right guy to do certain missions. So I do what I have to and then I go home. I don't need anyone to know. In the end, I'd rather be good than great.'

As Lily had got older—and followed Jack on his adventures with the Ramesean Stones, the Great Games and the Three Secret Cities; and gone abroad to study at Stanford—she had grown to admire his brand of humble heroism more and more.

There were, especially at Stanford, lots of guys who had money and flashiness—and sometimes she fell under their spell, as in the case of Dion—but as she matured, she found herself looking for a guy with that same quiet heroism underneath the surface.

Of course, she found it in Alby.

★ ★ ★

As for Alby, during the three-week period after the team had found the Three Secret Cities, he had also done a lot of thinking.

He'd lost a hand during the mission to find the cities: that had been Dion's cruel revenge when Alby had been captured by him and the Knights of the Golden Eight.

It cut at Alby's self-image more than he thought it would. As a child, Alby had always been small, nerdy and geeky. His mother had been a little over-protective and his father had not cared much for him.

And then he'd become friends with Lily at school and met Jack and discovered a whole new world, a world in which his intelligence had value and where physical stature meant nothing.

Still, while Alby had grown into a tall young man of twenty-one, losing his hand had brought back all his childhood anxieties of being the small, weak kid.

He had never forgotten the time Jack had stood up for him during a parent–teacher conference with an arrogant sportsmaster at his school.

(The sportsmaster, a garden-variety muscle-head, had not listened when Alby's mousy mother had asked him if Alby could be excused from gym class. He *had* listened when Jack had quietly crushed a softball in front of his eyes with his titanium left hand.)

That incident had long stayed with Alby because the way Jack interacted with people intrigued him.

Whether he was talking to a prince, a prime minister or a lowly minotaur like Easton, Jack treated everyone with the same courtesy. (Or, in the case of self-important sportsmasters, courteous but firm forcefulness.)

Alby's own father, a senior mining executive, didn't do that. He measured people by the titles on their business cards.

Alby had also seen various players in the shadow royal world—people like Dion and the Knights of the Golden Eight—showing obeisance to those they considered their 'betters' or of higher social rank.

But to Jack there didn't seem to be any such thing as social rank.

'There are only people,' Jack answered when Alby asked him about it just before Jack left for Mont Saint-Michel.

'Money comes and goes, and rank is relative to time and place. And if *having* money is the only thing that gives you rank, then you're living a life based on a foundation of sand. For what if you lose all your money? Way I see it, if you treat *everyone* with decency and respect, whether they're a prince or a pauper, you'll always do okay. It's worked for me so far.'

'Yes, but you're smart and tough and strong,' Alby said, nodding at Jack's physique. 'I'm deaf and kinda nerdy.'

Jack snuffed a laugh.

'Oh, really.' He rolled up his left sleeve, revealing his titanium forearm and hand.

'Look at this arm,' he said. 'I was a one-armed man before this.'

They both knew how it had happened: on the day of Lily's birth, inside a volcano in Uganda, to save Lily, Wizard and himself, Jack had thrust his arm through a waterfall of sizzling lava.

'I knew when I did it that I would probably never be a soldier again,' Jack said. 'The army doesn't have much use for a one-armed trooper. But then Wizard built this for me and it's fricking awesome. Better than the arm I was born with and it's got me out of a lot of sticky situations.'

He sighed. 'It's funny, sometimes what people think is your greatest weakness can actually be your greatest strength. Take, for instance, your deafness. Some might see that as a weakness. But because of it, you taught Lily, Zoe and me sign language, and thus made us more capable people. And hey, look at what just happened in Moscow. Because you're deaf, those bells don't affect you. The way I see it, that's an enormous strength in the battle ahead.'

That was Jack West Jr for you, Alby thought as he remained in Hades's estate while Jack's team was at Mont Saint-Michel and Zoe's team was in Rome.

No-one would ever call Jack a superhero but he did have one superpower: the ability to make you feel like you could do anything.

HADES'S ESTATE
ALSACE-LORRAINE, FRANCE
24 DECEMBER, 2250 HOURS

Alby blinked out of his thoughts.

It was late and all was silent at Hades's estate in the forests of eastern France.

Alby was manning the radio room, waiting anxiously for word from Mont Saint-Michel and Rome.

Easton was out near the lake house. He'd just finished the 'special task' Stretch had given him and was leaving the finished product—packed into a dozen boxes—in a special concrete-walled storage basement underneath the lake house.

As Alby had waited here, he'd done a deep dive into the five iron mountains and their connection to the moon.

The moon, it turned out, really was a strange celestial body.

That it perfectly blocked out the sun during an eclipse—by appearing to be the same size—was simply a coincidence beyond calculation: the sun is four hundred times larger than the moon, but it is also exactly four hundred times further away from the Earth. The moon also only ever shows the Earth the same face. In addition to this, like Jupiter, the moon protects the Earth from bombardment by rogue asteroids and meteorites. It is as if the Earth is somehow defended by it.

One thing that took Alby a lot of time was figuring out an astronomical track of the moon's orbit and spin, giving him the ability to note where it would be over certain points on the Earth at any given time, but he eventually got it done.

Then he set about following Jack's order to discover whatever he could about the Supreme Labyrinth.

Using some hieroglyph translation programs, he found a few references to mazes and labyrinths in Jack's collection of artefacts and documents from the farm; the ones relating to his mission involving the Seven Ancient Wonders and the Great Pyramid at Giza.

The first reference he found was a partial Greek scroll, torn and in terrible condition, that mentioned the most famous labyrinth in all of history: King Minos's elaborate maze on the island of Crete that housed his dreaded monster, the Minotaur.

Alby gazed at the image of the partial Greek scroll on his computer screen.

According to the translation program it read: —I ventured into—labyrinth accompanied by—brother's son, the noble Theseus, and a—man named Asterion sent by—my other brother—

The rips in the scroll made it a little hard to read, but it appeared to be just another retelling of the Theseus legend.

Alby knew the story well. Like many young boys, he'd loved it all his life. It was one of the world's most enduring myths of heroism and bravery.

Every nine years, the tyrannical King Minos demanded that the city of Athens send seven young men and seven maidens to him as tribute. Upon arriving at Crete, these poor youngsters would be sent into the labyrinth to be hunted down and killed by the Minotaur.

Appalled by this, Theseus—the Athenian king's son—volunteered to go as one of the sacrificial victims. He entered the labyrinth, slayed the Minotaur and, aided by a length of thread given to him by King Minos's daughter, Ariadne, he managed to find his way back out of the labyrinth.

The second reference to a labyrinth that Alby found was far more exciting.

It was a photo of some Egyptian hieroglyphics on the wall of a tomb underneath the Step Pyramid in Saqqara, Egypt, and it was in

much better condition. As soon as he read its first line, Alby leaned forward with interest.

For these hieroglyphs had been written by Imhotep the Great himself, the designer and builder of that pyramid.

It read:

> *I, Imhotep, beheld the Labyrinth. It is the most magnificent*
> *structure in the whole world, the greatest achievement*
> *of my illustrious forebears. It is beyond compare. I am*
> *honoured to have seen it with my own eyes.*
> *Oh, what a terrible and terrifying thing it is. Woe betide*
> *any who would seek to conquer it! You would rather count*
> *the stars in the sky than attempt such a task unaided.*
> *It took me many days to penetrate its fearsome depths and*
> *countless tunnels, and I had the wisdom of the ancients*
> *to guide me and the benefit of travelling mostly via the*
> *Emperor's Route. Even then I barely escaped with my life.*
> *When I returned, I imparted the secrets of that maze to my*
> *body in the manner of the ancients. When I die, let the next*
> *head-priest of Amon-Ra replicate those markings in the*
> *same manner. Then seal me in stone in my tomb dedicated*
> *to Thoth within the great hill of the Oracle under the sea,*
> *with the secrets of the maze buried with me.*

'The secrets of the maze,' Alby said. 'You had them imparted to your body *in the manner of the ancients* and buried with you. So what's the manner of the ancients?'

Whatever it was, worryingly, Imhotep had also suggested future head priests of the Cult of Amon-Ra do it. Which meant the Catholic Church—the modern face of that cult—might already have this information.

'And what is this *Emperor's Route?*' he thought aloud. 'Hmmm.'

Alby did a quick search on Imhotep.

Put simply, Imhotep the Great was a towering figure in Egyptian history.

High priest, royal adviser, brilliant astronomer and gifted doctor, he had lived around 2700 B.C.E., just before the building of the Great Pyramid. The reigning genius of his time, he was one of only two people who were *not* pharaohs whom the Egyptians had made a god.

In honour of this status, the ancient Egyptians had produced many statues and images of him.

All depicted him in the same way: holding a papyrus scroll and wearing a multi-coloured neck-ring around his throat and a solid-looking skullcap on his head.

He was ancient Egypt's greatest architect, perhaps history's greatest. He designed the Step Pyramid, the first giant pyramid ever built, before anyone else had even contemplated the idea of a pyramid.

He was a man thousands of years ahead of his time.

Alby also knew there was a connection between Imhotep and one of Jack's previous missions.

Jack had told him how several brilliant priests honoured with the name *Imhotep* had built many of the trap systems that Jack had overcome in his search for the capstone of the Great Pyramid.

These connections to the ancient world—including knowledge of the Supreme Labyrinth—made Alby wonder if Imhotep the Great might have had some *extra* help in acquiring his advanced skills.

Had he had access to the wisdom of the advanced civilisation that had built all these Falling Temples and the Labyrinth?

A man who knew the Word of Thoth could easily dazzle a primitive culture like that of early Egypt.

'So if you took the secrets of the Labyrinth to your grave, Imhotep, where were you buried?' Alby asked aloud. 'Where is *the great hill of the Oracle under the sea*?'

At the sight of the word *Oracle* Alby naturally thought of Lily. She was, after all, the current Oracle of Siwa.

Maybe Imhotep had been buried at Siwa. The desert town of Siwa did have a high rocky hill filled with tombs and catacombs, but Siwa was nowhere near any seas or oceans. It was located deep in the Sahara Desert, near the Libyan–Egyptian border, hundreds of miles from the nearest coast.

Alby looked up Imhotep's tomb more generally, only to discover that no tomb dedicated to him had ever been found.

Alby made a note to come back to that. He moved on to the next hit.

It was a big one.

His translation program had found mentions of the search terms 'impossible maze' and 'sacred mountaintop' in another of Jack's old Great Pyramid files: an aged British photo of some hieroglyphics carved into a wall of the King's Tomb within the Great Pyramid itself.

The glyphs appeared to have been written at the order of the builder of the pyramid, the all-powerful pharaoh Khufu, or, as the Greeks called him, Cheops.

The translation read:

> *Oh, great and wise Overlords,*
> *I have done as you commanded!*
> *I have built the mighty structure that will capture and*
> *contain the awesome power of Ra's Destroyer.*

I built it near Aker, who, ever alert, watches over the impossible maze from his sacred mountaintop perch. When death takes me, I will be laid inside this same mighty structure and use it as my tomb.

'That's interesting,' Alby said.

Ra's Destroyer was the ancient Egyptians' name for the Tartarus Sunspot, the deadly hotspot on the surface of the sun that would have destroyed the Earth had Jack not re-erected the capstone of the Great Pyramid and caught the sunspot's rays in its crystal array.

But Alby's eyes were locked on one particular paragraph:

I built it near Aker, who, ever alert, watches over the impossible maze from his sacred mountaintop perch.

'*Who watches over the impossible maze*,' Alby said aloud. 'The Supreme Labyrinth.'

Alby quickly looked up the Egyptian term: *Aker*.

For a moment, he thought it might be the Great Sphinx—it was, without doubt, 'ever alert'—but that couldn't be right. The Great Sphinx sat in a depression *below* the pyramids, not on a mountaintop.

Aker, it turned out, was an Egyptian god; specifically, the god who welcomed dead pharaohs to the Underworld and guided them through it.

He was also a *very* old god, even by Egyptian standards.

Aker appeared in the first Egyptian myths, predating the more well-known ones about Osiris, Isis, Horus and even Ra. He predated the pyramids.

'He watches over the maze *from his mountaintop perch* . . .' Alby said.

The tallest mountain range in Egypt was in the Sinai Peninsula across the Gulf of Suez, quite a way from Giza. A closer range was the Eastern Desert Mountains, which stood where the Sahara Desert met the Red Sea.

Alby scowled. This would require further study.

He decided to do that later, because he very much wanted to chase up something Iolanthe had said before she'd left for Mont Saint-Michel with Jack.

She'd said that since ancient times, scholars like Newton, Pythagoras and Albert Einstein had debated the identities of the five iron mountains.

Einstein, Alby thought.

Lily had mentioned Einstein, too, in her quickly scrawled note to Jack: something about Einstein, Alexander Friedmann and $k>0$.

Alby knew what that referred to.

The Friedmann Equation. It was a complex equation that explained the expansion of the universe. But if one element of it—k—was greater than 0, it meant that the universe would collapse in on itself in an almighty singularity.

The Omega Event.

Einstein was also Alby's hero—his hero of heroes—and had been for a long time.

As a nerdy bespectacled boy, when his brother and other boys his age had been putting up posters of sports stars and rock bands on their bedroom walls, Alby had stuck up a poster of Albert Einstein and his famous quote: GREAT SPIRITS HAVE ALWAYS ENCOUNTERED VIOLENT OPPOSITION FROM MEDIOCRE MINDS.

This also meant that Alby knew more about the world's most famous scientist than most.

Of course, he knew all about Einstein's most famous equation, $E=mc^2$, his theories of special and general relativity, and his famous letter to President Franklin Roosevelt about the power of the atom to make a nuclear weapon: the letter that had led to the creation of the Manhattan Project.

But Alby also knew some more obscure facts about Albert Einstein.

Like how Einstein had *disappeared* during World War II.

After penning his famous letter to the president, Einstein was, bizarrely, banned from participating in the Manhattan Project. U.S. Army Intelligence felt that his left-leaning political views made him a security risk.

The U.S. Navy, however, thought otherwise and happily employed him for the duration of the war. What Einstein actually did for the Navy for four years, Alby knew, had long been shrouded in mystery.

And so Alby decided to check it out and look into anything and everything connected to Einstein in U.S. Navy records.

It took some searching and a little skirting of military firewalls, but soon Alby hit on Einstein's Navy codename: Mr Light.

That led to several documents including one that blew Alby's mind.

A second letter to the president, dated 10 April 1945.

Plastered across it was a series of bold red stamps warning:

DO NOT SEND
DO NOT SEND
DO NOT SEND

Alby read it:

Dear President Roosevelt,

I once wrote to you about a most grave matter: the notion of an atomic weapon and the necessity that the Allied powers acquire one before the Nazi state does.

Now, I write to you about a far greater and more worrisome event. It will occur long after you and I are dead but it threatens no less than our universe's very existence.

In theology the study of this event is known as *eschatology*, and various religions have called it the end-times, doomsday or the Omega Event. Through my scientific studies, I call it real. It is coming.

Without getting into the mathematics of it all, this event concerns notions of the universe's *reversal* from expansion

to contraction. This event has occupied the mind of Sir Isaac Newton and, for a very long time, the Catholic Church.

It boils down to this equation:

$$E^u = mc^c$$

This equation modifies my other equation. It represents a signal—or, more precisely, the *energy* of a signal: E^u—that must be sent out from the Earth at the requisite time. (The energy of this signal is beyond enormous: 'c' is the speed of light, a huge number; in this equation, it is multiplied *to the power of itself*, which creates a number of astonishing size.)

I call this signal the *quantum pulse*. Somehow, when a certain ceremony is performed in an ancient maze, this signal, this pulse, will be sent out into the cosmos at extraordinary speed to stave off the contraction of the universe and save our planet.

Alby sat bolt upright.

Einstein was describing—in scientific terms, not those of a historian or mythic storyteller—what would happen in the Supreme Labyrinth.

A quantum pulse.

A signal that shot across the universe at superluminal speed to tell the—what?—the intelligence at the centre of the universe—that sentient life still existed on Earth.

The Navy must have thought Einstein had lost his mind, thus the many stamps screaming **DO NOT SEND**.

Except Einstein had not lost his mind at all.

Einstein may not have been aware of the Great Games, the Three Secret Cities, the Five Iron Mountains or a throne at the centre of the Supreme Labyrinth, but he had discovered the essence of the Omega Event and the quantum mechanics behind how to stop it.

'Awesome . . .' Alby breathed.

Easton returned from the lake house. 'All boxes in storage basement,' he said.

'Nice work,' Alby said. 'Those things'll come in handy, I'm sure.'

And then, as the clock struck eleven, some images started coming in from Mae in Rome.

Minutes later, their radio started pinging as the two teams called in.

'*Folks, are you there?*' Jack's voice came in over the speaker.

Alby leapt to the microphone. 'I'm here, Jack.'

Zoe's voice came in a second later. '*We're here, too.*'

'*What did you find in Rome?*' Jack asked.

Zoe said, '*Jack, your mother was taken—alive—by a new player, a guy named Rastor. We also had to leave without Agnes. I don't know if she's alive or not. Rastor shot her up pretty bad.*'

'Rastor?' Jack said.

'*He was a brilliant general who served the four kingdoms, but then fell out of favour,*' Lynda explained. '*He is formidable and ruthless. Your mother will be safe, at least for a time, because he will want to hold her as leverage against you. Agnes will have no such value to him. If she's not already dead, I fear for her.*'

Silence.

Jack said, '*Tell us about Rome.*'

Zoe said, '*Like Moscow, the whole city is asleep. We discovered that the Pope ordered an assassination attempt on the expert on the bells, the ex-nun Dr Tracy Smith, but it failed. We also bumped into some Omega monks and met the aforementioned asshole named General Rastor.*

'*Rastor has his own V-88 Condor and is more than happy to use it. He blew away the dome of St Peter's with it before he annihilated the Omega monks. He also mentioned that the monks might be getting assistance from Catholic soldiers in the Romanian military, which is a little unsettling. Then he took your mother. Long story short, he's a big shot from the shadow royal world who's returned to make his play.*'

Jack said, '*Tell us what you learned about the mountains.*'

Lynda said, '*Before Rastor took her, Mae sent through some photos of the documents we saw in the Vatican Secret Archives: photos of the Great Sphinx at Giza and letters from Francis Xavier to the Pope of his day.*'

'*Give us the executive summary,*' Jack said.

'*Okay. The second mountain is Mont Blanc. The third is in Lhasa, Tibet. Your mother and I are convinced it's under Potala Palace. The Church thinks the fourth mountain is somewhere in Italy, along the strip of locations known as the Sword of St Michael, but that's not certain. We need to study that some more.*'

'And the fifth mountain?' Alby asked as he scanned the photos that Mae had sent from the Secret Archives.

'*Sorry, we didn't find anything about that one,*' Lynda said.

Zoe said, '*What about you, Jack? How did it go at Mont Saint-Michel?*'

'*It was bad,*' Jack said. '*Sphinx did the Fall and then had Hades killed. Sphinx is on his way to the Supreme Labyrinth now, with some guide notes about it written by Imhotep the Great—*'

'Wait,' Alby interjected. 'Those notes by Imhotep. Were they the actual notes or a copy?'

Jack said, '*Uh, a copy, I think. Sphinx or Mendoza said they were the Church's copy of Imhotep's notes. Why?*'

Alby said, 'I've been doing some research into the originals. Imhotep knew all about the Labyrinth, including something called the Emperor's Route through it. Lynda? Any idea what that is?'

Lynda said, '*The Labyrinth is famously large and complex, but it has a single straight route that runs directly to its holy centre. This is the Emperor's Route. It's designed for the King of Kings. It makes his passage through the Labyrinth easy and simple, a mere procession. This is the route Zeus took, because he went to the Labyrinth as the unchallenged King of Kings or Emperor. But, if an Emperor is challenged, things are very different. If someone else does a Fall and enters the Labyrinth via one*

of its other four gates, then the Emperor's Route will be closed off and it becomes a race through the vast maze to the throne, a race that must be completed before the Omega Event occurs on December 29th.'

Jack said, *'Which is why we desperately need to do a Fall ourselves at one of the other iron mountains, then get to the Labyrinth to stop Sphinx.'*

'We're a long way behind, Jack,' Alby said.

'While we're still breathing, we keep chasing.'

Alby looked at Easton. 'Oh, Jack. Easton finished his task. The boxes are in the storage basement under the lake house, should you need them.'

'Thanks, Easton,' Jack said. *'I know that wasn't easy. Okay, folks, here's what we're gonna do. I'll take Nobody, Iolanthe and our new friend, Bertie, to Mont Blanc, the second mountain. Zoe, Rufus and Lynda, I want you to go to the third one underneath Potala—'*

'Attention, Jack West. Attention people of the world,' another voice came over the line, cutting Jack off.

Alby's blood went ice cold.

It was Sphinx's voice.

But the voice hadn't come from the radio. It had come from the bank of TVs behind Alby . . .

. . . *every* TV.

Every television had cut to an emergency broadcast screen and Sphinx's voice was coming from all of them.

Just as the Knights of the Golden Eight had done a few weeks ago, Sphinx was taking over the airwaves of every commercial radio and television signal in the world.

He sounded like God himself.

'People of the world, by now you know about Moscow and Rome. Resist me and you will suffer the same fate. Or, if I feel so disposed, you might suffer this.'

All the TV screens cut to a shot of a low dusty city nestled among some brown snow-capped mountains.

Alby recognised the mountain city instantly, seeing the imposing white-and-red palace perched atop a hill in its centre.

It was Lhasa, Tibet, and the palace was Potala Palace.

Then, with shocking suddenness, a missile lanced down from the sky, slammed into the massive palace in the middle of the city and detonated.

A colossal nuclear explosion followed.

It rippled across the city with astounding force, flattening buildings and shaking the ground, until finally, as the camera was struck by the expanding concussion wave, the image cut to hash.

Sphinx's voice returned. '*People of the world, a new dawn awaits you. My name is Hardin Lancaster the Twelfth. The Sphinx. Soon, most of you will fall into a peaceful slumber. When you wake, you will wake in a new world. For now, just wait while those of us with the requisite knowledge perform the requisite deeds on your behalf. One must earn the right to rule and that is what I must do now.*

'*Oh, and if you should see this man, Captain Jack West Jr*'— a picture of Jack appeared on all the televisions—'*kill him. Anyone who kills Captain West and brings me his corpse will be rewarded with riches beyond measure in my new world order.*'

Jack said to the group, '*Everyone, quick. Switch all comms to this roaming frequency.*' He picked one at random on his radio. '*We can't have him or his people listening in on us.*'

Sphinx wasn't finished.

'*You cannot beat me, Captain. You can chase me, but you chase in vain. I know more than you do, both about the mountains and the Labyrinth. I also know where you've been hiding. In the late Lord Hades's estate in eastern France.*'

The signal clicked off a moment later.

Alby never saw it.

Never saw all the TVs resume their regular programming.

Because he was already running out of the radio room, yelling to Easton to grab the rolling beds of Lily, Aloysius Knight and Stretch and get them downstairs.

As he ran past a window he saw them—saw them emerging from the tree line of the forest surrounding the lush estate: one hundred bronzemen led by Yago DeSaxe.

Coming for him and his friends.

Coming to kill them.

Deep below the main house of Hades's estate was a large World War II–era loading dock, part of the ouvrage from the Maginot Line that lay under the property.

Almost everything in the dock was made of faded grey concrete: the walls, floor, ceiling . . . and the train platform.

In the midst of all this decaying ninety-year-old concrete was a very 21st-century vehicle.

A little train: an engine car and one carriage.

It sat beside the platform on shiny railway tracks that disappeared into an old tunnel that itself led to the maze-like subway system of the Maginot Line.

Alby burst out of the elevator, frantically pushing two wheeled hospital beds containing the immobile figures of Lily and Stretch. Also on the beds were some of his laptops and documents.

Easton came next, pushing the gurney with Aloysius Knight's sleeping body on it.

Jack's falcon, Horus, sat perched on Lily's headboard while his two dogs—the feisty black poodle Roxy and the more placid labrador Ash—chased after them.

Alby thrust his two beds into the carriage and then raced forward to the engine car to start it up.

Easton had just pushed Aloysius's bed onto the carriage when an explosion rang out from somewhere above them—they couldn't see it from down here, but the Knights had fired a missile at Hades's beautiful mansion and blown it into a million pieces.

The whole loading dock shook violently and two beams of concrete dropped away from the ceiling and came crashing down *between* the train carriage and the two dogs.

Roxy, smaller and nimbler than Ash, just dodged out of the way, hurdled the obstacle and leapt into the train.

But Ash was cornered, fenced in by the fallen concrete, and freaking out. She whimpered as she searched desperately for a way over it.

Standing at the doorway of the carriage, Easton saw her, trapped and helpless—

—just as the elevator beyond her opened—

—to reveal six bronzemen and a Knight of the Golden Eight standing in it.

'Doggy . . .' he breathed.

'Easton! We gotta go!' Alby shouted from the engine car. 'Are we all aboard?'

Easton stared in horror at Ash. Her eyes were wide and panicked, fearful of being left behind by her pack.

Easton wasn't going to let that happen.

'No!' he called back to Alby. 'Get train going! We catch up!'

And then he bolted off the train, side-jumped over one of the concrete beams and lifted Ash into his arms.

The train started moving.

The bronzemen swept out of the elevator, charging after it.

Easton was only a short distance ahead of them, struggling as he ran with the ungainly mass of the yellow labrador in his arms.

He arrived beside the rear door of the moving carriage and tossed Ash into it. She landed clumsily with her paws splayed wide, but she was okay.

Easton was running full speed now alongside the accelerating train and he crouched to jump for the doorway—

—at the exact moment that the Knight fired his Steyr AUG assault rifle and hit Easton in the right calf.

Looking back from the engine car, Alby saw Easton's leg collapse beneath him and the Neanderthal fell, inches from the open door of the carriage.

Easton went sprawling onto the platform, crying out in pain, while the train shot off into the tunnel, disappearing into the underground darkness.

Alby could only peer back in dismay, knowing that he'd had no choice.

'Oh, Easton, I'm so sorry,' he said as he turned from the sight and drove the train away.

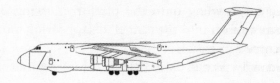

A few hours later, Easton sat glumly in the enormous cargo hold of one of Sphinx's C-5M Super Galaxy military aeroplanes.

His hands were cuffed behind his back and he was alone . . .

. . . except for the sixty bronzemen standing to attention in twelve rows of five down the length of the hold.

They did not move.

They did not make a sound.

The Lockheed Martin C-5M Super Galaxy is the largest plane in the U.S. Air Force's inventory.

It is not so much a plane as a flying warehouse. Designed to convey heavy payloads around the world without stopping, its dimensions are staggering.

At 250 feet long with a wingspan of 222 feet, it is propelled by four enormous General Electric TF39 turbofan jet engines. For something so large, it is also quite elegant: it looks like a big grey windowless 747 with an oversized jaw.

Having said that, the Super Galaxy's greatest asset is its cargo hold. There is nothing like it in the world. It is immense.

It could carry—if required—five double-decker London buses parked end-to-end; an entire Chinook helicopter; or the fuselage of a C-130 Hercules cargo plane.

Adding to its sheer size is its accessibility: the Super Galaxy has both a rear loading ramp and a huge hinged nose assembly that can be raised for loading and unloading from the front.

Easton didn't care.

He sat slumped in his chair in the vast hold, a prisoner.

The commander of the plane came down from the upper deck.

He was a tall man, barrel-chested and imposing. Easton had heard one of the crew members address him as 'Lord Yago'.

Yago stood over Easton, glaring down at him with disgust. He said nothing.

Then Yago's radio squawked.

'*What did you find in the ruins of Hades's secret estate?*' a voice said over the line.

'A single pathetic minotaur,' Yago said. 'The others fled through the Maginot tunnels. I am sorry, Hardin.'

'*A shame,*' the voice said. '*I was hoping you might acquire some individuals we could use to torment Captain West. I can't imagine he would care for a lowly minotaur.*'

Easton said, 'Captain Jack is my friend. He will come for me.'

Yago snorted.

So did the voice on the other end of the radio. '*What is your designation number, minotaur?*'

'My name is Easton,' Easton replied proudly. 'It is the name I chose myself—'

Yago guffawed. 'A minotaur with a *name*. What is the world coming to?'

'I am a friend of Captain Jack. He will rescue me,' Easton said defiantly.

Yago said, 'Minotaur, what can you possibly mean to West? You are nothing. You are one of thousands of nameless grunts from the Underworld. Why would he expend even a scintilla of effort saving you?'

Easton hesitated, doubt creeping into his voice. 'Because—I— I am . . . his friend.'

Yago said into the radio: 'Sire, you said to take all captives alive. What do you want me to do with this one?'

There was a brief pause.

'*I have a half a mind to keep him as a hostage. West is prone to caring about such individuals. But no. Throw him out of the plane. I have to go. We are arriving at the Labyrinth.*'

The radio clicked off.

Yago shrugged to Easton. 'Sorry, minotaur.'

He held up his hand, indicating the thick signet ring on it.

'See this ring? Sphinx gave it to me. While I wear it, I command these bronzemen. They will do whatever I say. *Whatever* I say. Allow me to demonstrate.'

He turned to the nearest pair of bronzemen. 'You two! Come here.'

The two bronzemen took three sharp steps forward and stood to attention before Yago.

'A minotaur with a name . . .' Yago said again, shaking his head. 'Bronzemen. Hold this man.'

The two bronzemen grasped Easton firmly by his arms, lifting him to his feet.

Yago calmly stepped over to the side door of the hold and opened it. Wind rushed into the cabin from outside.

Horror shot through Easton. He started struggling desperately, but it was no use. They were far too strong.

'Now walk out this door with him.'

The two faceless bronzemen lifted Easton off the ground and began moving toward the open door—

—when abruptly the plane rocked wildly.

A sickening, sudden lurch.

Both Yago and the two bronzemen were jolted off their feet, so unexpected was the move.

Easton fell to the floor, released.

'*Sir!*' a voice came over the C-5's internal speakers. '*This is the flight deck! We have a problem! Someone's hacking the plane!*'

Yago staggered for the stairs leading to the upper deck and the cockpit.

'What do you mean, hacking the plane?' he shouted angrily.

The plane banked wildly the other way, and Yago had to clutch the rail of the stairs so as not to go tumbling back down them.

'*Somebody's taken control of our avionics! Looks like they hacked the navigation system! We no longer have control of this plane!*'

Easton watched all this in both terror and confusion. The bronzemen who had been tasked with walking out of the plane with him had just been getting back to their feet when the second sudden banking move had sent them falling the other way.

And then, as if all this hadn't been surprising enough, the most unexpected thing of all happened.

The rear ramp of the enormous plane began to rumble open.

A mini-cyclone of wind rushed into the hold, whistling around all the bronzemen standing in it.

Then, following the inrushing wind, came *an entire seaplane*, bouncing into the hold from behind, crashing through the ranks of bronzemen and knocking them down like bowling pins!

The plane was a little ICON A10 emblazoned with the name *Sexy Prince One*.

It skidded to a halt . . .

. . . and out of it leapt Jack West Jr, with two Remington shotguns raised, his teeth clenched and his eyes furious.

'I'm looking for my friend, Easton!' he shouted.

Of course, it wasn't just Jack behind the daring rescue.

It was everybody.

And it hadn't been easy.

As soon as Jack had heard from Alby that Easton had been taken by Sphinx's forces at Alsace-Lorraine, he had got Alby to get a fix on the plane that had taken him.

The Super Galaxy had been found and, after a quick stop at Hades's estate, Jack had asked Nobody to fly after it in their much smaller—but speedier—seaplane.

When they were within sight of the giant cargo plane, he'd told Alby—sitting in a black Mercedes-Benz Sprinter van that had been waiting at the other end of his escape tunnel and using Aloysius Knight and Rufus's top-secret GPS-satellite/nav-system hack—to hack the Super Galaxy, take control of it, and open its rear ramp.

And then Jack had got Nobody to fly the little A10 seaplane *into* the Super Galaxy.

If anyone had been up in the sky to see it, it was, quite simply, an astonishing sight.

They would have seen the massive C-5M Super Galaxy thundering through the moonlit sky . . .

. . . only to then spy the tiny seaplane swooping up suddenly from below and behind it. Then the seaplane hit the gas and pressed forward, disappearing inside the bigger plane's rear end!

★ ★ ★

The cargo hold of the Super Galaxy was a maelstrom of furious wind.

The seaplane lay tilted at a thirty-degree angle, with at least a dozen bronzemen pinned beneath it or hurled off their feet. But forty of them still stood, impassive and silent, unmoved by the spectacular entrance of the little seaplane into the hold.

Jack stood in front of the plane, his silver shotguns raised. Nobody sprang out beside him.

Standing near Easton, Yago pointed his ringed finger at them: 'Bronzemen! Kill those men!'

The still-standing bronzemen turned their faceless heads toward Jack and Nobody . . .

. . . just as Jack levelled his two guns at them.

Yago laughed. 'Your bullets are useless here, West!'

Jack gave him a wry grin.

'Are they?'

And with those words, he raised his guns and fired them at the nearest bronzeman's head.

The bullets slammed into the metal head of the bronzeman—*and tore right through it*, blasting out the back—and the bronzeman stopped dead in its tracks . . .

. . . and fell, immobilised, dead.

The look on Yago's face said it all.

'That can't be . . .' he gasped.

He couldn't have known about Stretch's project back at the estate, the one that had involved working away at the blade of the fabled sword Excalibur with a metal grinder.

The one that had involved affixing—by hand, with glue, one by one—a shaving of Excalibur's gleaming blade to the tips of hundreds and hundreds of bullets.

That had been Easton's tedious task.

He had spent many hours at it: affixing shavings to bullets and shotgun shells, hundreds of them, and then loading those rounds into clips.

Jack hadn't had those rounds for the Moscow mission, but he had them now, having picked them up during his quick stop at the estate on the way here.

Jack and Nobody fired hard as they advanced together down the windblown hold—Jack with Aloysius's silver shotguns, Nobody with two pistols.

Bronzemen fell on all sides as they were shot in the head.

But only shots to their heads dropped them. Anything astray of that—shots to the chest or limbs—only left holes in their metal skins but did nothing to slow them.

The C-5's hold was now a bizarre scene: a crashed seaplane lying askew, many fallen bronzemen, many standing bronzemen, Jack and Nobody firing their guns as they moved forward from the rear and Yago and Easton up at the forward end of the long space.

'Kill them! Kill them! Kill them!' Yago roared.

There were bronzemen everywhere: too many of them, no matter how many special bullets Jack and Nobody had.

Easton looked from Yago to Jack and Nobody to the bronzemen and he knew he had to do something to help, so he sprang upward—his hands still bound behind his back—and shoulder-charged Yago from behind, knocking him to the metal floor of the hold.

As he himself hit the floor, Easton pulled up his knees and rolled his hands under his feet, bringing them in front of his body.

Jack and Nobody kept firing hard: left and right, right and left.

Jack's shotguns boomed. Nobody's pistols blazed.

But the bronzemen just kept coming, their faceless faces showing no fear as they advanced into the storm of specially tipped bullets coming at them.

Then Jack's Remingtons ran dry so he holstered them and drew his Desert Eagle pistols from a pair of shoulder-holsters and resumed firing.

Nobody kept shooting as well, then he too went dry and hurriedly reloaded.

But they just kept coming.

And in that moment Jack knew.

He'd miscalculated.

There were just too many bronzemen.

He kept firing, even though in his heart he knew it was hopeless.

The bronzemen were all around him and Nobody.

Jack 'killed' a bronzeman with a shot to the forehead at point-blank range, just as another bronzeman swung a razor-sharp claw at his head.

Jack ducked the blow and shot that one, too.

Nobody covered their left flank, firing repeatedly. But for every bronzeman he shot, another took its place.

'There're too many!' he yelled.

'We gotta . . . keep trying . . .' Jack called back just as the slide of one of his guns racked back, dry.

Out of the corner of his eye he saw Easton and Yago rolling around on the floor, struggling, grappling, fighting.

And then a bronzeman smacked Jack's other gun clean out of his hand and it went flying away. Jack dove against the wall of the hold, now totally defenceless.

The bronzeman advanced on him quickly, raised its clawed hand and without any hesitation swung at his throat and Jack shut his eyes—

—as a voice called, 'Bronzemen! Stop!'

The bronzeman's claw halted in mid-swing, inches from Jack's neck.

Jack snapped round to see who had spoken and his eyes widened when he saw that it had been Easton.

The sweet little minotaur had kicked himself clear of Yago and was standing apart from him.

His hands were still cuffed in front of him but on one of them, he was now wearing Yago's signet ring.

Every bronzeman in the hold stopped where it stood.

Jack was still pressed against the wall, but the bronzeman that seconds before had been about to slay him now stood dumbly and silently in front of him, motionless.

Yago sprang up from the ground, only for Easton to round on him and yell, 'Bronzemen! Seize him!'

The two nearest bronzemen snatched hold of the furious Yago, gripping him by his arms.

And suddenly Yago and Easton's roles were reversed: now the bronzemen held Yago in front of the short minotaur.

Wind whistled through the hold, but with the battle over, it was now much more quiet and still. It was only then that the other two passengers in the ICON A-10 dared to peer out from it: Iolanthe and Bertie. Iolanthe hopped lightly out of the plane. Bertie looked shell-shocked.

'Nobody, Iolanthe,' Jack said, 'go up to the flight deck and bring down the crew.'

Nobody reloaded his guns and headed upstairs with Iolanthe.

Jack joined Easton, removed his handcuffs, and stared impassively at Yago.

Easton turned to Jack, clearly confused. 'Captain Jack come to save Easton? Why?'

'Because you're part of my family now. Alby told me you got captured saving Ash. That in itself warrants a full-scale five-alarm rescue.'

'But Captain Jack could have died. Saving Easton might have ruined your plan to save world.'

Jack gave Easton a kind smile. 'We all get through this or we all die trying. No-one gets left behind, Easton.'

'Thank you, Captain Jack.'

He handed Jack the signet ring. 'Here. Easton think it is best for Captain Jack to have this. It command bronzemen.'

Jack turned the ring over in his fingers. It was exceedingly old and very striking.

Easton nodded at it. 'If you wear ring, bronzemen will do whatever you command. He was going to have the bronzemen walk me out that door.'

Jack looked at Yago. 'Is that so?'

Yago glared at Jack. 'I should have killed you when you were at Erebus.'

'As I recall, you were quite happy to let me rot there for the rest of my life,' Jack said. 'I was also at Hades's penthouse in New York when you had all his servants killed. You're a nasty piece of work, Yago.'

'*You can't win this!*' Yago spat. 'Sphinx is already at the gates to the Supreme Labyrinth. You will soon be living under his rule.'

Jack nodded sagely . . .

. . . as he slid the signet ring on his finger.

'But you won't. Live by the sword, die by the sword. Bronzemen, walk him out that rear ramp.'

Yago gaped in horror as the two bronzemen gripping him carried him toward the still-open rear ramp of the C-5.

Yago thrashed and screamed—'No! *Nooooo!*'—as they dragged him to the edge of the ramp and without so much as a pause simply stepped off it and dropped out of sight, taking Yago with them.

He fell twenty thousand feet, screaming all the way down, before he and the two bronzemen slammed into the Earth together.

Jack was kinder to the two pilots of the Super Galaxy.

He bound their hands behind their backs and put parachutes on them. Then he shoved them out the back of the plane, yanking on the ripcords as he did so, causing the parachutes to open. The two pilots would survive the fall.

Then, standing there inside the hold of the massive Super Galaxy with Easton and surrounded by bronzemen, Jack did something unexpected.

He handed Easton the signet ring.

'I think this should be yours, Easton,' he said. 'What we have here is a mini-legion of bronzemen and I can't think of a better guy to command them. Thanks for saving my dog.'

He gave Easton a big hug, a hug that the short minotaur returned in full.

Jack gazed around the hold and his searching eyes landed on some paint cans. They appeared to be filled with pale blue Air Force paint, the colour one applied to the exterior of a plane.

'Easton, you may want to use some of that paint to make sure we know which bronzemen are ours,' he said.

Easton nodded. 'Leave that to Easton, Captain Jack.'

'*Jack*,' Nobody's voice came in over the plane's intercom. '*Where to now?*'

Jack keyed the intercom. 'Mont Blanc. In a hurry.'

★ ★ ★

While all this was happening, Hades's estate lay eerily empty and silent.

Someone arrived at the estate.

Two someones.

A pair of men who gazed around at the evidence of the brutal assault that had taken place there.

The main house had literally been torn apart. Hit by the missile, its roof had been completely blown off. The once-gorgeous chateau was now a charred, open-air ruin.

The two men stared at the damage, taking it all in.

Then they strode away toward the lake.

THIRD OFFENSIVE

THE SECOND IRON MOUNTAIN: MONT BLANC

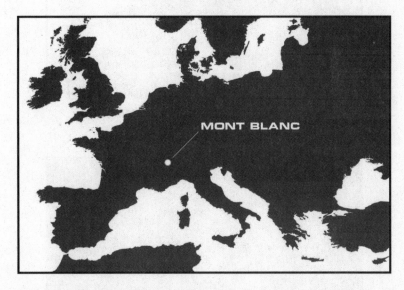

MONT BLANC

Apparently, buried within [Mont Blanc's] rocky core is a strange hollow structure that dates back over five thousand years. Once, when I politely asked to inspect it, the then King of Land—my own father—would not let me.

IOLANTHE COMPTON-JONES
THE THREE SECRET CITIES, P. 173
(MACMILLAN, SYDNEY, 2018)

**THE AIGUILLE DU MIDI MOUNTAIN
IN THE MONT BLANC MASSIF**

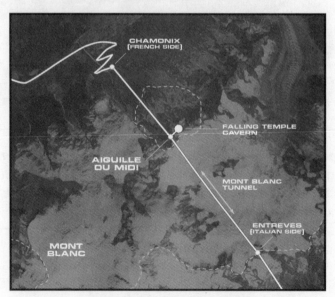

CHAMONIX
(FRENCH SIDE)

FALLING TEMPLE
CAVERN

AIGUILLE
DU MIDI

MONT BLANC
TUNNEL

ENTREVES
(ITALIAN SIDE)

MONT
BLANC

**THE AIGUILLE DU MIDI
AND THE MONT BLANC TUNNEL**

MONT BLANC MASSIF
FRENCH–ITALIAN BORDER
24 DECEMBER, 0340 HOURS

It wasn't a long flight to the French Alps—barely thirty minutes—so Jack got there quickly in his new Super Galaxy cargo plane.

What he wasn't expecting was all the activity on the airwaves as he arrived.

For as the snow-capped peaks of the Alps came into view—shimmering silver in the light of the full moon—frantic shouts and explosions blared out from his digital radio scanner.

Dion DeSaxe's voice was yelling: '*Keep firing! Keep firing, damn it!*'

Another voice shouted: '*Jaeger Eins, I got more enemy vehicles coming in from the Italian end of the motorway tunnel! Looks like the monks brought Romanian special forces with them.*'

Jaeger Eins called: '*Jaeger Drei, get over there with the bronzemen! Lord Dion and I are pinned down on the temple. Hold them off! We need more time in here!*'

And behind it all, the roar of helicopter rotors.

As Jack beheld the colossal mountain range before him—with the great bulk of Mont Blanc lording over all the other peaks—he listened to the voices of his enemies.

It sounded like chaos down there.

When he'd initiated the radio interception algorithm, Jack had hoped to hear a few bland sit-reps or sentry check-ins that might give him a clue as to the location of the Falling Temple within the mountain range.

What he heard was gunfire, explosions, panicked orders and helicopters.

Dion's voice again, furious: '*Fucking Omega monks! Cut them down! CUT THEM DOWN!*'

Jaeger Eins's voice was calmer: '*Knights, I repeat, hold off their reinforcements in the motorway tunnel. We can't do the Fall in here until the clearing pod has removed all the ice and snow from the moon shaft. Jaeger Vier, report.*'

'*Sir, this is Vier. All quiet here in the observa—*'

Gunfire.

An explosion.

Screams.

'*Sir! This is Vier! Correction! We have hostile contacts attacking us up in the observatory! Maybe ten men in total. Paratroopers. Coming in from the air!*'

'*Hold that observatory, Vier, till we do the Fall. Then carry out your orders. Eins, out.*'

Jack listened in stunned silence.

Beside him in the cockpit of the stolen Super Galaxy, Nobody, Iolanthe, Bertie and Easton did the same.

Jack's mind spun: temples, observatories, a clearing pod, the Knights of the Golden Eight . . . and one specific detail.

'The motorway tunnel,' he said. 'That's the way in. There must be a side tunnel branching off it somewhere under the mountain, a tunnel that gives access to the Falling Temple. Iolanthe, you once told me that there was a hollow structure inside Mont Blanc that your father wouldn't let you see. It must be the Hall of the Falling Temple. Looks like you get to it via the motorway tunnel that runs underneath the massif.'

Bertie asked, 'What's a clearing pod?'

'It's a little cable-mounted elevator-cage that you use to clean out mine shafts that have been clogged up with debris,' Jack said. 'Mont Blanc isn't like Mont Saint-Michel. It's been open to the elements for centuries, so its moon shaft must have got filled with ice and snow. Dion has to clear it out before the moon arrives directly overhead.'

Nobody said, 'But it sounds like someone else came here as well: the Omega monks, with Romanian muscle.'

That was when a second set of voices—hushed, cooler and calmer—came in over the intercepts:

'*Brother Esrael. Take that temple chamber. If we are to help Brother Ezekiel, we must have control of this temple before the shaft is cleared, the moon is overhead and the DeSaxe boy can do the Fall—*'

'*Copy that—*'

Brother Ezekiel, Jack thought, hearing the familiar name.

The leader of the Order of the Omega, the secretive brotherhood of monks from Venice who knew more about the Omega Event than anyone and who had vanished a few weeks ago. Mae and Lynda had encountered a few of them in Rome and now more of them were here, evidently trying to perform the Fall and thus get access to the Supreme Labyrinth, and also, from what they were saying, to somehow help their leader, Brother Ezekiel, who was elsewhere.

'The Omega monks,' Jack said, his eyes narrowing. 'This could be a break for us. While these two forces fight, we might be able to slip past them and do the Fall. Hit the gas. We have to get to that motorway.'

Opened in 1965, the Mont Blanc motorway tunnel connects France with Italy. It is over ten kilometres long.

An incredible feat of engineering, it is an important trade route that allows freight trucks from both countries to go under the otherwise impassable Alps.

As Jack knew, however, it is also slightly misnamed.

For the Mont Blanc Tunnel does not actually pass beneath Mont Blanc. Rather, it passes directly underneath the summit of another mountain of the Mont Blanc Massif: the high peak known as the Aiguille du Midi—the Needle of Midday.

The Aiguille du Midi is a truly striking mountain, tall and slender, with almost vertical flanks dropping away from its pointed peak.

A cluster of man-made structures sits atop that summit, perched precariously above the drop, looking out over the glorious mountain range.

Among these structures—all connected by walkways and bridges—is a cable-car station, some tourist viewing balconies, a twelve-storey-tall astronomical observatory with a domed roof encasing its telescope and, on the mountain's summit, a high needle-like antenna.

As their huge plane began its descent, Jack looked out at the snow-covered mountains below him. The Mont Blanc Massif was a mini mountain range of eleven peaks that were part of the larger French Alps.

'We don't have time to be pretty about this,' he said grimly. 'We go in hard and we go in ugly but most of all, we go in fast.'

Fifteen minutes later, with the blazing full moon now almost directly over the Mont Blanc Massif, Jack's stolen Super Galaxy zoomed in low over the Alps.

Alby had done the calculations. The moon, with its pedestal, would be directly overhead at 4:03 a.m.

Suddenly, two tiny figures—Nobody and Iolanthe, dressed in high-altitude parachute gear—dropped out of the Galaxy's rear ramp and plummeted through the sky toward the moonlit mountains.

Back in the Super Galaxy, Jack, Easton and four of their newly-painted bronzemen manoeuvred the A10 seaplane—still sitting askew in the hold—toward the open rear ramp.

Since the heads of Easton's bronzemen were all now splattered with pale blue Air Force paint, Jack had decided to call them 'palemen'.

Jack tethered the seaplane to the Super Galaxy with a cable and ordered Easton and the four palemen into it.

As they jumped inside, Jack went over to Bertie, the last remaining member of their team on the plane and the only one who would stay on it, with the remaining thirty palemen.

Bertie looked doubtfully at the little seaplane. 'The landing gear looks like it took a beating when you crashed this plane inside the hold. You sure you can land it?'

Jack shrugged. 'It'll be okay. Landing gear isn't necessary for my plan.'

'Okay,' Bertie said. 'What about this plane? Tell me again how this cargo plane is going to land safely without anyone flying it?'

In answer, Jack hit his radio. 'Alby? You there?'

'*Copy, Jack,*' came Alby's voice.

'Have you got full control of the C-5M now?'

Alby said, '*Banking left now.*' The plane banked gently to the left.

Jack nodded to Brother Bertie. 'Alby has control of this plane. He'll land you at a private airport outside Dijon. It's the best I can do, unless you want to join me in a hellish firefight.'

'Well, I . . . I mean—' Bertie stammered.

'You'll be fine,' Jack said. 'I gotta go.'

'But will *you* be fine?' Bertie said. 'That nasty DeSaxe boy, the Omega monks, the Knights of the Golden Eight, plus who knows how many bronzemen. You don't know what you're flying into.'

Jack pursed his lips and nodded. 'We still have to try. See you on the ground.'

He strode back to the seaplane, now perched on the edge of the Super Galaxy's rear ramp.

He untethered it, then climbed in and nodded to Easton, who called to the first row of palemen still standing in the hold: 'Push this vehicle out!'

The palemen did so and with a sudden lurch . . .

. . . the seaplane dropped, rear-end first, out of the cargo plane.

It fell through the sky backwards at first, before reorienting itself nose-down . . .

. . . when its engines kicked in and the plane swooped away, guided by Jack in the pilot's seat, heading full tilt toward Mont Blanc and the Aiguille du Midi.

Jack recalled Dion saying over the radio that the Omega monks' forces were attacking from the Italian end of the car tunnel, so he aimed for the northern end, the French end, near the town of Chamonix.

Jack flew low and tight against the mountains, keeping to the valleys and canyons so as to avoid being detected by any radars, until at the very last moment, as his little seaplane approached Chamonix, it sprang out from behind a mountainside, banking hard and zooming fast.

As Jack had hoped, Dion's forces had gone into the tunnel to tackle the Omega threat coming from the other end, which meant there were only a few vehicles here: three troop trucks and a couple of machine gun–mounted jeeps.

Dion's troops were all caught by surprise by the sudden appearance of the seaplane whipping out from the darkness behind a nearby mountain.

They were doubly surprised when the little plane, flown determinedly by Jack, *didn't stop*.

It swept in over the road, zooming just above the vehicles parked near the tunnel's entrance, impossibly low, before—*whoosh!*—it shot like a bullet into the motorway tunnel!

From Jack's point of view, it was hair-raising.

One second he was soaring in the silver moonlight through snow-covered canyons flanked by rocky mountainsides.

The next, he was blasting out over the road and some military vehicles and then—

—*whoosh!*—

—the walls of the tunnel were shooting past him on either side in superfast blurs of motion.

The tunnel was modern and wide, with two broad lanes big enough to accommodate two full-sized semitrailers travelling in opposite directions, plus raised sidewalks on either side in case of breakdowns.

Which is to say the car tunnel was just wide enough for Jack's seaplane to *fly down it* at insane speed.

It took all of Jack's concentration to keep from hitting the tunnel's walls with his wingtips, but he managed it and after a short time,

he saw them: a larger cluster of parked trucks, motorcycles, jeeps—and *dead bodies*, perhaps twenty of them—arrayed around an open escape door set into the left-hand wall of the tunnel.

He turned to Easton and his four palemen. 'Hang on! This is gonna be really ugly!'

What he'd said about not needing landing gear was true.

Jack pressed forward on his steering yoke and brought the seaplane into a controlled skid against the asphalt surface of the tunnel's roadway.

The sleek A10 touched down . . . its landing pontoons screaming against the asphalt before snapping off . . . and then the little plane skidded on its belly, kicking up a thousand sparks . . . right into the midst of the vehicles parked at the side door.

The runaway seaplane drove through the cluster of vehicles, sending them flying every which way, before it hit a jeep, bounced off it and slammed up against a parked troop truck.

Jack was already moving, unbuckling his seatbelt and kicking open his door.

Easton and his palemen did the same, following him.

In his radio earpiece, Jack heard gunfire, the roaring of chopper rotors and the desperate shouts of Dion and the Omega monks doing battle inside the temple chamber.

Jack pointed at the large escape door set into the left-hand wall.

'Easton! Get your palemen into formation around us. We're going into a hornets' nest, where two groups of hornets are already fighting.'

With those words they ran from the crumpled seaplane—*Sexy Prince One*, once Dion's pleasure flyer but now a battered wreck—through the side door that led to the Hall of the Falling Temple of this Iron Mountain.

They ran for about a hundred metres down a wide rough-walled tunnel.

At the end of the tunnel was an enormous ancient archway

covered in Thoth glyphs and, on its magnificent keystone, a primitive version of Newton's drawing of the moon poised over the
Earth, its lone mountain aimed down at one on the surface of
the Earth.

Artificial light from floodlights leaked out through the archway
from within.

Flashes of gunfire strobed.

The *thump-thump-thump* of a helicopter shook the air.

And Jack caught glimpses of running men—or bronzemen, he
couldn't tell—racing across the entryway, silhouetted against the
light.

He swallowed.

It was a hornets' nest all right.

Then he arrived at the archway and gazed out into the space and
said, 'What have we walked into?'

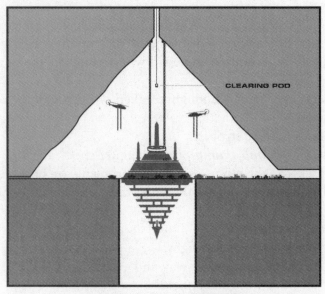

THE FALLING TEMPLE
INSIDE THE AIGUILLE DU MIDI
(SIDE VIEW)

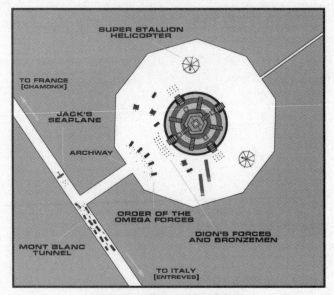

THE FALLING TEMPLE
(OVERHEAD VIEW)

It was absolute pandemonium.

The battle raging inside the chamber of this Falling Temple was big, wild, loud and *bitter*.

There was movement everywhere and it took Jack a moment to take it all in.

First, there was the place itself.

It looked broadly similar to the Hall of the Falling Temple he'd seen at Mont Saint-Michel: a gigantic rock-walled cavern with a gorgeous multi-levelled spinning top-shaped temple in its centre. As at Mont Saint-Michel, this Falling Temple was suspended by ancient chains above a broad shaft that plummeted into the bowels of the Earth.

Likewise, directly *above* the temple was a much narrower shaft—barely wider than a man—that shot upward, presumably, Jack figured, all the way up through the body of the Aiguille du Midi to its summit.

A tiny cable snaked out from this smaller shaft, reaching down to the top level of the Falling Temple where it ended at a little man-sized cage.

The cage had a motorised winch of some kind attached to it, plus a lever. It was the shaft-clearing pod that Dion's men had used to clean out the moon shaft, preparing it for the moon's arrival overhead.

Jack figured that among the many structures perched on top of the Aiguille du Midi, one was basically a cap that concealed the moon shaft. But those structures hadn't been built till recent times.

Centuries of hard-packed snow must have filled the shaft and Dion had had to clean it out.

But that was just the place.

Then there were the two rival forces in it—men, vehicles and weapons.

The two forces were positioned simply: one was in the centre of the cavern, either on or defending the Falling Temple. That was Dion and his people.

The second force was arrayed *around* the temple, trying to move in on it and take it. That was the Order of the Omega and their troops.

Jack took in the battle from the centre outward.

Standing on the temple itself, taking cover behind its obelisks and podiums, were Dion DeSaxe and Jaeger Eins, firing their guns desperately.

They were on the second-to-top level of the temple, trying to reach the enormous main obelisk on the topmost level, and they were flanked by two Knights of the Golden Eight, their guns also raised and firing.

Ringing the base of the Falling Temple—just outside the narrow gap between it and the edge of the shaft—were perhaps fifty bronzemen, facing outward and now armed with glistening bronze spears. Jack didn't know where they'd got those from.

But the Knights and the bronzemen were not Dion's only allies.

Not one but two Super Stallion helicopters hovered in the air above the temple, tongues of fire blazing out from their side-mounted cannons, defending Dion.

It was an impressive and bizarre sight: seeing two of the world's biggest military choppers flying *inside* an enclosed space like this.

They fired heavy-bore tracer rounds and their already deafening rotor-noise echoed off the walls of the giant cavern, making it hard to hear anything else above the din.

Thick hauling chains dangled from the two choppers, flailing around like dangerous whips as the two choppers banked and fired.

Why bring helicopters here? Jack thought.

And then he saw the chains above the Falling Temple and he understood.

The chains were frozen solid, encased in thick ice. Dion had brought the choppers in to haul up the Falling Temple—with him on it—after he'd performed the Fall.

Three tanks, three troop trucks and two long flatbed transporter trucks—which must have brought in the choppers with their rotors folded on their backs—were parked at the near edge of the temple.

Jack then took in the second, outer force trying to reach the Falling Temple.

It comprised five military jeeps, each mounted with a powerful 23-millimetre anti-aircraft cannon and marked with a blue-yellow-and-red flag on its flanks.

The jeeps were parked just inside the archway, their cannons pointed both upward at the choppers and downward at the bronzemen, the camouflaged soldiers on their rear trays firing relentlessly at both targets. Unlike regular pistol and rifle rounds, the larger anti-aircraft rounds hurled the bronzemen off their feet, forcing them back but not killing them.

Jack saw the blue-yellow-and-red flag painted on the jeeps.

The Romanian flag.

Romanian troops, he thought. *The Omega Order's muscle. Probably a handful of ultra-conservative Catholic regiments from an ultra-conservative Catholic country, glad to assist the ultra-conservative order of monks.*

Sure enough, Jack saw then that the two men leading the Romanian troops, barking orders at them, were Omega monks.

And, last of all, there was Easton and him and their four palemen.

'Okay,' Jack said, 'how are we gonna do this—?'

At that moment, a rogue bronzeman appeared right beside Jack, emerging from underneath a toppled vehicle, and lunged at him, only for two of the palemen to cut between it and Jack, tackle it and fight it off.

'Sheesh . . .' Jack gasped.

'*Jack!*' Alby's voice burst through his earpiece. '*The moon is coming into position above the Aiguille du Midi! It'll be in place directly above you in about ten seconds and stay there for fourteen minutes. If you want to do the Fall here, you better get moving!*'

'Right,' Jack said, his mind spinning.

Suddenly, one chopper's tracer fire hit one of the jeeps and there was a huge explosion and the jeep flew backwards through the air, slamming into the wall a metre to Jack's right.

Return fire from three of the other jeeps hit that Super Stallion and its engines blew apart. It wheeled in the air and began to list . . . falling . . .

. . . and with a colossal noise, the great chopper crashed down on top of twenty bronzemen, its rotors slashing against the stone floor of the chamber, kicking up sparks, emitting an ear-splitting squeal before the entire chopper exploded and shrapnel showered out like bullet-fire in every direction.

Every man in the cavern, including Jack, ducked for cover as sizzling pieces of the chopper lodged in the walls.

The bronzemen didn't duck. Those that were in the direct line of the explosion were knocked down by the force of the blast or the shrapnel, but not killed.

It was exactly the distraction Dion needed.

For right then, it happened.

The clock struck 4:03 and the moon moved into position directly above the Aiguille du Midi and a laser-like beam of green light shot down from it into the mountain's moon shaft and *slammed* into the obelisk atop the Falling Temple, illuminating the entire cavern in an unearthly green glow.

Jack looked at the brilliantly illuminated temple in dismay. 'No!'

He could only watch helplessly as, at that moment, while everyone else in the cavern was still taking cover, Dion bounded up onto the topmost level of the Falling Temple.

There, covered by Jaeger Eins and the other two Knights of the

Golden Eight, their guns extended and firing hard, Dion planted his right hand on one of the palm symbols at the base of the main obelisk and suddenly the whole massive sixteen-storey temple dropped from Jack's sight, disappearing into the shaft.

The temple fell fast, the walls of the shaft whipping upward on every side of it.

On the temple, Dion knew what he had to do, and with Jaeger Eins by his side, after holding his palm to the altar as it passed through the upper annulus, he sprinted down the many levels of the temple—its eight upper levels and its eight lower ones—until he came to the bottommost level, where he planted his palm on a hand image cut into the second altar there just as the temple shot through the lower annulus set into the shaft's curving walls.

He now had the vital key-marks seared onto his hand.

And then, just as had happened with Sphinx at the Falling Temple at Mont Saint-Michel, the 'brakes' of this temple extended out from its middle level and grinded loudly against the stone walls of the shaft, bringing the great falling structure to a spectacular halt.

Gasping with relief and exhilaration, Dion and Jaeger Eins looked at each other and clasped hands.

Dion had performed the Fall.

Dion clambered back up onto the upper half of the Falling Temple.

He looked up the shaft.

High above him, tiny in the distance, he saw his remaining Super Stallion chopper, its rotors spinning in a blurring circle.

He keyed his radio. 'Chopper Two, get down here and pick us

up. With Chopper One down, we won't be able to haul this temple back up. Come down and get us!'

He caught his breath and keyed his radio again. 'Observatory team. We're done down here. You good up there?'

'*We're fine, sir,*' came the reply from the Knight up there, Jaeger Vier. '*We held them off and killed them all. They appear to have been Romanian paratroopers.*'

Dion said, 'Use the lunar rover to cover the pedestal again with the Kapton foil sheet and then destroy the uplink to the rover. No-one else can be allowed to do another Fall at *any* other mountain now.'

Dion turned to Jaeger Eins. 'My friend, we did it. Let's get the fuck out of this place and go join Sphinx at the Labyrinth.'

Jack heard Dion's words over his earpiece.

The first part about not being able to haul the temple back up was bad enough. But the last part gave Jack a chill:

'*Use the lunar rover to cover the pedestal again with the Kapton foil sheet and then destroy the uplink to the rover. No-one else can be allowed to do another Fall at* any *other mountain now.*'

As he listened, he watched the remaining Super Stallion lower itself *into* the wide stone shaft into which the ancient temple had dropped. It was going down to pick up Dion.

His mind raced.

They'd arrived here minutes too late and now Dion had performed the Fall, granting him the ability to enter the Supreme Labyrinth.

Worse, it also looked like he had people remotely operating a lunar rover on the moon and using it to cover the pedestal up there with thermal foil, the pedestal that was crucial to performing another Fall.

The lunar mountain, an ancient pedestal, thermal foil, a rover, plus iron mountains and multiple forces down here. It was all too much.

Then the Super Stallion reappeared from the shaft and Jack glimpsed Dion and Jaeger Eins in it, flanked by Knights and bronzemen.

A missile streaked out of the chopper's right-side pod and shot down into the shaft. A few seconds later, an explosion boomed from deep down there.

Jack reeled.

'He just destroyed the Falling Temple,' he said. 'So no-one can lift it up again and do a Fall. He's ensuring no-one can follow him and Sphinx into the Supreme Labyrinth.'

The Super Stallion carrying Dion and Jaeger Eins pivoted in the air, turning toward the entrance tunnel.

But as it did, Jack heard a series of muffled booms coming from that tunnel.

Boom . . .

Boom . . .

Boom . . .

Jack frowned.

They didn't sound like explosions. They sounded more like . . . like a truck or large vehicle pounding through smaller ones—

With a mighty roar, a massive Mack truck with a metal snow-plough mounted on its nose thundered into the cavern from the entrance tunnel!

It was a huge thing and it pushed two jeeps and a troop truck ahead of it, having collected them on its way in.

As it sped out into the wider cavern, two 50-millimetre anti-aircraft cannons mounted on the truck's rear bed mowed down the bronzemen in the hall with tracer fire, ripping their heads off, so large and powerful were the rounds.

The mighty Mack truck took out the other vehicles parked near the entrance, sending them tumbling left and right as they bounced off its huge grille.

As it did so, its guns kept blazing wildly and Jack saw one of his palemen over by a jeep near the fall shaft—it was one of the two that had saved his life—get decapitated by one of the huge rounds and fall instantly, dead.

Then a second identical Mack truck—also with a snowplough and anti-aircraft cannons—came in behind the first one and it

stopped right in the archway of the cavern, blocking the exit almost completely.

A giant of a man stepped out of the first Mack truck and gazed over the cavern as if he owned it.

He took in the scene: Dion's force and the Omega force, but he did not see Jack and Easton behind a toppled jeep.

Jack didn't recognise him.

'Who is this guy?' he breathed. Could it be the general named Rastor that Zoe had talked about?

The giant looked up at Dion in his hovering chopper and smiled a wicked, amused grin.

'Hades Junior!' the giant called. 'You have performed the Fall! Respect to you!'

From his hiding spot, Jack watched the exchange closely: Dion's chopper hovering inside the cavern, facing off against this huge fellow and his two trucks blocking the exit. Oddly, despite Dion's clear advantage in firepower, the giant seemed to dominate the situation.

Dion's voice came over the Super Stallion's speakers: '*General Rastor! A new era is upon us! A new world order! Join Sphinx and me! Be our general!*'

So this is Rastor, Jack thought.

The giant smiled again.

A truly sinister grin.

'I work for no man,' he boomed. 'I have been freed from Erebus, and with the world open for the taking, I will impose my own order. Run, Hades Junior! Run to the maze, because I will meet you there soon enough!'

Jack saw Dion shout some orders to his pilots and, to Jack's astonishment, the chopper immediately banked *away* from General Rastor and made for the opposite side of the cavern . . .

. . . where Jack spied a lone jeep parked at the mouth of a small tunnel, a tunnel Jack hadn't seen until now.

'There's another exit,' he whispered. 'A priests' tunnel. I should've known.'

Before Jack could do anything more, the chopper hovered close to the ground, allowing Dion and Jaeger Eins to jump down directly into the jeep. They sped away into the little tunnel in the jeep, fleeing, while the chopper immediately took to the air again to defend them.

As the jeep shoomed off into the darkness of the tunnel, Jack saw Jaeger Eins toss a couple of grenades behind it and the grenades detonated.

Two short, sharp explosions . . .

. . . and the entryway to the little escape tunnel caved in, filling with rocks and dust.

And suddenly Jack and Easton were stuck in the cavern of the Falling Temple with the monks of Omega and the fearsome General Rastor.

What happened next happened really fast.

A grey-clad masked trooper sprang from Rastor's Mack truck with an RPG launcher on his shoulder and fired it at the Super Stallion that had unloaded Dion.

The shot hit its mark and the chopper exploded and wheeled around wildly inside the enclosed space of the cavern, engines squealing, smoke belching from its wound.

The huge helicopter slammed down against the stone floor of the cavern nose-first, its rotor blades snapping off instantly.

As this happened, the chopper's tail got entangled in one of the mighty ancient chains dangling from the ceiling of the cavern and the whole sorry helicopter ended up nose down, ass up: its nose balanced on the edge of the fall shaft, its tail hanging from the ancient frozen chains.

Five Omega monks and five of their Romanian troops tried to make for the exit tunnel, but more of Rastor's troops—perhaps twenty of them—sprang from his Mack trucks and quickly encircled them, guns up, and the monks and the Romanians dropped their weapons and raised their hands.

And Jack and Easton—hiding behind their overturned jeep—got to watch a most unusual exchange.

Rastor stood over the lead monk, gripped by two of his grey-clad, masked troops.

'What is your name, monk?'

'Brother Esrael.'

'And your position in your order?'

'I am second to Brother Ezekiel.'

Rastor nodded. 'I know your ways, monk, for I was once one of you. Tell me, did Ezekiel succeed at Potala before the iron mountain there was destroyed by Sphinx's missile?'

Jack shot bolt upright at that.

So did Brother Esrael.

'I . . . he . . . how did you know . . . ?' the monk stammered in surprise.

Rastor reached down and grabbed Brother Esrael by the throat with one of his massive hands.

He lifted the helpless monk two feet off the ground.

'I said, did your brother monk perform the Fall at the iron mountain underneath Potala Palace in Lhasa, Tibet, before Sphinx destroyed that mountain with a nuclear missile?'

Gasping for air, his hands clawing at the mighty fist gripping his throat, Brother Esrael choked: 'Yes . . . yes, Ezekiel did.'

'And he is now heading to the Supreme Labyrinth?' Rastor asked.

'Yes . . .'

Jack watched in stunned silence, his mind now spinning even more at what he was hearing.

Sphinx had performed his Fall at Mont Saint-Michel.

And Dion had just done the same here at Mont Blanc.

But Ezekiel had also performed the Fall at another iron mountain in Tibet and was right now on his way to the Supreme Labyrinth.

Still holding the monk high above the floor, Rastor shook his head in disappointment.

'Your order seeks a world where women and their bodies are the property of men. If your Brother Ezekiel succeeds at the great maze, that is the world he will fashion.'

The monk named Esrael continued to choke.

Rastor continued. 'What a petty philosophy.' He held the choking monk's face up to his own. 'Why have men, women, or even a universe at all?'

And with those words, the giant general broke the monk's neck and Brother Esrael's body went limp, dead.

Rastor threw his corpse to the floor.

'Kill these other monks and their Romanian friends,' he said to his troopers as he strolled casually toward the fall shaft.

Machine-gun fire rang out. The remaining monks and Romanians were shot to bits where they knelt.

Reaching the edge of the fall shaft, Rastor paused at a body on the ground. It was the body of a bronzeman that had been shot clean through the head by one of his huge 50-millimetre rounds.

'What have we here?'

The bronzeman's head and shoulders were marked with pale blue Air Force paint. It was one of Easton's palemen. The one Jack had seen get shot before.

'A bronzeman marked with paint . . .' Rastor said. 'Most irregular. But clever. Now who would think of such a thing?'

The giant turned and raised his voice. 'Captain West! Are you in here? If you are, you might as well reveal yourself, because we will find you eventually.'

Jack's heart almost stopped.

'What do we do?' Easton whispered.

Jack didn't answer.

He just stood up, revealing himself to Rastor.

Rastor stared evenly at Jack.

'Captain West,' he said slowly. 'The man who tore asunder the system of the four kingdoms. Word of your remarkable exploits at the Great Games reached all the way to the innermost dungeon of Erebus. Why, I believe we were both residents there at the same time, for a short while at least.'

'Who are you?' Jack said.

'My name is General Garthon Rastor. As a young man, I was a member of the Omega Order. There I learned about the end of all things. But monastic life did not suit me, so I joined an army. Ruthlessness served me well and I rose in rank until I was a general of the four kings.

'I was their sword, their finest general . . . until I was not. Until they came to fear me. Then one day they drugged my wine and abducted me and locked me away in the bowels of Erebus.'

As Rastor spoke, Jack pushed Easton backwards, toward the downward-tilted Super Stallion helicopter tangled in the chains above the fall shaft.

'Why would the four kings fear you?' he asked.

'Why does any king fear a general of his? Because the general was becoming too beloved by his troops. Because he was becoming a threat. And because I—and those who follow me—believe in nothing.'

'Nothing? What does that mean?' Jack said. The chopper was now right behind him and Easton.

Rastor grinned that grin of his.

'I believe in the Omega Event. The end of all things. The *nothing* that must follow the moment when the universe collapses in on itself.

'I don't seek to rule the world like Sphinx and his ilk. I don't seek to enslave women like the monks of Omega wish to. I want to enter the Supreme Labyrinth in order to *stop* Sphinx and the monks from sitting on the World Throne. I desire that no-one sits on that throne when Omega comes. I want to *let* the Omega Event happen as it should. I want the universe to collapse as it is meant to.'

In that moment, Jack saw madness—pure yet calculated madness—in Rastor's eyes.

'We have to get out of here, *now*,' Jack whispered to Easton. 'Just follow me, okay.'

Without warning, Jack dived into the cockpit of the downturned Super Stallion and pulled the missile-launch trigger on its control stick.

A missile blasted out from the chopper's port-side pod and, with a *whoosh*, flew right into Rastor's lead Mack truck and blew it apart in a booming explosion.

The truck was lifted completely off the ground and slammed back against the stone wall behind it.

Rastor's men dived for cover. Rastor hardly even flinched.

Easton was watching all this in amazement when Jack yanked hard on his arm, pulling him up onto the roof of the steeply-tilted helicopter's fuselage . . .

. . . and all of a sudden the two of them were running up the length of the crashed helicopter, toward its tail, still entangled in one of the ancient chains hanging from the cavern's ceiling.

Easton had no idea what Jack was thinking when he saw it.

A short distance from the chopper's tail was the clearing pod, still suspended from its cable, the cable that ran up into the slender moon shaft at the very peak of the temple chamber.

When the Falling Temple had been in its resting position, the pod had been hanging above its upper levels. But after the temple had fallen, the pod had simply been left to hang from its cable above the yawning fall shaft.

As Jack and Easton came to the tail of the downturned chopper, Jack called, 'Jump!'

He and Easton dived together off the tail of the chopper.

Jack caught the bottom edge of the clearing pod and Easton caught Jack.

The pod was little more than an open-air cage with a diesel motor and some ice-drills for chipping away at obstructions in the shaft.

Rastor called, 'Kill them!'

Hanging from the bottom of the pod by his titanium left hand, Jack reached up with his natural right hand and yanked on the lever that activated the pod's motorised winch.

And suddenly the little pod shot upward on its cable, zooming up into the moon shaft, and as their enemies opened fire and the hard stone roof of the cavern was strafed with bullets, Jack and Easton whizzed up into the hole in the middle of ceiling.

Jack and Easton shoomed up the tight, dark shaft on their pod, its cable-winch whirring shrilly.

The cylindrical stone walls rushed by close beside them, barely a foot away.

As they whizzed upward, Jack spoke into his throat-mike: 'Nobody! Iolanthe! I don't know if you're up at the observatory yet, but Easton and I are on our way there via the moon shaft!'

They shot vertically upward for quite a distance before they burst out into bright light inside a room at the summit of the Aiguille du Midi. Their pod hung from a sturdy tripod that straddled the moon shaft.

The pod jerked to a halt and Jack and Easton swung dumbly as their upward journey abruptly ceased.

They looked around themselves—

—to see many dead bodies arrayed around them. The bodies of dead Romanian paratroopers.

'Jack!' someone called and Jack spun to see Iolanthe and Nobody running into the room.

Nobody lifted Jack and Easton out of the pod. 'We got lucky. Musta missed the firefight by minutes. Dion's people just left here in a chopper.'

'Jack, come on,' Iolanthe said. 'There's something up here we have to show you.'

SUMMIT OF THE AIGUILLE DU MIDI

Nobody and Iolanthe guided Jack and Easton through the collection of structures that sat perched atop the Aiguille du Midi mountain.

It was an odd assortment of buildings—some new, some old; some made of concrete and steel, others of faded wood—all constructed at different times in history.

Jack and Easton had emerged at the very peak of the mount, far from the tourist viewing balconies, the public cafeteria and the enormous cable-car station. Their shaft had literally bored down through the spine of the mountain. It had been capped by a high antenna which Dion's people had moved to one side for the Fall.

Nobody and Iolanthe guided them further away from the public areas, toward the 'professional area' on the other side of the Aiguille du Midi; a group of structures that included weather huts, satellite dishes and, most striking of all, the observatory.

Twelve storeys tall, silver and cylindrical, more than anything else, the Aiguille du Midi Astronomical Observatory resembled a wheat silo.

Its curving silver walls gleamed in the moonlight, looking like something out of a science fiction movie.

Its top was domed, and poking out from it was the tip of a massive optical telescope.

'This way,' Nobody urged, guiding Jack inside the observatory.

Moments later, Jack stood inside the main chamber of the observatory.

The huge telescope dominated the space, rising high above him, its colossal lens pointed almost vertically upward, directly at—

'The moon,' Jack said.

Iolanthe nodded as she raced to the base of the massive telescope and its eyepiece. A rolling trolley stacked with computers and other devices sat beside it.

One of the computers, Jack glimpsed as he went past it, was horribly smashed and broken, as if someone had taken to it with a sledgehammer.

'Quickly, Jack, you have to see what it's pointed at,' she said.

Jack hurried over to the eyepiece. It was so strange, he thought, that this massive device served a single human eye.

Jack peered into the eyepiece—

—and saw the surface of the moon in astonishingly close-up detail.

He saw a grey sandy expanse, a crater, some mountains, and in the exact middle of the image—

—two small vehicles with square metal bodies, spindly arms and six fat tyres each.

'Lunar rovers,' Jack breathed.

'Look at what's beside them,' Iolanthe said.

Jack did.

And he swallowed deeply.

Beside the lunar rovers, on the otherwise barren surface of the moon was a perfectly rectangular slab of rock.

'Nature doesn't build in straight lines,' he said softly.

'It sure doesn't,' Iolanthe said. 'It's the pedestal. The one that aligns with each iron mountain and sends down its beam of green light during which one performs the Fall.'

Jack said, 'There's something on it.'

He could see a rumpled sheet of material lying on top of the altar-like pedestal.

'It's thermal foil,' Iolanthe said. 'Aluminised Kapton foil. It's an insulation material used on spacecraft to protect them from solar radiation. That pedestal is located in a range of mountains on the moon known as the Apennines, beside a flat section of land called the Sea of Rains, which is where—'

'—the *Apollo 15* astronauts landed on the moon. The fourth Apollo mission,' Jack said. 'Hades said it was the important one. It was also the first mission to use a lunar rover.'

'But there are two rovers there,' Nobody said.

Jack said, 'The Soviet Union never landed *people* on the moon, but they did successfully land several remotely operated probes and rovers to perform experiments. Looks like they drove one of those rovers here.'

'That was probably at the direction of royal operatives,' Iolanthe added.

Jack leaned back from the eyepiece.

A screen beside it showed the coordinates of the lunar site it was aimed at.

Latitude Deg N (Davies system)	Longitude Deg E
26.13333	3.62837
26.13407	3.62981
26.13224	3.63400

Jack gazed at them thoughtfully. 'I've seen these coordinates before . . .'

Then he remembered where: in Venice, at the abandoned head-quarters of the Order of the Omega.

He looked at Iolanthe. 'The Omega monks had all this information. And I just heard downstairs that they successfully performed the Fall at Potala Palace before it was destroyed. I also heard Dion say something about destroying the uplink to the rover.'

Iolanthe jerked her chin at the destroyed computer on the trolley beside the telescope's eyepiece.

'That would be that uplink computer,' she said flatly. 'His people covered the top of the pedestal with the Kapton foil and then they smashed the uplink to the only thing that can *uncover* it: the rovers. Jack, even if we knew where the last two mountains were, while that pedestal is covered, *we can't perform the Fall.*'

Jack took this all in, biting his lip in thought.

'Goddamn it,' he said. 'Goddamn it all . . .'

As if in answer, the monitor on one of the computers beside Jack came to life and a face appeared on it.

'*Hello there, Captain West.*'

On the computer screen, smirking at Jack and the others, was the disfigured face of Dion DeSaxe.

'*You seem to have arrived at the party a little late, Captain.*' Dion seemed to be standing on a runway of some sort, in front of a jet aircraft and some military vehicles. The Alps rose in the background behind him.

He wasn't far away, maybe down in Chamonix.

'I figure things out eventually,' Jack said.

Dion snorted. '*Like you did at the Games. Don't worry, you didn't miss all of this party. For instance, you haven't missed the fireworks. Fire.*'

That final word was spoken to someone offscreen.

Dion stepped aside to allow Jack to see the large vehicle on the runway behind him.

It was an M270 mobile missile launcher.

On its back was a pod containing two Lockheed Martin MGM-140E surface-to-surface tactical missiles.

With twin blazes of white-hot tail fire, the two missiles launched, shooting off into the sky.

'*Goodbye, Captain West. Enjoy the fireworks. Because you're about to be a part of them*,' Dion said a moment before the computer screen went black.

Jack heard them before he saw them.

Heard the distinct *whoosh-whoosh* of the two surface-to-surface missiles sweeping around the peak of the Aiguille du Midi.

The missiles had not needed to travel far to reach their target.

Jack didn't have any time to react.

No time to run or flee.

One after the other, the two MGM-140E missiles slammed into the twelve-storey observatory perched on the mountaintop.

The first struck the base of the tall cylindrical building, its quarter-ton warhead detonating in a shockingly powerful explosion.

The building shuddered.

The walls squealed.

The foundations cracked.

That was when the second missile hit and, just as it was designed to do, finished the job.

The blast of its warhead caused the entire twelve-storey observatory—with its shiny silver flanks and its huge domed roof—to break free from its foundations and topple off the mountain . . .

. . . with Jack and the others inside it.

When the two missiles had struck the building, Jack had been thrown to the floor. Now he was hurled sideways as the building around him suddenly tilted crazily.

The squeal of rending steel filled the air and he looked up as the great telescope above him broke free of its mountings and fell.

'Look out!' Jack tackled Nobody and Iolanthe out of the way as the hundred-foot-tall telescope crashed down right where they'd been standing and smashed through a section of the wall.

Then things got *really* crazy.

From where he was inside the observatory, Jack saw everything around him tilt: computers slid off desks, cabinets toppled.

This was because, seen from the outside, the observatory was falling *away* from its perch on the mountain.

Like a hand on a clock, the observatory fell through one o'clock, then two, then three—at which point the whole building was horizontal.

At five o'clock—*wham!*—the observatory slammed down against the snow-covered mountainside, kicking up a cloud of white . . .

. . . before it began to slide, roof-first, down the flank of the mountain.

Jack had just got back to his feet when he felt the building start sliding.

He swapped a horrified look with Nobody.

'We're *sliding* . . .' Nobody breathed.

Jack didn't know what to do.

The interior of the observatory looked like a bomb had hit it, which was actually the truth.

Fires burned—windows were smashed—power cords swung like whips—and the great telescope rolled dangerously around.

Through a broken window beside him, Jack saw the snowy flank of the mountain rushing by outside.

His mind tried to comprehend the situation.

They were inside a building, an astronomical observatory, an upside-down observatory, sliding down a mountain.

And gaining speed.

Jack looked down the length of the sliding building and peered out through the wide slit-like aperture that had until recently been its roof, but which was now its lowest point, its leading edge.

'Oh, you have *got* to be kidding me . . .'

Through the aperture he saw the slope ahead of them.

Covered in snow, it extended steeply for about another thousand metres before it ended abruptly at a rocky edge above a sheer three-kilometre drop.

They and their building were about to rush off a cliff.

And in that moment, Jack knew.

They were sliding too fast.

They couldn't escape this time.

There was nothing they could do, nowhere they could leap to, no clever thing they could construct into some life-saving parachute.

This time—he gulped deeply—they really had run out of options.

They were going to die.

Then his earpiece crackled.

'Jack! Jack! Are you in there? Can you hear me?' a voice yelled. 'We're coming in on your right side! Get to a window or a door and get ready to jump!'

The voice had a distinct accent, one that Jack knew well.

A New Zealand accent.

It was Sky Monster.

In a dark corner of his mind, Jack puzzled at how Sky Monster could be here.

Sky Monster was dead. He'd died with Pooh Bear when their Tupolev had been blown apart in the sky outside Moscow, shot down while they had slept in the coma of the bell and the plane had been flying on autopilot. Why, he'd even read their Messages from the Other Side.

Think about that later! his mind screamed.

Jack sprang into action.

'Everybody! This way! Now, now, now!'

Inside the huge sliding building, Jack clambered over the rubble and debris, arriving at a side door, which he kicked open . . .

. . . to reveal an amazing sight.

An ICON A10 seaplane was *right there*, flying fast and low, skimming along inches above the steep snowy slope only metres away from the sliding observatory!

On its flank, Jack saw its name:

Sexy Prince Two.

The second seaplane from the lake at Hades's estate.

And there at its controls he saw Sky Monster, performing an aerobatic feat that only a handful of pilots in the whole world could do, while beside him, reaching out from the seaplane's open side door, waving them over, was Pooh Bear!

Honestly, it defied description.

The twelve-storey silver-sided observatory—sliding down the mountainside, roof-first, out of control, racing toward the cliff edge and a bottomless drop—flanked by a tiny seaplane zooming along beside it with a figure waving from its side door.

Because the observatory was sliding on its side, its door had opened downward, turning it into a little platform on which Jack and his people could stand.

They stood facing Pooh Bear, separated by about ten feet of rushing wind and snow. Owing to the plane's wingspan, however, Pooh's doorway was too far for them to transfer into.

Pooh Bear pointed at the seaplane's left pontoon.

'Grab onto the pontoon!'

Iolanthe went first, stepping off their little door-platform and grabbing hold of the pontoon. Nobody went next, then Easton.

Buffeted by the rushing wind, hammered by the snow, they clung desperately to the pontoon's struts.

But there was no more room.

No more room for Jack.

Pooh Bear saw this, too, and he locked eyes with Jack . . .

. . . and extended one hand while gripping the doorframe with the other.

'Jump! I'll catch you, my friend!' he yelled.

And as the speeding building hit the edge of the cliff, knocking snow down into the alpine chasm below it, Jack leapt full-length out of the doorway, reaching for Pooh Bear's hand—

—and they caught each other's forearms and clasped tightly.

The observatory shot off the cliff and sailed down into the chasm.

Down, down, down it went, the twelve-storey silver tower becoming smaller and smaller, dwarfed by the scale of the mountains around it—

—while the tiny seaplane shot laterally off the same cliff edge, staying aloft, with three figures clutching its left pontoon and another figure hanging from its left-side door.

The seaplane soared away into the night-time sky, bathed in the light of the moon, shooming off to safety.

Many seconds later, somewhere in the depths of the alpine chasm, there came a resounding boom as the observatory hit the bottom.

Ten minutes later, the seaplane touched down gently on a remote mountaintop lake in nearby Switzerland and cruised to a stop on its shore.

After everyone had leapt to the ground, hugged and thanked Sky Monster for an incredible piece of flying, Jack said, 'Where did you guys come from? I thought you were dead.'

Sky Monster said, 'We parachuted out of the *Sky Warrior* just before she got hit by that missile. You know me, Jack. I only use the best headphones when I fly: military-grade noise-cancelling. We weren't asleep, just jammed.'

Pooh Bear added, 'We landed in some godforsaken farmland outside Moscow, literally the middle of nowhere, so we couldn't get in touch with you. We've been making our way back ever since. Eventually, we stole a plane from a regional airport and got back to Hades's estate in Alsace-Lorraine . . . well, what was left of it. Place was a smoking wreck. Picked up a bunch of signals here—some mentioning you—so we hot-footed it this way. We've been trying to hail you on the radio, but you must've switched to another frequency.'

'We did. We flicked over to a roaming frequency after Sphinx hacked the commercial airwaves. But I'm sure glad you arrived when you did,' Jack said.

He looked at the tranquil mountain lake beside them. They were still in the Alps, to the east of Mont Blanc, in the Swiss section of the range, but a long way from anywhere.

Jack gazed out at the mountains, deep in thought.

Iolanthe came up beside him. 'What do we do now?'

'By now, Sphinx is either at or close to the Supreme Labyrinth,' Jack said. 'When I was down inside the mountain, I heard that the Omega monks performed the Fall at Potala Palace before Sphinx destroyed the mountain there. And now Dion has done a Fall, too, so he can join Sphinx at the Labyrinth and help him . . .'

His voice trailed away.

'Which leaves us—broken, sleeping and scattered—and still far behind. We need to do a Fall. But to do that, we need to find one of the two lost mountains and also uncover that pedestal on the moon.'

Saying it all out loud seemed only to reinforce the hopelessness of their situation.

No-one said anything.

They all just stared despondently at the beautiful mountain land-scape in the moonlight.

THE FIVE FORTIFIED MONASTERIES
A DESERT SOMEWHERE
25 DECEMBER, 0900 HOURS

By the light of the morning sun, Sphinx's mighty land force rumbled across a vast desert plain, kicking up a sandstorm in its wake.

Fifty vehicles of all shapes and sizes thundered over the relentlessly flat plain, both on it and above it.

Apache attack helicopters, bristling with guns and missiles.

Chinook transports containing thousands of bronzemen.

And, of course, Sphinx's big Russian Mi-4000 quadcopter.

Speeding along the desert floor were many troop trucks and car-carriers containing more bronzemen.

Their destination: a low mountain range that rose up out of the otherwise flat plain.

Nestled up against the base of one of these barren rocky hills was a little collection of five long-abandoned monasteries not unlike the famous one near Mount Sinai dedicated to St Catherine.

Like St Catherine's these five fortified monasteries were isolated in the extreme, a thousand kilometres from anywhere. A hermit's dream.

Also like St Catherine's, they each burrowed into the low brown mountain behind them.

They were arrayed around a tan-coloured mountain—arranged in a rough semi-circle, about five hundred metres from each other—and all were in similar states of ruin and disrepair. For unlike St Catherine's, they had all been abandoned for over a millennium.

According to the locals, a small band of dedicated Christian monks had lived in them and defended them during the rise of Mohammed and his armies in the 8th century, but a vicious bout of the plague had wiped them out.

The rampaging Islamic army had arrived at the five fortified monasteries soon after and, seeing the infected corpses inside them, sealed their doors and painted warnings on all of their gates: DO NOT ENTER, PLAGUE WITHIN.

And so the location and the importance of the five monasteries had been lost.

Until now.

The great land force pulled to a halt in front of the first abandoned monastery, the middle one of the five. Sphinx's huge four-rotored chopper landed in front of all the vehicles and he stepped out of it.

Sphinx gazed up at the low mountain.

Brown and wrinkled, it was wider than it was tall. It looked like it was made of melted rock, a single slab of the stuff.

The monastery's ancient gate—still bearing the centuries-old Muslim warning about the plague on its thick iron-studded slats—creaked open and a lone figure emerged.

It was Cardinal Mendoza. He had been sent ahead.

Only now he looked different.

Before, Mendoza had had black hair which he usually wore slicked back, underneath a cardinal's red skullcap.

Now, he wore no cap and at some point between Mont Saint-Michel and here, he had *shaved his head completely*, exposing the scalp.

Mendoza bowed to his master . . .

. . . and in doing so revealed a complex tattoo on the skin of his skull.

The tattoo wrapped completely around his head, from temple to temple, and it featured many strange swirls and geometric shapes, plus lines of text in the ancient Word of Thoth.

'Sire,' he said. 'This is it. The end of our long mission. This is the Emperor's Gate to the Supreme Labyrinth and I have, marked in the ancient way on my scalp, the clues to successfully navigating it.'

Sphinx's people moved quickly.

While Sphinx strode inside the monastery, his army sprang into action, forming a defensive perimeter around the low brown mountain.

Four thousand bronzemen were unloaded from the various choppers, troop trucks and car-carriers.

A thousand of them formed up in ranks in front of this monastery's gate. They stood to attention, dead still, impervious to the blazing heat of the desert, something no human army could do.

The remaining three thousand bronzemen began to march toward the four other fort-monasteries arrayed around the mountain containing the four other gates to the Supreme Labyrinth, where they would assume similar defensive positions.

Sphinx was going to perform this final trial of the Omega Event and he was determined to do it unchallenged.

Sphinx entered his gate.

Immediately inside the entrance was a small chapel, dusty and bare.

That was it. That was all there was inside. Just a ruined chapel, little more than a cave with smooth walls.

It was ten paces deep and covered in centuries of dust, sand and spiderwebs. The walls were crumbling. A sad ruin.

At the rear of the chapel was a high stone wall.

This wall was carved in the shape of a high arched doorway and it had a small votive altar protruding from it. This was what archaeologists called a 'false door', a wall carved to look like a door.

It was all rather shabby and unremarkable.

Unless you knew something more about this place.

For carved into the floor at the base of the blank wall was a raised stone symbol that Sphinx recognised.

A five-pointed symbol, roughly the size of a human hand.

Sphinx smiled.

'Welcome to the first of the Five Gates to the Supreme Labyrinth,' Mendoza said, standing behind Sphinx with Chloe Carnarvon.

Chloe said, 'The plague-ridden bodies left here by those monks 1200 years ago did their job. They kept intruders away until this place was forgotten.'

Mendoza said, 'This middle entrance is the Emperor's Gate. A special entrance. For once you open it and enter the Supreme Labyrinth, its outer gate and *all the other outer gates* will begin to close.'

'We must waste no time,' Sphinx said. 'Others have already performed the Fall and will try to enter via the other gates. Get all our gear and gather our entry team. Let's do this.'

Thirty minutes later, wearing military fatigues, a helmet and carrying a pack filled with a week's worth of food and water, Sphinx stood before the inner wall of the chapel.

He was flanked by Mendoza, Chloe and three Knights of the Golden Eight—knights six, seven and eight—all similarly dressed and equipped for an extended journey on foot. The Knights carried large packs and rolling Samsonite cases with all manner of equipment and weapons inside them.

A fourth Knight, Jaeger Fünf, stood to the side, brandishing only a rifle.

Last of all were the eight short red-skinned Vandals. They shifted impatiently from side to side.

Mendoza, bald as a cue ball, his tattooed head gleaming, said, 'It is an honour to serve you, sire, during this momentous occasion.

To bear Imhotep's clues to the maze on my body and have you use them makes me very proud.'

Sphinx gazed up at the inner wall of the chapel, but said nothing.

He reached out with his right hand—his five fingers seared with the five-pointed symbol during his Fall at Mont Saint-Michel—and pressed it against the matching raised marking on the floor.

With a deep rumble, the stone wall slid upward—dust and cobwebs falling off it as it did so—and the grand ancient gateway opened.

It yawned wide, a high square of darkness.

Beyond the gateway, Sphinx glimpsed broad stairs going steeply downward.

Then suddenly there came a momentous grinding sound from *behind* them and Sphinx spun . . .

. . . to see *another* far heavier stone slab slowly begin to lower into the chapel's outer doorway.

The immense slab moved slowly, gradually, by some unseen superancient mechanism.

Mendoza said, 'By opening the Emperor's Gate, you have initiated the closing of all five outer gates. Just as this outer gate is now closing, so too are the outer gates at the other four gates around this mountain.'

'How long until they close fully?' Sphinx growled.

'According to the ancient texts, a single rotation of the Earth. Twenty-four hours, give or take,' Mendoza said.

Sphinx turned to the fourth Knight, Jaeger Fünf, and handed him a signet ring. 'Get all our forces into position outside each of the other gates. Make sure they close fully. Allow no-one to get in before they do.'

'Aye-aye, sire,' Jaeger Fünf acknowledged.

Sphinx pulled out a sat-phone.

'Jaeger Eins,' he said into it, 'how did you go with Dion at Mont Blanc?'

'*Lord Dion successfully performed the Fall, sire,*' Jaeger Eins's voice replied. '*We are ready to assist you if you need us.*'

'Get here. The outer armoured doors have begun to close. They will seal completely in twenty-four hours. I'll take some precautions of my own just in case any of our rivals penetrate the Labyrinth. But if they do, I want Dion and some squires to come in and assist me. You will command the defence outside with the assistance of Jaeger Fünf.'

'*Copy that, sire.*'

'Are all the bells in position?' Sphinx asked.

'*Yes, sire, they are. We sent Siren bells to London, New York, Washington D.C., Los Angeles, Shanghai, Beijing, plus the ancient and religious centres of Jerusalem, Mecca and Cairo. The men manning the bells await your command.*'

'Put them all to sleep,' Sphinx said firmly. 'Then get here.'

'*As you command, sire.*'

Sphinx clicked off the sat-phone and turned to Chloe.

'Ms Carnarvon. Take some squires and find the blue bell. It is vital to my new world, for it will determine whom I wake from the sleep.'

'It will be done, sire,' Chloe said, bowing respectfully.

Sphinx turned back to face the entry to the maze.

'This is the final trial to be completed in advance of the Omega Event: the long journey through the Supreme Labyrinth to the World Throne. Come, it is time.'

And with those words, followed by Mendoza, his three remaining Knights and the eight diminutive Vandals, Sphinx passed through the Emperor's Gate.

On the floor on the inner side of the gate was a second raised five-pointed asterisk symbol.

Once all his people were through, Sphinx bent down and pressed his hand against it. Once again the seared markings on his palm matched it perfectly.

Immediately, the inner gate slid shut behind him and his team.

No-one else could pass through this gate. Anyone else desiring to enter the maze would have to access it through one of the four other gates, soon to be guarded by Sphinx's massive force of bronzemen and silvermen, and which in a day's time would be shut off forever when their outer gates closed completely.

The inner gate boomed loudly as it slid shut, cutting off the view of Sphinx and his team descending into the gigantic maze.

Inside the maze, Sphinx keyed his radio. 'Jaeger Fünf, do you copy?'

There was no reply.

'We can't get a signal in here?' Sphinx said.

'It's the Labyrinth,' the cardinal replied. 'It emits a peculiar electromagnetic field which is inimical to radio waves. The maze is not of this planet, sire. Radio signals mean nothing to it.'

Which was why, moments later, Sphinx never heard Jaeger Fünf shout into his radio, '*Missile teams! Get a lock on that incoming jet and fire, fire, fire!*'

For at that moment, outside the entrance to the Labyrinth, a Learjet came zooming in low over the desert, crash-landed and skidded across the dusty ground toward the entrance gate to the left of the one Sphinx had used.

It kicked up a tornado of sand and dust as it roared forward, aimed right at the gate.

Sphinx's bronzemen had not yet reached the other gates and they broke into a run as the jet slid to a halt in front of the second gate and six figures burst out of its cockpit and raced desperately inside the gate.

It was Brother Ezekiel and five Omega monks.

They were inside the second gate before anyone knew what was happening and by the time Jaeger Fünf's people got there, that second gate's inner slab was firmly closed behind them.

'Fuck!' Jaeger Fünf growled. He turned to the man behind him. 'Call Lord Dion and Jaeger Eins. Tell them to get here as soon as possible. Dion is now officially required inside the maze.'

As Christmas Day dawned around the world, several drone Chinook helicopters rose, unnoticed, above nine major cities of the world—London, New York, Washington D.C., Los Angeles, Shanghai, Beijing, Jerusalem, Mecca and Cairo—and rang their Siren bells.

And those cities joined Moscow and Rome in the mysterious slumber of the bells.

In New York City, just before the bell rang, Sphinx's people hacked into the many television screens of Times Square, replacing their advertisements with a final taunting message that blazed from every single screen:

YOU
WILL
WAKE
AS
SLAVES

FOURTH OFFENSIVE

THE TWO LOST MOUNTAINS

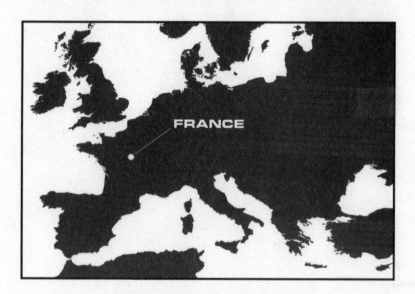

What does the mountain care?

ROBERT BROWNING
'ANDREA DEL SARTO'

It was Christmas Day but it didn't feel like it.

Usually December 25th was a day of gifts, joy, family and frivolity but today the world was silent, quiet, cowed.

After seeing almost a dozen major cities felled by the mysterious sleep and the Tibetan city of Lhasa obliterated by a nuclear strike, people around the world hid in their homes, afraid.

No-one knew which city would be next.

Jack's team regrouped at an airport outside Dijon, France.

The gigantic Super Galaxy cargo plane—flown there remotely by Alby earlier—was parked at one end of the airport's runway.

Beside it, dwarfed by it, was the black Mercedes-Benz Sprinter van that Alby had driven here from Alsace-Lorraine plus two smaller planes: the little seaplane named *Sexy Prince Two* which had landed on a set of roll-out wheels and Rufus's Sukhoi Su-37, freshly returned from Rome with Zoe and Sister Lynda.

Stretching away from the little airport to the horizon on every side were farms and fields of classic French countryside. It was all empty. Whoever lived here was remaining in their homes.

Lily, Stretch and Aloysius Knight all lay on gurneys in the Sprinter van, still gripped by the sleep of the bells.

Mae was gone: taken by Rastor who hopefully saw a benefit in keeping her alive. And they feared the worst for Agnes.

A sombre silence hung over the group.

At least, Jack thought, *Pooh Bear and Sky Monster are here, alive and well, and back with the team.*

Jack whispered to Sky Monster, 'I read your Message from the Other Side. Thought you were dead. Nice stuff.'

Sky Monster nodded. 'I meant every word.'

Jack turned to the others. They were all gathered around the communications console of the Super Galaxy.

'Play it again,' he said.

The recent exchange between Sphinx and Jaeger Eins came through the speakers one more time:

Sphinx: *Get here. The outer armoured doors have begun to close. They will seal completely in twenty-four hours. I'll take some precautions of my own just in case any of our rivals penetrate the Labyrinth. But if they do, I want Dion and some squires to come in and assist me. You will command the defence outside with the assistance of Jaeger Fünf.*

Jaeger Eins: *Copy that, sire.*

Sphinx: *Are all the bells in position?*

Jaeger Eins: *Yes, sire, they are. We sent Siren bells to London, New York, Washington D.C., Los Angeles, Shanghai, Beijing, plus the ancient and religious centres of Jerusalem, Mecca and Cairo. The men manning the bells await your command.*

Sphinx: *Put them all to sleep. Then get here.*

The group stared at the speakers in grim silence.

'So, here's how things stand,' Jack said. 'Sphinx has entered the Labyrinth. By entering the maze, it looks like he activated some outer protective doors which will seal completely in one day. Which means we now have twenty-four—no, twenty-three—hours to find one of the two lost mountains, perform the Fall at one of them and get to that Labyrinth.'

Alby added, 'Don't forget, to perform the Fall, we also need to make sure the pedestal on the moon is uncovered.'

'Yeah . . .' Jack said. 'It's no understatement to say we've got our work cut out for us. Okay, everybody, tell me what you got.'

★ ★ ★

The team members laid out the various pieces of ancient knowledge they had accumulated over the last few days.

Zoe mentioned the strange reference to 'Albano's emissary' that she had found in the Pope's private study. 'According to the Pope, the Church's notes about the location of the blue bell were taken to Albano's emissary, whoever that is. We'll have to figure this out since I have a feeling we'll be needing that bell.'

Lynda described the enormous sandstone cobra statue that she and Mae had seen in Vault XXII of the Vatican Secret Archives: the lost uraeus from the head of the Great Sphinx.

'The Omega monks who were examining it were comparing it to two old pictures of the Great Sphinx: the Denon sketch and an old aerial photo of the Sphinx from the 1920s.'

Alby nodded. 'That uraeus had supposedly never been found. Not even Napoleon's army of scientists could find it when they did detailed studies of the Sphinx and the pyramids in the 1790s. Turns out the Church had it all along.'

Iolanthe turned to Bertie. 'Were you aware of this?'

Bertie shook his head. 'I'd heard rumours but nothing more than that.'

'There were also two stone slabs with carved images that looked like the Sephirot Tree of Life and the Norse Tree of Death,' Lynda said. 'I don't know where they came from or what they refer to.'

'What about the last two iron mountains?' Jack said.

Sister Lynda held up a photo of a page from Francis Xavier's journal, the one that she and Mae had found in the Vatican Secret Archives, and quoted out loud:

> 'In his secret report to the Pope, the great wandering monk, the Venerable Laurent of the Levant, wrote that "He who wields the blade of the archangel will find the fourth mountain."
>
> Ignatius and I both believe this means that the fourth mount is either Sacra di San Michele in Turin or the Sanctuary to the Archangel at Mount Gargano near Foggia.'

'"He who wields *the blade of the archangel* will find the fourth mountain",' Lynda said. 'We believe this is a reference to the Sword of St Michael.'

'A sword?' Pooh Bear said. 'You mean some kind of legendary weapon like Excalibur?'

Lynda shook her head. 'No. This isn't an actual sword. It's a metaphor. It's actually a line, a straight line known as a ley line. Ley lines are geographical links between ancient structures—megalithic sites, churches, abbeys—often built far apart, sometimes on different continents.'

Jack nodded. 'We encountered this with Stonehenge, its quarry and the Great Pyramid. They all lie on a single straight line.'

'This is just as impressive as that one,' Lynda said. 'The Sword of St Michael is a very curious line of *seven* churches, abbeys and monasteries that stretches all the way from Britain to Israel. The reason for its name is that *all* of these churches, abbeys and monasteries are dedicated to the same saint, the Archangel Michael, including the two monasteries named by Javier, the Sacra di San Michele in Turin and the Sanctuary to the Archangel at Mount Gargano. Let me show you.'

Lynda pulled up an image from the internet:

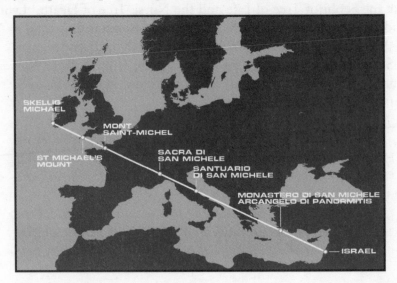

Jack saw some names on the image that he had already encountered: St Michael's Mount in Cornwall and Mont Saint-Michel in France. He also noticed that the ley line passed almost directly through the Mont Blanc Massif.

Lynda said, 'Here's the most common depiction of the line, showing it as a sword.'

Sister Lynda explained, 'The Archangel St Michael was seen as God's leader in the war against the Devil, so this line of holy places was named St Michael's Sword. As you can see, it starts in Ireland, at Skellig Michael, and ends in the Holy Land, in modern Israel.'

Jack gazed hard at the two images.

'*He who wields the blade of the archangel . . .*' he said. '*Wields* the blade.'

He looked up sharply.

'The handle. If you wield the blade of the sword, you're gripping it by the handle. The mountain is at the grip-end of the ley line.'

Jack pointed at both ends of the Sword of St Michael. 'The line of holy sites extends from Ireland to Israel. You say it starts in Ireland? At Skellig Michael?'

Lynda shrugged. 'That's where, historically, it has been held to begin.'

Jack frowned. 'Skellig Michael is a barren rock with a very basic monastery built on top of some pagan ruins. It's been dug up many times over the years by archaeologists. There's nothing there. But what if—what if—the sword points up, not down? What if it starts down here . . .'

Jack pointed to the other end of the line.

'. . . in Israel? What's the holy site in Israel that sits on the ley line?'

Lynda said, 'There are two candidates. First, the "Our Lady Star of the Sea" monastery in Haifa. But it was sacked and destroyed by Muslim forces during the Crusades, so no-one's quite sure where it really stood.'

'And the second option?' Jack asked.

Lynda hesitated.

'Well, I mean . . . if you extend the line further . . . well—'

Jack leaned forward. 'What's the second possibility?'

Sister Lynda swallowed. 'It's the Dome of the Rock in Jerusalem.'

'The Dome of the Rock?' Alby said. 'The *holiest* site in the whole of the Jewish faith?'

Pooh Bear added, 'And the third holiest in Islam.'

'And a place that both religions have been fighting over for more than a thousand years,' Bertie said.

'And reputedly built on top of the ruins of Solomon's Temple,' Zoe said.

Jack remained silent.

Then he said, 'It makes sense. Everything we've encountered on this quest has had *some* connection to existing religions. Certain places are often considered sacred or holy long before they become modern places of worship.'

'It's the same with dates,' Alby observed. 'Look at today, Christmas Day. December the 25th was originally celebrated by pagan peoples simply because it was the date of the northern vernal equinox, the moment of the year when the days become longer. It heralds the end of winter and the arrival of spring and thus new life.'

Jack added, 'Modern churches have long been built on local religious shrines. The Dome of the Rock—the *whole* old city of Jerusalem for that matter—is considered sacred by three religions. The reason it has tremendous significance today might well stem from a significance it had well before Judaism and Islam even existed. And it's at one end of the Sword of St Michael. Given all that, I like it as a potential site of the fourth iron mountain—'

'It's Jerusalem,' Rufus said firmly.

Everyone turned.

The big kindly pilot wasn't exactly an expert on historical matters. Yet he had spoken with absolute authority and conviction.

'How do you know that, big fella?' Jack asked.

'Because of that.' Rufus pointed at a small television at his end of the communications console.

It was tuned to BBC World and on it was an incredible black-and-white shot captured by a closed-circuit security camera in Jerusalem at very long range.

The newsreader was saying: '. . . *an extraordinary sight captured on a security camera shortly after the entire city of Jerusalem succumbed to the mysterious sleep that has affected ten other cities around the world . . .*'

The TV showed a gigantic four-rotored aeroplane bristling with cannons and missile pods hovering above the glittering roof of the Dome of the Rock.

In the dusty air of Israel, the giant plane loomed above the ancient mount, flanked by smaller choppers.

It was Rastor's V-88 Condor.

And it was already in Jerusalem.

Jack stared at the plane on the TV screen.

'Shit, he's there already and he has my mother.' Jack spun. 'Alby. Quick. What time will the moon be over Jerusalem tonight?'

Alby tapped away on his computer for a few moments.

'It'll be directly above Jerusalem at exactly 10:05 p.m. It'll stay in that position for fourteen minutes.'

'We have to get there now.'

Nobody said, 'Jack, what about the small matter of *the moon*? It's no use getting to that lost mountain if we can't uncover the pedestal on the lunar surface.'

Jack turned to Alby. 'What have you found?'

'I found one option that might work, but I have to be honest, it's a really shitty option,' Alby said.

Jack shrugged wearily. 'Right now, son, a shitty option is better than none at all. Hit me.'

Alby told them.

When he was finished, Jack nodded.

'That really is a truly terrible option. The way I see it, this General Rastor wouldn't be in Jerusalem if he didn't have someone handling the moon issue. We'll go to Jerusalem and hope to piggy-back on his knowledge. As a back-up, Alby, I want you to execute the shitty option. Rufus? Are you game to fly Alby to his destination and help him there?'

Rufus looked from Jack to the sleeping figure of his friend, Aloysius, lying on a stretcher nearby.

'I'm all in, Cap'n. Hundred per cent.'

Alby turned to Easton. 'Where I'm going, I can't take the dogs. You okay to look after them again?'

Easton nodded. 'Always.'

Jack looked over at Iolanthe and Bertie, huddled in a corner of the comms room, discussing something between themselves.

'Iolanthe? Bertie?' he said. 'Anything you'd like to share?'

Bertie said, 'Captain West, I've been thinking about what your wife, Zoe, learned at the Vatican about the location of the blue bell. Specifically, that the Church's notes about it were taken to "Albano's emissary". I have an idea about that and would like to investigate it further . . . in Italy.'

'Do it,' Jack said. 'Nobody, Iolanthe, can you go with him and keep us informed?'

'Will do,' Nobody said.

'Sure,' Iolanthe said.

Sister Lynda looked up from her computer. 'Captain, I think I've got a hit on Tracy Smith's location. It could be nothing, but I found a report from some U.S. forces in Aleppo, Syria. Last month, as a bunch of bombs fell on the city, they tried to extract a white female ENT surgeon from Doctors Without Borders but she refused to go. They never got her name, but that sounds like Tracy.'

'Go,' Jack said. 'We need all the help we can get with the Siren sleep. Zoe?'

'I can fly Lynda there,' Zoe said. 'We can take the A-10, and squeeze Lily, Stretch and Aloysius in the back. If this lady knows the cure to that sleep, maybe she can wake them.'

'All right, people, get moving,' Jack said. 'The battle's already started in Jerusalem.'

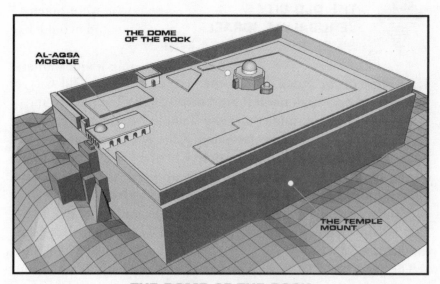

**THE DOME OF THE ROCK
ON THE TEMPLE MOUNT
JERUSALEM, ISRAEL**

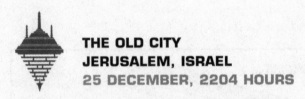

THE OLD CITY
JERUSALEM, ISRAEL
25 DECEMBER, 2204 HOURS

The Dome of the Rock sits on the very edge of the Old City of Jerusalem atop a high natural hill known as the Temple Mount.

Over the last two millennia, the Temple Mount has gradually been encased by towering retaining walls and battlements—first by Herod the Great and later by both Christian and Muslim forces during the Crusades—so that today it appears less like a natural hill and more like an imposing square-walled fortress that gazes out over the lesser hills and valleys of modern Jerusalem.

It is considered sacred to Judaism and Islam and, to a lesser extent, Christianity.

The Jews consider it to be the site of Solomon's Temple, long lost to history.

More than that, they believe that the Temple of Solomon's most inviolable chamber, the Holy of Holies—the sealed room that housed the Ark of the Covenant, the chest that held the Ten Commandments—was situated on the Mount.

(Jack, of course, knew differently about the Ten Commandments. Rather than containing the ten primary laws sent by God to Moses, they were actually two identical tablets carved with an incantation written in the Word of Thoth. The biblical figure known as Moses was actually Thuthmosis, a renegade Egyptian priest who stole the two tablets from their resting place inside the second pyramid at Giza.

Jack had ultimately obtained the two tablets in a mine underneath the stone churches at Lalibela in Ethiopia during the adventure involving the six Ramesean Stones.)

In any case, devout Jews dare not even set foot on the Temple Mount, out of fear that they might accidentally step on the location of the Holy of Holies. Since the Mount is governed by Muslim authorities, the closest Jews can get to it is a segment of the Mount's western flank which has become known as the Western or 'Wailing' Wall.

For Muslims, it is a little different.

While they revere the site and claim it as their own with great zeal, oddly, the sacred structure that they built on the Mount—the Dome of the Rock, with its striking hemispherical gold roof—is *not* a mosque.

It is simply a shrine.

An actual consecrated mosque—the Al-Aqsa Mosque—sits a few hundred metres from it, on the southern precipice of the Mount.

Indeed, the Dome's original roof was not even made of gold, and for many centuries, Muslims cared little for it. While it was said to house the spot from which Mohammed had ascended to Heaven, the Dome lay in forlorn condition until the 20th century when, as religious tensions mounted in the region, the King of Jordan restored it and added the golden roof.

Jack and his sub-team—Pooh Bear and Easton—had sped across the Mediterranean from France to Israel in the C-5 Super Galaxy. By the time they arrived above Israel, after taking into account the time difference, night had fallen on Jerusalem . . .

. . . and a laser-like beam of ethereal green light was lancing down from the moon . . .

. . . and General Rastor had totally and completely blown apart the Temple Mount.

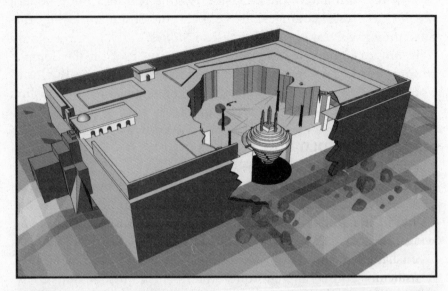

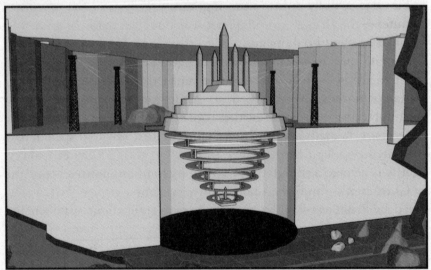

THE TEMPLE MOUNT . . .
. . . AFTER RASTOR

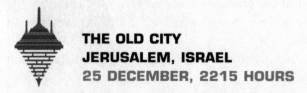

THE OLD CITY
JERUSALEM, ISRAEL
25 DECEMBER, 2215 HOURS

As he rocketed down through the night-time sky on a pair of gull-wings, Jack saw the extremely thin but amazingly bright beam of green light stretching down from the heavens and slamming into Jerusalem.

He was acutely aware that the beam would vanish in a few minutes—

Then he saw the damage.

'Good God,' he breathed as he saw what Rastor had done to the Temple Mount.

Rastor hadn't just blasted open the Dome of the Rock. He had torn open *one whole side* of the Temple Mount.

A giant ragged hole yawned wide in the eastern wall of the Mount.

It was a huge and ugly gash at least a hundred metres broad.

Giant bricks from the once-mighty retaining wall—blasted outward by what must have been multiple gigantic explosions—had tumbled down the slope away from the hole and come to rest on the road there.

Floodlights ringed the site, bathing it in a white sodium glare.

But there was no movement.

No people were visible.

Two dozen abandoned military excavation vehicles were parked above and to the side of the great gash: bulldozers and

cranes that had cleared away the debris to make access to the hole easier.

But their drivers and operators were gone.

And the citizens of Jerusalem, put to sleep by Sphinx's bell hours earlier, hadn't been able to offer any resistance to Rastor's explosive actions.

There was no sign of the huge hover-capable V-88 Condor plane Jack had seen on the television and which Zoe and the others had encountered in Rome.

'Alby,' Jack said into his throat-mike. 'How long till that beam from the moon vanishes?'

'*Four more minutes*,' came Alby's reply.

Jack swooped in toward the gash, aiming for the now-exposed Falling Temple inside it.

Jack landed inside the enormous space, the whole area bathed in the eerie green glow of the beam shooting down from the moon.

The scale of the wreckage around him was monstrous. Boulders the size of buses surrounded him. Rastor's excavation efforts had turned the Falling Temple's once-underground space into a huge open-air grotto.

Jack hurried to the Falling Temple that, until tonight, had been hidden for thousands of years directly beneath the Dome of the Rock.

Like the ones at Mont Saint-Michel and Mont Blanc, this temple was shaped like a spinning top, with an eight-storey-high upper half made of stone and a spindlier lower half of eight open-sided levels connected by ladders on its slim golden pillars.

With the collapse of the cavern's roof, the temple's chains had fallen away and yet still, somehow, the structure was poised above the fall shaft.

It was then that Jack noticed four thick steel beams—man-made and modern—holding up the waist-section of the Falling Temple.

What was this? A trap?

Beneath the temple, Jack saw the fall shaft into which it had to drop in order for someone to perform the Fall.

Everything was lit by Rastor's abandoned floodlights and the green beam from the moon.

This is wrong . . . Jack's mind warned him.

He stood before the enormous Falling Temple, at the edge of the dark shaft underneath it.

Suddenly a radio squawked, shattering the silence. It was followed by a voice.

'*Greetings, Captain West.*'

Rastor's voice.

Jack whirled around, his eyes searching, and he saw a lone radio lying on the ground a few feet from him, beside the edge of the fall shaft.

'*You're too late. Both to perform the Fall and to save your mother.*'

Jack drew one of his guns and spun, looking for Rastor.

But there was no-one else here.

He was alone in the giant demolished space.

Then he spotted it: a small camera mounted on one of the abandoned bulldozers a short distance away.

Rastor was watching him from somewhere else.

Jack picked up the radio as Rastor spoke again: '*Your reputation precedes you, Captain. A reputation for determination, for acts of remarkable heroism when all seems lost, for saving others when they cannot save themselves.*'

'While there's still a chance, I don't give up,' Jack said into the radio.

'*Yes, but you are now officially out of chances,*' Rastor's voice said. '*I have performed the Fall already. I did it before you arrived here and hauled the temple back up with my plane. You, however, will get no such chance.*'

At that moment, as if on cue, the green laser beam from the moon winked out.

'Alby?' Jack whispered into his throat-mike.

Alby's voice said, '*Jack, the light's still on up there—you still have three minutes—but something's blocking it. He must've just replaced the reflective Kapton cover on the pedestal on the moon.*'

'*That's precisely what I have just done,*' Rastor said. '*But come now, Captain. There's something else you want to ask me.*'

'Where's my mother?' Jack said flatly.

'*She is closer to you now than she is to me,*' Rastor said lightly.

Jack turned, his eyes searching the broken cavern around him.

'Mum! Can you hear me? Mum!' he shouted.

'Jack . . . ! Jack . . . !'

It was Mae's voice.

But muted, echoing, and in pain.

Jack stepped back from the Falling Temple so that he could peer down at its spindly lower levels.

'Jack!' his mother called again.

And he glimpsed her.

'Holy fucking shit . . .' he gasped.

He could just see Mae down at the lowest level of the Falling Temple.

She lay with her back pressed against the underside of the temple, her head facing downwards, looking directly into the dark abyss like some gruesome kind of figurehead on the leading edge of the falling structure.

Although Jack couldn't see the terrible sight fully, Mae Merriweather had been crucified with masonry nails to the underside of the Falling Temple's lowest level.

Rastor's monstrous intent was clear: when the temple fell and hit the bottom of the shaft, she would be crushed to nothing as the rest of the heavy temple landed on top of her a split second later.

A sinister chuckle came from the radio. '*What happens when you* can't *save someone, Captain? Someone you truly love.*'

Jack ignored him. 'Mum!' he yelled.

Mae turned her head as best she could and saw him.

Her arms were spreadeagled, cruelly affixed to the stone floor of the temple.

'Jack!'

'Don't worry, I'll save you!'

'No! You have to leave!'

Jack's mind raced.

This was out of control.

The wrecked Temple Mount—the green moonbeam blocked—the Falling Temple—and his mother nailed to the bottom of it poised above the drop.

'Cubby,' Mae said.

She said it calmly, firmly, despite her predicament.

'You can't save me *and* the world. Everything I need to say to you is in my Message from the Other Side. Now, go! Please!'

'I can't leave you to die . . .'

'Jack! You have to! You have to GET OUT OF HERE AND SAVE THE WORLD! I love you, Cub! Fight to the end. That's what you do. I'm so proud of you.'

'*Oh, Captain,*' Rastor's voice said. '*This is all so touching. But you have no idea what I am prepared to do to destroy this world. One thing I must do along the way, however, is break your spirit.*'

Then it happened.

Explosive bolts on the steel beams holding up the Falling Temple at its waist blew and the beams snapped, and suddenly the temple dropped into the shaft with Mae attached to it.

Jack shouted helplessly as the temple dropped away from him.

With a loud *whooshing* sound, it shot down into the fall shaft that bored into the Earth beneath the Temple Mount . . . with Mae attached to its leading edge.

The Falling Temple plummeted through the darkness of the shaft.

And as it did, Jack West's mother closed her eyes and took a deep calm breath—

—an instant before the whole massive structure *slammed* into the hard stone base and the heavy upper half of the temple crashed down on its spindly lower half, blasting through its thin pillars as if they were matchsticks and crushing Mae Merriweather to nothing.

Up at the top of the shaft, Jack heard the temple hit the bottom with a distant, resounding boom.

'Oh, Mum . . .' he breathed. 'Oh, no.'

The following hour was a blur to Jack.

The shock of watching Mae fall to her death, horrifically attached to the Falling Temple, had rattled him terribly.

'*Jack!*' Pooh Bear's voice called in his ear. '*Get to the Jaffa Gate! We'll meet you there to extract you!*'

Then he was stumbling through the rabbit warren of alleyways that was the Old City of Jerusalem, heading westward for the Jaffa Gate.

Through the alleys he staggered, bouncing off walls in a daze, his mind racing with images of falling temples and his mother's awful violent death.

Bumping off one wall as he rounded a corner, his headphones were knocked off his ears and dangled around his neck.

As he ran, he heard Rastor's cackling laugh and at first he thought he was imagining it, until he realised that he'd put the general's radio in his pocket earlier and the laugh was coming from it, live and in real-time.

At length, Jack came to the Jaffa Gate, a high medieval battlement situated at the western end of the Old City, embedded in its monumental outer walls.

The famed Walls of Jerusalem stretched away from the gate to the south for hundreds of metres, fading off into the gloomy night air. Built over two thousand years ago and augmented in the Crusades, they were high, solid and formidable.

Jack didn't care.

Everything had gone to Hell.

Rastor had performed the Fall before Jack had got here and was no doubt on his way to the Supreme Labyrinth.

Jack had not performed a Fall at all and until he did, the Supreme Labyrinth would be closed to him. Christ, he didn't even know where the Labyrinth *was*.

Things had been tough for him before, but they had never been this bad.

His daughter was adrift in a deadly slumber.

Stretch and Aloysius Knight, too.

He'd lost Hades at Mont Saint-Michel.

And now his mother.

As Jack saw Pooh Bear and Easton pull up in a van outside the Walls of Jerusalem, he wondered how this could possibly get any worse.

And then it got worse.

Jack saw it rising above the darkened tree-covered hills to the south, above modern Jerusalem's dimly lit suburban streets, and his mouth fell open in dismay.

A lone helicopter—a Chinook—its twin rotors thumping, its floodlights panning the area.

It rose straight up.

Up and up and up.

Jack froze in horror as he saw the object hanging from the underbelly of the Chinook.

A giant metal sphere.

A Siren bell.

He hadn't seen one since Moscow. He'd forgotten how big they were.

'Oh, no. No, no, no . . .'

He waved frantically to Pooh Bear and Easton and, oddly, in that instant, he noticed that Easton had Roxy with him.

Jesus Christ, Jack thought. *Amid all this craziness, my dog is here.* He blinked away the thought.

'Guys! Put on your headphones! Sphinx still has people here!'

He clutched for his own headphones, dangling around his neck.

But before he could get them on his head, the helicopter rocked and the great bell swung . . .

. . . and rang . . .

. . . and to his absolute horror, Jack heard it, heard the singular sound of its ring, and in that terrifying instant he knew that he was going to fall asleep.

★ ★ ★

Because he'd been wearing protective headphones in Moscow when the bell had gone off there, Jack hadn't actually heard the song of a Siren bell before.

It was oddly beautiful, *eerily* beautiful even, like a gong being struck, only lighter, sweeter.

His brain ate up the noise the bell made, the pleasure centres inside it going wild.

Jack saw Pooh Bear fall out of the van he had arrived in; saw Easton slump in his seat.

And then the sweet, sweet sound of the bell overwhelmed Jack himself and as his strength waned and darkness closed around him, he was able to mumble one final word.

'No . . .'

Then his world went black.

The Siren sleep.

It was a very strange kind of sleep, Jack discovered. More like a twilight state than deep slumber.

It was like being asleep but also partially awake. His eyes were closed and to any outside observer, he would have appeared asleep, lost in the coma of the bell.

Yet while his eyes might have been closed, Jack could hear the world outside him, albeit distantly, dimly, in a muffled kind of way, as if he were underwater.

But he could not move.

No matter how hard he willed his muscles to act, he couldn't get them to obey.

He was paralysed. Paralysed and blind, yet sentenced to hear, from an eerie distance, the goings-on around him.

For instance, he heard the Chinook helicopter sweep by overhead, its normally deafening rotor-noise a faraway thumping.

He actually felt it land on the broad boulevard outside the Jaffa Gate, a boulevard that by day was packed with tourist buses.

Then he heard and felt the footfalls.

Many footfalls, heavy footfalls, all of them stepping in perfect unison.

The sound of bronzemen . . .

Getting louder.

Getting closer.

Coming toward him.

And it was then, right then, again very distantly, that he heard, of all things, a dog barking.

Jack couldn't see it himself, but if he could have, he would have seen himself lying flat on his back, out cold, on the wide boulevard outside the Jaffa Gate, beneath the high Walls of Jerusalem.

Near him was the parked van, with the slumped figures of Pooh Bear and Easton, also out cold.

The Chinook helicopter had landed about two hundred metres from him. Its floodlights—blinding white—were pointed directly at Jack.

Out of its rear ramp marched about twenty bronzemen.

They marched in rows, in unison, toward the sleeping figure of Jack West Jr.

At their rear, sauntering along with easy confidence, was Jaeger Zwei, the Knight of the Golden Eight who had failed to kill Jack in Moscow.

Wearing military-grade headphones, Zwei grinned nastily.

He couldn't believe his luck.

He'd got a second chance to kill Jack West Jr.

After ringing his Siren bell over Jerusalem and putting all its citizens to sleep, Jaeger Zwei had been about to leave the city when Rastor had shown up with his awesome force.

Zwei and his chopper had lain low and observed Rastor blowing apart the Temple Mount and performing the Fall in the light of the powerful green moonbeam. Using the bell on Rastor wasn't an option, as he and his people were all wearing protective headphones. And losing his bell to Rastor—who had a far more powerful plane than Zwei did—was to be avoided at all costs.

Then Rastor had left and West had appeared and Zwei had seen his opportunity for revenge.

And now he had Jack, paralysed and defenceless, completely at his mercy.

It was then that something truly odd happened.

A small black poodle sprang from the van near West and raced to his side.

Jaeger Zwei frowned.

In the glare of the helicopter's floodlights, the little black dog stood over West's body protectively, forepaws spread wide, growling at Zwei and his advancing company of bronzemen.

And then the dog did what dogs do.

It started barking at them.

Zwei drew his gun. He'd shoot the fucking dog, too.

It was quite possibly the sweetest sight in the world.

The tiny Roxy barking fiercely at the approaching ranks of impassive bronzemen.

The bronzemen did not stop.

Roxy kept barking.

Seeing that this strategy wasn't working, she reached down and, with her teeth, snagged hold of Jack's collar and started trying to drag him back toward the van.

Now it was the most extraordinary sight in the world.

The little black poodle, barely knee-high, all fifteen kilograms of her, with one crooked hind leg, trying desperately to pull her full-sized human master out of harm's way.

But Jack was just too big, too heavy.

Whimpering with the effort, Roxy lost her grip on his collar a few times and Jack's limp body slumped to the ground.

But every time he fell, Roxy just bit into his collar again and started dragging him again, in a determined but futile effort to get him to safety.

In the hazy world of Jack's mind, this was all happening far, far away.

He heard the barks and the footfalls and the chopper's rotor blades. He even felt the jolting movement of being dragged, but it was an alien sensation that in his current state, his mind couldn't interpret.

And then he heard something his mind *could* understand: a voice, also remote and distant.

A woman's voice.

One that he knew.

A *young* woman's voice.

But as he recognised it, he knew for certain that he was dreaming because it was impossible that she could be here.

For it was Lily's voice.

She was saying, '*It's okay, Roxy. Good girl. Good girl. We got him now. We got him. Zoe?*'

'*Okay, Tracy, do it,*' Zoe's voice said.

In his current state, imprisoned in his own body, Jack didn't know what to think.

Obviously, Lily wasn't here. She was asleep herself.

And Zoe couldn't be here either. She had gone somewhere else, on some other mission, somewhere Jack couldn't quite remember now.

Maybe this was what happened at the end, at your death. As death overtook you, you heard the voices of the people you loved the most, which for him was Lily and Zoe.

And then he felt sharp pricks behind each of his ears and—

—Jack West Jr sprang up into a sitting position on the roadway outside the Jaffa Gate, awake and fully fucking alive!

The glare of the helicopter's floodlights blinded him and he held up his forearm to shield his eyes.

Suddenly several things happened at once:

Something small, black and furry leapt onto his lap.

Roxy.

She licked his face furiously, slobbering all over him with unbridled adoration.

Then human arms wrapped Jack in the tightest of embraces and Lily's voice called.

'Dad!'

As his eyes adjusted to the glare, he saw that it was indeed Lily— his Lily, awake and alive—wrapping him in her arms.

Then gunfire rang out, loud and close, as beside Lily, Jack saw three figures standing over him, all of them firing at the advancing ranks of bronzemen.

Zoe.

And Stretch.

And Aloysius Knight.

But how could that be? The last time Jack had seen Stretch and Aloysius, they'd been asleep . . .

It didn't matter to Jack now.

They must have been using the team's specially tipped bullets because the bronzemen were falling and Jaeger Zwei was racing for cover.

Jack still wasn't sure this wasn't all some acid-trip dream caused by the bell.

And then, covered by the still-firing Stretch and Aloysius, he was lifted by Lily and Zoe—accompanied by a brown-haired woman he'd never met—back to the van, where he saw Sister Lynda at the wheel.

'Fucking hurry up!' the old nun shouted over the gunfire.

Might still be a whacked-out dream, Jack thought.

In seconds he was inside the van alongside the still-comatose bodies of Pooh Bear and Easton, fleeing from the Old City of Jerusalem, looking back out through the rear window to see Jaeger Zwei furiously watching him get away.

As the van zoomed through the deserted streets of modern Jerusalem, Jack's mind strained to return to normal.

Sister Lynda drove like a demon, taking turns at high speed through a residential neighbourhood packed with apartment complexes.

'Lynda!' Zoe yelled. 'We can't outrun that chopper once it's airborne! We need to hide! Get us underground now!'

In response, Sister Lynda yanked the steering wheel hard over and they went bouncing down a ramp into an underground parking garage beneath an apartment building.

They descended for three levels until Lynda hit the brakes and the van squealed to a halt.

Jack was still lying on his side, taking in this sudden unexpected rescue.

Stretch and Aloysius scanned the garage outside, guns up.

Zoe and Lily knelt above Jack.

They both smiled broadly.

'Hey, you,' Zoe said. 'Wakey, wakey.'

'Hi, Dad,' Lily said. 'I'm *back*.'

ALEPPO, SYRIA
4 HOURS EARLIER

While Jack had been dashing to Jerusalem, Zoe and Sister Lynda had been racing in their little ICON A-10 plane—with the sleeping figures of Lily, Stretch and Aloysius lying against each other in the back—to Syria, to the town of Aleppo.

It took some doing, but there, amid the bombed-out ruins of the once-magnificent Roman city—its citizens living under constant bombardment by the brutal Syrian regime—they found a small mobile hospital run by Médecins Sans Frontières, Doctors Without Borders.

They'd found this field hospital by asking the local women if they knew of a female doctor who specialised in hearing and breathing difficulties. It turned out, many did. They spoke of the brilliant lady ear doctor who had saved the hearing of many of their children after bombs had landed close to them.

A brilliant lady ear doctor.

That sounded like Dr Tracy Smith.

Which was how, on Christmas Day, among the dusty ruins of Aleppo, Zoe and Sister Lynda had found a striking woman with her sleeves rolled up and her brown hair pulled back in a careless ponytail peering intently into a small child's ear with an otoscope.

'Tracy!' Lynda called.

The doctor turned. She was in her mid-forties, sharp-eyed and attractive.

She nodded in acknowledgement.

'Why, hi, Lynda. With all these Siren bells going off around the world, I was wondering if someone might come looking for me.'

Brief introductions were made and Zoe quickly saw just how disillusioned Tracy Smith had become with the secret royal world.

Tracy said, 'There's an old African proverb: *When elephants fight, it is the grass that suffers*. I got tired of all the palace intrigue with the nuns and the Church and the royal households. I figured I'd never have a voice in the throne rooms of the world and get to sway the elephants, so I decided—fuck it—I'd just go help the grass: the poor, the dispossessed, the ones who lose their homes while the lords of everything squabble.'

'You're more important than you know,' Zoe said with genuine sympathy. 'The Catholic Church wants you dead. They ordered a hit on you. I'm guessing this is because of your work on the Siren bells.'

Tracy Smith gave a single short nod. 'I imagine so.'

'*Do* you know how to undo the Siren sleep?' Zoe asked.

Another single nod. 'The Siren sleep isn't magic or some kind of religious hocus-pocus. It's just science. The bells affect the inner ear, specifically the semicircular canals within the inner ear. It's kind of like a supercharged version of Ménière's disease.'

'What's that?'

'The bells disrupt the delivery of a special kind of fluid in those canals known as endolymph fluid. The bells don't affect animals because their semicircular canals are larger than ours. My theory is that you undo the sleep by injecting a synthetic endolymph serum into the semicircular canal in each ear.'

Zoe's eyes widened with hope.

'Dr Smith. I work with Jack West Jr and we need your help. If you come with me and test out your theory on a very important young woman named Lily, you'll not only be deeply hurting the throne rooms of the world, you might just help save the whole world from enslavement.'

Tracy Smith looked up at that.

Zoe began to speak, but the doctor held up her hand.

'It's okay, Miss Kissane,' she said. 'You had me at "deeply hurting the throne rooms of the world". Let's go and fuck them up.'

Thirty minutes later, on a bombed-out runway in Syria, in the back of Zoe's plane, Dr Tracy Smith inserted a long-tipped needle into the soft tissue behind Lily's right ear and injected some serum into it.

Then she did the left ear.

Everyone waited, watching Lily intently.

Nothing happened.

Lynda looked at Tracy. 'How long will it—'

'Wait!' Zoe exclaimed. Her eyes had never left Lily's.

Lily's eyelids fluttered.

Then, very slowly, they opened—blinking quickly, regaining focus—and Lily sat up and looked at the cluster of women gathered around her.

'I . . . I . . . Thank you,' she said.

Zoe dived forward and hugged her adopted daughter tightly, tears flowing down her cheeks.

Lily hugged her back. 'You won't believe how hungry I am. Do you have any food and water?'

'We sure do,' Zoe said, reaching for a canteen and some energy bars in her pack.

As she handed Lily the water, Lily froze, suddenly remembering the moment she had succumbed to the sleep.

'Where's Dad? I tried to warn him . . . in Moscow . . . with a note.'

'He got your note, Lily, and it saved him from the bells,' Zoe said. 'And because of that note, we're still in the game. But the game has got kinda crazy and we're a long way behind the bad guys. As usual, Jack's in the middle of it all and we need to go help him in Jerusalem right now.'

With those words, they'd got moving, heading directly for Jerusalem, with a new member added to their ragtag team, Dr Tracy Smith.

On the way to Jerusalem, Tracy had used her serum to awaken Stretch and Aloysius.

Stretch groaned. 'What happened? Is everybody okay?'

Aloysius Knight rubbed the back of his head. 'I have got the worst headache. Feels like the hangover from Hell.'

He spun to face Zoe. His first question wasn't about Jack or the sleep or the end of the world.

'Where's Rufus?'

'He's okay,' Zoe said kindly. 'He's on a mission with Alby Calvin. They're going to a remote location to try and tap into a lunar rover on the surface of the moon.'

Aloysius stared at her blankly. 'The surface of the moon? Just how long have I been out?'

'Long enough.' Zoe turned to Tracy Smith. 'We can't wake entire cities with this serum. We'll need to find the blue bell to do that. But this totally changes everything.'

From there they'd raced to Jerusalem and found Jack beneath the walls of the Old City just in time to inject the serum behind his ears and whisk him away from Jaeger Zwei and his bronzemen.

Once they were safe in the underground garage, Tracy woke Pooh Bear and Easton, too.

Everyone praised little Roxy and her desperate dragging of Jack. The few precious seconds the little poodle had bought him may well have saved his life.

Jack scratched Roxy behind the ear and her tail wagged with joy.

At which point, they got a call from Alby.

Alby was delighted to hear about Lily's awakening and the effectiveness of Tracy's serum.

'*Rufus and I are at the spaceport,*' he reported. '*Looks like it's still in working order. And one other thing: I did some extra research on the way here. I think I've found the last iron mountain.*'

FIFTH OFFENSIVE

THE LAST IRON MOUNTAIN

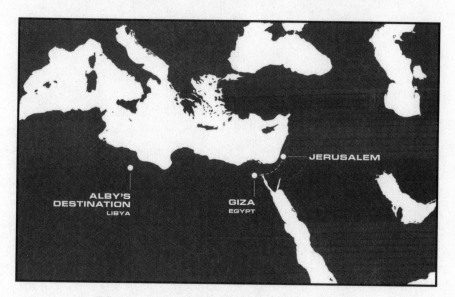

'My name is Ozymandias, king of kings;
Look on my works, ye Mighty, and despair!'
Nothing beside remains. Round the decay
Of that Colossal wreck, boundless and bare
The lone and level sands stretch far away.

PERCY BYSSHE SHELLEY
'OZYMANDIAS'

AIRSPACE OVER LIBYA
25 DECEMBER, 2020 HOURS

Alby had figured it out on the way to his peculiar destination.

While Rufus had flown the Sukhoi, Alby had sat in the rear gunner's seat, absorbed in his research, looking for the location of the fifth and last iron mountain, all the while aware that the clock to reaching the Supreme Labyrinth was ticking relentlessly downward.

After two hours, he discovered something promising.

He found it when he glanced back at the research he'd been doing at Hades's estate in Alsace-Lorraine—just before it had been raided by Sphinx's bronzemen—and the information buried in Jack's old documents relating to his mission regarding the Seven Ancient Wonders and the Great Pyramid at Giza.

Alby pulled up the translation from Khufu's edict that had been found inside the Great Pyramid:

> *Oh, great and wise Overlords,*
> *I have done as you commanded.*
> *I have built the mighty structure that will capture and*
> *contain the awesome power of Ra's Destroyer.*
> *I built it near Aker, who, ever alert, watches over the*
> *impossible maze from his sacred mountaintop perch.*
> *When death takes me, I will be laid inside this same mighty*
> *structure and use it as my tomb.*

When he had first read this, Alby had been drawn to the mention of an impossible maze.

This time, he decided to delve further into the idea of mountains near the Giza necropolis.

Nothing of note came up with his standard internet and library database searches.

Although he did get one hit for a PDF document titled: CITY OF CAIRO: DEPARTMENT OF CIVIL ENGINEERING GPR REPORT INTO AL-QADIR APARTMENT COMPLEX IN WESTERN CAIRO. It was dated January 2007.

It was one of those obscure things you got when you did an online search.

Alby clicked on it anyway, just to see what it was.

What he found was a very dry and very boring engineering report by some civil engineers into a new apartment complex that was being built on the western outskirts of Cairo near the pyramids.

When they had done a Ground Penetrating Radar study of the bedrock below the site of the new buildings, the engineers had struck solid granite.

The report read:

> GPR soundings indicate a large sub-stratum level of granite. Seems to rise gradually in the direction of the nearby Giza plateau [ref: image attached below].
>
> Lateral cross-sections show the outline of a conical underground mass that by our reckoning would peak near the plateau. We might have to refer this to the Antiquities Department . . .

Alby frowned.

A conical *underground* mass? On the western edge of Cairo, near the Giza plateau?

He thought about that.

The movement of desert sands in Egypt could be profound. Entire temples had been buried by encroaching sand. The Sphinx itself had been buried to the neck for many centuries in sand that had crept in from the desert to the west of it.

If something as big as the Sphinx could be covered in sand, it was entirely possible that, if left unchecked for thousands of years, the sands of the desert could conceal a low mountain.

Alby clicked further through the engineering document and suddenly he found a picture.

'Son of a bitch,' he said.

The picture leapt out at him.

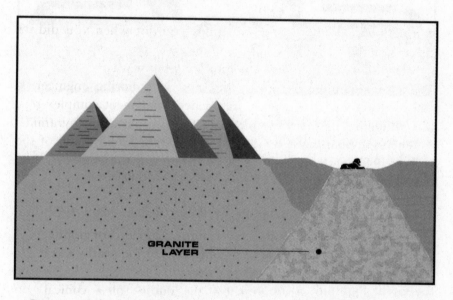

It may not have meant anything to some city engineers, but there it was, as clear as day: the Sphinx sitting atop a different kind of subterranean stone, an underground mountain.

Alby hurriedly typed 'Aker, images' into his search engine, expecting to find some kind of bird, given that Khufu had mentioned Aker watching over the maze from his sacred mountaintop *perch*.

But when he saw the first image that came up, he reared back in surprise.

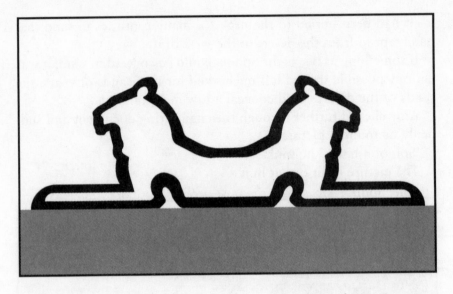

The image of Aker was of two recumbent lions facing in opposite directions, their bodies joined.

'Oh, man . . . why didn't I see it before?' Alby breathed. 'The uraeus in the Vatican. The photos Mae and Lynda saw there. It was right in front of us all along.'

In the pilot's seat in front of Alby, Rufus could hear him muttering.

'What's got your goat, kid?' he asked.

'Rufus,' Alby said, 'someone ordered the pharaoh Khufu to build the Great Pyramid, so he did, near a thing he called Aker. Now, this Aker is *very* important to us right now, because not only does it look out over the labyrinth we're searching for, I'm pretty sure it also sits on the summit of the fifth iron mountain. Rufus, I think I know what Aker is.'

'What?'

'Aker is the most famous statue on Earth. Aker is the Great Sphinx at Giza.'

'If the Sphinx sits atop the last iron mountain,' he reasoned, 'where's the entrance to its internal temple?'

Like a lightning bolt, it hit him.

'Wait, I've *seen* that entrance!' he said aloud.

Rufus was still flying. 'Kid, what are you talking about?'

Alby started tapping furiously on his laptop until he found them: the photos Mae had taken at the Vatican Secret Archives and sent to the team.

Two images of the Sphinx.

The first was the famous sketch that Vivant Denon had drawn during Napoleon's expedition to Egypt in 1798:

View of the Sphinx, near Cairo.

'Oh, wow . . .' Alby breathed as he looked at the sketch again.

He must have seen this image a dozen times before, but this time he focused not on the gigantic stone head sticking up from the sand but on the *men* standing on top of it.

'I never saw what they were doing before.'

Now that he had a reason to look more closely at the drawing, the figures in it stood out.

The men had not just been included in the drawing to give the Sphinx scale. They were doing things.

Two things, to be precise.

Three men stood on top of the Sphinx.

One, standing at the forward edge of the massive head, held a weighted rope in front of its forehead, as if taking a measurement.

Alby said, 'He's trying to recreate the uraeus.'

More importantly for Alby, however, was one of the other two men.

He was climbing out of the Sphinx's head.

'That's the entrance,' Alby breathed.

To confirm it, he brought up the other photo Mae had sent from the Vatican, the aerial shot of the Great Sphinx taken some time in the 1920s:

And there it was.

On the crown of the Sphinx's head was a round hole, no doubt the same hole Napoleon's men had been using in Denon's sketch.

A quick search of French museum pieces recording Napoleon's famous visit to Egypt brought up an obscure diary entry written by Napoleon himself:

> *My men found a narrow shaft that delved down into the head of the great stone beast. Only a single man could fit inside this mysterious shaft.*
>
> *But our explorations ended in disappointment. The shaft ended abruptly two fathoms down, blocked by centuries of clogged sand that had become solid stone.*

Alby shook his head.

Two fathoms was about twelve feet.

If only Napoleon had dug *through* the stone floor at the base of the narrow shaft, he might have found something incredible.

'Rufus, I just found what we need,' he said.

'Do you want to go somewhere else now?' Rufus asked.

Alby did some quick calculations of the moon's orbit.

It would be directly over Giza in a few hours, at 2:25 a.m. local time, and it would stay there for thirteen minutes.

'No,' he said firmly. 'We still have to get to our destination. Because while Jack goes inside the Sphinx at Giza, we have to uncover that pedestal on the moon.'

AIRSPACE OVER EGYPT
26 DECEMBER, 0155 HOURS

As the massive C-5 Super Galaxy cargo plane made the short hop from Jerusalem to Cairo, Jack sat down in the hold of the plane with Lily.

After all the chaos in Jerusalem—Rastor and the blasted-open Temple Mount, Mae's death, Jack's brush with the Siren sleep—it was their first real chance to catch up.

Indeed, it had been almost a month since Jack had actually spoken with Lily: the last time had been back in London, before she had been kidnapped by the Knights of the Golden Eight and delivered to Sphinx.

'I was a blubbering mess, kiddo,' Jack said, 'when I thought you were dead.'

Lily nodded. 'I appreciate that.'

'I do it all for you. Just trying to make sure there's a world for you to live in.'

'I know, Dad.'

'It's all gonna come to a head soon,' Jack said softly. 'At the Labyrinth. There's no comeback after that. No catching up. No second chances. This is about to become an all or nothing scenario.'

'Yeah,' Lily said.

'It might get crazy,' Jack said. 'Might have to do some desperate things.'

'More desperate than usual?'

'I'm thinking a whole new level of "drastic",' Jack said. 'It's so good to be with you again. It's all I ever want or need.'

Lily reached over and gave him a hug. 'You're the best, Dad.'

As she released him, Jack pulled out his cell phone. 'Oh, speaking of parents.'

He opened a secure file in his phone and brought up an email from his mother.

It was titled 'MY MESSAGE FROM THE OTHER SIDE'.

Jack clicked on it.

The first line read:

Jack, please read this with Zoe and Lily.

Jack called for Zoe to come down to the hold and join them. When she arrived, they read Mae Merriweather's last words together.

My dearest Cubby, Lily and Zoe,

I suppose it's over, if you're reading this.

As I think back on my life, I'm actually very proud of it. It was a good life, an interesting one. I married a brilliant man whom everyone called 'Wolf', so of course you, Jack, became 'Cub'. I loved Wolf once, but brilliant as he was, he turned out not to be so nice. But then, life after him— after I left him—turned out to be wonderful. I spent those years happily delving into my one true love: history.

But of all the things I've accomplished, the greatest one is you, Cubby.

The quiet little boy who became a man. And the best kind of man. Not some nerveless hero or even some famous warrior of legend, just a man for others. No mother could be prouder.

Cubby, the loyalty you receive from your merry band of friends—Zoe and Lily, Zahir and Benjamin, Sky Monster (I confess I don't know what his actual name is) and even your dogs—is merely the universe giving back to you what you gave first.

Zoe: thank you for loving my son. Like most men, he probably doesn't say it enough, but he adores you. Thank you.

And Lily. Kid. You are unique. And not because you can translate some ancient language. It's because you are you. With your blazingly inquisitive mind and your delightful personality. You have a light. Shine it. Don't let anyone dim it.

(Oh, and look after your dad. He worries about you. And date that Alby kid. I like him. Girls throughout history have always learned this lesson way too late: it's not the guys in motorcycle jackets who you want to be with; it's the ones with glasses and smarts and kind hearts. And Alby's got all of those and more. Sorry, nosy grandma moment there.)

Well, I guess I'd better sign off. I imagine you still have work to do.

Thanks for letting me join you on your adventures. History was never more fun.

I had the time of my life.

Mae

Lily sniffed back sobs.

Zoe put her arm around Jack.

None of them said anything.

Jack thought about his mother. Small in stature but big in brains, she'd been tough and strong, unbending and formidable. She'd been a gifted teacher, an inspirational historian and a great mum.

'We'll miss you, Mum,' Jack whispered.

Then Sky Monster's voice squawked over the intercom: '*Jack, we've started our descent into Cairo. The city looks asleep—from the ringing of a bell, it seems—but I can see some floodlights over by the pyramids. Someone got here ahead of us.*'

CAIRO INTERNATIONAL AIRPORT
CAIRO, EGYPT
26 DECEMBER, 0200 HOURS
7 HOURS TILL LABYRINTH GATES CLOSE

Cairo International Airport lay completely still.

Nothing stirred.

Even though it was two in the morning, normally there would be *some* movement at the airport—the odd maintenance truck or catering van; the usual night-time comings and goings of an international airport.

But tonight, thanks to a Siren bell, all of Cairo, including its airport, lay silent and empty.

The various vans, trucks and police cars at the airport all sat motionless, some of them with drivers slumped over their steering wheels.

Even the military vehicles in one corner of the airport—a Hercules cargo plane, two attack choppers and some jeeps mounted with 50-millimetre cannons—sat on the tarmac, completely still, with soldiers, pilots and maintenance crews lying on the ground beside them.

This was how Jack's massive C-5 Super Galaxy landed unimpeded at Cairo Airport, without so much as a challenge from the tower.

As it touched down, Jack turned to the two most important people in his life.

'Zoe. Lily. I want you both to do this Fall with me. Only a person with the mark on their hand can sit on the throne at the centre of the Supreme Labyrinth at the end of all this. I hate to say it, but we may not all make it that far, so having three of us with the mark gives us a better chance. You good with that?'

'Yes,' Lily said solemnly.

'Sure,' Zoe said.

No sooner had the big Super Galaxy rumbled to a halt than the three of them ran out of it, flanked by Pooh and Stretch.

They leapt into a nearby abandoned police car, fired it up and sped away into Cairo.

Aloysius, still groggy from his Siren sleep, stayed with Easton to guard the plane alongside Easton's mini-legion of palemen in the hold. Sister Lynda and Tracy Smith remained on board as well, to do more research and to look into ways of making larger batches of Tracy's serum.

Jack's police car sped toward the pyramids that towered over the western edge of the city.

It was 2:01 a.m.

The moon would be directly over Giza at 2:25.

They had twenty-four minutes.

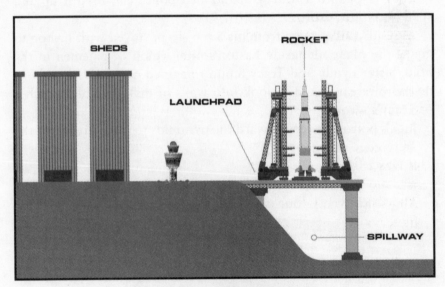

SHEDS

ROCKET

LAUNCHPAD

SPILLWAY

**ZAPADNY COSMODROME
LIBYA**

ZAPADNY COSMODROME
LIBYAN DESERT
26 DECEMBER, 0200 HOURS

At the same time as Jack and his team were arriving in Cairo, Alby and Rufus were arriving at their destination . . . in Libya.

It was a spaceport.

A working satellite launch facility located in the middle of the vast Libyan desert about a hundred miles from the Mediterranean coast.

Alby's jaw dropped at the sight of it.

Its scale was incredible. It was, quite simply, enormous in every way.

There was a reason for this.

While modern privately-owned satellite launch facilities are rather compact affairs, with slender rockets and minimal footprints, this spaceport had been built in the 1970s by the Soviet Union at the height of the Cold War.

The Soviets had built the facility in Muammar Gaddafi's Libya—of course after paying Gaddafi a giant bribe—to perform equatorial launches of satellites destined for geosynchronous orbits.

It was much more difficult to attain such orbits from the USSR's other main launch sites, the Baikonur Cosmodrome in Kazakhstan and the Vostochny—or 'eastern'—Cosmodrome in Siberia. Indeed this facility's original name was the Zapadny—or western—Cosmodrome.

Since it had been built by Soviet engineers, it was very grey, very ugly and very, very big.

The three towering sheds that had once housed multi-stage Russian rockets were twenty storeys tall. The tracks that led from them to the launchpad were as wide as four trucks parked side by side.

And then there was the launchpad itself, the centrepiece of the spaceport.

It was built in the same brutish Soviet style as the one at Baikonur, which was to say that the launchpad was a gigantic iron platform that, thanks to two colossal concrete pillars, jutted out from a cliff edge over a vast cement spillway two hundred feet deep.

During a launch, when the rocket blasted off from the elevated pad, it sent a downblast of fire and smoke into the spillway below, safely away from the command buildings atop the cliff.

After many superhot launches over the last forty years, the concrete surface of the spillway was charred black, like the walls of an old fireplace.

For the spaceport was indeed a working one. After the fall of the Soviet Union in 1989, it had fallen into disrepair. But with the recent rise of privately-owned satellite-launch companies, it had been bought by a European corporation and retrofitted for launches.

Indeed, as the Sukhoi came in closer to the spaceport, in the dull orange glare of its security lights, Alby saw a modern rocket—tall, white and slim—mounted on the launchpad, ready for launch.

Rufus was also clearly impressed. 'Holy moly, look at the size of this place.'

As they came nearer, however, Alby's face fell.

He saw the spaceport's control tower, a four-storey building that looked like a stunted version of an airport's air-traffic control tower.

All of its windows were smashed to pieces, blown apart by a fierce explosion.

And in that moment Alby realised.

'Rastor's people must have had the same idea we had,' he said. 'They used this place's communications gear to make contact with that second rover on the moon and uncover the pedestal up there when Rastor did the Fall at Jerusalem. When they were done, they replaced the foil cover and then destroyed the control tower behind them, so rivals like us couldn't use the communications gear afterward. *Shit!*'

Rufus gazed out over the deserted spaceport. Its towering structures and single rocket glowed orange in the glare of the security lights.

'I ain't no genius or anything,' Rufus said, 'but maybe there's still a way we can create an uplink to that rover on the moon.'

'Say that again, Rufus,' Alby said.

CAIRO, EGYPT
26 DECEMBER, 0210 HOURS

Jack boomed through the centre of Cairo in his stolen police car, racing through intersections unimpeded, running red lights at speed.

The city was empty.

Nothing moved on the roads. Any cars on them were stopped, either parked by the kerb or crashed against walls or each other.

The whole of Cairo was asleep.

With Zoe by his side, and Lily, Pooh Bear and Stretch in the back seat, Jack swept up a ramp onto an elevated freeway that cut across the city. He kept the headlights off, lest anyone spot their movement.

The high overpass wound between the modern buildings of the Egyptian capital. The skyline of central Cairo is generally low, with a few dozen office buildings and western hotels poking up out of a jumble of mosques, alleyways and markets.

Looming over it all to the west are Egypt's pride and joy.

Ancient and gigantic, the three mighty pyramids of Giza dominate the city's western horizon. Several project towers have been built near them in the suburb of Giza, but none of these, no matter how tall, can match the pyramids' awesome presence.

They are built to a different scale.

They are of another time.

As he dashed westward across the city, whizzing past stationary cars on the freeway, Jack eyed the pyramids.

He recalled his wild battle on the summit of the Great Pyramid over a decade ago, when he had re-erected its capstone.

And now he was back here.

It seemed almost appropriate, actually. In ancient matters, all roads led to Egypt.

Right then, his scanner picked up radio signals from whoever was already at the Giza necropolis.

Voices spoke hurriedly:

'—Lucifer base, this is Brother Eli with the Giza team. Are you ready?'

'—Copy, Giza team, this is Lucifer base in Arizona. Uplink has been established. We're ready when you are, Eli.'

'—We just broke through the bottom of the shaft cut into the Sphinx's head and can see a vast space with a Falling Temple in its middle. We are entering it now. Stand by.'

Zoe's eyes widened. 'They've found the temple underneath the Sphinx.'

'Who are these guys?' Lily asked.

'Monks from the Order of the Omega,' Jack said. 'More pals of Brother Ezekiel's. We think Ezekiel performed the Fall at Potala Palace, before Sphinx blew it up with a nuke. He's probably on his way to the Supreme Labyrinth now, if he's not already there. Looks like his buddy Eli is trying to perform the Fall here so they can double their chances in the Labyrinth. We're behind in this race again.'

'What's Lucifer?' Pooh Bear asked. 'Seems odd for some Catholic boys to have a base called Lucifer.'

Jack said, 'It's a high-tech astronomical observatory run by the Catholic Church at Mount Graham in Arizona, about 150 miles east of Tucson. Lucifer is the nickname for the state-of-the-art telescope there. That must be where the Omega monks are uplinking to a rover on the moon to uncover the pedestal.'

Their car rounded a bend in the freeway—its headlights still off—and suddenly the pyramids rose up in front of them, dark triangles against the night sky.

And there in front of the three pyramids, lying serenely in the spot it had occupied for thousands of years, staring sightlessly eastward, its paws outstretched, its head perfectly poised, mysterious and enigmatic as ever, was the Great Sphinx.

In the harsh glare of their floodlights, three men wearing miners' headlamps could be seen crawling on top of the huge statue's head.

A fourth man stood by a van at its base.

The three men on the head of the Great Sphinx had erected an A-frame over the hole. A cable from a motorised winch on the A-frame stretched down into the hole.

Suddenly their radio barked:

'—*Giza team, we just picked up something incoming to our location here at Lucifer. Wait, what—!*'

The signal cut to tone.

Jack looked at Zoe. 'What the hell just happened?'

Stretch answered by holding up his smartphone. He had a live stream of CNN on it.

On the phone, the TV news anchor looked confused. 'We're getting . . . wait a minute now . . . we're getting unconfirmed reports out of Tucson, Arizona, of a nuclear explosion near there. We're awaiting images but early reports are of an explosion east of the city . . .'

Lily gasped. 'Like 150 miles east?'

A few moments later, a grainy image appeared on the live stream.

It showed a hellish mushroom cloud rising above the Arizona desert. The chyron below the image read: BREAKING NEWS: NUCLEAR BLAST OUTSIDE TUCSON, AZ.

The response from the monks at the Great Sphinx was instantaneous.

'—*Lucifer team, report!*'

No answer.

'—*Lucifer team, come in!*'

Still nothing.

Jack swallowed. Then he keyed his own satellite radio.

'Alby, have you arrived at the spaceport yet?'

'We just got here, Jack. Got some issues, but we might have a way to create an uplink to one of the rovers on the moon.'

'Whatever you have to do, do it,' Jack said simply. 'And watch your back. The bad guys clearly don't want anyone else performing a Fall and they may come for you.'

**ZAPADNY COSMODROME
LIBYAN DESERT**

Over in Libya, a very skilful piece of flying was taking place.

Carefully manoeuvred by Rufus, the Sukhoi Su-37 edged in toward the pointed tip of the two-hundred-foot-tall rocket standing on the launchpad of the Zapadny Cosmodrome.

The rocket resembled a giant spear pointing skyward, supported by a kind of metal framework.

For until it lifted off, the rocket was encased on four sides by gantry scaffolding: a criss-crossing lattice of elevators, ladders, platforms, water pipes, gas pipes, fuel pipes and workrooms. The amazing thing was that the whole four-sided lattice would fold back on huge hinges—like the petals of a flower opening—when the rocket blasted off in a blaze of fire and fury.

When the Sukhoi reached the tip of the rocket, the canopy of the fighter-bomber's cockpit opened and the tiny figure of Alby crept out onto its wing and *leapt down* onto the uppermost platform of the gantry structure.

Then he ran to the very tip of the rocket.

Buffeted by wind, Alby stood at the peak of the rocket, high above the world. With the additional two hundred feet of drop to the spillway beneath the launchpad, it felt extra high and dizzying.

From this spot, he could see for miles in every direction, across the dead-flat landscape to the dark horizon.

Out here in the desert, the stars winked brightly.

The full moon, huge and round and so bright you could read by its light, was off to the east—almost directly over Giza in Egypt.

Alby didn't have time to marvel at the view.

Using a powered screwdriver, he hurriedly removed a panel on the rocket's nose-cone, revealing a bank of data monitors, cables, blinking lights and a small keyboard with a computer screen.

It was the rocket's guidance and communications system.

The bulk of any rocket is fuel. That's the two-hundred-foot-tall part. The business end is the nose. This is where you find all the avionics and electronics—including guidance and communications gear—and whatever satellite (which is often quite small) that the rocket is delivering into orbit.

Using a T3 cable, Alby plugged his laptop into the rocket's communications unit and suddenly he was in.

'*How's it going, kid?*' Rufus's voice said in his earpiece.

'Connecting to the rocket's comms system now,' Alby said.

This was Rufus's brilliant idea.

They needed an uplink powerful enough to reach the moon 240,000 miles away. Not many vehicles in the world had such a system. But an orbital rocket did. And Alby was now going to use it to control one of the rovers on the moon.

Alby tapped on some keys, getting the rocket's communications system to search for a receiver on the surface of the moon—

—and suddenly the rocket's system beeped and a screen read:

1 RECEIVER FOUND
I.D. #: RC-7D4 RUSSIAN SPACE PROGRAM
TYPE: LUNAR ROVER MODEL VS-12-D

Alby ordered the computer to take over the Russian lunar rover's controls and abruptly an image appeared on the rocket's computer screen: an image of the moon taken from ground level.

'Whoa . . .' Alby breathed.

The landscape that he saw was just like what he'd seen on every documentary he'd ever watched about the lunar surface.

Everything was grey: the ground, the rocks, the boulders. Every shadow was dark, really dark.

Another rover, the original American rover from *Apollo 15*, sat parked nearby.

And there beside it was an object that while also grey in colour was not natural to the moon.

The pedestal.

That it was alien there was no doubt.

It was rectangular in shape, with sharply cut edges and a perfectly flat upper surface.

But it was covered by a thin sheet of rumpled silver material: Kapton foil that would block its light from bursting forth.

'Bingo,' Alby said.

It took him a minute to figure out how to drive the rover and manipulate its gripping prongs. It wasn't easy. The technology was super old and not very responsive. When he managed to grip the Kapton foil with the prongs, they locked in place, refusing to release it.

He had just grabbed the foil when Rufus said in his ear, '*Er, kid. We got a problem. Somethin' incoming and incoming fast.*'

Alby snapped around to look up at the sky, worried that it was another nuke, coming to obliterate the spaceport.

And he saw it.

A speck of light among the stars.

Only this 'star' was moving. Quickly.

Coming from the north.

Coming toward him.

An incoming plane of some kind.

Alby checked his watch.

2:24 a.m.

One minute till the moon was over Giza. Then Jack would have thirteen minutes to do the Fall.

At that moment, something detached from the incoming speck of light, something dark and rectangular that fell toward the spaceport.

Whatever it was, it wasn't a missile.

It came roaring out of the sky and *slammed* into the ground barely three hundred metres from Alby's rocket, kicking up a monstrous cloud of dust and sand.

Alby peered at the dust cloud, wondering what the hell this was.

Gradually, the cloud cleared and in its place he saw a long black armoured box about the size of a shipping container.

It was an ADS-IRM—Aerial Delivery System for Impact Resistant Material—identical to the ones that had delivered four loads of bronzemen to Novodevichy Convent in Moscow.

With four simultaneous *whams*, the walls of the container dropped open, revealing sixty bronzemen who immediately began marching toward the rocket on the launchpad.

'Oooooh, shit,' Alby said.

He keyed his radio. 'Jack! Are you at the temple under the Great Sphinx yet? I have an uplink to the moon. Please hurry because a bunch of bronzemen just landed here and are coming for us right now!'

In Cairo, Jack's car skidded to a dusty halt behind some museum buildings a hundred metres from the Great Sphinx, just out of sight from it.

The handful of Omega monks on the head of the giant statue didn't see him. In any case, they were swapping confused looks because of the recent nuclear destruction of their uplink in Arizona.

Jack keyed his radio. 'Expose the pedestal, Alby! We're going in!'

At the tip of the rocket high above the spaceport, with the bronzemen advancing down the length of the launchpad toward him, Alby worked the controls on the rocket's communications system . . .

. . . manoeuvring the Russian lunar rover on the surface of the moon, causing it to creep backwards and, with its extendable

mechanical prongs gripping the Kapton foil, pull the reflective silver sheet off the ancient pedestal up there . . .

. . . when something happened.

The rover up on the moon abruptly rolled *forward*—of its own accord—pushing the silver foil *back onto* the pedestal, covering it again.

'Damn Russian systems!' Alby shouted. He fiddled hurriedly with the controls until he figured out what was happening.

It was a glitch, some kind of automated movement programmed into the rover many years ago. The upshot was: every time he reversed it, the rover would move forward again, retracing its steps, *replacing* the Kapton foil over the pedestal.

'All right, okay, I can do this,' Alby said quickly to himself. He'd just have to man the controls the whole time. He reversed the rover again, pulling the Kapton foil off the pedestal, as . . .

. . . the clock struck 2:25 . . .

. . . and—*bam!*—a blinding beam of brilliant green light shot out from the pedestal, lancing down toward the Earth, toward Giza.

The three Omega monks on the head of the Great Sphinx sprang back in surprise as, in an instant, a blazing beam of green light extended down from the moon and shot between them *into* the hole in the head of the statue.

Their leader, Brother Eli, was quick-witted enough to realise what had happened.

'Someone else has exposed the pedestal on the moon!' he called, his face illuminated by the otherworldly green glow. 'Guard the entrance! I must do the Fall!'

He hurried to the hole in the Great Sphinx's head, leaping into a slender steel basket hanging from the A-frame that straddled the hole, and with a whizzing whir, he plunged into the shaft while the other two monks turned to keep guard.

An instant later, two shots felled them and Jack West Jr, Zoe and Lily appeared on the head of the Great Sphinx.

Jack peered down into the hole.

Brother Eli's motorised winch was still whirring loudly as it unspooled, lowering the monk into the inky darkness.

'You both still okay to do this Fall?' Jack asked.

'Ready as I'll ever be,' Lily said.

'Not a doubt in my mind,' Zoe said.

With a loud *clank*, the motorised winch stopped unspooling.

'He's landed on the temple! We don't have much time. Lily, hang on to me. Zoe, you slide down after us!'

Lily wrapped her arms around Jack's neck as Jack stepped into

the beam of green light and grabbed hold of the cable with his gloved hands.

Then he wrapped his boots around it and slid down the cable into the tight vertical shaft bored into the head of the Great Sphinx of Giza.

A few seconds later, bathed in the green glow of the moon-pedestal's light, Jack and Lily slid out from the ceiling of a high, domed cavern.

As at the other mountains, the Falling Temple lay directly below them.

It was identical to the others: shaped like a giant spinning top, with a heavy upper half and a spindly lower half. It hung from mighty ancient chains attached to the ceiling. An imposing main obelisk stood on its peak surrounded by four smaller ones.

Brother Eli was just stepping out of his steel basket at the bottom of the cable, right next to the main obelisk, when he saw them.

He dashed for the altar at the base of the main obelisk and reached for one of the four images of a human hand on its sides, the images with raised markings that looked like a W.

Eli pressed his palm against one of the images . . .

. . . and the Falling Temple was released from its chains and dropped with a heavy lurch . . .

. . . just as Jack and Lily, and then Zoe, whizzing down the cable, released their grips on it and hurled themselves at the temple's uppermost level, landing on it just as the heavy ancient structure dropped and began its ceremonial Fall.

In Libya, Alby was manning the controls atop the rocket while looking frantically below him.

Gunfire rang out as Rufus brought the Sukhoi around and fired on the advancing company of bronzemen.

His bullets took out some but the simple fact was there were too many of them.

Forty of the bronzemen arrived at the base of the rocket's gantry tower and started to climb it, heading for Alby.

But he couldn't leave. He had to make sure the rover didn't replace the foil on the pedestal until Jack and the others were done.

'Oh, this is very bad . . .' Alby said grimly.

Released from its chains, the Falling Temple dropped with frightening speed toward the yawning mouth of the wide round shaft below it.

It fell fast, accelerating quickly.

The monk named Eli looked shocked to see Jack, Lily and Zoe land beside him and place their hands on the other three palm images just as the temple shot through the upper annulus of the fall shaft.

The three lines of the W were seared onto all their thumbs, index and middle fingers as the Falling Temple plummeted down the shaft.

'Now, run!' Jack called. 'We gotta get to the lower altar before the temple passes through the second ring!'

And the race was on.

Wind whipped all around Jack, Lily, Zoe and Eli as they bounded down the slanting levels of the temple's upper half, running as it fell, with the Omega monk, Brother Eli, always a short distance in the lead.

The walls of the shaft sped by, rushing upward.

The green glow of the beam from the moon lit up everything.

Jack, Lily and Zoe came to the waist of the temple, its widest point, and hurried down a ladder built into it, coming to its spindly lower half.

Jack glimpsed Eli a few paces ahead of them, racing across the width of this level to another ladder at its opposite end.

He gave chase, followed by Lily and Zoe.

At the same time in Libya, the forty bronzemen were now halfway up Alby's gantry tower, closing in on him at the top of the rocket.

Alby glanced down nervously at them as he continued to operate the controls that kept the pedestal on the moon open.

'Jack! You done yet? I've got a real problem here!'

'Not yet, Alby!' Jack called into his radio-mike as he leapt down onto the next lower level.

'You gotta keep that light from the moon blazing for a little longer, just till we reach the lower altar!'

Down he went, back and forth across each level, sliding down ladders until he slid down a final one and found himself on the bottommost and smallest level of the entire temple—

—where he was confronted by the bulky frame of Brother Eli, blocking the way to the temple's lower altar two paces behind him.

The walls of the drop shaft continued to whoosh by around them.

'You have failed, Captain!' Eli yelled above the wind. 'In moments, we will pass through the second electromagnetic ring and you will not have your hand pressed against this altar—'

Jack didn't have time for speeches so he just launched himself forward and tackled Eli—hard—knocking the big monk sideways while Lily and Zoe raced past the two of them and quickly pressed their palms against two of the hand-shaped images on the lower altar.

On the rocket tower in Libya, the bronzemen were now only one level away from Alby, climbing, climbing.

The first bronzeman's head poked up onto Alby's level.
Blam!
Alby levelled his pistol and shot the bronzeman in the head with one of his special bullets.
The bronzeman snapped back and fell.
'Hurry, Jack . . . !' Alby urged.

Eli and Jack fought on the lowest level of the Falling Temple.
Eli—a big man with speed and strength—quickly slithered behind Jack and wrapped one of his huge forearms around Jack's neck.
Then he drew a long curved blade and readied to slash it across Jack's throat when Jack twisted suddenly and lurched *forward*, pulling Eli with him so that the big monk's forehead slammed with shocking violence against the hard stone edge of the altar.
It was a horrific blow.
Blood flew.
The monk recoiled, stunned but not killed.
Jack took care of that a moment later.
Freed from Eli's grip, he kicked him square in the chest, hurling the big monk clear off the platform of the Falling Temple. Eli screamed as he toppled off the still-dropping temple.
On his knees, Jack crawled over to the altar and slammed his palm down on one of the hand images . . .
. . . just as the entire temple whizzed through a second silver ring embedded in the circular wall of the fall shaft . . .
. . . and he roared in pain—as did Lily and Zoe—as the markings were seared into their palms, creating the five-pronged mark on their fingers.
Instantly, the temple's braking system was activated and it squealed to a halt.
The monk Eli kept falling, screaming shrilly as he vanished into the darkness of the shaft.
He hit the bottom a few seconds later and the screaming stopped.

★ ★ ★

Breathless and panting, Jack looked at Lily and Zoe.

They all held up their hands.

All three of them bore the five-pointed mark on their right palms.

Jack keyed his radio. 'Alby! We did it! Get out of there!'

Alby was now firing wildly and repeatedly at the swarm of bronze-men assailing his position.

His gantry tower was completely crawling with them.

They just kept coming. No sooner would he blast one away with a special bullet than another would appear in the first one's place.

Alby kept firing grimly, while also manning the rover controls. It would have been comical if it hadn't been so vitally important.

He had to keep the green light beam on the moon alive until Jack and the others completed the Fall.

Another bronzeman sprang up suddenly from below him, so close that Alby could see not only its beak-like proboscis, but the many intricate markings engraved all over its shiny bronze skull.

A mixture of swirls, geometric shapes and Thoth text, the markings looked like tattoos etched into the automaton's metal pate.

Right now, Alby didn't care what they were.

He shot the bronzeman in the face and the back of its head blew out and it toppled off the rocket.

And then Jack's voice exploded in his ear:

'*Alby! We did it! Get out of there!*'

Alby was thrilled to hear Jack's command but actually getting out of his predicament was another thing entirely—

Clang!

Something banged against the bridge connecting his platform to the gantry tower.

A cage hanging from a cable.

A cable that hung from the belly of the Sukhoi!

Rufus had brought the fighter-bomber into a hover directly above the rocket and unspooled the cage from the plane's bomb bay.

'*Get in, kid!*' his voice rang in Alby's earpiece.

Alby moved instantly.

He dived for the cage, catching it with his fingertips as the bronzemen overwhelmed his position atop the rocket. No sooner had he gone than the Russian rover on the moon once again automatically rolled forward, covering the pedestal again with the Kapton foil.

The cage swung wildly as Alby hung from it and Rufus peeled the Sukhoi away from the gantry tower now teeming with bronzemen.

Rufus and Alby flew away into the night.

They had done what they came here to do.

They'd uncovered the pedestal on the moon long enough for Jack and others to perform the Fall at Giza.

Now it was time to help Jack face the final challenge: finding and entering the Supreme Labyrinth.

FINAL OFFENSIVE

THE FIVE GATES OF THE SUPREME LABYRINTH

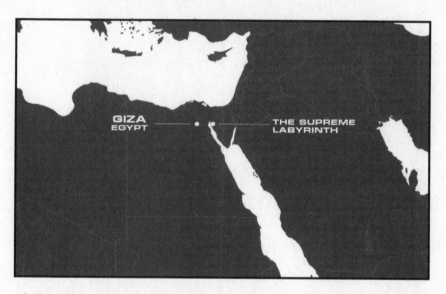

GIZA
EGYPT

THE SUPREME
LABYRINTH

It has been staring unblinking in that direction for eternity,
but what, I ask you, is the Great Sphinx looking at?

NAPOLEON BONAPARTE

After Jack, Zoe and Lily emerged from the Hall of the Falling Temple beneath the Great Sphinx at Giza, they sped back with Stretch and Pooh Bear to Cairo International Airport.

When they pulled up outside their parked C-5 Super Galaxy, they found Sister Lynda waiting for them, very excited.

'I know where the Labyrinth is,' she said.

'*Sixteen schoinos from my eyes,*' she explained once they were all gathered inside the Super Galaxy. 'That's what one of the Omega monks said in the Vatican when he was examining the uraeus from the Great Sphinx. Mae and I didn't know what he meant at the time, but I do now. It all makes sense from here, or more precisely, from Giza.'

'Slow down, now. We're gonna need a little more explanation,' Jack said.

Lynda took a breath. 'A *schoinos* is an ancient Egyptian unit of measurement. It's about ten and a half kilometres. Now, those Omega monks said: *Sixteen schoinos from my eyes.* Like us and Rastor, those monks were searching for the Supreme Labyrinth. They were looking for something they called the *multiple*: which was how far—how many *schoinos*—the Labyrinth is from a certain starting point. The monks knew the starting point. They just didn't know how far the Labyrinth was from it.'

'So what's the starting point?' Zoe asked.

'The Great Sphinx,' Lynda said. 'That uraeus in the Vatican was once mounted on its forehead. *Sixteen schoinos from my eyes* means about 160 kilometres from *the Great Sphinx's eyes.*'

Lynda pointed due east. 'The Supreme Labyrinth is approximately 160 kilometres that way. Napoleon himself once asked, "What is the Sphinx looking at?" That's what it's been looking at for thousands of years: the Supreme Labyrinth.'

A map was brought up on a computer.

Jack overlaid a line on it stretching due east of Giza and scaling it to 160 kilometres.

They all scanned it closely.

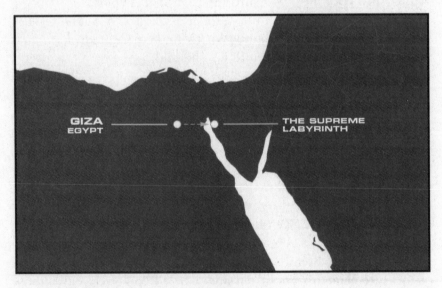

GIZA
EGYPT ——————— ○ - - ○ ——————— THE SUPREME
LABYRINTH

'Looks like it's in the Sinai Desert,' Zoe said.

'Literally the middle of nowhere,' Lynda agreed.

Jack frowned.

He'd seen something like this before.

Then he remembered.

He quickly brought up a photo on his smartphone, one he had taken while he and Lily had been inside the innermost vault of the Order of the Omega in Venice, something that seemed a lifetime ago.

It was the shot of a very old sheet of papyrus titled in Latin: MAGNUM VIAM PORTAE QVINQVE. The Five Gates to the Great Labyrinth.

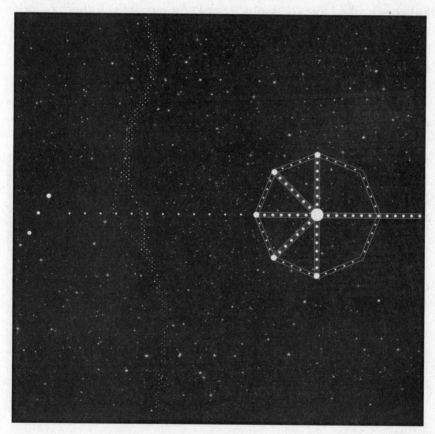

'I can't believe I didn't see it before,' he said. 'It looks like a star map, but it's not. *It's a map of Egypt.*

'Those three bright stars on the left that look like Orion's Belt are the three pyramids at Giza. The bending vertical line of stars in the

middle is the Nile. And that wagon-wheel thing on the right—
the one with five spokes leading to a central hub—that must be the
Labyrinth with its five entrances. The monks knew the starting
point all right. They just needed to know the distance using the
multiple.'

'It's not that far away,' Lily said. 'Maybe an hour by plane.'

Jack frowned. 'Sphinx got there a full day ago and entered the
Labyrinth. We have to assume that Dion has arrived there by now
as well. It's also likely that Sphinx has stationed some guards at
the other gates, to stop competitors like us, the monks and General
Rastor from getting inside.'

He keyed his radio. 'Alby? Rufus? You guys still alive out there?'

'*We're here, Jack*,' Alby's voice replied. '*Leaving the spaceport
now.*'

'How far from Cairo are you?'

'*Maybe forty minutes*,' Rufus replied.

'We can't wait for you,' Jack said. 'We have to get to the
Labyrinth right away. Meet us there. Hurry. I'll send you the
coordinates.'

Jack bit his lip, thinking about what he had to work with: people, planes, vehicles, guns. 'We need a plan . . .'

And he blinked as it struck him.

Zoe saw it happen. 'Just what kind of plan are you thinking of,
Jack?'

Jack turned to face her.

'I'm gonna call it the Russian Doll Plan. Let me explain.'

As Rufus flew the Sukhoi at full speed toward Egypt, Alby sat in the gunner's seat, exhausted.

He gazed dumbly at the plane's interactive digital map of the landscape below them: the barren Sahara Desert, Libya and Egypt.

Like all aeroplane maps, this one crept along in real time, moving with the plane's movement, and included on it were the names of various towns and topographical land formations.

As he gazed at the map, Alby abruptly saw the name of one town that he recognised.

There it was, tucked near the Libyan–Egyptian border, just on the Egyptian side. They were going to fly almost directly over it.

The designation read: **SIWA OASIS (-19)**

The Siwa Oasis, Alby thought.

It was, in a way, where this whole adventure had begun: Lily was, after all, the last in a long line of Oracles from that very place.

As he looked at the digital map, Alby saw the notation beside the name: **(-19)**.

For a moment, he wondered what that meant and then, seeing similar numbers beside other towns and landforms, he realised.

It was that place's height above sea level.

But in the case of Siwa, it was a negative number: minus 19.

'*The Siwa Oasis is below sea level*,' Alby said, realising.

'What are you mumbling about this time, kid?' Rufus said.

'The Siwa Oasis lies just off the western tip of the Qattara Depression, a vast hollow in the floor of the Sahara, one of the lowest points in all of Africa. According to this map, it lies nineteen metres below sea level—'

He cut himself off.

'Imhotep's tomb,' he said suddenly. 'Imhotep wrote that his tomb was located *within the great hill of the Oracle under the sea.* I thought he meant under an ocean so I discounted Siwa, but I was wrong. He was referring to Siwa being below sea level.'

Alby scooped up his laptop and started typing furiously.

'What are you doing?' Rufus asked, swivelling in his seat.

Alby didn't look up as he typed.

'I might be finding something that Jack's gonna need: some ancient clues that can guide him safely through the Supreme Labyrinth.'

CAIRO, EGYPT

At Cairo International Airport, Jack's team was making hurried preparations.

Jack had given everyone instructions—including assigning Aloysius and Easton a particularly important task—and they'd scattered to get their jobs done.

While all this was going on, Jack took Stretch and Pooh Bear aside.

'You two aren't going to the Labyrinth,' he said seriously. 'I have another mission for you.'

'Yes?' Pooh said cautiously.

Jack said, 'Assuming *somebody* succeeds inside the Labyrinth, the world is going to be pretty crazy afterwards. A whole bunch of major cities will still be asleep. And everyone associated with the four kingdoms knows this. Whether they support Sphinx or not, the royal assholes of the world will have a plan for what comes *after* the Omega Event. I don't know how, but I want you guys to find these royal assholes and figure out their plan. Take Sister Lynda and Tracy Smith with you. They might be able to help. Oh, and, guys, if I should die, at least make things hard for these bastards.'

Stretch nodded. 'You got it, Jack.'

'While we're on the subject of my death . . .' Jack pulled a sealed envelope from his pocket and handed it to Pooh Bear.

'I've sent this to Zoe and Lily in an email, but I want you guys to have it, too,' he said softly.

'What is it?' Pooh Bear said, although he had an idea.

Jack said, 'It's my letter. My Message from the Other Side. To be opened in the event that I don't get out of this alive.'

'Jack, don't think like that—' Stretch began.

'If everything goes well, I'll be going into the maze with Lily and Zoe,' Jack said. 'We each have the mark on our hands, so any one of the three of us can save the world if we can get to the throne at the centre. I just . . . well . . . I just don't know about this one. There are no guarantees here. Hades and my mum were both murdered and I don't know how long my luck will last. I just, well, I just have a feeling I might not . . . Listen, if I don't make it out of there, I want you guys to have my letter and to read it, okay?'

Pooh Bear nodded grimly. 'You got it, Jack. We'll take care of it.'

Stretch—a stoic guy at the best of times and not a man given to emotional gestures—leaned forward and hugged Jack fiercely.

'You'll get out, buddy. You always do. You always do.'

'I don't know this time,' Jack said, his eyes downcast.

Then he walked away to get to work.

A short time later, they all took off, heading eastward for the Sinai Peninsula and the five fortified entrances to the Supreme Labyrinth, knowing that they were flying into the fight of their lives.

THE SIWA OASIS
WESTERN EGYPT
26 DECEMBER, 0655 HOURS
2 HOURS 05 MINUTES TILL GATES CLOSE

While Jack was preparing to take off from Cairo, Alby and Rufus were diverting from their original flight path and swooping down toward Lily's ancestral home, the Siwa Oasis.

With its wide spring-fed lakes and thousands of date palms, the Siwa Oasis is simply remarkable, a true wonder of nature: a vibrant burst of lush greenery amid an otherwise endless sea of sand.

In any other circumstances, Alby would have loved to take his time and absorb the history of the place, but not now.

Now he was in a hurry.

Roaring out of the moonlit sky, the Sukhoi boomed into a hover above the main landform of the remote oasis: the Hill of the Dead.

It was a high cone-shaped sandstone formation that towered over Siwa's vast main lake and which was named for the many tombs and burial niches within its catacombs.

Alby sprang out of the fighter-bomber, calling, 'Come on, Rufus! If I'm right, I'm gonna need you in here. Bring the hammer and chisel.'

Leaving the Sukhoi parked on the peak of the hill, the two of them raced into its catacombs.

There are hundreds of tombs inside Siwa's Hill of the Dead, but—as Alby had discovered on the way here—only four were

of a size that would be regarded as worthy of a high priest of the Cult of Amon-Ra, and only one of those was named the Tomb of Niperpathoth: the tomb of 'he who belongs to the House of Thoth'.

Alby recalled Imhotep's words:

Then seal me in stone in my tomb dedicated to Thoth within the great hill of the Oracle under the sea, with the secrets of the maze buried with me.

They found the tomb quickly. It was a minor tourist attraction for the few hardy tourists who ventured this far into the desert. A bare square room, it stank of centuries-old musk.

Alby and Rufus trained their flashlights over it. It was extraordinary in its plainness, with only a couple of crude paintings of the beaked god of wisdom, Thoth, on its walls.

Rufus sighed. 'Kid, there's nothing here.'

The tomb was indeed glaringly empty.

Grave robbers and archaeologists had long ago seized anything of value that wasn't nailed down.

'That's okay,' Alby said. 'What we're looking for won't be in plain sight.'

He moved his flashlight beam over the tomb's floorstones, his eyes searching.

He was looking for something he had seen before in the ancient royal world—

'There!' he exclaimed, pointing at one long floorstone.

It was slightly darker than the others.

It was made of a different kind of stone.

'Greystone . . .' Alby said aloud. '*Seal me in stone*, Imhotep commanded. After they mummified him, he got his followers to seal his mummy in greystone. Let's do this.'

And so Alby and Rufus started assaulting the floor of the ancient tomb with their hammer and chisel, chipping away at the stone until, after a few minutes . . .

. . . they struck something . . .

. . . something wrapped in linen.

'Careful now,' Alby said as they cleared away the broken grey-stone and revealed . . .

. . . the mummy of Imhotep the Great.

'Whoa, mama,' Rufus whispered.

Alby unwrapped the mummy's headcloth, revealing for the first time in almost five thousand years the face of Imhotep the Great.

As with other mummies, the skin was dry, desiccated and black. The eye sockets were sunken and the mouth hung open, its ghastly teeth bared in an eternal scream.

'Are you sure it's him?' Rufus asked.

'It's him,' Alby said. 'He's wearing his skullcap.'

And what a thing it was.

The old statues of Imhotep hadn't done justice to his signature domed cap.

For it wasn't made of just any metal.

It was made of glorious polished silver that gleamed in the light of their flashlights. Etched Thoth markings ringed it.

Alby gazed at the silver metal cap in awe. It was a strange silver, dull, non-reflective, like that of the—

'The silvermen . . .' Alby breathed. 'Imhotep's skullcap was taken from the head of a silverman. Silvermen are the guards of ancient places like the Labyrinth. I wonder if Imhotep took his cap from a dormant silverman during his venture into the Labyrinth.'

Slowly, carefully, Alby reached into the broken-open floor and removed the silver cap from the mummy, revealing the black skin of its scalp.

That was the main reason he was here.

It had struck him as they had flown here.

An image he'd seen at the spaceport.

He recalled seeing the tattoo-like markings etched into the metal heads of the bronzemen—much like he was seeing now on the silver cap—swirls and Thoth symbols engraved into the crowns of their shiny skulls.

> *I imparted the secrets of that maze to my body*
> *in the manner of the ancients.*

To my body.

In the manner of the ancients.

Like the ancients had done with the heads of the bronzemen and silvermen.

'That was why he always wore that skullcap,' Alby said. 'To cover the markings on his scalp.'

Alby shone his flashlight at the blackened skin of Imhotep the Great's mummified skull. Being sealed in airtight greystone had kept it in very good condition.

The markings on it were dim, but they were there, drawn in grey ink on the age-blackened skin.

Swirls.

Geometric shapes.

And lines of text in the Word of Thoth.

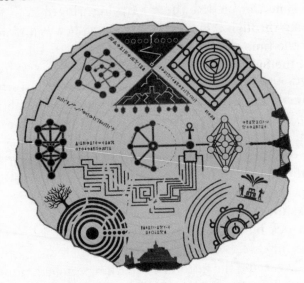

As he scanned the tattooed text and images, Alby recalled another line from Imhotep's message:

When I die, let the next head-priest of Amon-Ra replicate those markings in the same manner.

'The next head-priest of Amon-Ra,' Alby said. 'I'm guessing someone high up in the Catholic Church has these same secrets tattooed onto his scalp. My first guess would be Cardinal Mendoza.'

Rufus nodded at the mummy with its head exposed but its body still sealed in the greystone. 'So, are we gonna take him with us? If so, how?'

Alby said, 'Don't tell any archaeologists I did this, okay.'

Without any ceremony or reverence, and with a sharp cracking sound, Alby roughly yanked Imhotep's head off his body. Then he tossed it into his backpack.

'We're taking the *head* with us?' Rufus gaped.

'Sure are.' Alby slung the backpack over his shoulder. 'Let's move. We gotta get this to Jack before he reaches the Labyrinth.'

The two of them raced out of the tomb.

By the time they reached the surface, they could hear a police siren cutting through the night. Someone had called the local cops.

But by the time the lone Siwan police car arrived at the Hill of the Dead, the Sukhoi had flown off, heading east, in the direction of greater Egypt and the Supreme Labyrinth.

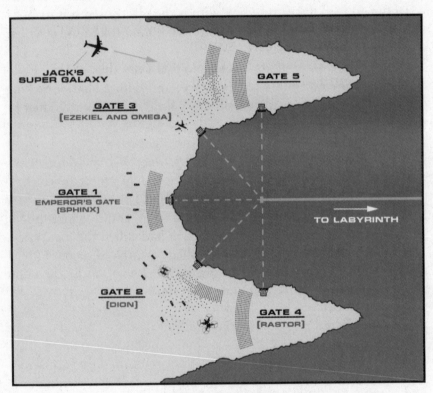

**THE FIVE GATES
OF THE SUPREME LABYRINTH**

THE GATES OF THE SUPREME LABYRINTH
SINAI DESERT, EGYPT
26 DECEMBER, 0830 HOURS
30 MINUTES TILL GATES CLOSE

Jack's Super Galaxy raced toward the newly risen sun, soaring over the mouth of the Suez Canal at the northern tip of the Red Sea.

The rugged desert landscape of the Sinai Peninsula lay spread out before it.

It was brutal terrain, stark and brown, rugged and mountainous, dry, arid and hotter than Hell. A land of rubble and rock, sand and dust.

Nothing lived here. Not trees, not even weeds.

And somewhere in there, Jack thought as he gazed out the cockpit windshield of the Super Galaxy, *is a semicircle of five ancient gates that give access to a gigantic subterranean labyrinth.*

Having plotted a course on their sat-nav system that led due east from the Great Sphinx at Giza—or more specifically, from the eyes of the cobra-shaped uraeus that had once adorned its forehead—they hoped to come across the site approximately 160 kilometres from their start point.

It turned out not to be that difficult to spot, for three reasons.

First, the four thousand–strong *army* of bronzemen standing in defensive formations around the gate complex, accompanied by Sphinx's hovering Russian quadcopter plus men on the ground in anti-aircraft jeeps.

Second, because of the remnants of a plane crash that had clearly already occurred at one of the gates.

And third, because of the gigantic and explosive battle raging there.

Rastor's immense hovering aeroplane was raining hell on Sphinx's defensive forces.

The huge V-88 Condor was even larger than Sphinx's Mi-4000 quadcopter. It hovered to the right of a low mountain, launching missiles at the quadcopter at the same time as it spewed tracer fire at the ground, blowing anti-aircraft jeeps to pieces and mowing down the ranks of bronzemen.

Explosions rang out.

Bronzemen were thrown everywhere.

Parts of the mountain blew off in geysers of dust and sand.

Then—shockingly—Sphinx's Mi-4000 was struck by a missile and the huge quadcopter wheeled wildly through the air before it slammed hard against the side of the mountain and blew apart in a colossal spray of fire and dirt.

The low tan-coloured mountain jutted out from a larger mass of rugged peaks as if it were aimed *back* toward the Great Sphinx so many miles distant. It was shaped like a rough hemisphere flanked by a pair of narrow valleys.

From the air, Jack could make out some tiny square structures on the edges of the hemisphere: brown stone cubes that were the same tawny colour as the mountain.

The gates to the Labyrinth.

They were spaced about five hundred metres apart from each other and would have been hard to spot were it not for the objects in front of some of them. There was, for instance, *a private jet* crashed in front of one gate. (Jack guessed that it had brought Ezekiel and some of his Omega monks here the previous day after they had successfully performed their Fall.)

In front of two of the gates—the two at either extremity of the low mountain—were line upon line of bronzemen, a thousand of them for each gate, arrayed in sweeping defensive arcs to protect the landward approach to them.

Closer still to the two gates were smaller phalanxes of silvermen, perhaps forty silvermen each. They were clustered right in front of the gates themselves, in case someone got through the outer force of bronzemen.

Clearly, Sphinx had left orders to prevent anyone from entering the Labyrinth after him and those two gates must have still been unused.

Jack stared at the giant V-88 raining fire on the right-most gate. He'd seen it on a TV screen in Jerusalem, but seeing it up close reinforced just how huge it was. It was the ultimate flying fortress.

'I'm guessing Rastor used that plane to blast open the Temple Mount,' he said.

Zoe nodded. 'He also used it to blow the dome off St Peter's Basilica in Rome.'

'And now he's using it here,' Lily said.

As she said this, Jack saw the giant plane land in front of the right-most gate, blowing the silvermen in front of it to pieces, and a group of small figures with Rastor at their head raced inside it.

Jack turned to the members of his team.

He'd already outlined the Russian Doll Plan. It was very high-risk. At any of three different times, it could fail and they'd be dead before they knew it.

'All right, folks,' he said, 'our target is that last gate, the one over on the far left-hand side. This is what it all comes down to. Thank you for your friendship and your help over the years. I hope I see you later, if and when it's all over. Sky Monster, my old friend, bring us in. Bring us in *hard*.'

With those words, the mighty Super Galaxy, flown by Sky Monster, began its descent toward the gate complex of the Supreme Labyrinth.

Anti-aircraft fire came at them, but the Super Galaxy was a tough bird with thick skin and some of the best countermeasures in the world, and the incoming missiles whizzed wildly by it while the uprushing rounds bounced off its armoured fuselage.

And then, without warning, a second plane sprang out from behind the Super Galaxy! It had flown in behind the bigger C-5, out of view.

It was an Egyptian Air Force Hercules, purloined from Cairo International Airport by Aloysius Knight—his special task—and it swooped in front of the descending Super Galaxy and landed right in front of it!

In most scenarios, a Hercules would have been the biggest plane in attendance, but here it was dwarfed by the enormous Super Galaxy.

Flown by Aloysius, the Hercules touched down on the flat desert plain in front of the gate complex—closely followed by the Super Galaxy.

It kicked up a billowing cloud of dust and sand as it landed and then it was rushing headlong toward the low mountain, straight at the legions of bronzemen.

It didn't slow down.

The Hercules ploughed *right into* the ranks of bronzemen, crushing fifty of them in a single instant . . .

. . . creating a path through them . . .

. . . which the Super Galaxy, touching down a moment later, used as its taxiway.

It was an astonishing sight.

The two massive planes, travelling one after the other across the desert floor, mowing down the ranks of bronzemen.

'Take that, you bronze motherfuckers!' Aloysius yelled as he swung his Hercules to port, toward the left-most gate of the complex, watching bronzemen go under his bow by the dozen.

But the sheer number of bronzemen on the ground was always going to stop him eventually.

The metal automatons—twisted and crushed like rag dolls—got caught up in the plane's wheels, jamming them, and just as the Hercules got about two-thirds of the way through their ranks, the big plane began to slow.

At this point, Aloysius yanked his plane hard to the right and the cargo plane came to a lurching halt . . .

. . . as the Super Galaxy behind it, spared from hitting all the first ranks of bronzemen, swept by, continuing on toward the left-most gate.

Now the Super Galaxy ploughed over many bronzemen, crushing them beneath its nose, getting closer to the left gate of the Labyrinth.

Then its wheels also began to jam with the crumpled bodies of bronzemen—despite the damage to them, the bronzemen were still 'alive', clawing and grasping like metal zombies, even as the wheels crushed them en masse—and the Super Galaxy came to a rending halt on the desert floor . . .

. . . three hundred metres from the left gate and with at least five hundred bronzemen *still* blocking the way.

A cloud of dust and sand veiled the whole sorry scene: the broken-down planes, the bronzemen scattered around them.

The many bronzemen still standing began to advance on the motionless Super Galaxy.

At which moment the front section of the Super Galaxy— its entire massive nose cone—rose up on a hinge, exposing its

enormous hold, and suddenly a truck came blasting out of the hold, bouncing down the plane's forward ramp into the throng of still-standing bronzemen, mowing them down in the same manner that the two planes had, aiming for the left-most gate!

Jack was at the wheel, with Lily and Zoe beside him. He drove hard, bending and swerving, trying to reach the gate in the low mountain.

The truck bounced wildly as bronzemen disappeared under its bonnet.

Some bronzemen managed to jump onto the sides of the truck, clamping their razor-sharp claws into its metal flanks.

'Jesus!' Zoe shouted as the claws of one bronzeman smashed the window of her door.

Blam!

She blew the bronzeman's head off with a specially tipped bullet fired from point-blank range.

Thus they rampaged through the many ranks of bronzemen, with Jack driving and Lily and Zoe firing guns left and right, edging ever closer to the gate.

But like the plane before it, the truck was eventually over-whelmed by the sheer number of bronzemen.

It got to within a hundred metres of the gate by the time it was stopped . . .

. . . when the third element of Jack's Russian Doll plan—a vehicle within a vehicle within a vehicle—leapt out of the rear bed of the truck: a motorcycle with a sidecar, with Jack driving and Lily and Zoe in the sidecar!

Jack's eyes were focused and hard as the motorbike bounced down to the ground and skidded around. Jack aimed it for the gate—

—and his face fell.

The remaining bronzemen closed ranks quickly.

Three hundred of them.

Blocking the way.

And still with the silvermen behind them.

'Fuck,' Jack said. 'We got so close.'

No sooner had Jack said this than two lines of heavy-bore 50-millimetre rounds strafed the ground on either side of him, knocking down the bronzemen in front of him, carving a clear path to the gate for his motorcycle.

'*We're here, Jack!*' Alby's voice called in his ear as the *Black Raven* swooped in low overhead and pulled up into a hover, the guns on its wings blazing, tearing open a path in the bronzemen's ranks.

Jack gunned the motorbike's engine and rushed into the now-open pathway, bronzemen whooshing by him on either side.

It was chaos, absolute chaos.

The Sukhoi blazing away above him, opening the way; and Zoe and Lily firing left and right from the sidecar with specially tipped bullets from their guns.

Jack kept his eyes forward, focusing on the gate as they got closer and closer to it.

And as they got nearer, he saw a thick stone slab lowering into the gateway: the outer door, closing slowly, designed to seal it, and now almost completely shut.

It only had about two more feet to go before it shut fully and was closed forever.

They were only sixty metres away now—

—when a shoulder-launched missile fired by one of Sphinx's human defenders hit the *Black Raven* and it peeled away in the sky, wounded, trailing black smoke, and slammed down onto the dusty ground forty metres from the left-most gate, turned

sideways to the gate, one of its wings almost completely snapped in half and—

—the final group of silvermen closed ranks in front of Jack's motorbike and sidecar, blocking the way.

Jack wanted to scream in frustration.

He spun to check on the Sukhoi, to see if Alby and Rufus were all right, just as the Sukhoi's canopy popped open and Rufus and Alby sprang out of it, guns up and firing more special-tipped rounds at the remaining silvermen guarding the gate.

They were okay, and still desperately helping, giving Jack the opening he needed . . .

. . . a clear path to the gate.

He gunned the bike for it, going all out . . .

. . . when, without warning, another enemy troop truck swept in from the side and stopped right in his path, blocking the gate!

The truck was driven by a Knight of the Golden Eight—Jaeger Zwei again, Jack's nemesis from Moscow and Jerusalem—and it was loaded with twenty more silvermen who quickly leapt down from it!

'You have *got* to be kidding me . . .' Jack breathed.

'We were so close!' Lily shouted.

Jack couldn't believe it.

His eyes darted from the twenty newly arrived silvermen to the furious scowl on the face of Jaeger Zwei in the truck to the lowering stone slab in the doorway of the gate—almost fully closed now—and the original force of toppled silvermen behind him who were now getting to their feet and staggering toward him.

And then it got worse.

From out of nowhere, *another* troop truck speared across Jack's path and at the sight of it, all of Jack's hopes fell.

It skidded to a halt in between Jack's bike and Zwei's truck, throwing up a huge cloud of dust and sand as it ground to a halt near the gate.

As the dust cloud settled, Jack saw the shadows of more automatons emerge from the newly arrived truck and his heart sank.

More reinforcements for the bad guys.

But then the cloud of dust parted and he saw one of the bronze-men more clearly: it had pale blue Air Force paint on its head and shoulders.

They were Easton's palemen!

And, directed by little Easton—leaping down from the truck which Jack now saw was driven by Aloysius Knight—they threw themselves at the silvermen: automaton versus automaton.

Aloysius shouted, 'Go, Jack, go!'

And in that moment of respite that Easton and Aloysius had given him, Jack saw the way to do this.

'Thanks!' he shouted. Then to Lily and Zoe: 'Follow me!'

They were only forty metres from the gate now, but still blocked from reaching it by silvermen, many of them now fighting Easton's palemen.

They raced on foot across the dusty ground, not toward the gate but off to one side of it, toward . . .

. . . the crashed Sukhoi.

They scrambled up onto the wing of the crumpled fighter-bomber.

'Alby! Rufus!' Jack called as he ran past them. 'You use the second one to get out of here!'

Rufus frowned. 'The second *what*?'

Alby threw something to Jack as he ran by him: his backpack.

'Jack! Something to help you in there!' he yelled.

'Thanks, kid!' Jack caught the backpack and plonked himself in the pilot's seat of the Sukhoi.

'Lily!' he said as she joined him. 'On my lap. Zoe, wrap yourself around Lily!'

As the two women jumped on top of Jack on the pilot's seat, Jack reached out with his shotgun and—very strangely—fired it *at the right wing of the Sukhoi*.

After three booming shots, the already cracked wing broke and the whole plane lurched wildly, rocking over onto its side . . .

. . . so that the top of its cockpit now faced the ancient closing gate.

Zoe saw the future. 'You are not thinking of . . . ?'

'Oh, yes, I am,' Jack said grimly. 'Hang on.'

Then he yanked on the ejection lever of the pilot's seat and did the impossible.

The pilot's seat came shooting out of the side-turned Sukhoi like a champagne cork out of a bottle, rocketing laterally across the dusty desert, flying horizontally two feet off the ground, heading *straight for* the closing gate.

Zoe yelled.

Lily screamed.

Jack just clenched his teeth as the ejection seat bounced across the sand like a stone skimming across a pond, whipping between all the silvermen.

The gate rushed up to meet them before, with a loud *clang!*, the reinforced back of the ejection seat slammed against the stone slab lowering into the outer doorway of the gate and stopped with a bone-jarring lurch.

Jack quickly unfastened his seatbelt and pushed Lily and Zoe under the lowering slab and into the darkness beyond.

'Go! Go! Go!' he urged.

He turned and caught a final glimpse of Alby, Aloysius and Rufus on the Sukhoi, jumping back into its cockpit while firing their guns at the plane's other wing, righting the plane again. A moment later, the Sukhoi's second ejection seat, the rear gunner's seat, shot skyward out of the plane, hopefully to land safely some distance away.

But then Jack's view of them was cut off by a silverman appearing right beside him, looming over him.

Quick as a snake, the silverman grabbed Jack by the head and began to squeeze and twist—

—it was going to rip his head off—

—when suddenly the silverman was bowled aside by two pale-men, crash-tackling it, and the silverman released Jack from its grip and suddenly Easton was at Jack's side, lifting him to his feet and shoving him toward the lowering slab in the doorway.

The slab was only a foot off the ground now.

With a final look at the sky and the mountains and the desert behind him, Jack rolled through the gap at the base of the ancient doorway, followed by Easton and four of his palemen.

There was so little room now, that as the last paleman successfully rolled under the lowering slab, the slab scratched some deep lines across its blank metal face.

A moment later, with a reverberating *boom*, the slab hit the ground, closing off the maze to the outside world.

Jack, Lily and Zoe stood in pitch darkness, flanked by Easton and the four palemen.

Jack flicked on the small flashlight mounted on his fireman's helmet.

Zoe lit up the penlight on the barrel of her MP-7.

Jack, Zoe and Lily all wore light packs on their backs, variously filled with canteens, protein bars, night-vision goggles and, in Jack and Zoe's cases, spare clips loaded with specially-tipped ammunition, ropes, climbing gear and a mini-Maghook each.

Jack checked the backpack Alby had thrown to him outside.

A severed mummified head stared up out of it.

'Not what I was expecting,' Lily said.

The mummified head wore a burnished silver skullcap and suddenly Jack realised who it was.

'Imhotep,' he said.

A Post-it note was stuck to the silver cap, with a message in Alby's handwriting:

Jack, meet Imhotep.
Take off his skullcap.
The tattoos help with the maze.
Assume Mendoza has this, too.
Alby

Jack took the silver cap off the desiccated skull and looking closely at the mummified skin of its crown, saw the tattoos:

a complex array of shapes and Thoth text marked on the black skin in a paler grey.

'Lily, what do those Thoth markings say?' he asked.

Lily scanned them. 'Hmm. Stuff like: *Move forward or die, for the Labyrinth closes itself: each maze remains open for but one rotation—Once you pass the shining stair, there is no going back—To find the endless tunnel, take the doorway below the image of Ningizzida—In the tunnel, always take the sinister fork—Speak not in the presence of the gold ones: only in silence may you pass—Look not in their faces, or thine eyes will not see again—Beware the liquid fire.* And lastly, *Life is rule, death is life. But there is no escaping the ultimate choice. In the face of Omega, you cannot conceal your true desires.*'

'They're instructions for the maze . . .' Zoe said. 'Oh, Alby, nice work. *Nice work.*' She turned to Lily. 'If we get out of here alive, honey, marry that boy.'

'The thought had crossed my mind,' Lily replied.

Jack put the skull back in the pack and looked at the space around them.

They were inside a small chapel, dusty and silent.

Guided by their flashlight beams, and followed by Easton and his palemen, they stepped over to the inner wall. It was carved to look like an arched doorway.

On the floor before it they saw a raised marking: the five-pointed mark.

Jack, Zoe and Lily each bore the same mark on their palms, acquired during the Fall.

Jack pressed his hand against the raised mark on the floor and with a deep ominous rumbling, the ancient inner door above it opened.

On the other side of the door, descending into darkness, was a wide set of stairs.

'The Supreme Labyrinth,' Lily said solemnly. 'The ultimate maze. The final trial to overcome before the Omega Event, the end of all things.'

'And we're the last to get here,' Zoe added. 'Our enemies are already inside, way ahead of us.'

Jack nodded at them and Easton.

'True. But, then, you know what I always say: we didn't come this far just to come *this* far. Zoe, Lily, Easton, I'm so pleased to have you all with me on this final mission. Let's do this.'

With those words, followed by the four palemen, the four of them stepped through the ancient doorway and ventured down the dark stairs beyond it into the Supreme Labyrinth.

THE END

OF

THE TWO LOST MOUNTAINS

JACK WEST JR WILL RETURN . . .

. . . ONE FINAL TIME

AN INTERVIEW WITH MATTHEW REILLY

SPOILER WARNING!

The following interview contains **SPOILERS** from *The Two Lost Mountains*. Readers who have not yet read the novel are advised to avoid reading this interview as it does give away major plot moments in the book.

You scared us when you almost killed Lily off at the end of The Three Secret Cities—*but early in this book, we find out what really happened and about poor Alexander's fate!*

Yes, I wanted to take readers to the very edge with Lily and the sacrificial ritual. In fact, in the very first draft of *The Three Secret Cities* I did *not* include the epilogue where it is suggested that Lily is okay. A few of the people who read that draft really believed I'd killed her off and were quite upset with me.

I am a reader. I *love* reading. In this way, I am *just like* my fans. And as a reader, when I finish a novel and close that book for the final time, I firmly believe I should smile, nod and mentally say to myself, 'Mmmm, that was satisfying. I enjoyed that.'

I apply that standard to my own novels. When a reader finishes one of my books, I hope they smile, nod and mentally say, 'Mmmm, that was satisfying. I enjoyed that.'

So.

I didn't want readers to finish *3SC* and say, 'What the hell! The bad guys won and they killed Lily!' Finishing a book with a cliffhanger

is one thing (and that can be fun, like with *The Six Sacred Stones*), but it's all about that feeling of satisfaction.

And so I decided to add the epilogue. I think this made *The Three Secret Cities* better, since it ended the novel on an uptick and not a downer, giving readers a hopeful ending, not a hopeless one . . . and thus they closed the book feeling satisfied in the knowledge that Lily may still be alive and there's more to be revealed.

This is why *The Two Lost Mountains* addresses Lily's fate immediately. I felt I owed readers that. I really enjoyed starting the book with Lily on the steps on St Basil's Cathedral in Moscow, in the cold, flanked by two beheaded nuns. It's a jarring way to start a novel, which I love (a bit like the way I started *The Four Legendary Kingdoms* with Jack waking with a startled gasp and finding himself inside an ancient cell with his head shaved—it instantly makes readers curious and invites them to lean in).

With every Jack West book, we wonder what kind of new piece of mythology or shocking ancient technology we'll discover. How did you come up with the Siren bells? When Jack falls 'asleep' and gets to fully experience it, it sounds terrifying!

As I think the Jack West books clearly show, I'm a huge fan of mythology. More than that, I'm an even bigger fan of explaining ancient myths in modern, realistic terms.

It goes all the way back to *Seven Ancient Wonders*, where I imagined the Hanging Gardens of Babylon. Or in *The Four Legendary Kingdoms*, where I tried to formulate what the Labours of Hercules might have actually been. My answer: a set of competitive deadly challenges!

When it comes to the Siren bells and the sleep they cause, I was directly inspired by the Greek myth of the 'Sirens': beautiful maidens who, with their entrancing song, caused sailors to crash their boats on the shore. I first read about the Sirens in *The Voyage of the Argonauts* by Apollonius of Rhodes and I thought they were just terrific (it's a super book, too, by the way). Just as good was Odysseus's typically inquisitive desire to hear their song and be able to describe it afterward. His method of achieving that was great: he had himself bound to the mast of the ship while the rest of the crew rowed with wax in their ears.

So, instead of the hypnotising song of some sweet-voiced maidens, I chose advanced bells which, when rung, would put people into a sleep-like state. (I particularly like how Jack can actually hear the world around him while he is sleeping, which makes that scene in Jerusalem even more dramatic.)

On a narrative level, with the series racing toward its conclusion, I wanted to raise the stakes and put the population of the whole world in jeopardy. Rather than have Jack 'save the world' in an over-all way, he now has to rouse everyone from this terrible sleep or else they will freeze or starve to death. And if Sphinx wins, he just won't wake millions of people. The stage is thus set for the final book.

Will we see some more myths realised like this in the final book?

Oh, yes! Absolutely. I've kept a few awesome ones up my sleeve. In the final book of the series, I'll address a couple of the ancient world's greatest myths.

The fate of the world (or galaxy, or universe) is always at stake, but it's usually Jack West and his team who are the ones on the front line of the action. There have been some exceptions—like the incident in London in The Three Secret Cities—*but you really put the people of the world in immediate danger in* The Two Lost Mountains: *Moscow being trashed, scared sites in Jerusalem being destroyed, whole cities being put to sleep . . .*

Go big or go home, I say. But seriously, in many of the earlier books, Jack worked away at the extreme corners of the world, far from its major cities and population centres. I found, though, as the stakes rose, his adventures necessarily brought him closer to civilisation: like with the scene on the Thames in London and the action at Hades's penthouse in New York in *The Three Secret Cities*.

On some level, I suppose I felt it was time for the people of the world to know about Jack's efforts on their behalf. The poor guy is constantly saving the world and no-one knows about it! While this is fine with Jack—indeed, an integral part of his character is *not* wanting to be celebrated; more than anything, Jack wants to go home to his farm and remain far from the world—it's not fine with me.

Also, we're getting near the end of what has become a gigantic seven-book series, so I have to make sure we finish with a bang, which means everything has to be at stake.

You first teased the importance of the Apollo 15 mission in The Three Secret Cities. What inspired you to use the moon as a key component in the Trial of the Mountains?

I just wanted to give Jack a completely impossible task: having to do something on the surface of the moon!

First of all, I just love anything to do with the moon landings. I think they were the pinnacle of human achievement, exploration and *daring*. One of my all-time favourite books is *Moondust* by Andrew Smith. The author interviewed every living astronaut who had set foot on the surface of the moon. All had been changed by the experience and the descriptions of the landings—including Armstrong's, which is as thrilling a piece of writing as you'll ever read—are simply awesome.

I loved the idea of linking one of the moon landings—*Apollo 15*, which really was the first mission to use a rover—to a specific requirement of the four kings. I had the idea of doing this a while back, which is why I slipped the clue into *The Three Secret Cities*.

Since I jumped back into the Jack West Jr series with *The Four Legendary Kingdoms*, I've been doing this sort of thing more: inserting clues in an earlier book and revealing the twist or twists in later ones. (I always loved the image of five warriors standing behind four kings that I put in *The Six Sacred Stones* way back in 2006 only to reveal who the four kings were ten years later in *The Four Legendary Kingdoms*—that was a very long-term clue!)

I think this is because, in my mind, I view the last three books in this series as one big story.

Once I committed to writing *The Four Legendary Kingdoms*, I knew I was committing to counting all the way down to *The One Something Something*. In my mind, *The Four Legendary Kingdoms* sets up the chessboard for the final stages of this story and in the last three books, I just go hell-for-leather for the finish line.

Oh, and just FYI, and there are still things lurking in the early books that I will refer to in *The One Something Something*.

And we head back to Egypt in this book! It feels very nostalgic for long-time Jack West fans. Could you possibly have imagined when first writing Seven Ancient Wonders that you'd ever bring Jack back here, or use the Great Sphinx somehow?

I have been waiting for so long to put the Great Sphinx in one of these novels. It's taken all my restraint to wait this long.

In the Jack West books, I've tried to link all the strange ancient sites dotted around our planet into one big story and the Great Sphinx

is one of the strangest. I just think it's the *best* one! When I visited Egypt years ago, I sat down and just gazed at the Great Sphinx for ages. It is truly mysterious.

Oh, and the two images of it in this book are real.

Let's talk about the other Sphinx—the villainous Hardin Lancaster XII, Watchman of the City of Atlas. As a member of the Trismagi, he's first teased as a character in The Four Legendary Kingdoms *and proves a tough opponent for Jack in* The Three Secret Cities. *Jack hasn't faced such a clever adversary since defeating his father, Wolf. It must be fun to turn yet another myth on its head—that one of the three wise men uses his knowledge not for noble purposes, but to greedily seek power.*

Once again, I enjoy taking mythical figures and reimagining them. I actually considered for a time making one of the 'three wise men from the East' a mystic from China.

As I considered the big finish for the series, I wanted to set up some new villains and, the way I see it, a guy like Hardin Lancaster/Sphinx has a great motivation to do what he does. Because of the way royalty works, he's been passed over by Orlando, despite the fact that he's smarter and better informed than Orlando. (I honestly find hereditary systems fascinating, precisely because they really do have a fatal flaw: mentally weak princes and princesses. Good kings and queens may have dunces as children, but the system demands that the dunces wear the crown. Very peculiar.)

And if a villain is going to go up against Jack over the final three novels, then he has to be smart, tough and totally committed to his cause and Sphinx is all of those and more, as we see when he does the Fall.

On that, tell us more about the Fall.

As a writer, I'm always thinking about villains and villainy. Because when it's all said and done, your hero really is only as good as your villain. So I'm always trying to find ways to make my villains tougher and tougher to beat.

Let me first say that it took me a *really* long time to design the Fall. I'd always had the idea of a death-defying plummet that Jack would have to do to 'qualify' for the final labyrinth, but until I sat down to map out *The Two Lost Mountains*, it only existed in my mind as a vague idea. Making it real meant designing the structure that would actually fall. The clinching moment came as I dabbled with various sketches of the Falling Temple and drew one with a skeletal lower half that would crumple underneath a heavier upper half when it hit the bottom of the shaft.

Having said that, the Fall was designed for another important reason: to establish Sphinx (and Ezekiel and Rastor) as villains willing to risk their lives to attain the power that is at stake.

In my quest to create better villains I've found that the best villains these days are totally committed to their goal, to the point where they are willing to sacrifice anything in pursuit of it. A good recent example is Thanos, the villain in *Avengers: Infinity War* and *Endgame*. I very much enjoyed watching him because he was utterly committed to his goal and would do anything for it.

On that point, there's another big *new player in this book—the nihilistic General Rastor. Can you tell us anything more about him?*

As we race toward the climax of this whole series, I wanted to have a character in the mix who *doesn't* want to rule the world or save anybody.

He was a fun villain to create because not only is he absolutely committed to his goal of destroying the universe, he can't be reasoned with or talked out of it. There is no way to bargain with Rastor. There is no-one he loves or cares about who can be held against him. And he's also big and ruthless and a genocidal maniac.

Jack and his team are several steps behind the bad guys the whole way through this book. Sphinx, Rastor and the Omega monks all know way more about the Trial of the Mountains and how to get to the Supreme Labyrinth for the Omega Event while Jack and our heroes can't seem to catch a break. Tell us how you came up with this structure.

The way I see it, *The Two Lost Mountains* is really the middle part of a three-book story that started with *The Three Secret Cities* and will finish with *The One Something Something*. This whole three-book story was set up in *The Four Legendary Kingdoms*, which laid down the key ideas of the four kingdoms, the trials and the Omega Event.

This means that *The Two Lost Mountains* is essentially the headlong race to the final battle which will take place (mostly) in a giant maze called the Supreme Labyrinth. I wanted Jack's challenge in this book to be that he was *always* behind, *always* chasing, *always* with less information. I wanted to stack the odds against him and make his mission absolutely and utterly desperate. (Indeed, as I mentioned earlier, just when it seems that his mission is completely impossible, he learns that he has to physically move something *on the moon*!)

A notable, shocking death in the book is the gruesome decapitation of Hades. Then poor Mae! Crucified and crushed! How will the death of Jack's mother affect him going forward?

Hades had to go. I wish I could explain it in a more profound way, but that's the truth.

He was a fun character to create, especially as a kind of 'dark mentor' to Jack (who kind of replaced Wizard, the nice mentor). He also had lots of money, which allowed me to give him many cool toys, planes and estates! And his knowledge of the kingdoms and their rituals was important. But I felt I'd reached the point in the story where Jack needed to press on alone, without his dark mentor's help.

Mae is a little different. While also something of a mentor to Jack, she also represents his heart and soul. She was a good mother who, in counterpoint to his father, fostered Jack's senses of empathy and compassion. Just as Jack needs to press on in his adventure without Wizard's wisdom and Hades's knowledge, now he must move on without Mae's guidance. If he is to truly be a hero, he must face the final challenges alone.

Mae's death also served to establish Rastor as a worthy rival to Jack. Rastor pays a big role in the final book and now he and Jack have some serious unfinished business.

That Russian Doll plan was one crazy, wild ride of an ending, Matthew! We're all set for the big finish in the Supreme Labyrinth. Any hints about what the ONE in the series will refer to?

As I mentioned above, much of this book is about putting all manner of insane obstacles in front of Jack and his goal. The final obstacle was an army of bronzemen and silvermen to get past.

The Russian Doll plan was my solution to that obstacle: gradually advance then stop . . . only to reveal another, smaller vehicle; advance further, and stop . . . and reveal a third, even smaller vehicle. At which point, it's the combination of all of Jack's friends coming to help him that gets him over the line.

As for the title of the final book, as always, I'll reveal it a few months before that book comes out. People may not realise this, but I don't even tell my publisher what the title of the next Jack West book is until the day I deliver it! It's a secret I like to hold until the last moment, making it something that, for about a year or two, only I know.

Is it the next book you are writing?

Yes, it's the next book I'm writing. I figure I can't bring readers all this way, right to the doors of the Supreme Labyrinth, four days from the Omega Event, only to go off and write another book. I'm making good progress with it already. Writing-wise, it's very helpful to continue straight into the next book. I did this once before with *The Six Sacred Stones* and *The Five Greatest Warriors* and it really smoothed the flow of the story between them.

How have you been holding up in L.A. during the coronavirus pandemic?

It's certainly been a strange and difficult time, but I've been healthy and my thoughts go out to those who have lost loved ones or their jobs or even just felt financial stress.

Like everyone else, I sheltered in place and just stayed at home. I had a couple of short stories up my sleeve—*Roger Ascham and the Dead Queen's Command* and *Jack West Jr and the Chinese Splashdown*—so I was pleased to release them online for free during the lockdown. I enjoy releasing free stories at the best of times, just to be able to give something back to my readers. To do it during a time when everyone was sheltering in their homes, made me feel I was, in some small way, making the lockdown a little more bearable.

Being locked down prevented me from attending a writers festival in Margaret River which was a real shame. Hopefully I can get there in the future. The lockdown pretty much postponed all the extraneous stuff I do, so in the end, with my calendar pretty empty, I took the opportunity to write, write, write.

Ultimately, I tried to make the best out of a bad situation and use the time to be productive. I completed a couple of short novels—including a very cool superhero story—plus a new screenplay, and, of course, I got started on that final Jack West novel.

And after that? What comes next? Will there be any more Jack West novels?

Ha! Ha! No, after *The One Something Something*, that's it! That's all. The story will come to its end with that book. I've enjoyed writing this series so much, I wouldn't want to overdo it by extending it beyond what I originally intended. And I planned to finish it with *The One*.

I have thrown pretty much everything into the Jack West series: everything I know about history and myths and ancient places. *Seven Ancient Wonders* was released in 2005. My goal when I decided to write sequels to it was to write a *giant, massive, truly epic* series that linked all the strange ancient places around the world—from Stonehenge to Easter Island to the Great Sphinx—and by the end of the last book, I think I will have done that.

Hopefully readers found the journey enjoyable, but . . . it is a journey with an end. My sole goal right now is to make sure that ending, that final seventh book, is *satisfying* to all those readers who have taken the time to join me on it. Finishing the series is actually something of a challenge for me: I've never actually ended a series before; the Scarecrow series can keep on going, but to close out a long story in a satisfying way requires lots of thought and I've embraced the challenge.

And then it will be time to start something new, which brings me a whole other kind of joy.

As always, I hope you enjoyed this book. The next one will be a doozy.

Matthew Reilly
Los Angeles
May 2020

MORE BESTSELLING TITLES FROM MATTHEW REILLY

Ice Station

THE DISCOVERY OF A LIFETIME

At a remote ice station in Antarctica, a team of US scientists has found something buried deep within a 100-million-year-old layer of ice. Something made of *metal*.

THE LAW OF SURVIVAL

In a land without boundaries, there are no rules. Every country would kill for this prize.

A LEADER OF MEN

A team of crack United States marines is sent to the station to secure the discovery. Their leader – Lieutenant Shane Schofield, call-sign: SCARECROW. They are a tight unit, tough and fearless. They would follow their leader into hell. They just did . . .

Temple

Deep in the jungle of Peru, the hunt for a legendary Incan idol is under way – an idol that in the present day could be used as the basis for a terrifying new weapon.

Guiding a US Army team is Professor William Race, a young linguist who must translate an ancient manuscript which contains the location of the idol.

What they find is an ominous stone temple, sealed tight. They open it – and soon discover that some doors are meant to remain unopened . . .

The Great Zoo of China

AN IMPOSSIBLE DISCOVERY

It is a secret the Chinese government has been keeping for forty years. They have found a species of animal no one believed even existed.

THE WORLD'S GREATEST ATTRACTION

The Chinese are ready to unveil their fabulous creatures in the greatest zoo ever constructed. VIPs and journalists, including reptile expert Dr Cassandra Jane 'CJ' Cameron, are invited to see the beasts for the first time.

ONE FALSE PROMISE

The visitors are assured by their Chinese hosts that they are perfectly safe, that nothing can go wrong.

Of course it can't . . .

The Secret Runners of New York

THE COMING END

When Skye Rogers and her twin brother Red move to Manhattan, rumours of a coming global apocalypse are building.

But the young elite of New York keep partying without a care.

CAN YOU KEEP A SECRET?

And then suddenly Skye is invited to join an exclusive gang known as the Secret Runners of New York.

This is no ordinary clique – they have access to an underground portal that can transport them into the future.

And what Skye discovers in the future is horrifying . . .